SPOOKY SEA STORIES

EDITED BY

CHARLES G. WAUGH
AND
FRANK D. McSHERRY

INTRODUCTION BY

TONY GIBBS

Former Editor of Yachting

YANKEE BOOKS
Camden, Maine

Cover illustration and design by Anthony Bacon Venti
Text design by Amy Fischer, Camden, Maine
Typeset by Camden Type 'n Graphics, Camden, Maine
Printed and bound in the United States

Library of Congress Cataloging-in-Publication Data

Spooky sea stories / edited by Charles G. Waugh & Frank D.
   McSherry, Jr.
      p. cm.
   ISBN 0-89909-337-X
   1. Ghost stories, American. 2. Ghost stories, English. 3. Sea
stories, American. 4. Sea stories, English. I. Waugh, Charles.
II. McSherry, Frank D.
PS648.G48S66   1991
813'.0873308–dc20   91-2446
                                                                CIP

To Marty, who made it all possible

CONTENTS

INTRODUCTION

Seafarers have always been notoriously superstitious, and the reasons are not far to seek. After all, what other class of people subject their existence to the whim of so a mysterious, implacable, deeply inhuman element as the sea? Recognizing their helplessness, sailors at first tried to make the great adversary understandable by giving it the status of a god, whether the Greek Poseidon or the Babylonian Tiamat. A god, after all, could be placated with prayers and offerings, and the early seamen did their best in that line, up to and including human sacrifice.

But sooner or later came the same stark realization that has chilled the sailor throughout history: The sea can't be bribed; the sea simply doesn't care—about human beings, or anything else. That icy, elemental indifference is somehow worse than honest enmity, and many seamen refused to accept it (still refuse, for that matter, and probably always will).

For them, magic was the answer, elaborate taboos and rituals they would have found laughable ashore. Never leave port on a

Friday; never sail with a parson aboard; never change a ship's name—the list is endless, and many of the items on it receive shamefaced observation even today. I've sailed with a skipper who, when the wind went flat, would sidle up to the mast and scratch it, muttering *"perkele, perkele"* under his breath. The wind, I have to say, would often oblige him—but then he was a Finn, and Finns have for centuries been considered supreme in the techniques of nautical witchcraft.

Whether the rituals work or not, practicing them leads to a tacit acceptance of the supernatural afloat—an acceptance bolstered by the abiding sense of mystery the sea carries with it. Even now, when we can say with some confidence what the surface of another planet looks like, we have only a keyhole glimpse of what goes on beneath the surface of our oceans. For all we know, the Loch Ness monster may be a pilot-fish for something far greater that no man has yet seen.

Or seen and lived to talk about. And that is the burden of two of the tales in this collection: The emergence from the sea of a homicidal creature outside our knowledge. Morgan Robertson's *From the Darkness and the Depths* conjures up a monster of the ultimate deep, pushed up to the surface by the very historical eruption of Krakatoa in 1883. The event, which raised immense tidal waves and scattered volcanic ash over 300,000 square miles, was perhaps the single greatest natural phenomenon of the Victorian age—the perfect keynote for a story that exemplifies an early science-fiction style in spooky tales (or, if you prefer, spooky strain in science fiction). Beginning with a real event, and concealing his design behind a screen of technical and scientific detail, Robertson lures us toward a gradual acceptance of his creation's possible existence—a possibility made more credible by Robertson's own observation of known sea creatures and their peculiar attributes. It's the same technique that Michael Crichton, among current storytellers, has mastered to near-perfection. Robertson's turn-of-the-century "science" may seem a little quaint to us, but the story's premises are no more unbelievable than some of the bottom-dwelling fish that ichthyologists now take for granted.

By contrast, William Hope Hodgson, in the *The Derelict*, gives only a perfunctory nod to realism. His conceptual monster springs full blown from the kernel of a single idea, and the necessary clue to its origin has been planted by the end of the story's third paragraph. Unlike the narrator, the alert reader will soon figure out what makes that derelict vessel so quick to welcome its visitors and so reluctant to let them go. Hodgson's art isn't mystification but imagination; the reader gets sucked in by atmospherics rather than probability. Even so, anyone who's seen the revolting things that can happen to a vessel's timbers under the combined influences of darkness, damp, and warmth may conclude that Hodgson's imagination hasn't had to strain unnecessarily far.

Hodgson's piece has stylistic echoes of Edgar Allan Poe, a writer for whom atmosphere was everything. Though *MS. Found in a Bottle* was Poe's first short story, written when he was 22, by the time it appeared he had already published two volumes and a pamphlet of poems, joined the U.S. Army under a false name, and been admitted to and expelled from West Point. The story won Poe a $50 cash prize and may well have done more to influence his subsequent writing career than his poems did. As a writer, Poe isn't usually connected to the sea, but he had crossed the Atlantic in both directions by sailing vessel as a boy, so he'd had plenty of time to pick up useful detail. Even so, *MS. Found in a Bottle* is less concerned with nautical atmosphere than with creating a gathering aura of doom— first aboard a passenger vessel crippled in a mysterious tempest, then on the ageless mystery ship that rams and sinks her. The crew are distant cousins of the *Wandering Jew* and the *Flying Dutchman*, ancient beyond reckoning, seeking the peace that only death can bring, and their destination has a momentary flash of Jules Verne about it.

The tale of the Flying Dutchman is arguably the prototype of the spooky sea story. *Spooky,* my dictionary says, means "relating to, resembling, or suggesting" ghosts, and the Dutchman, doomed to cruise the seas forever, is one of fiction's really durable specters. In most versions of the story, the awesome side of the Dutchman is leaned on heavily and his identity is often veiled, but in *A Strange Arrival* John William DeForest carries off the reincarnation in a more lighthearted fashion. His narrators, Captain Phineas Glover and his daughter, Mary Anne, are not unduly stunned by their mid-ocean encounter with the eternal wanderer; if anything, Phineas's Yankee self-possession gives him an edge over the undying crew who succor him and Mary Anne.

DeForest's accomplishment is particularly notable considering that we meet the Dutchman (and, perhaps surprisingly, his family) after the repentance that will allow him to gain salvation. Like so many reformed characters, the new, improved Dutchman is sometimes a little too effusive for ordinary mortals like the Glovers. But after 280 years without touching land, anyone might be a little emotional at finding the voyage was coming to an end. In DeForest's version, the Dutchman's original crime was a failure to give aid to a pair of mariners clinging to a piece of floating wreckage. Landlubbers may feel that the Dutchman's sentence was out of proportion to his crime, but any seafarer will recognize that rendering assistance to other sailors in peril has always been a first commandment afloat.

A most unusual alternative version of the Flying Dutchman legend is Wilhelm Hauff's *The Story of the Haunted Ship*. Here the classic is given a Muslim spin. The unnamed narrator is himself a Mohammedan, the accursed crew are Turkish, and the captain's crime is the murder of a holy man. Their punishment, however, is somewhat different, and the narrator plays a far more active role than did Captain Glover—and receives a far different recompense. Ethnic background aside, Hauff's story is cast in the style of the classic Arabian Nights fantasy; not that it is equipped with djinns and afrits, but the piece has essentially the same internal resonances that the Western mind seems to consider proper for a Middle Eastern narrative. Somewhat the same word cadences can be observed in several of Kipling's *Just So Stories* or even in the libretto of the Broadway musical *Kismet.*

In both Hauff's and DeForest's stories, the transgressors' sentence goes on forever—barring reformation in the one case or intercession in the other. It may be stretching a point, but one is tempted to see in the endlessness of the Flying Dutchman's ordeal the sailors' particular idea of the nature of punishment, rooted in their own lives. At some point in every long voyage, in every extended storm, it seems that things will go on in the same way forever, day after identical day.

Sometimes, of course, a terrible punishment may be visited on people who are innocent of any intended wrong. This is the theme of Henry Fielding's oddly entitled *The Police Officer's Tale.* (While the story has nothing whatever to do with police, Fielding himself was one of the founders of the modern metropolitan police force. He was also the author of *Tom Jones*.) In the spectrum of spookery, Fielding's piece falls in the category of stories dealing with objects that bear a communicable curse. In this case, the objects are the ship's entire cargo, bones bought in Egypt and destined to become fertilizer in America.

The bones are, of course, not those of animals but of human beings—of the thousands of unnamed soldiers who died in the numberless wars of the Middle East (and Fielding, we should remember, was writing in the mid-18th century, before that area's bloodiest mass conflicts had been fought). The ghosts of the dead object violently to being uprooted, carted across the ocean, and ground up to provide encouragement for vegetables; one can scarcely blame them. Curiously enough, only one of the ship's crew, a weak-headed Dane named Christiansen, can perceive what is going on—can actually see the spirits of the dead—even though the other sailors can feel their anger. Fielding is drawing here on one of the oldest traditions of the supernatural, that the mentally handicapped are better equipped than the rest of us to appreciate what is happening in the twilight world. (Not that Christiansen's psychic talents do him any good.)

Another subtheme makes its appearance here as well, and this one recurs in several of the book's selections. Fielding's captain is something of a thug, as are his two mates. And it is not clear that the captain is truly innocent of guilty knowledge about his cargo. Nineteenth-century nautical fiction really brought to center-stage the literary convention of the hardcase skipper and the bully mate, but fiction was only following fact.

In real life, alas, we can read again and again of monstrous officers retiring to wealthy, happy lives ashore. In Elizabeth Ward's *Kentucky's Ghost*, the evil mate finally gets his—but it takes a force from beyond the grave to do it. Mr. Whitmarsh, the mate of the *Madonna*, is as harddriving a bully as one could easily find, a nautical Simon Legree. There were many like him, and not until well into this century was his type largely rooted out. Ward's tale graphically illustrates the sailing-ship crew's collective helplessness in the face of such a man, and the power a sadistic officer could wield, particularly in the case of a stowaway, who had no legal rights at all. It's not hard to understand why, absent supernatural assistance, 18th and 19th century crews sometimes resorted to "lifting" an especially tyrannical officer over the side during a gale.

There is always the other side, though: Sailing-ship crews were seldom recruited from choir lofts, and the only way a captain could be sure of surviving was to be even tougher than the men he led. In *The Voodoo-Woman*, Mary S. Watts makes it clear that Captain Jed Slocum, of the *Laughing Sallie*, is just a harder, greedier, larger-scale version of his crew. In the end, when he leads his men in an ill-advised search for the voodoo priestess's hoard, he is no better than a buccaneer, though one has to admire the unflinching way he meets his fate.

Joseph Conrad's sea officers are as tough as any who ever sailed, but they are seldom brutish. Put it down, perhaps, to class feeling on Conrad's part—he was, after all, a merchant marine officer himself. In his story *The Brute*, the title character is not a bully mate, or a human being at all. This brute is the ship herself, a vessel with the curious name *Apse Family*. (Ship names are a fascinating study in themselves, and have distracted many a nautical writer.)

The *Apse Family*, named for her owners, is that sailor's particular hate object, a rogue vessel. Anyone who has been around ships has one or more examples to cite, from the mildly crank boat that never backs down the same way twice to real killers that are forever dropping blocks from the masthead or snagging one's clothing in their machinery. And what they so often have in common is the absence of a visible reason for their bad behavior. These are not, by and large, craft with some glaring design flaw. Intellect tells us that there's nothing personal in their apparent hostility, but experience says differently. (And it's curious that even the sophisticated seafarer, who can accept the sea's apparent malignities as nothing more than meteorology, will react like a rejected lover when his vessel double-crosses him.)

Charlie, the *Apse Family*'s first mate, is one of those matter-of-fact Conradian sea officers who won't let himself be pushed around by circumstance; the trouble here is that he's out of his depth. A rogue ship has her own tactics, her own rules, and even unceasing vigilance is not enough to keep her in line. Only a man lost to seafaring ethics can be an inadvertent match for her.

For the sailor, love is seldom smooth and often tragic. That doesn't mean he shies away from it, though—quite the opposite. The seaman in love can be driven by a dream, a memory, or, in the case of Arthur Conan Doyle's *The Captain of the Pole-Star*, the picture of a 19-year-old woman, identified only as "M.B." Captain Craigie is one of those mysteriously tragic figures the Victorians loved: A man of unknown nationality, despite his Scottish name, who simply disappears at the end of each whaling voyage and then materializes shortly before his ship's departure.

At first it's not clear what is driving Craigie to take the *Pole-Star* farther and farther north, into the pack ice. Even when we begin to suspect the nature of the wraith that flits over the ice ahead of them, there is no proof. What is clear is that Craigie is torn between his duty to the ship and her crew, and his need to pursue the figment of his past. And we all know what happens to men who do that.

The supernatural was an area that attracted Doyle throughout his life, and especially after the death of his son in World War I; but Doyle, like Poe, isn't thought of as a writer concerned with the sea. Yet it's surprising how many of his stories have scenes afloat. Perhaps the most easily remembered of his seafaring characters is Black Peter, the murdered skipper whose demise set Sherlock Holmes to harpoon practice in a butcher shop. Several other Holmes stories deal with the sea—as a road to escape, or fortune, or death. And Doyle's great historical novel, *The White Company*, has a splendid description of a medieval sea battle.

The return of the dead, drawn variously by love or a need for revenge, is a consistent theme in spooky tales. It pops up with great frequency in sea stories of the supernatural, and no wonder. Seafarers were particularly likely to be cut off young and—unlike their brethren ashore—to vanish, with or without their ship. Losing a crewmember over the side is every skipper's nightmare, and was in the age of sail one of the most common nautical accidents. But the disappearance over the side of Jim Benton, in F. Marion Crawford's *Man Overboard!*, has ramifications the reader is unlikely to suspect until the very end. Here again the cause is driven love, and as so often happens the returned spirit has lost whatever human kindness he may have had when alive.

In Dana Burnet's *Fog*, the young protagonist with the unusual name of Wessel's Andy is also drawn to doom by passion. In Andy's case the passion is for a ship and a woman, neither of which he has actually seen. We have all of us had obsessions (though seldom as obsessive as Andy's), and most of us have experienced the shuddery sensation of *déjà vu*. But to be called from beyond is, happily, something few people have undergone.

No collection of spooky stories would be complete without one that involved a shape-shifter. Jonas Lie, the author of *The Cormorants of Andvaer*, is not known in this country, but in his native Norway he achieved considerable renown as a novelist, playwright, and poet with a knack for mingling the realistic and fantastic. In this example of his art, he is mining a different vein, however. Few American readers will miss the very familiar Northern European atmosphere in this tale of the mysterious young woman who offers her would-be lovers a deadly trial. There is some Grimm here, and some Hans Christian Andersen, too, but the story has an aura all its own.

A more straightforward love story by far is Henry Van Dyke's *Messengers at the Window*. Nataline, the wise and beautiful French-Canadian lighthouse keeper, is one of those women who can exercise a moral superiority without being tiresome about it. And while her husband, Marcel, has committed a crime, he did it only for her, so we can forgive him easily enough. Fortunately for Marcel, he is given three warnings to repent, and his victim does not, apparently, hold a grudge once his very personal property is returned.

There is a Fairfield in Australia, and no less than 19 towns with that name in the United States, but none in England. Nonetheless, the Fairfield Richard Middleton describes in *The Ghost Ship*—"near the Portsmouth Road, about half way between London and the sea"—sounds like the kind of place that Baedecker would have singled out as an essential stop on any spook connoisseur's British tour. How could you pass up a place where the living and the dead co-exist in such casual harmony? Until, that is, the unexpected arrival of Captain Bartholomew Roberts, complete with pirate ship, in the middle of the innkeeper's field. Roberts is a Bad Influence, though mostly on the formerly living inhabitants of Fairfield. His hospitality is giving the town a very peculiar bad name, but how does one get rid of an immortal ship that's come to rest many miles from the sea?

There's no question that spookery afloat has come on hard times in the last few decades. Part of that ebb may be attributed to the technological revolution. Thanks to radar, depth sounders, range finders, and VHF-FM radio today's mariner has a whole new spectrum of phantoms—electronic ones—to curse and fear; you can't spare the time to worry about that translucent figure keening up in the crow's nest when your radar is showing you on a collision course with an island that doesn't exist.

But maybe it's just a matter of waiting till art catches up with science, and we have a whole new generation of spooky sea stories in which the haunting is done by ohm and megahertz. Because you can depend on one thing: The mariner will never, never give up superstition, as long as there's wood to rap his knuckles on.

Tony Gibbs
February, 1991

TONY GIBBS *has been Editor of* Yachting *and Executive Editor of* The New Yorker. *He now lives in Santa Barbara, California, where he is a Senior Editor of* Islands *magazine. He is the author of more than a dozen books, of which two—*Dead Run *and* Running Fix—*are thrillers with a nautical setting.*

DANA BURNET

FOG

I HAD COME OUT of the city, where storytelling is a manufac-
tured science, to the country where storytelling is a by-product of
life. Mr. Siles had arrived to paint my piazza, as per a roundabout
agreement between my cook, my cook's cousin, my cook's cousin's
wife, who had been a Miss Siles, and finally—Mr. Siles himself. If
that sentence is somewhat involved, so was my contract with Mr.
Siles. In the country, a semicircle is the shortest line between two
points.

I came at the strange story of Wessel's Andy in something of
the same circuitous manner. Mr. Siles, as I have said, had arrived to
paint my piazza; but after a long look at the heavens and the heaving
sea, he opined that it would be a wet day and that the painting had
best be left till tomorrow. I demurred. I was acquainted with the
tomorrows of this drowsy Maine village. But while we were arguing
the point, a white ghost began to roll in from the deep.

"Fog," said Mr. Siles.

"Yes," I admitted grudgingly.

He stared into the thickening mists with an expression that puzzled me. I have seen the same look upon the face of a child compelled to face the dark alone.

"I mistrust it," said Mr. Siles, simply.

"Mistrust the fog?"

He nodded, his iron-gray beard quivering with the intensity of the assent.

"Take a gale of wind," he said, "that's honest weather, though it blows a man's soul to Kingdom Come. But fog. . . ."

"I suppose strange things do happen in it," I replied. It was a chance shot, but it struck home.

"Strange!" cried Mr. Siles. "You may well say strange! There was somethin' happened right here in this village. . . ."

I settled myself comfortably against the naked piazza railing, and Mr. Siles told me this story.

He was born a thousand miles from deep water. His folks were small farmers in a midwestern grain state, and he was due to inherit the farm. But almost before he could talk they knew he was a queer one. They knew he was no more farmer than he was college professor. He was a land hater from the beginnin'. He hated the look and the feel and the smell of it. He told me afterward that turnin' a furrow with a plow set his teeth on edge like when you scrape your fingernail along a piece of silk. His name was Andy.

When he was about thirteen year' old he found a picture of a ship in a newspaper. It was like a glimpse of another world. He cut it out and pasted it on the attic wall over his bed. He used to look at it a hundred times a day. He used to get up in the middle of the night, and light a match and look at it. Got so, Andy's father came up early one mornin' with a can o' whitewash and blotted the whole thing out against the wall. The boy didn't say a word until the ship was gone. Then he laughed, a crazy sort o' laugh.

"That's the way they go," he says, "right into the fog," he says, "and never come out again!"

He was sick after that. Some sort of a fever. I guess it made him a little delirious. He told me he was afraid they were goin' to blot him out, same as the picture. Used to dream he was smotherin' to death, and pleasant things like that. Queer, too. . . .

When the fever finally burned out of him, he was nothin' but skin and bones. His people saw he was too sickly to work, so they let him mope around by himself. He used to spend most of his time in the woodshed, whittlin' pine models o' that whitewashed schooner. He was known all through those parts as Wessel's Andy, Wessel bein' his fam'ly name. See for yourself what Wessel's Andy meant. It didn't mean Andrew Wessel, by the grace o' God free and twenty-one. It meant "that good-for-nothin', brain-cracked boy over to Wessel's." That's what it amounted to in plain words.

But the strange thing about that name was how it followed him. It came east a thousand miles, and there wasn't a town but it crawled into, on its belly, like a snake into long grass. And it poisoned each place for him, so that he kept movin' on, movin' on, always toward deep water. It used to puzzle him how strangers knew to call his name hindside foremost. 'Twan't any puzzle to me. He hadn't been in my place two minutes askin' for a job, but I say "What's your name?" And he says, starin' hard at the model of the *Lucky Star* schooner that hung over my counter, "I'm Wessel's Andy," he says, never takin' his eyes off the schooner. Likely he'd done the same absent-minded trick all along the road, though not for just that reason.

I rec'llect the evenin' he came into my place. I was keepin' a ship's supply store in those days—fittin's and supplies, down by the Old Wharf. He shuffled in toward sundown, his belongin's done up in a handkerchief, his clothes covered half an inch thick with dust.

"I want a job," says he.

"What kind of a job?" says I.

"Oh, anything," says he.

"All right," I told him, "you can start in here tomorrow. I been lookin' for somebody to help around the store." Then I asked him his name and he answered "Wessel's Andy." Some of the boys was standin' 'round and heard him say it. He was never called anything but Wessel's Andy from that time on.

Quietest young fellow ever I saw—plenty willin' to work, but not very strong. I paid him four dollars a week and let him bunk in with me at the back o' the store. He could have made more money some'ers else, but he wouldn't go. Naturally there were a good many seafarin' men in and out o' the shop, and some evenin's they used to sit around yarnin' to one another. Often I've seen Wessel's Andy hunched up on a soap box behind the counter, his eyes burnin' and blinkin' at the model of the *Lucky Star* on the opposite wall, his head bent to catch the boys' stories. Seemed as if he couldn't get enough o' ships and the sea.

And yet he was afraid to go, himself. I found that out one night when we were lockin' up after the boys had gone.

"Have you ever felt yourself to be a coward, Mr. Siles?" he says, in one of his queer fits o' talkin'.

"Why as for that," I says, "I guess I been pretty good and scared, a time or two."

"Oh, I don't mean that," he says. "I don't mean scared. I mean afraid—day and night, sleepin' and wakin'."

"No," I says, "and nobody else with good sense would be. Ain't nothin' in this world to frighten a man steady like that, unless it's his own sin."

Wessel's Andy shook his head, smilin' a little.

"Maybe not in this world," says he, white and quiet, "but how about—other worlds?"

"What you drivin' at?" says I. "You mean ghosts?"

"Not ghosts," he says, lowerin' his voice and lookin' out the side window to where the surf was pawin' the sand. "Just the feelin' o' ghosts."

"Come to bed," I says. "You've worked too hard today."

"No. Please let me tell you. Please sit up awhile. This is one of the times when I can talk."

He grabbed my hand and pulled me down to a chair. His fingers were as cold as ice. Then he dragged his soap box out from the counter and sat opposite me, a few feet away.

"I'll tell you how I know I'm a coward," he says. And he told me everything up to the time of his leavin' home.

"You see," he says, "I had to come. It was in me to come East. I've been four years workin' my way to open water, and I've had a hell of a time . . . a hell of a time. But it was in me to come. There has been a ship behind my eyes ever since I can remember. Wakin' or sleepin' I see that ship. It's a schooner, like the *Lucky Star* there, with all her tops'ls set and she's disappearin' in a fog. I know," he says, lookin' at me so strange and sad it sent the shivers down my back, "I know I belong aboard o' that ship."

"All right," I says, as though I didn't think anything of his queer talk, "all right, then go aboard of her. You'll find a hundred vessels up and down the coast that look like the *Lucky Star*. Not to

4

a seafarin' man, maybe. But you're a farmer. You couldn't tell one from t'other. Take your pick o' the lot," I says, "and go aboard of her like a man."

But he just smiled at me, a sickly sort o' smile.

"There's only one," he says, "there's only one, Mr. Siles. When she comes I'll go aboard of her, but I . . . won't . . . go . . . like . . . a . . . man!"

Then all at once he jumped up with a kind o' moanin' noise and stood shakin' like a leaf, starin' out the window to the sea.

"There," he says, kind o' chokin'. "There, I saw it then! Oh, God, I saw it then!"

I grabbed him by the shoulders and shook him.

"You saw what?" I says. "Tell me!"

His fingers dug into my arm like so many steel hooks.

"At the end of the Old Wharf. A sail! Look, don't you see it?"

I forced him down onto the soap box.

"Sit there," I says, "and don't be a fool. It's low tide," I says, "and there ain't enough water off the Old Wharf to float a dory."

"I saw it," he says, draggin' the words out slow as death, "I saw it, just as I always knew I would. That's what I came East for . . . a thousand miles. And I'm afraid to go aboard of her. I'm afraid, because I don't know what it's for."

He was rockin' himself back and forth like a crazy man, so I ran and got a drop o' whiskey from the back room.

"Here," I says. "Drink this."

He swallowed it straight, like so much water. In a few minutes he quieted. "Now then," I says, "you come to bed. This night's entertainment is over."

But it wasn't. About midnight I woke up with the feelin' that somethin' was wrong. First thing I saw was the lamp burnin' high and bright. Next thing was Wessel's Andy, sittin' in his underclothes on the edge o' the bunk, my whiskey flask in his hands.

"Mr. Siles," says he, as straight and polite as a dancin' master, though his eyes burned, "I have made free with your whiskey. I have drunk it all, I think."

"Great Jehosophat," I says, "there was pretty nigh a quart in that flask!"

"I hope you don't begrudge it," says he, still smooth as wax, "because it has made me feel like a man, Mr. Siles, like a man. I could talk—and even laugh a little, I think. Usually I can only feel. Usually I am afraid. Afraid of what, Mr. Siles? Afraid of goin' aboard without knowin' what for. That's the fear to eat your heart out, Mr. Siles. That's the fear to freeze your blood. *The not knowin' what for!*"

I was wide awake by this time and wonderin' how I could get him back to bed. I didn't want to lay hands on him any more than you'd want to lay hands on a person with nightmare. So I started to argy with him, like one friend to another. We were a queer lookin' pair, I'll warrant, sittin' there in our underclothes, facin' each other.

"Look here," I says, calm as a judge, "if it's your fate to ship aboard of a vessel, why don't you go peaceable and leave the reasons for it to God Almighty? Ain't anything holdin' you, is there?"

"There is somethin' holdin' me," he says; and then, very low, "What is it, Mr. Siles, that holds a man back from the sea?"

"Saints and skittles!" I says, jolted out o' my play-actin', "you ain't gone and fallen in love, have you?"

He didn't answer. Just sat there starin' at me, his face whiter than I ever saw a livin' man's face. Then all at once he turned his head, exactly as he would have done if a third person had walked into the room. He was gazin' straight at the lamp now. His eyes had a sort o' dazzled look.

"No," he says. "No, I won't tell that. It's . . . too . . . beautiful."

And before I could jump to catch him he pitched in a dead faint onto the floor.

It was two or three days before he was well enough to go to work again. Durin' that time he hardly spoke a word. But one afternoon he came to me.

"Mr. Siles," he said. "I'm queer, but I'm not crazy. You've been kind to me, and I wanted you to know it wasn't that. There are people in this world," he said, "whose lives aren't laid down accordin' to the general rule. I'm one o' them."

And that's all he ever said about his actions the night he drank the whiskey.

It was a week or so later that Wessel's Andy heard the story o' Cap'n Salsbury and the *Lucky Star*. I suppose he was bound to hear it sooner or later, it bein' a fav'rite yarn with the boys. But the way of his hearin' it was an accident, at that.

One afternoon, late, a fisherman from Gloucester put into the harbor. He had carried away some runnin' gear on his way to the

Newf'n'land Banks and was stoppin' in port to refit. After supper the skipper came into the shop, where the boys was sittin' round as usual. First thing he saw was that model o' the *Lucky Star* on the wall.

"What has become o' Dan Salsbury?" says he, squintin' aloft. "What has become o' Dan Salsbury that used to go mackrelin' with the fleet?"

So they told him what had become o' Dan Salsbury, three or four o' them pitchin' in together. But finally it was left to old Jem Haskins to tell the story. In the first place, Jem had the longest wind and in the second place his cousin Allie used to keep house for Cap'n Dan. So Jem knew the ins and outs o' the story better than any o' the rest. As he began to talk, I saw Wessel's Andy pick up his soap box and creep closer. . . . And this is the story that he heard:

Cap'n Dan Salsbury was a deep-sea fisherman, owner and master o' the schooner *Lucky Star.* He had been born and raised in the village and was one of its fav'rite citizens. He was a fine, big man to look at, quiet and unassumin' in his ways and fair in his dealin', aship and ashore. If ever a man deserved to be happy, Dan Salsbury deserved it. But somehow happiness didn't come to him.

First his wife died. He laid her in a little plot o' ground on the hill back of his house, took his year-old girl baby aboard the *Lucky Star* and sailed for God knows where. He was gone ten months. Then he came back, opened his cottage on Salsbury Hill and set out to make little Hope Salsbury the richest girl in the village. He pretty nigh did it, too. His luck was supernat'ral. His catches were talked about up and down the coast. He became a rich man, accordin' to village standards.

Hope Salsbury grew up to be the prettiest girl in town. She was never very strong, takin' after her mother that way, and there was an air about her that kept folks at a distance. It wasn't uppish or mean. She was as kind as an angel, and just about as far-away as one. There wasn't a youngster in the village but would have died to have her, but she scared 'em speechless with her strange, quiet talk and her big misty eyes. Folks said Hope Salsbury wouldn't look at a man, and they were right. She looked straight *through* him.

It worried Cap'n Dan. He didn't want to get rid of Hope, by a long shot, but he knew he was failin' and he wanted to see her settled with a nice, dependable boy who could take care of her after he had

7

gone. There was a man for every woman, said Cap'n Dan. But Hope didn't seem to find her man. She got quieter and quieter, and lonelier and lonelier, till the Cap'n decided somethin' was wrong somewhere. So he asked her straight out if there was anyone she wanted, anyone she cared enough about to marry. She said no, there wasn't. But she said it so queer that the Cap'n began to suspect it was a case of the poor child lovin' somebody who didn't love her. It took him a long time to find the courage to ask that question. But when he did, she only smiled and shook her head.

"Hope," says the Cap'n, "there's only one thing in the world that makes a young girl wilt like you're wiltin', and that's love. Tell me what it is you want, and we'll go searchin' the seven seas till we find it."

"I don't know what it is myself," the girl answered. "It's as though I was in love with someone I had met long ago, and then lost."

"Lost can be found," says the Cap'n. "We'll go 'round the world in the *Lucky Star.*"

Within a month's time the old schooner was overhauled and refitted and made ready for sea. It was June when she sailed out o' the harbor, but she hadn't gone far enough to clear the Cape when a fog shut down and hid her from sight. Most of the village was standin' on the wharf to wave good-bye. But they never saw the *Lucky Star* again. The fog lasted all day and all night and by mornin' o' the second day Cap'n Dan Salsbury and his daughter were a part o' the blue myst'ry across the horizon. They never came back. The *Lucky Star* was lost with all hands in the big blow off Hatteras two years ago this summer. . . . So little Hope Salsbury never found her man, and that branch o' the Salsbury family died, root, stock, and branch.

As old Jem broke off, I glanced at Wessel's Andy. The boy was crouched forward on his soap box, his eyes burnin' like two coals in the shadow. When he saw me lookin' at him, he shrank back like a clam into its shell. That night, as we were undressin' in the back room, he turned to me all of a sudden.

"Mr. Siles," says he, "is there a picture o' Miss Hope Salsbury in this village?"

"Why," I answered, "I don't know as there is . . . and I don't know as there isn't. Come to think, I guess Cap'n Dan's cousin Ed

Salsbury might have a likeness. He inherited most of the Cap'n's prop'ty. Probably find one in the fam'ly album."

"Which house is Ed Salsbury's?"

"Third to the right after you climb the Hill. You aren't thinkin' o' goin' up there tonight, are you?"

Wessel's Andy was kind o' smilin' to himself. He didn't answer my question. But he got into bed all right and proper, turned his face to the wall and was soon breathin' quiet and regular. I never suspected for a minute that he was shammin'.

It was just four o'clock in the mornin' when the telephone in the store began to ring—I looked at the clock as I jumped up to answer the call. I was on a party wire and my call was 13—one long and three shorts. I had never thought about it bein' unlucky till that minute. But it struck me cold to hear that old bell borin' through the early mornin' silence . . .

"Hello," I says, takin' down the receiver.

"This is Ed Salsbury," says the other party. "Come up to my house right away and take your crazy clerk off my hands. I found him sittin' in the parlor when I came down to start the fires. Asked him what he was doin' and he said he had come to steal things. If you ain't up here in fifteen minutes I'll call the deputy sheriff."

I was up there in less than fifteen minutes. I cursed that fool boy every step of the way, but I went. I don't know why I took such trouble about him. Maybe I was a part o' that fate o' his.

Ed met me at the door of his cottage.

"Siles," says he, "there's somethin' queer about this. It's against nature. That boy—I've been talkin' to him—swears he came up here last night to steal. He pried open one o' the front windows and got into the parlor. That's enough to send him to jail for a good long bit, but I'm blessed if I want to send him. I've got a suspicion that the lad is lyin', though why any human should lie himself *into* the penitentiary instead of *out* of it, blamed if I know. You got any ideas on the subject?"

"What was he doin' when you found him?" says I.

"That was funny, too. He was sittin' at the table, with the lamp lit, as home-like as you please. And. . . ."

"And what?"

"Lookin' at that old fam'ly album of ours."

"Ed," I says, "I'll go bond for that boy. Don't say anything about this down at the village. Some day I'll tell you why he came up here at dead o' night to peek into that old album of yours. It ain't quite clear in my own mind yet, but it's gettin' clearer."

"Queer how he looked at me when I came in the door," says Ed. "Just as though he was the one belonged here and I was the trespasser. His eyes. . . ."

"I know," I said. "Where is the boy, Ed? I'll take him home now."

"He's in the kitchen," Ed answered, kind o' sheepish, "eatin' breakfast."

The Salsburys always were the biggest-hearted folk in the village.

So I took Wessel's Andy back to the store, but instead o' talkin' to him like I meant to, I never so much as opened my mouth the whole way home. I couldn't. He looked too *happy*. It was the first time I'd seen him look anything but glum and peaked. Now, he was a changed man. There was a light on his face, and when I say light I mean *light*. Once he burst out laughin'—and it wasn't the sort o' laugh that comes from thinkin' o' somethin' funny. It was just as though he'd seen some great trouble turned inside out and found it lined with joy. He made me think of a *bridegroom*, somehow, stridin' along there in the early dawn. . . .

I believe he would have gone straight on past the store, but for my hand on his arm. He followed me into the back room like a blind man, and there for the first time he spoke.

"I shan't work today," he says, drawin' a deep breath. Again I thought of a *bridegroom*.

"No," I says, "you'll go to bed and get some sleep."

"Yes," he says, "I must sleep." He began to peel off his clothes, and when I came back an hour later he was sleepin' like a baby, and smilin' . . .

He slept well into the afternoon. Then he got up, shaved, washed and put on the best clothes he owned. He didn't have but only the one suit, and he brushed it till it looked like new. Instead o' the blue shirt that he wore around the shop he had on a white one with a standin' collar and a *white tie*. I found him standin' by the window in the back room, lookin' out to sea.

"Mr. Siles," he says, not turnin' round, "I am goin' to leave you "

"Leave?" I says.

"Yes."

"When you goin'?"

"Soon," he says. And then he faced me.

"That ship," he says, "that ship I told you about"—he was speakin' slow and quiet—"it's comin' for me very soon. I shan't have to wait much longer now. I feel that it is near. And I am glad."

"I thought you didn't want to go?" I says, tryin' to get at the real meanin' of his words. I felt like a man in a dark room that's reachin' for somethin' he knows is there but can't quite locate.

"That was yesterday," he says, smilin' like he had smiled in his sleep. "Today I'm glad. Today I want to go. It's the natural thing to do, now. It's so natural—and good—that I don't mind talkin' about it any more. Sit down," he says, "and I'll tell you. You've been my friend, and you ought to know."

I sat down, feelin' kind o' weak in the knees. By this time it was beginning to grow dark. A slight mist was formin' on the water.

"I've already told you," he says, "about the ship that was always behind my eyes. There was somethin' else, Mr. Siles, somethin' I've never told a livin' soul. Ever since I was a little boy I've been seein' a face. It was a child's face to begin with, but it grew as I grew. It was like a beautiful flower, that changes but is always the same. At first I only dreamed it, but as I grew older I used to see it quite clearly, both day and night. I saw it more and more frequently, until lately"—he put his hand to his eyes—"it has become a livin' part o' me. It is a woman's face, Mr. Siles, and it calls me.

"Until last night I had never connected this face in any way with the ship in the fog. You see, one was the most beautiful thing in the world—the *only* beautiful thing in my world—and the other was horrible. But it called me, too, and I was afraid; afraid that I would have to go before I found *her.*"

He leaned forward and put his hand on my knee.

"Mr. Siles," says he, in the voice of a man speakin' of his bride, "I saw that face last night in Mr. Salsbury's old album. It was the face of Hope Salsbury."

I jumped up and away from him. My brain had been warnin' me all along that something like this was comin', but it was a shock, just the same.

"She's dead," I says. "She's dead!"

It was the only thing I could think to say. My mouth was dry as a bone. Words wouldn't come to me.

"Oh, no," he cried, and his voice rang. "Oh, no, Mr. Siles. There's no such thing as bein' dead. There are more worlds than one," he says. "As many more as a man needs," he says. "This is only a poor breath of a world. There are others, others! I know," he says—and laughed—"I know how it is with men. They think because their eyes close and their mouths are still and their hearts stop beatin' that it's the end o' happiness. And maybe it is with some. I can't say. Maybe if folks are entirely happy in this world they don't need the others. But it's every man's right to be happy, Mr. Siles, and the Lord God knows His business. Trust Him, Mr. Siles, trust Him. Don't I know? I used to be afraid, but now I see how it is."

"Lord help me," I says. "What am I to do?"

"Why, nothin'," he says pattin' my knee. "It's all right, Mr. Siles. You go ahead with your life," he says, "the same as though I had never come into it. Take all the happiness you can get, Mr. Siles, for that's as God intended. But never think it ends here."

I couldn't look at him. There was a blur before my eyes. I got up and went out o' the store, headin' down the beach. I wanted to be alone, to sit down quietly and *think*. My brain was spinnin' like a weathercock in a gale.

I must have blundered up the beach a good two miles before I noticed that the mist was thickenin'. I stopped dead still and watched it creep in, blottin' the blue water as it came. It was like the white sheet that a stage magician drops between him and the audience just before he does his great trick. I wondered what was goin' on behind it.

The sun was settin' behind Salsbury Hill. There was a sort o' glow to the fog. It began to shine like a piece of old silver that has been rubbed with a rag. All at once I heard Wessel's Andy say, clear as a bell, "Mr. Siles, I am goin' to leave you!"

I turned toward home, walkin' fast. But somethin' kept pesterin' me to hurry, hurry! I began to run, but I couldn't get ahead of the black fear that was drivin' me. I saw Wessel's Andy standin' at the window and lookin' out to sea. I heard him say, "It's comin' for me very soon." I ran till my heart pounded in my side . . .

The beach curved before me like the blade of a scythe, with the Old Wharf for the handle. The edge of it was glistenin' in the afterglow and the surf broke against it like grain against the knife. I was still half a mile from home when I saw a single figure walk out on that shinin' blade and stand with his arms folded, starin' into the fog. It was Wessel's Andy.

I tried to run faster, but the sand caught my feet. It was like tryin' to run in a dream. I called and shouted to him, but he didn't hear. All the shoutin' in the world wouldn't have stopped him then. Suddenly he threw out his arms and walked down into the water. I was so near by that time that I could see his face. It was like a lamp in the mist.

I called again, but he was in the surf now, and there were other voices in his ears. A wave broke over his shoulders. He struggled on, his hands kind o' gropin' ahead of him. I caught another glimpse of his face. He was smilin' . . .

I gathered myself to jump. I remember the foam on the sand and the water swirlin' underfoot and the new wave makin' and the fog over all. I remember thinkin' o' the strong tide, and how little a man looked in the sea . . .

And then I saw the *Lucky Star.*

I would have known her anywhere. She was just haulin' out o' the mist, on the starboard tack, with all her canvas set. As I looked she melted in the fog—she that should have been lyin' fathoms deep—and after that I only saw her by glances. But I saw her plain. She was no color at all, and there wasn't the sign of a light to mark her, but she came bow on through water that wouldn't have floated a dory, closer and closer until I could make out the people on her decks. They were like statues carved out o' haze. There was a great figure at the wheel, and others up for'ard, in smoky oilskins. And at the lee rail I saw a young girl leanin' against the shrouds, one hand to her heart, the other held out as though to tear aside the mist. . . .

I was in the water then, and it was cold. A wave picked me up and carried me forward. I saw Wessel's Andy flounderin' in the trough ahead o' me. I swam for him. My hand touched his shoulder. He twisted half about and looked at me. His hair was like matted seaweed over his eyes and his face was as pale as the dead. But again, in all that wildness, I thought of *a bridegroom* . . .

A great wave, with a cruel curved edge, lifted above us. I made ready to dive, but he flung his arms out and waited . . . I saw white bows ridin' on the crest of it, and the silver belly of a drawin' jib, and it seemed to me I heard a laugh! Then the wave hit me . . .

When I came to, I was lyin' on the beach with some o' the boys bendin' over me. They had heard me shoutin' and arrived just in time to pull me away from the tide. They never found *him*. They said it was because of the strong undertow. But I knew better. I knew that Wessel's Andy had gone aboard of his vessel at last, and that all was well with him.

Mr. Siles stopped abruptly and drew his hand across his eyes. I found myself staring at the gray wall of fog as though it had been the final curtain of a play. I longed for it to lift—if only for an instant—that I might see the actors out of their parts. But the veil was not drawn aside.

Then I heard someone speaking monotonously of a piazza that would be painted on the morrow, and turning a moment later saw Mr. Siles just vanishing in the mist, a smoky figure solely inhabiting an intangible world.

I went into my house and closed the door.

EDGAR ALLAN POE

MS. FOUND
IN A BOTTLE

OF MY COUNTRY AND of my family I have little to say. Ill usage and length of years have driven me from the one, and estranged me from the other. Hereditary wealth afforded me an education of no common order, and a contemplative turn of mind enabled me to methodize the stories which early study diligently garnered up. Beyond all things, the works of the German moralists gave me great delight: not from my ill-advised admiration of their eloquent madness, but from the ease with which my habits of rigid thought enabled me to detect their falsities. I have often been reproached with the aridity of my genius; a deficiency of imagination has been imputed to me as a crime; and the Pyrrhonism of my opinions has at all times rendered me notorious. Indeed, a strong relish for physical philosophy has, I fear, tinctured my mind with a very common error of this age—I mean the habit of referring occurrences, even the least susceptible of such reference, to the principles of that science. Upon the whole, no person could be less liable than myself to be led away from the severe precincts of truth by the *ignes fatui* of superstition. I have thought proper to premise thus much, lest the incredible tale I have to tell should be considered rather the raving of a crude imagination, than the positive experience of a mind to which the reveries of fancy have been a dead letter and a nullity.

After many years spent in foreign travel, I sailed in the year 18——, from the port of Batavia, in the rich and populous island of Java, on a voyage to the Archipelago Islands. I went as passenger—having no other inducement than a kind of nervous restlessness which haunted me as a fiend.

Our vessel was a beautiful ship of about four hundred tons, copper-fastened, and built at Bombay of Malabar teak. She was freighted with cotton-wool and oil, from the Lachadive Islands. We had also on board coir, jaggeree, ghee, coconuts, and a few cases of opium. The stowage was clumsily done, and the vessel consequently crank.

We got under way with a mere breath of wind, and for many days stood along the eastern coast of Java, without any other incident to beguile the monotony of our course than the occasional meeting with some of the small grabs of the Archipelago to which we were bound.

One evening, leaning over the taffrail, I observed a very singular isolated cloud, to the N. W. It was remarkable, as well from its color as from its being the first we had seen since our departure from Batavia. I watched it attentively until sunset, when it spread all at once to the eastward and westward, girting in the horizon with a narrow strip of vapor, and looking like a long line of low beach. My notice was soon afterward attracted by the dusky-red appearance of the moon, and the peculiar character of the sea. The latter was undergoing a rapid change, and the water seemed more than usually transparent. Although I could distinctly see the bottom, yet, heaving the lead, I found the ship in fifteen fathoms. The air now became intolerably hot, and was loaded with spiral exhalations similar to those arising from heated iron. As night came on, every breath of wind died away, and a more entire calm it is impossible to conceive. The flame of a candle burned upon the poop without the least perceptible motion, and a long hair, held between the finger and thumb, hung without the possibility of detecting a vibration. However, as the captain said he could perceive no indication of danger, and as we were drifting in bodily to shore, he ordered the sails to be furled, and the anchor let go. No watch was set, and the crew, consisting principally of Malays, stretched themselves deliberately upon deck. I went below—not without a full presentiment of evil. Indeed, every appearance warranted me in apprehending a simoon. I told the captain of my fears; but he paid no attention to what I said, and left me without deigning to give a reply. My uneasiness, however, prevented me from sleeping, and about midnight I went upon deck. As I placed my foot upon the upper step of the companion-ladder, I was startled by a loud, humming noise, like that occasioned by the rapid revolution of a mill-wheel, and before I could ascertain its meaning, I found the ship quivering to its centre. In the next instant a wilderness of foam hurled us upon our beam-ends, and, rushing over us fore and aft, swept the entire decks from stem to stern.

The extreme fury of the blast proved, in a great measure, the salvation of the ship. Although completely water-logged, yet, as her masts had gone by the board, she rose, after a minute, heavily from the sea, and, staggering awhile beneath the immense pressure of the tempest, finally righted.

By what miracle I escaped destruction, it is impossible to say. Stunned by the shock of the water, I found myself, upon recovery, jammed in between the sternpost and rudder. With great difficulty I regained my feet, and looking dizzily around, was at first struck with the idea of our being among breakers; so terrific, beyond the wildest imagination, was the whirlpool of mountainous and foaming ocean within which we were engulfed. After a while I heard the voice of an old Swede, who had shipped with us at the moment of leaving port. I hallooed to him with all my strength, and presently he came reeling aft. We soon discovered that we were the sole survivors of the accident. All on deck, with the exception of ourselves, had been swept overboard; the captain and mates must have perished while they slept, for the cabins were deluged with water. Without assistance we could expect to do little for the security of the ship, and our exertions were at first paralyzed by the momentary expectation of going down. Our cable had, of course, parted like pack-thread, at the first breath of the hurricane, or we should have been instantaneously over-whelmed. We scudded with frightful velocity before the sea, and the water made clear breaches over us. The framework of our stern was shattered excessively, and, in almost every respect, we had received considerable injury; but to our extreme joy we found the pumps unchoked, and that we had made no great shifting of our ballast. The main fury of the blast had already blown over, and we apprehended little danger from the violence of the wind; but we looked forward to its total cessation with dismay; well believing, that in our shattered condition, we should inevitably perish in the tremendous swell which would ensue. But this very just apprehension seemed by no means likely to be soon verified. For five entire days and nights—during which our only subsistence was a small quantity of jaggeree, procured with great difficulty from the forecastle—the hulk flew at a rate defying computation, before rapidly succeeding flaws of wind, which, without equalling the first violence of the simoon, were still more terrific than any tempest I had before encountered. Our course for the first four days was, with trifling variations, S. E. and by S.; and we must have run down the coast of New Holland. On the fifth day the cold became extreme, although the wind had hauled round a point more to the northward. The sun arose with a sickly yellow lustre, and clambered a very few degrees above the horizon—emitting no decisive light. There were no clouds apparent, yet the wind was upon the increase, and blew with a fitful and unsteady fury. About noon, as nearly as we could guess, our attention was again arrested by the appearance of the sun. It gave out no light, properly so called, but a dull and sullen glow without reflection, as if all its rays were polarized. Just before sinking within the turgid sea, its central fires suddenly went out, as if hurriedly extinguished by some unaccountable power. It was a dim, silver-like rim, alone, as it rushed down the unfathomable ocean.

We waited in vain for the arrival of the sixth day—that day to me has not yet arrived—to the Swede never did arrive. Thenceforward we were enshrouded in pitchy darkness, so that we could not have seen an object at twenty paces from the ship. Eternal night continued to envelop us, all unrelieved by the phosphoric sea-brilliancy to which we had been accustomed in the tropics. We observed, too, that, although the tempest continued to rage with unabated violence, there was no longer to be discovered the usual appearance of surf, or foam, which had hitherto attended us. All around were horror, and thick gloom, and a black sweltering desert of ebony. Superstitious terror crept by degrees into the spirit of the old Swede, and my own soul was wrapt in silent wonder. We neglected all care of the ship, as worse than useless, and securing ourselves as well as possible, to the stump of the mizen-mast, looked out bitterly into the world of ocean. We had no means of calculating time, nor could we form any guess of our situation. We were, however, well aware of having made farther to the southward than any previous navigators, and felt great amazement at not meeting with the usual impediments of ice. In the meantime every moment threatened to be our last—every mountainous billow hurried to overwhelm us. The swell surpassed anything I had imagined possible, and that we were not instantly buried is a miracle. My companion spoke of the lightness of our cargo, and reminded me of the excellent qualities of our ship; but I could not help feeling the utter hopelessness of hope itself, and prepared myself gloomily for that death which I thought nothing could defer beyond an hour, as, with every knot of way the ship made, the swelling of the black stupendous seas became more dismally appalling. At times we gasped for breath at an elevation beyond the albatross—at times became dizzy with the velocity of our descent into some watery hell, where the air grew stagnant, and no sound disturbed the slumbers of the kraken.

We were at the bottom of one of these abysses, when a quick scream from my companion broke fearfully upon the night. "See! see!" cried he, shrieking in my ears, "Almighty God! see! see!" As he spoke I became aware of a dull sullen glare of red light which streamed down the sides of the vast chasm where we lay, and threw a fitful brilliancy upon our deck. Casting my eyes upwards, I beheld a spectacle which froze the current of my blood. At a terrific height directly above us, and upon the very verge of the precipitous descent, hovered a gigantic ship of perhaps four thousand tons. Although upreared upon the summit of a wave more than a hundred times her own altitude, her apparent size still exceeded that of any ship of the line or East Indiaman in existence. Her huge hull was of a deep dingy black, unrelieved by any of the customary carvings of a ship. A single row of brass cannon protruded from her open ports, and dashed from the polished surfaces the fires of innumerable battle-lanterns which swung to and from about her rigging. But what mainly inspired us with horror and astonishment, was that she bore up under a press of sail in the very teeth of that supernatural sea, and of that ungovernable hurricane. When we first discovered her, her bows were alone to be seen, as she rose slowly from the dim and horrible gulf beyond her. For a moment of intense terror she paused upon the giddy pinnacle as if in contemplation of her own sublimity, then trembled, and tottered, and—came down.

At this instant, I know not what sudden self-possession came over my spirit. Staggering as far aft as I could, I awaited fearlessly the ruin that was to overwhelm. Our own vessel was at length ceasing from her struggles, and sinking with her head to the sea. The shock of the descending mass struck her, consequently, in that portion of her frame which was nearly under water, and the inevitable result was to hurl me, with irresistible violence, upon the rigging of the stranger.

As I fell, the ship hove in stays, and went about; and to the confusion ensuing I attributed my escape from the notice of the crew. With little difficulty I made my way, unperceived, to the main hatchway, which was partially open, and soon found an opportunity of secreting myself in the hold. Why I did so I can hardly tell. An indefinite sense of awe, which at first sight of the navigators of the ship had taken hold of my mind, was perhaps the principle of my concealment. I was unwilling to trust myself with a race of people who had offered, to the cursory glance I had taken, so many points of vague novelty, doubt, and apprehension. I therefore thought proper to contrive a hiding-place in the hold. This I did by removing a small portion of the shifting-boards, in such a manner as to afford me a convenient retreat between the huge timbers of the ship.

I had scarcely completed my work, when a footstep in the hold forced me to make use of it. A man passed by my place of concealment with a feeble and unsteady gait. I could not see his face, but had an opportunity of observing his general appearance. There was about it an evidence of great age and infirmity. His knees tottered beneath a load of years, and his entire frame quivered under the burthen. He muttered to himself, in a low broken tone, some words of a language which I could not understand, and groped in a corner among a pile of singular-looking instruments, and decayed charts of navigation. His manner was a wild mixture of the peevishness of second childhood, and the solemn dignity of a God. He at length went on deck, and I saw him no more.

A feeling, for which I have no name, has taken possession of my soul—a sensation which will admit of no analysis, to which the lessons of bygone time are inadequate, and for which I fear futurity itself will offer me no key. To a mind constituted like my own, the latter consideration is an evil. I shall never—I know that I shall never—be satisfied with regard to the nature of my conceptions. Yet it is not wonderful that these conceptions are indefinite, since they have their origin in sources so utterly novel. A new sense—a new entity—is added to my soul.

It is long since I first trod the deck of this terrible ship, and the rays of my destiny are, I think, gathering to a focus. Incomprehensible men! Wrapped up in meditations of a kind which I cannot divine, they pass me by unnoticed. Concealment is utter folly on my part, for the people *will not* see. It is but just now that I passed directly before the eyes of the mate; it was no long while ago that I ventured into the captain's own private cabin, and took thence the materials with which I write, and have written. I shall from time to time continue this journal. It is true that I may not find an opportunity of transmitting it to the world, but I will not fail to make the endeavor. At the last moment I will enclose the MS in a bottle, and cast it within the sea.

An incident has occurred which has given me new room for meditation. Are such things the operation of ungoverned chance? I had ventured upon deck and thrown myself down, without attracting any notice, among a pile of ratlin-stuff and old sails, in the bottom of the yawl. While musing upon the singularity of my fate, I unwittingly daubed with a tar-brush the edges of a neatly-folded studding-sail which lay near me on a barrel. The studding-sail is now bent upon the ship, and the thoughtless touches of the brush are spread out into the word DISCOVERY.

I have made my observations lately upon the structure of the vessel. Although well armed, she is not, I think, a ship of war. Her rigging, build, and general equipment, all negative a supposition of this kind. What she *is not*, I can easily perceive; what she *is*, I fear it is impossible to say. I know not how it is, but in scrutinizing her strange model and singular cast of spars, her huge size and overgrown suits of canvas, her severely simple bow and antiquated stern, there will occasionally flash across my mind a sensation of familiar things, and there is always mixed up with such indistinct shadows of recollection, an unaccountable memory of old foreign chronicles and ages long ago.

I have been looking at the timbers of the ship. She is built of a material to which I am a stranger. There is a peculiar character about the wood which strikes me as rendering it unfit for the purpose to which it has been applied. I mean its extreme *porousness*, considered independently of the worm-eaten condition which is a consequence of navigation in these seas, and apart from the rottenness attendant upon age. It will appear perhaps an observation somewhat over-curious, but this would have every characteristic of Spanish oak, if Spanish oak were distended by any unnatural means.

In reading the above sentence, a curious apothegm of an old weatherbeaten Dutch navigator comes full upon my recollection. "It is as sure," he was wont to say, when any doubt was entertained of his veracity, "as sure as there is a sea where the ship itself will grow in bulk like the living body of the seaman."

About an hour ago, I made bold to trust myself among a group of the crew. They paid me no manner of attention, and, although I stood in the very midst of them all, seemed utterly unconscious of my presence. Like the one I had at first seen in the hold, they all bore about them the marks of a hoary old age. Their knees trembled with infirmity; their shoulders were bent double with decrepitude; their shrivelled skins rattled in the wind; their voices were low, tremulous, and broken; their eyes glistened with the rheum of years; and their gray hairs streamed terribly in the tempest. Around them, on every part of the deck, lay scattered mathematical instruments of the most quaint and obsolete construction.

I mentioned, some time ago, the bending of a studding-sail. From that period, the ship, being thrown dead off the wind, has continued her terrific course due south, with every rag of canvas packed upon her, from her truck to her lower studding-sail booms, and rolling every moment her top-gallant yardarms into the most appalling hell of water which it can enter into the mind of man to imagine. I have just left the deck, where I find it impossible to maintain a footing, although the crew seem to experience little inconvenience. It appears to me a miracle of miracles that our enormous bulk is not swallowed up at once and forever. We are surely doomed to hover continually upon the brink of eternity, without taking a final plunge into the abyss. From billows a thousand times more stupendous than any I have ever seen, we glide away with the facility of the arrowy seagull; and the colossal waters rear their heads above us like demons of the deep, but like demons confined to simple threats, and forbidden to destroy. I am led to attribute these frequent escapes to the only natural cause which can account for such effect. I must suppose the ship to be within the influence of some strong current, or impetuous undertow.

I have seen the captain face to face, and in his own cabin—but, as I expected, he paid me no attention. Although in his appearance there is, to a casual observer, nothing which might bespeak him more or less than man, still, a feeling of irrepressible reverence and awe mingled with the sensation of wonder with which I regarded him. In stature, he is nearly my own height; that is, about five feet eight inches. He is of a well-knit and compact frame of body, neither robust nor remarkable otherwise. But it is the singularity of the expression which reigns upon the face—it is the intense, the wonderful, the thrilling evidence of old age so utter, so extreme, which excites within my spirit a sense—a sentiment ineffable. His forehead, although little wrinkled, seems to bear upon it the stamp of a myriad of years. His gray hairs are records of the past, and his grayer eyes are sybils of the future. The cabin floor was thickly strewn with strange, iron-clasped folios, and mouldering instruments of science, and obsolete long-forgotten charts. His head was bowed down upon his hands, and he pored, with a fiery, unquiet eye, over a paper which I took to be a commission, and which, at all events, bore the signature of a monarch. He murmured to himself—as did the first seaman whom I saw in the hold—some low peevish syllables of a foreign tongue; and although the speaker was close at my elbow, his voice seemed to reach my ears from the distance of a mile.

*

The ship and all in it are imbued with the spirit of Eld. The crew glide to and fro like the ghosts of buried centuries; their eyes have an eager and uneasy meaning; and when their fingers fall athwart my path in the wild glare of the battle-lanterns, I feel as I have never felt before, although I have been all my life a dealer in antiquities, and have imbibed the shadows of fallen columns at Balbec, and Tadmor, and Persepolis, until my very soul has become a ruin.

When I look around me, I feel ashamed of my former apprehension. If I trembled at the blast which has hitherto attended us, shall I not stand aghast at a warring of wind and ocean, to convey any idea of which, the words tornado and simoon are trivial and ineffective? All in the immediate vicinity of the ship, is the blackness of eternal night, and a chaos of foamless water; but, about a league on either side of us, may be seen, indistinctly and at intervals, stupendous ramparts of ice, towering away into the desolate sky, and looking like the walls of the universe.

As I imagined, the ship proves to be in a current—if that appellation can properly be given to a tide which, howling and shrieking by the white ice, thunders on to the southward with a velocity like the headlong dashing of a cataract.

To conceive the horror of my sensations is, I presume, utterly impossible; yet a curiosity to penetrate the mysteries of these awful regions predominates even over my despair, and will reconcile me to the most hideous aspect of death. It is evident that we are hurrying onward to some exciting knowledge—some never-to-be-imparted secret, whose attainment is destruction. Perhaps this current leads us to the southern pole itself. It must be confessed that a supposition apparently so wild has every probability in its favor.

The crew pace the deck with unquiet and tremulous step; but there is upon their countenance an expression more of the eagerness of hope than of the apathy of despair.

In the meantime the wind is still in our poop, and, as we carry a crowd of canvas, the ship is at times lifted bodily from out the sea! Oh, horror upon horror!—the ice opens suddenly to the right, and to the left, and we are whirling dizzily, in immense concentric circles, round and round the borders of a gigantic amphitheatre, the summit of whose walls is lost in the darkness and the distance. But little time will be left me to ponder upon my destiny! The circles rapidly grow small—we are plunging madly within the grasp of the whirlpool—and amid a roaring, and bellowing, and thundering of ocean and tempest, the ship is quivering—oh God! and—going down!

F. MARION CRAWFORD

MAN OVERBOARD!

YES—I HAVE HEARD "Man overboard!" a good many times since I was a boy, and once or twice I have seen the man go. There are more men lost in that way than passengers on ocean steamers ever learn of. I have stood looking over the rail on a dark night, when there was a step beside me, and something flew past my head like a big black bat—and then there was a splash! Stokers often go like that. They go mad with the heat, and they slip up on deck and are gone before anybody can stop them, often without being seen or heard.

Now and then a passenger will do it, but he generally has what he thinks a pretty good reason. I have seen a man empty his revolver into a crowd of emigrants forward, and then go over like a rocket. Of course, any officer who respects himself will do what he can to pick a man up, if the weather is not so heavy that he would have to risk his ship; but I don't think I remember seeing a man come back when he was once fairly gone more than two or three times in all my life, though we have often picked up the life buoy, and sometimes the fellow's cap. Stokers and passengers jump over; I never knew a sailor to do that, drunk or sober. Yes, they say it has happened on hard ships, but I never knew a case myself. Once in a long time a man is fished out when it is just too late, and dies in the boat before you can get him aboard, and—well, I don't know that I ever told that story since it happened—I knew a fellow who went over, and came back dead. I didn't see him after he came back; only one of us did, but we all knew he was there.

No, I am not giving you "sharks." There isn't a shark in this story, and I don't know that I would tell it at all if we weren't alone, just you and I. But you and I have seen things in various parts, and maybe you will understand. Anyhow, you know that I am telling what I know about, and nothing else; and it has been on my mind to tell you ever since it happened, only there hasn't been a chance.

It's a long story, and it took some time to happen; and it began a good many years ago, in October, as well as I can remember. I was mate then; I passed the local Marine Board for master about three years later. She was the *Helen B. Jackson*, of New York, with lumber for the West Indies, four-masted schooner, Captain Hackstaff. She was an old-fashioned one, even then—no steam donkey, and all to do by hand.

There were still sailors in the coasting trade in those days, you remember. She wasn't a hard ship, for the Old Man was better than most of them, though he kept to himself and had a face like a monkey wrench. We were thirteen, all told, in the ship's company; and some of them afterwards thought that might have had something to do with it, but I had all that nonsense knocked out of me when I was a boy. I don't mean to say that I like to go to sea on a Friday, but I *have* gone to sea on a Friday, and nothing has happened; and twice before that we have been thirteen, because one of the hands didn't turn up at the last minute, and nothing ever happened either—nothing worse than the loss of a light spar or two, or a little canvas. Whenever I have been wrecked, we had sailed as cheerily as you please—no thirteens, no Fridays, no dead men in the hold. I believe it generally happens that way.

I dare say you remember those two Benton boys that were so much alike? It's no wonder, for they were twin brothers. They shipped with us as boys on the old *Boston Belle*, when you were mate and I was before the mast. I never was quite sure which was which of those two, even then; and when they both had beards it was harder than ever to tell them apart. One was Jim, and the other was Jack; James Benton and John Benton. The only difference I ever could see was that one seemed to be rather more cheerful and inclined to talk than the other; but one couldn't even be sure of that. Perhaps they had moods. Anyhow, there was one of them that used to whistle when he was alone. He only knew one tune, and that was "Nancy Lee," and the other didn't know any tune at all; but I may be mistaken about that, too. Perhaps they both knew it.

Well, those two Benton boys turned up on board the *Helen B. Jackson.* They had been on half a dozen ships since the *Boston Belle,* and they had grown up and were good seamen. They had reddish beards and bright blue eyes and freckled faces; and they were quiet fellows, good workmen on rigging, pretty willing, and both good men at the wheel. They managed to be in the same watch— it was the port watch on the *Helen B.,* and that was mine, and I had great confidence in them both. If there was any job aloft that needed two hands, they were always the first to jump into the rigging; but that doesn't often happen on a fore-and-aft schooner. If it breezed up, and the jibtopsail was to be taken in, they never minded a wetting, and they would be out at the bowsprit end before there was a hand at the downhaul. The men liked them for that, and because they didn't blow about what they could do.

I remember one day in a reefing job, the downhaul parted and came down on deck from the peak of the spanker. When the weather moderated, and we shook the reefs out, the downhaul was forgotten, until we happened to think we might soon need it again. There was some sea on, and the boom was off and the gaff was slamming. One of those Benton boys was at the wheel, and before I knew what he was doing, the other was out on the gaff with the end of the new downhaul, trying to reeve it through its block. The one who was steering watched him, and got as white as cheese. The other one was swinging about on the gaff end, and every time she rolled to leeward he brought up with a jerk that would have sent anything but a monkey flying into space. But he didn't leave it until he had rove the new rope, and he got back all right. I think it was Jack at the wheel; the one that seemed more cheerful, the one that whistled "Nancy Lee." He had rather have been doing the job himself than watch his brother do it, and he had a scared look; but he kept her as steady as he could in the swell, and he drew a long breath when Jim had worked his way back to the peak-halliard block, and had something to hold on to. I think it was Jim.

They had good togs, too, and they were neat and clean men in the forecastle. I knew they had nobody belonging to them ashore— no mother, no sisters, and no wives; but somehow they both looked as if a woman overhauled them now and then. I remember that they had one ditty bag between them, and they had a woman's thimble in it. One of the men said something about it to them and they looked at each other; and one smiled, but the other didn't. Most of their clothes were alike, but they had one red guernsey between them. For some time I used to think it was always the same one that wore it, and I thought that might be a way to tell them apart. But then I heard one asking the other for it, and saying that the other had worn it last. So that was no sign either.

The cook was a West Indies man, called James Lawley; his father had been hanged for putting lights in coconut trees where they didn't belong. But he was a good cook, and knew his business; and it wasn't soup-and-bully and dog's-body every Sunday. That's what I meant to say. On Sunday the cook called both those boys Jim, and on weekdays he called them Jack. He used to say he must be right sometimes if he did that, because even the hands on a painted clock point right twice a day.

What started me trying for some way of telling the Bentons apart was this. I heard them talking about a girl. It was at night, in our watch, and the wind had headed us off a little rather suddenly, and when we had flattened in the jibs, we clewed down the topsails, while the two Benton boys got the spanker sheet aft. One of them was at the helm. I coiled down the mizzen-topsail downhaul myself, and was going aft to see how she headed up, when I stopped to look at a light, and leaned against the deckhouse. While I was standing there I heard the two boys talking. It sounded as if they had talked of the same thing before, and as far as I could tell, the voice I heard first belonged to the one who wasn't quite so cheerful as the other—the one who was Jim when one knew which he was.

"Does Mamie know?" Jim asked.

"Not yet," Jack answered quietly. He was at the wheel. "I mean to tell her next time we get home."

"All right."

That was all I heard, because I didn't care to stand there listening while they were talking about their own affairs; so I went aft to look into the binnacle, and I told the one at the wheel to keep her so as long as she had way on her, for I thought the wind would back up again before long, and there was land to leeward. When he answered, his voice, somehow, didn't sound like the cheerful one. Perhaps his brother had relieved the wheel while they had been speaking, but what I had heard set me wondering which of them it was that had a girl at home. There's lots of time for wondering on a schooner in fair weather.

After that I thought I noticed that the two brothers were more silent when they were together. Perhaps they guessed that I had overheard something that night, and kept quiet when I was about. Some men would have amused themselves by trying to chaff them separately about the girl at home, and I suppose whichever one it was would have let the cat out of the bag if I had done that. But, somehow, I didn't like to. Yes, I was thinking of getting married myself at that time, so I had a sort of fellow-feeling for whichever one it was, that made me not want to chaff him.

They didn't talk much, it seemed to me; but in fair weather when there was nothing to do at night, and one was steering, the other was everlastingly hanging round as if he were waiting to relieve the wheel, though he might have been enjoying a quiet nap for all I cared in such weather. Or else, when one was taking his turn at the lookout, the other would be sitting on an anchor beside him. One kept near the other, at night more than in the daytime. I noticed that. They were fond of sitting on that anchor, and they generally tucked away their pipes under it, for the *Helen B.* was a dry boat in most weather, and like most fore-and-afters was better on a wind than going free. With a beam sea we sometimes shipped a little water aft. We were by the stern, anyhow, on that voyage, and that is one reason why we lost the man.

We fell in with a southerly gale, southeast at first; and then the barometer began to fall while you could watch it, and a long swell began to come up from the south'ard. A couple of months earlier we might have been in for a cyclone, but it's "October all over" in those waters, as you know better than I. It was just going to blow, and then it was going to rain, that was all; and we had plenty of time to make everything snug before it breezed up much. It blew harder after sunset, and by the time it was quite dark it was a full gale. We had shortened sail for it, but as we were by the stern we were carrying the spanker close reefed instead of the storm trysail. She steered better so, as long as we didn't have to heave to. I had the first watch with the Benton boys, and we had not been on deck an hour when a child might have seen that the weather meant business.

The Old Man came up on deck and looked round, and in less than a minute he told us to give her the trysail. That meant heaving to, and I was glad of it; for though the *Helen B.* was a good vessel enough, she wasn't a new ship by a long way, and it did her no good to drive her in that weather. I asked whether I should call all hands, but just then the cook came aft, and the Old Man said he thought we could manage the job without waking the sleepers, and the trysail was handy on deck already, for we hadn't been expecting anything better. We were all in oilskins, of course, and the night was as black as a coal mine, with only a ray of light from the slit in the binnacle shield, and you couldn't tell one man from another except by his voice.

The Old Man took the wheel; we got the boom amidships, and he jammed her into the wind until she had hardly any way. It was blowing now, and it was all that I and two others could do to get in the slack of the downhaul, while the others lowered away at the peak and throat, and we had our hands full to get a couple of turns round the wet sail. It's all child's play on a fore-and-after compared with reefing topsails in anything like weather, but the gear of a schooner sometimes does unhandy things that you don't expect, and those everlasting long halliards get foul of everything if they get adrift. I remember thinking how unhandy that particular job was. Somebody unhooked the throat-halliard block, and thought he had hooked it into the head-cringle of the trysail, and sang out to hoist away, but he had missed it in the dark, and the heavy block went flying into the lee rigging, and nearly killed him when it swung back with the weather roll. Then the Old Man got her up in the wind until the jib was shaking like thunder; then he held her off, and she went off as soon as the head-sails filled, and he couldn't get her back again without the spanker.

Then the *Helen B.* did her favourite trick, and before we had time to say much we had a sea over the quarter and were up to our waists, with the parrels of the trysail only half becketed round the mast, and the deck so full of gear that you couldn't put your foot on a plank, and the spanker beginning to get adrift again, being badly stopped, and the general confusion and hell's delight that you can only have on a fore-and-after when there's nothing really serious the matter. Of course, I don't mean to say that the Old Man couldn't have steered his trick as well as you or I or any other seaman; but I don't believe he had ever been on board the *Helen B.* before, or had his hand on her wheel till then; and he didn't know her ways. I don't mean to say that what happened was his fault. I don't know whose fault it was. Perhaps nobody was to blame. But I know something happened somewhere on board when we shipped that sea, and you'll never get it out of my head. I hadn't any spare time myself, for I was becketing the rest of the trysail to the mast. We were on the starboard tack, and the throat-halliard came down to port as usual, and I suppose there were at least three men at it, hoisting away, while I was at the beckets.

Now I am going to tell you something. You have known me, man and boy, several voyages; and you are older than I am; and you have always been a good friend to me. Now, do you think I am the sort of man to think I hear things when there isn't anything to hear, or to think I see things when there is nothing to see? No, you don't. Thank you.

Well now, I had passed the last becket, and I sang out to the men to sway away, and I was standing on the jaws of the spanker-gaff, with my left hand on the bolt-rope of the trysail, so that I could feel when it was board taut, and I wasn't thinking of anything except being glad the job was over, and that we were going to heave her to. It was as black as a coal-pocket, except that you could see the streaks on the seas as they went by, and abaft the deckhouse I could see the ray of light from the binnacle on the captain's yellow oilskin as he stood at the wheel—or, rather, I might have seen it if I had looked round at that minute. But I didn't look round. I heard a man whistling. It was "Nancy Lee," and I could have sworn that the man was right over my head in the crosstrees. Only somehow I knew very well that if anybody could have been up there, and could have whistled a tune, there were no living ears sharp enough to hear it on deck then. I heard it distinctly, and at the same time I heard the real whistling of the wind in the weather rigging, sharp and clear as the steam-whistle on a peanut-cart in New York. That was all right, that was as it should be; but the other wasn't right; and I felt queer and stiff, as if I couldn't move, and my hair was curling against the flannel lining of my sou'wester, and I thought somebody had dropped a lump of ice down my back.

I said that the noise of the wind in the rigging was real, as if the other wasn't, for I felt that it wasn't, though I heard it. But it was, all the same; for the captain heard it too. When I came to relieve the wheel, while the men were clearing up decks, he was swearing. He was a quiet man, and I hadn't heard him swear before, and I don't think I did again, though several queer things happened after that. Perhaps he said all he had to say then; I don't see how he could have said anything more. I used to think nobody could swear like a Dane, except a Neapolitan or a South American; but when I had heard the Old Man I changed my mind. There's nothing afloat or ashore than can beat one of your quiet American skippers, if he gets off on that tack. I didn't need to ask him what was the matter, for I knew he had heard "Nancy Lee," as I had, only it affected us differently.

He did not give me the wheel, but told me to go forward and get the second bonnet off the staysail, so as to keep her up better. As we tailed on to the sheet when it was done, the man next me knocked his sou'wester off against my shoulder, and his face came so close to me that I could see it in the dark. It must have been very white for me to see it, but I only thought of that afterwards. I don't see how any light could have fallen upon it, but I knew it was one of the Benton boys. I don't know what made me speak to him. "Hullo, Jim! Is that you?" I asked. I don't know why I said Jim, rather than Jack.

"I am Jack," he answered.

We made all fast, and things were much quieter.

"The Old Man heard you whistling 'Nancy Lee' just now," I said, "and he didn't like it."

It was as if there were a white light inside his face, and it was ghastly. I know his teeth chattered. But he didn't say anything, and the next minute he was somewhere in the dark trying to find his sou'wester at the foot of the mast.

When all was quiet, and she was hove to, coming to and falling off her four points as regularly as a pendulum, and the helm lashed a little to the lee, the Old Man turned in again, and I managed to light a pipe in the lee of the deckhouse, for there was nothing more to be done till the gale chose to moderate, and the ship was as easy as a baby in its cradle. Of course the cook had gone below, as he might have done an hour earlier; so there were supposed to be four of us in the watch. There was a man at the lookout, and there was a hand by the wheel, though there was no steering to be done, and I was having my pipe in the lee of the deckhouse, and the fourth man was somewhere about decks, probably having a smoke too. I thought some skippers I have sailed with would have called the watch aft, and given them a drink after that job; but it wasn't cold, and I guessed that our Old Man wouldn't be particularly generous in that way. My hands and feet were red hot, and it would be time enough to get into dry clothes when it was my watch below; so I stayed where I was, and smoked. But by and by, things being so quiet, I began to wonder why nobody moved on deck; just that sort of restless wanting to know where every man is that one sometimes feels in a gale of wind on a dark night.

So when I had finished my pipe I began to move about. I went aft, and there was a man leaning over the wheel, with his legs apart and both hands hanging down in the light from the binnacle, and his sou'wester over his eyes. Then I went forward, and there was a man at the lookout, with his back against the foremast, getting what shelter he could from the staysail. I knew by his small height that he was not one of the Benton boys. Then I went round by the weather side, and poked about in the dark, for I began to wonder where the other man was. But I couldn't find him, though I searched the decks until I got right aft again. It was certainly one of the Benton boys that was missing, but it wasn't like either of them to go below to change his clothes in such warm weather. The man at the wheel was the other, of course. I spoke to him.

"Jim, what's become of your brother?"

"I am Jack, sir."

"Well, then, Jack, where's Jim? He's not on deck."

"I don't know, sir."

When I had come up to him he had stood up from force of instinct, and had laid his hands on the spokes as if he were steering, though the wheel was lashed; but he still bent his face down, and it was half hidden by the edge of his sou'wester, while he seemed to be staring at the compass. He spoke in a very low voice, but that was natural, for the captain had left his door open when he turned in, as it was a warm night in spite of the storm, and there was no fear of shipping any more water now.

"What put it into your head to whistle like that, Jack? You've been at sea long enough to know better."

He said something, but I couldn't hear the words: it sounded as if he were denying the charge.

"Somebody whistled," I said.

He didn't answer, and then, I don't know why, perhaps because the Old Man hadn't given us a drink, I cut half an inch off the plug of tobacco I had in my oilskin pocket, and gave it to him. He knew my tobacco was good, and he shoved it into his mouth with a word of thanks. I was on the weather side of the wheel.

"Go forward and see if you can find Jim," I said.

He started a little, and then stepped back and passed behind me, and was going along the weather side. Maybe his silence about the whistling had irritated me, and his taking it for granted that because we were hove to, and it was a dark night, he might go forward any way he pleased. Anyhow, I stopped him, though I spoke good-naturedly enough.

"Pass to leeward, Jack," I said.

He didn't answer, but crossed the deck between the binnacle and the deckhouse to the lee side. She was only falling off and coming to, and riding the big seas as easily as possible, but the man was not steady on his feet and reeled against the corner of the deckhouse and then against the lee rail. I was quite sure he couldn't have had anything to drink, for neither of the brothers were the kind to hide rum from their shipmates, if they had any, and the only spirits that were aboard were locked up in the captain's cabin. I wondered whether he had been hit by the throat-halliard block and was hurt.

I left the wheel and went after him, but when I got to the corner of the deckhouse I saw that he was on a full run forward, so I went back. I watched the compass for a while, to see how far she went off, and she must have come to again half a dozen times before I heard voices, more than three or four, forward; and then I heard the little West Indies cook's voice, high and shrill above the rest:

"Man overboard!"

There wasn't anything to be done, with the ship hove to and the wheel lashed. If there was a man overboard, he must be in the water right alongside. I couldn't imagine how it could have happened, but I ran forward instinctively. I came upon the cook first, half dressed in his shirt and trousers, just as he had tumbled out of his bunk. He was jumping into the main rigging, evidently hoping to see the man, as if anyone could have seen anything on such a night, except the foam-streaks on the black water, and now and then the curl of a breaking sea as it went away to leeward. Several of the men were peering over the rail into the dark. I caught the cook by the foot, and asked who was gone.

"It's Jim Benton," he shouted down to me. "He's not aboard this ship!"

There was no doubt about that. Jim Benton was gone; and I knew in a flash that he had been taken off by that sea when we were setting the storm trysail. It was nearly half an hour since then; she had run like wild for a few minutes until we got her hove to, and no swimmer that ever swam could have lived as long as that in such a sea. The men knew it as well as I, but still they stared into the foam as if they had any chance of seeing the lost man. I let the cook get into the rigging, and joined the men, and asked if they had made a thorough search on board, though I knew they had and that it could not take long, for he wasn't on deck, and there was only the forecastle below.

"That sea took him over, sir, as sure as you're born," said one of the men close beside me.

We had no boat that could have lived in that sea, of course, and we all knew it. I offered to put one over, and let her drift astern two or three cable lengths by a line, if the men thought they could haul me aboard again; but none of them would listen to that, and I should probably have been drowned if I had tried it, even with a life belt; for it was breaking sea. Besides, they all knew as well as I did that the man could not be right in our wake. I don't know why I spoke again.

"Jack Benton, are you there? Will you go if I will?"

"No, sir," answered a voice; and that was all.

By that time the Old Man was on deck, and I felt his hand on my shoulder rather roughly, as if he meant to shake me.

"I'd reckoned you had more sense, Mr. Torkeldsen," he said. "God knows I would risk my ship to look for him, if it were any use; but he must have gone half an hour ago."

He was a quiet man, and the men knew he was right, and that they had seen the last of Jim Benton when they were bending the trysail—if anybody had seen him then. The captain went below again, and for some time the men stood around Jack, quite near him, without saying anything, as sailors do when they are sorry for a man and can't help him; and then the watch below turned in again, and we were three on deck.

Nobody can understand that there can be much consolation in a funeral, unless he has felt that blank feeling there is when a man's gone overboard whom everybody likes. I suppose landsmen think it would be easier if they didn't have to bury their fathers and mothers and friends; but it wouldn't be. Somehow the funeral keeps up the idea of something beyond. You may believe in that something just the same; but a man who has gone in the dark, between two seas, without a cry, seems much more beyond reach than if he were still lying on his bed, and had only just stopped breathing. Perhaps Jim Benton knew that, and wanted to come back to us. I don't know, and I am only telling you what happened, and you may think what you like.

Jack stuck by the wheel that night until the watch was over. I don't know whether he slept afterwards, but when I came on deck four hours later, there he was again, in his oilskins, with his sou'wester over his eyes, staring into the binnacle. We saw that he would rather stand there, and we left him alone. Perhaps it was some consolation to him to get that ray of light when everything was so dark.

It began to rain, too, as it can when a southerly gale is going to break up, and we got every bucket and tub on board, and set them under the booms to catch the fresh water for washing our clothes. The rain made it very thick, and I went and stood under the lee of the staysail, looking out. I could tell that day was breaking, because the foam was whiter in the dark where the seas crested, and little by little the black rain grew grey and steamy, and I couldn't see the red glare of the port light on the water when she went off and rolled to leeward. The gale had moderated considerably, and in another hour we should be under way again. I was still standing there when Jack Benton came forward. He stood still a few minutes near me. The rain came down in a solid sheet, and I could see his wet beard and a corner of his cheek, too, grey in the dawn. Then he stooped down and began feeling under the anchor for his pipe. We had hardly shipped any water forward, and I suppose he had some way of tucking the pipe in so that the rain hadn't floated it off.

Presently he got on his legs again, and I saw that he had two pipes in his hand. One of them had belonged to his brother, and after looking at them a moment I suppose he recognized his own, for he put it in his mouth, dripping with water. Then he looked at the other fully a minute without moving. When he had made up his mind, I suppose, he quietly chucked it over the lee rail, without even looking round to see whether I was watching him. I thought it was a pity, for it was a good wooden pipe, with a nickel ferrule, and somebody would have been glad to have it. But I didn't like to make any remark, for he had a right to do what he pleased with what had belonged to his dead brother.

He blew the water out of his own pipe, and dried it against his jacket; putting his hand inside his oilskin, he filled it, standing under the lee of the foremast, got a light after wasting two or three matches, and turned the pipe upside down in his teeth, to keep the rain out of the bowl. I don't know why I noticed everything he did, and remember it now; but somehow I felt sorry for him, and I kept wondering whether there was anything I could say that would make him feel better. But I didn't think of anything, and as it was broad daylight I went aft again, for I guessed the Old Man would turn out before long and order the spanker set and the helm up. But he didn't turn out before seven bells, just as the clouds broke and showed blue sky to leeward—"the Frenchman's barometer," you used to call it.

Some people don't seem to be so dead, when they are dead, as others are. Jim Benton was like that. He had been on my watch, and I couldn't get used to the idea that he wasn't about decks with me. I was always expecting to see him, and his brother was so exactly like him that I often felt as if I did see him and forgot he was dead, and made the mistake of calling Jack by his name; though I tried not to, because I knew it must hurt. If ever Jack had been the cheerful one of the two, as I had always supposed he had been, he had changed very much, for he grew to be more silent than Jim had ever been.

One fine afternoon I was sitting on the main hatch, overhauling the clockwork of the taffrail log, which hadn't been registering very well of late, and I had got the cook to bring me a coffee cup to hold the small screws as I took them out, and a saucer for the sperm oil I was going to use. I noticed that he didn't go away, but hung round without exactly watching what I was doing, as if he wanted to say something to me. I thought if it were worth much he would say

38

it anyhow, so I didn't ask him questions; and sure enough he began of his own accord before long. There was nobody on deck but the man at the wheel, and the other man away forward.

"Mr. Torkeldsen," the cook began, and then stopped.

I supposed he was going to ask me to let the watch break out a barrel of flour, or some salt horse.

"Well, doctor?" I asked, as he didn't go on.

"Well, Mr. Torkeldsen," he answered, "I somehow want to ask you whether you think I am giving satisfaction on this ship, or not?"

"So far as I know, you are, doctor. I haven't heard any complaints from the forecastle, and the captain has said nothing, and I think you know your business, and the cabin boy is bursting out of his clothes. That looks as if you are giving satisfaction. What makes you think you are not?"

I am not good at giving you that West Indies talk, and shan't try; but the doctor beat about the bush awhile, and then he told me he thought the men were beginning to play tricks on him, and he didn't like it, and thought he hadn't deserved it, and would like his discharge at our next port. I told him he was a damned fool, of course, to begin with; and that men were more apt to try a joke with a chap they liked than with anybody they wanted to get rid of; unless it was a bad joke, like flooding his bunk, or filling his boots with tar. But it wasn't that kind of practical joke. The doctor said that the men were trying to frighten him, and he didn't like it, and that they put things in his way that frightened him. So I told him he was a damned fool to be frightened, anyway, and I wanted to know what things they put in his way. He gave me a queer answer. He said they were spoons and forks, and odd plates, and a cup now and then, and such things.

I set down the taffrail log on the bit of canvas I had put under it, and looked at the doctor. He was uneasy, and his eyes had a sort of hunted look, and his yellow face looked grey. He wasn't trying to make trouble. He was in trouble. So I asked him questions.

He said he could count as well as anybody, and do sums without using his fingers, but that when he couldn't count any other way he did use his fingers, and it always came out the same. He said that when he and the cabin boy cleared up after the men's meals there were more things to wash than he had given out. There'd be a fork more, or there'd be a spoon more, and sometimes there'd be a spoon and a fork, and there was always a plate more. It wasn't that he complained of that. Before poor Jim Benton was lost they had a man more to feed, and his gear to wash up after meals, and that was in the contract, the doctor said. It would have been if there were twenty in the ship's company; but he didn't think it was right for the men to play tricks like that. He kept his things in good order, and he counted them, and he was responsible for them, and it wasn't right that the men should take more things than they needed when his back was turned, and just soil them and mix them up with their own, so as to make him think. . . .

He stopped there, and looked at me, and I looked at him. I didn't know what he thought, but I began to guess. I wasn't going to humour any such nonsense as that, so I told him to speak to the men himself, and not come bothering me about such things.

"Count the plates and forks and spoons before them when they sit down to table, and tell them that's all they'll get; and when they have finished, count the things again, and if the count isn't right, find out who did it. You know it must be one of them. You're not a green hand; you've been going to sea ten or eleven years, and don't want any lessons about how to behave if the boys play a trick on you."

"If I could catch him," said the cook, "I'd have a knife into him before he could say his prayers."

Those West Indies men are always talking about knives, especially when they are badly frightened. I knew what he meant, and didn't ask him, but went on cleaning the brass cogwheels of the patent log and oiling the bearings with a feather.

"Wouldn't it be better to wash it out with boiling water, sir?" asked the cook, in an insinuating tone. He knew that he had made a fool of himself, and was anxious to make it right again.

I heard no more about the odd platter and gear for two or three days, though I thought about his story a good deal. The doctor evidently believed that Jim Benton had come back, though he didn't quite like to say so. His story had sounded silly enough on a bright afternoon, in fair weather, when the sun was on the water, and every rag was drawing in the breeze, and the sea looked as pleasant and harmless as a cat that has just eaten a canary. But when it was toward the end of the first watch, and the waning moon had not risen yet, and the water was like still oil, and the jibs hung down flat an helpless like the wings of a dead bird—it wasn't the same then.

More than once I have started then, and looked round when a fish jumped, expecting to see a face sticking up out of the water with its eyes shut. I think we all felt something like that at the time.

One afternoon we were putting a fresh service on the jibsheet-pennant. It wasn't my watch, but I was standing by looking on. Just then Jack Benton came up from below, and went to look for his pipe under the anchor. His face was hard and drawn, and his eyes were cold like steel balls. He hardly ever spoke now, but he did his duty as usual, and nobody had to complain of him, though we were all beginning to wonder how long his grief for his dead brother was going to last like that. I watched him as he crouched down and ran his hand into the hiding-place for the pipe. When he stood up he had two pipes in his hand.

Now, I remembered very well seeing him throw one of those pipes away, early in the morning after the gale; and it came to me now, and I didn't suppose we kept a stock of them under the anchor. I caught sight of his face, and it was greenish-white, like the foam on shallow water, and he stood a long time looking at the two pipes. He wasn't look-to see which was his, for I wasn't five yards from him as he stood, and one of those pipes had been smoked that day, and was shiny where his hand had rubbed it, and the bone mouthpiece was chafed white where his teeth had bitten it. The other was water-logged. It was swelled and cracking with wet, and it looked to me as if there were a little green weed on it.

Jack Benton turned his head rather stealthily as I looked away, and then he hid the thing in his trousers pocket, and went aft on the lee side, out of sight. The men had got the sheet-pennant on a stretch to serve it, but I ducked under it and stood where I could see what Jack did, just under the fore-staysail. He couldn't see me, and he was looking about for something. His hand shook as he picked up a bit of half-bent iron rod, about a foot long, that had been used for turning an eye-bolt, and had been left on the main hatch. His hand shook as he got a piece of marline out of his pocket and made the waterlogged pipe fast to the iron. He didn't mean it to get adrift either, for he took his turns carefully, and hove them taut and then rode them, so that they couldn't slip, and made the end fast with two half-hitches round the iron, and hitched it back on itself. Then he tried it with his hands, and looked up and down the deck furtively, and then quietly dropped the pipe and iron over the rail, so that I didn't even hear the splash. If anybody was playing tricks on board, they weren't meant for the cook.

I asked some questions about Jack Benton, and one of the men told me that he was off his feed, and hardly ate anything, and swallowed all the coffee he could lay his hands on, and had used up all his own tobacco and had begun on what his brother had left.

"The doctor says it ain't so, sir," said the man, looking at me shyly, as if he didn't expect to be believed; "the doctor says there's as much eaten from breakfast to breakfast as there was before Jim fell overboard, though there's a mouth less and another that eats nothing. I says it's the cabin boy that gets it. He's bu'sting."

I told him that if the cabin boy ate more than his share, he must work more than his share, so as to balance things. But the man laughed queerly, and looked at me again.

"I only said that, sir; just like that. We all know it ain't so."

"Well, how is it?"

"How is it?" asked the man, half angry all at once. "I don't know how it is, but there's a hand on board that's getting his whack along with us as regular as the bells."

"Does he use tobacco?" I asked, meaning to laugh it out of him, but as I spoke I remembered the waterlogged pipe.

"I guess he's using his own still," the man answered, in a queer, low voice. "Perhaps he'll take someone else's when his is all gone."

It was about nine o'clock in the morning, I remember, for just then the captain called to me to stand by the chronometer while he took his fore observation. Captain Hackstaff wasn't one of those old skippers who do everything themselves with a pocket watch, and keep the key of the chronometer in their waistcoat pocket, and won't tell the mate how far the dead reckoning is out. He was rather the other way, and I was glad of it, for he generally let me work the sights he took, and just ran his eye over my figures afterwards. I am bound to say his eye was pretty good, for he would pick out a mistake in a logarithm, or tell me that I had worked the "Equation of Time" with the wrong sign, before it seemed to me that he could have got as far as "half the sum, minus the altitude." He was always right, too, and besides he knew a lot about iron ships and local deviation, and adjusting the compass, and all that sort of thing.

I don't know how he came to be in command of a fore-and-aft schooner. He never talked about himself, and maybe he had just been mate on one of those big steel square-riggers, and something had put him back. Perhaps he had been captain, and had got his ship aground, through no particular fault of his, and had to begin over again. Sometimes he talked just like you and me, and sometimes he would speak more like books do, or some of those Boston people I have heard. I don't know. We have all been shipmates now and then with men who have seen better days.

Perhaps he had been in the Navy, but what makes me think he couldn't have been, was that he was a thorough good seaman, a regular old windjammer, and understood sail, which those Navy chaps rarely do. Why, you and I have sailed with men before the mast who had their master's certificates in their pockets—English Board of Trade certificates, too—who could work a double altitude if you would lend them a sextant and give them a look at the chronometer, as well as many a man who commands a big square-rigger. Navigation ain't everything, nor seamanship either. You've got to have it in you, if you mean to get there.

I don't know how our captain heard that there was trouble forward. The cabin boy may have told him, or the men may have talked outside his door when they relieved the wheel at night. Anyhow, he got wind of it, and when he had got his sight that morning he had all hands aft, and gave them a lecture. It was just the kind of talk you might have expected from him. He said he hadn't any complaint to make, and that so far as he knew everybody on board was doing his duty, and that he was given to understand that the men got their whack, and were satisfied. He said his ship was never a hard ship, and that he liked quiet, and that was the reason he didn't mean to have any nonsense, and the men might just as well understand that too. We'd had a great misfortune, he said, and it was nobody's fault. We had lost a man we all liked and respected, and he felt that everybody in the ship ought to be sorry for the man's brother, who was left behind, and that it was rotten lubberly childishness, and unjust and unmanly and cowardly, to be playing schoolboy tricks with forks and spoons and pipes, and that sort of gear. He said it had got to stop right now, and that was all, and the men might go forward. And so they did.

It got worse after that, and the men watched the cook, and the cook watched the men, as if they were trying to catch each other; but I think everybody felt that there was something else. One evening, at supper-time, I was on deck, and Jack came aft to relieve the wheel while the man who was steering got his supper. He hadn't got past the main hatch on the lee side, when I heard a man running in slippers that slapped on the deck, and there was a sort of a yell and I saw the cook going for Jack, with a carving knife in his hand. I jumped to get between them, and Jack turned round short, and put out his hand. I was too far to reach them, and the cook jabbed out with his knife. But the blade didn't get anywhere near Benton. The cook seemed to be jabbing it into the air again and again, at least four feet short of the mark. Then he dropped his right hand, and I saw the whites of his eyes in the dusk, and he reeled up against the pinrail, and caught hold of a belaying pin with his left. I had reached him by that time, and grabbed hold of his knife-hand and the other too, for I thought he was going to use the pin, but Jack Benton was standing staring stupidly at him as if he didn't understand. But instead, the cook was holding on because he couldn't stand, and his teeth were chattering, and he let go of the knife, and the point stuck into the deck.

"He's crazy!" said Jack Benton, and that was all he said; and he went aft.

When he was gone, the cook began to come to, and he spoke quite low, near my ear.

"There were two of them! So help me God, there were two of them!"

I don't know why I didn't take him by the collar and give him a good shaking; but I didn't. I just picked up the knife and gave it to him and told him to go back to his galley, and not to make a fool of himself. You see, he hadn't struck at Jack, but at something he thought he saw, and I knew what it was, and I felt that same thing, like a lump of ice sliding down my back, that I felt that night when we were bending the trysail.

When the men had seen him running aft, they jumped up after him, but they held off when they saw that I had caught him. By and by, the man who had spoken to me before told me what had happened. He was a stocky little chap, with a red head.

"Well," he said, "there isn't much to tell. Jack Benton had been eating his supper with the rest of us. He always sits at the after corner of the table, on the port side. His brother used to sit at the end, next to him. The doctor gave him a thundering big piece of pie to finish up with, and when he had finished he didn't stop for a smoke, but went off quick to relieve the wheel. Just as he had gone, the doctor came in from the galley, and when he saw Jack's empty plate he stood stock still staring at it; and we all wondered what was the matter, till we looked at the plate. There were two forks in it, sir, lying side by side. Then the doctor grabbed his knife, and flew up through the hatch like a rocket. The other fork was there all right, Mr. Torkeldsen, for we all saw it and handled it; and we all had our own. That's all I know."

I didn't feel that I wanted to laugh when he told me that story; but I hoped the Old Man wouldn't hear it, for I knew he wouldn't believe it, and no captain that ever sailed likes to have stories like that going round about his ship. It gives her a bad name. But that was all anybody ever saw except the cook, and he isn't the first man who has thought he saw things without having any drink in him. I think, if the doctor had been weak in the head as he was afterwards, he might have done something foolish again, and there might have been serious trouble. But he didn't. Only, two or three times I saw him looking at Jack Benton in a queer, scared way, and once I heard him talking to himself.

"There's two of them! So help me God, there's two of them!"

He didn't say anything more about asking for his discharge, but I knew well enough that if he got ashore at the next port we should never see him again, if he had to leave his kit behind him, and his money too. He was scared all through, for good and all; and he wouldn't be right again till he got another ship. It's no use to talk to a man when he gets like that, any more than it is to send a boy to the main truck when he has lost his nerve.

Jack Benton never spoke of what happened that evening. I don't know whether he knew about the two forks, or not; or whether he understood what the trouble was. Whatever he knew from the other men, he was evidently living under a hard strain. He was quiet enough, and too quiet; but his face was set, and sometimes it twitched oddly when he was at the wheel, and he would turn his head round sharp to look behind him. A man doesn't do that naturally, unless there's a vessel that he thinks is creeping up on the quarter. When that happens, if the man at the wheel takes a pride in his ship, he will almost always keep glancing over his shoulder to see whether the other fellow is gaining. But Jack Benton used to look round when there was nothing there; and what is curious, the other men seemed to catch the trick when they were steering. One day the Old Man turned out just as the man at the wheel looked behind him.

"What are you looking at?" asked the captain.

"Nothing, sir," answered the man.

"Then keep your eye on the mizzen-royal," said the Old Man, as if he were forgetting that we weren't a square-rigger.

"Ay, ay, sir," said the man.

The captain told me to go below and work up the latitude from the dead-reckoning, and he went forward of the deckhouse and sat down to read, as he often did. When I came up, the man at the wheel was looking round again, and I stood beside him and just asked him quietly what everybody was looking at, for it was getting to be a general habit. He wouldn't say anything at first, but just answered that it was nothing. But when he saw that I didn't seem to care, and just stood there as if there were nothing more to be said, he naturally began to talk.

He said that it wasn't that he saw anything, because there wasn't anything to see except the spanker sheet just straining a little, and working in the sheaves of the blocks as the schooner rose to the short seas. There wasn't anything to be seen, but it seemed to him that the sheet made a queer noise in the blocks. It was a new manilla sheet; and in dry weather it did make a little noise, something between a creak and a wheeze. I looked at it and looked at the man, and said nothing; and presently he went on. He asked me if I didn't notice anything peculiar about the noise. I listened a while, and said I didn't notice anything. Then he looked rather sheepish, but said he didn't think it could be his own ears, because every man who steered his trick heard the same thing now and then—sometimes once in a day, sometimes once in a night, sometimes it would go on a whole hour.

"It sounds like sawing wood," I said, just like that.

"To us it sounds a good deal more like a man whistling 'Nancy Lee'." He started nervously as he spoke the last words. "There, sir, don't you hear it?" he asked suddenly.

I heard nothing but the creaking of the manilla sheet. It was getting near noon, and fine, clear weather in southern waters—just the sort of day and the time when you would least expect to feel creepy. But I remembered how I had heard that same tune overhead at night in a gale of wind a fortnight earlier, and I am not ashamed to say that the same sensation came over me now, and I wished myself well out of the *Helen B.*, and aboard of any old cargo-dragger, with a windmill on deck, and an eighty-nine forty-eighter for captain, and a fresh leak whenever it breezed up.

Little by little during the next few days, life on board that vessel came to be about as unbearable as you can imagine. It wasn't that there was much talk, for I think the men were shy even of speaking to each other freely about what they thought. The whole ship's company grew silent, until one hardly ever heard a voice, except giving an order and the answer. The men didn't sit over their meals when their watch was below, but either turned in at once or sat about on the forecastle smoking their pipes without saying a word. We were all thinking of the same thing. We all felt as if there were a hand on board, sometimes below, sometimes about decks, sometimes aloft, sometimes on the boom end; taking his full share of what the others got, but doing no work for it. We didn't only feel it, we knew it. He took up no room, he cast no shadow, and we never heard his footfall on deck; but he took his whack with the rest as regular as the bells, and —he whistled "Nancy Lee." It was like the worst sort of dream you can imagine; and I dare say a good many of us tried to believe it was nothing else sometimes, when we stood looking over the weather rail in fine weather with the breeze in our faces; but if we happened to turn round and look into each other's eyes, we knew it was something worse than any dream could be; and we would turn away from each other with a queer, sick feeling, wishing that we could just for once see somebody who didn't know what we knew.

There's not much more to tell about the *Helen B. Jackson* so far as I am concerned. We were more like a shipload of lunatics than anything else when we ran in under Morro Castle and anchored in Havana. The cook had brain fever, and was raving mad in his delirium; and the rest of the men weren't far from the same state. The last three or four days had been awful, and we had been as near to having a mutiny on board as I ever want to be. The men didn't want to hurt anybody; but they wanted to get away out of that ship, if they had to swim for it; to get away from that whistling, from that dead shipmate who had come back, and who filled the ship with his unseen self! I know that if the Old Man and I hadn't kept a sharp lookout the men would have put a boat over quietly on one of those calm nights, and pulled away, leaving the captain and me and the mad cook to work the schooner into harbour. We should have done it somehow, of course, for we hadn't far to run if we could get a breeze; and once or twice I found myself wishing that the crew were really gone, for the awful state of fright in which they lived was beginning to work on me too. You see, I partly believed and partly didn't; but, anyhow, I didn't mean to let the thing get the better of me, whatever it was. I turned crusty, too, and kept the men at work on all sorts of jobs, and drove them to it until they wished I was overboard too. It wasn't that the Old Man and I were trying to drive them to desert without their pay, as I am sorry to say a good many skippers and mates do, even now.

Captain Hackstaff was as straight as a string, and I didn't mean those poor fellows should be cheated out of a single cent; and I didn't blame them for wanting to leave the ship, but it seemed to me that the only chance to keep everybody sane through those last days was to work the men till they dropped. When they were dead tired they slept a little, and forgot the thing until they had to tumble up on deck and face it again.

That was a good many years ago. Do you believe that I can't hear "Nancy Lee" now without feeling cold down my back? For I heard it too, now and then, after the man had explained why he was always looking over his shoulder. Perhaps it was imagination. I don't know. When I look back it seems to me that I only remember a long fight against something I couldn't see, against an appalling presence, against something worse than cholera or yellow Jack or the plague —and, goodness knows, the mildest of them is bad enough when it breaks out at sea. The men got as white as chalk, and wouldn't go about decks alone at night, no matter what I said to them. With the cook raving in his bunk the forecastle would have been a perfect hell, and there wasn't a spare cabin on board. There never is on a fore-and-after. So I put him into mine, and he was more quiet there, and at last fell into a sort of stupor as if he were going to die. I don't know what became of him, for we put him ashore alive and left him in the hospital.

The men came aft in a body, quiet enough, and asked the captain if he wouldn't pay them off, and let them go ashore. Some men wouldn't have done it, for they had shipped for the voyage, and had signed articles. But the captain knew that when sailors get an idea into their heads they're no better than children; and if he forced them to stay aboard he wouldn't get much work out of them, and couldn't rely on them in a difficulty. So he paid them off, and let them go. When they had gone forward to get their kits, he asked me whether I wanted to go too, and for a minute I had a sort of weak feeling that I might just as well. But I didn't, and he was a good friend to me afterwards. Perhaps he was grateful to me for sticking to him.

When the men went off he didn't come on deck; but it was my duty to stand by while they left the ship. They owed me a grudge for making them work during the last few days, and most of them dropped into the boat without so much as a word or a look, as sailors will. Jack Benton was the last to go over the side, and he stood still a minute and looked at me, and his white face twitched. I thought he wanted to say something.

"Take care of yourself, Jack," said I. "So long!"

It seemed as if he couldn't speak for two or three seconds; then his words came thick.

"It wasn't my fault, Mr. Torkeldsen. I swear it wasn't my fault!"

That was all; and he dropped over the side, leaving me to wonder what he meant.

The captain and I stayed on board, and the ship-chandler got a West Indies boy to cook for us.

That evening, before turning in, we were standing by the rail having a quiet smoke, watching the lights of the city, a quarter of a mile off, reflected in the still water. There was music of some sort ashore, in a sailors' dance-house, I dare say; and I had no doubt that most of the men who had left the ship were there, and already full of jiggy-jiggy. The music played a lot of sailors' tunes that ran into each other, and we could hear the men's voices in the chorus now and then. One followed another, and then it was "Nancy Lee" loud and clear, and the men singing "Yo-ho, heave-ho!"

"I have no ear for music," said Captain Hackstaff, "but it appears to me that's the tune that man was whistling the night we lost the man overboard. I don't know why it has stuck in my head, and of course it's all nonsense: but it seems to me that I have heard it all the rest of the trip."

I didn't say anything to that, but I wondered just how much the Old Man had understood. Then we turned in, and I slept ten hours without opening my eyes.

I stuck to the *Helen B. Jackson* after that as long as I could stand a fore-and-after; but that night when we lay in Havana was the last time I ever heard "Nancy Lee" on board of her. The spare hand had gone ashore with the rest, and he never came back, and he took his tune with him, but all those things are just as clear in my memory as if they had happened yesterday.

After that I was in deep water for a year or more, and after I came home I got my certificate, and what with having friends and having saved a little money, and having had a small legacy from an uncle in Norway, I got the command of a coastwise vessel, with a small share in her. I was at home three weeks before going to sea, and Jack Benton saw my name in the local papers, and wrote to me.

He said that he had left the sea, and was trying farming, and he was going to be married, and he asked if I wouldn't come over for that, for it wasn't more than forty minutes by train; and he and Mamie would be proud to have me at the wedding. I remembered how I had heard one brother ask the other whether Mamie knew. That meant, whether she knew he wanted to marry her, I suppose. She had taken her time about it, for it was pretty nearly three years then since we had lost Jim Benton overboard.

I had nothing particular to do while we were getting ready for sea; nothing to prevent me from going over for a day, I mean; and I thought I'd like to see Jack Benton, and have a look at the girl he was going to marry. I wondered whether he had grown cheerful again, and had got rid of that drawn look he had when he told me it wasn't his fault. How could it have been his fault, anyhow? So I wrote to Jack that I would come down and see him married; and when the day came I took the train, and got there about ten o'clock in the morning. I wish I hadn't. Jack met me at the station, and he told me that the wedding was to be late in the afternoon, and that they weren't going off on any silly wedding trip, he and Mamie, but were just going to walk home from her mother's house to his cottage. That was good enough for him, he said. I looked at him hard for a minute after we met. When we had parted I had a sort of idea that he might take to drink, but he hadn't. He looked very respectable and well-to-do in his black coat and high city collar; but he was thinner and bonier than when I had known him, and there were lines in his face, and I thought his eyes had a queer look in them, half shifty, half scared. He needn't have been afraid of me, for I didn't mean to talk to his bride about the *Helen B. Jackson.*

He took me to his cottage first, and I could see that he was proud of it. It wasn't above a cable length from high-water mark, but the tide was running out, and there was already a broad stretch of hard, wet sand on the other side of the beach road. Jack's bit of land ran back behind the cottage about a quarter of a mile, and he said that some of the trees we saw were his. The fences were neat and well kept, and there was a fair-sized barn a little way from the cottage, and I saw some nice-looking cattle in the meadows; but it didn't look to me to be much of a farm, and I thought that before long Jack would have to leave his wife to take care of it and go to sea again. But I said it was a nice farm, so as to seem pleasant, and as I don't know much about these things I dare say it was, all the same. I never saw it but that once. Jack told me that he and his brother had been born in the cottage, and that when their father and mother died they leased the land to Mamie's father, but had kept the cottage to live in when they came home from sea for a spell.

It was as neat a little place as you would care to see: the floors as clean as the decks of a yacht, and the paint as fresh as a man-o'-war. Jack always was a good painter. There was a nice parlour on the ground floor, and Jack had papered it and had hung the walls with photographs of ships and foreign ports, and with things he had brought home from his voyages: a boomerang, a South Sea club, Japanese straw hats, and a Gibraltar fan with a bull-fight on it, and all that sort of gear. It looked to me as if Miss Mamie had taken a hand in arranging it. There was a brand-new polished iron Franklin stove set into the old fireplace, and a red tablecloth from Alexandria embroidered with those outlandish Egyptian letters.

It was all as bright and homelike as possible, and he showed me everything, and was proud of everything, and I liked him the better for it. But I wished that his voice would sound more cheerful, as it did when we first sailed in the *Helen B.*, and that the drawn look would go out of his face for a minute. Jack showed me everything, and took me upstairs, and it was all the same: bright and fresh and ready for the bride. But on the upper landing there was a door that Jack didn't open. When we came out of the bedroom I noticed that it was ajar, and Jack shut it quickly and turned the key.

"That lock's no good," he said, half to himself. "The door is always open."

I didn't pay much attention to what he said, but as we went down the short stairs, freshly painted and varnished so that I was almost afraid to step on them, he spoke again.

"That was his room, sir. I have made a sort of storeroom of it."

"You may be wanting it in a year or so," I said, wishing to be pleasant.

"I guess we won't use his room for that," Jack answered in a low voice.

Then he offered me a cigar from a fresh box in the parlour, and he took one, and we lit them, and went out; and as we opened the front door there was Mamie Brewster standing in the path as if she were waiting for us. She was a fine-looking girl, and I didn't wonder that Jack had been willing to wait three years for her. I could see that she hadn't been brought up on steam heat and cold storage, but had grown into a woman by the seashore. She had brown eyes and fine brown hair and a good figure.

"This is Captain Torkeldsen," said Jack. "This is Miss Brewster, Captain, and she is glad to see you."

"Well, I am," said Miss Mamie, "for Jack has often talked to us about you, Captain."

She put out her hand and took mine and shook it heartily, and I suppose I said something, but I know I didn't say much.

The front door to the cottage looked towards the sea, and there was a straight path leading to the gate on the beach road. There was another path from the steps of the cottage that turned to the right, broad enough for two people to walk easily, and it led straight across the fields through gates to a larger house about a quarter of a mile away. That was where Mamie's mother lived, and the wedding was to be there. Jack asked me whether I would like to look round the farm before dinner, but I told him I didn't know much about farms. Then he said he just wanted to look round himself a bit, as he mightn't have much more chance that day, and he smiled and Mamie laughed.

"Show the captain the way to the house, Mamie," he said. "I'll be along in a minute."

So Mamie and I began to walk along the path and Jack went up towards the barn.

"It was sweet of you to come, Captain," Miss Mamie began, "for I have always wanted to see you."

"Yes," I said, expecting something more.

"You see, I always knew them both," she went on. "They used to take me out in a dory to catch codfish when I was a little girl, and I liked them both," she added thoughtfully. "Jack doesn't care to talk about his brother now. That's natural. But you won't mind telling me how it happened, will you? I should so much like to know."

Well, I told her about the voyage and what happened that night when we fell in with a gale of wind, and that it hadn't been anybody's fault, for I wasn't going to admit that it was my old captain's, if it was. But I didn't tell her anything about what happened afterwards. As she didn't speak, I just went on talking about the two brothers, and how like they had been and how when poor Jim was drowned and Jack left, I took Jack for him. I told her that none of us had ever been sure which was which.

"I wasn't always sure myself," she said, "unless they were together. Leastways, not for a day or two after they came home from sea. And now it seems to me that Jack is more like poor Jim, as I remembered him, than he ever was, for Jim was always more quiet, as if he were thinking."

I told her I thought so, too. We passed the gate and went into the next field, walking side by side. Then she turned her head to look for Jack, but he wasn't in sight. I shan't forget what she said next.

"Are you sure now?" she asked.

I stood stock-still and she went on a step, and then turned and looked at me. We must have looked at each other while you could count five or six.

"I know it's silly," she went on, "it's silly and it's awful, too, and I have got no right to think it, but sometimes I can't help it. You see, it was always Jack I meant to marry."

" Yes," I said stupidly, " I suppose so."

She waited a minute and began walking on slowly before she went on again.

"I am talking to you as if you were an old friend, Captain, and I have only known you five minutes. It was Jack I meant to marry, but now he is so like the other one."

When a woman gets a wrong idea into her head there is only one way to make her tired of it, and that is to agree with her. That's what I did, and she went on talking the same way for a little while and I kept on agreeing and agreeing until she turned round on me.

"You know you don't believe what you say," she said, and laughed. "You know that Jack is Jack, right enough, and it's Jack I am going to marry."

Of course I said so, for I didn't care whether she thought me a weak creature or not. I wasn't going to say a word that could interfere with her happiness, and I didn't intend to go back on Jack Benton; but I remembered what he had said when he left the ship in Havana: that it wasn't his fault.

"All the same," Miss Mamie went on, as a woman will, without realizing what she was saying, "all the same, I wish I had seen it happen. Then I should know."

Next minute she knew that she didn't mean that and was afraid that I would think her heartless, and began to explain that she would really rather have died herself than have seen poor Jim go overboard. Women haven't got much sense anyhow. All the same, I wondered how she could marry Jack if she had a doubt that he might be Jim after all. I suppose she had really got used to him since he had given up the sea and had stayed ashore, and she cared for him.

Before long we heard Jack coming up behind us, for we had walked very slowly to wait for him.

"Promise not to tell anybody what I said, Captain," said Mamie, as girls do as soon as they have told their secrets.

Anyhow, I know I never did tell anyone but you. This is the first time I have talked of all that, the first time since I took the train from that place. I am not going to tell you all about the day. Miss Mamie introduced me to her mother, who was a quiet, hard-faced old New England farmer's widow, and to her cousins and relations, and there were plenty of them, too, at dinner, and there was the parson besides. He was what they call a Hard-shell Baptist in those parts, with a long, shaven upper lip and a whacking appetite, and a sort of superior look, as if he didn't expect to see many of us here-after—the way a New York pilot looks round and orders things about when he boards an Italian cargo-dragger, as if the ship weren't up to much anyway, though it was his business to see that she didn't get aground. That's the way a good many parsons look, I think. He said

54

grace as if he were ordering the men to sheet home the topgallant sail and get the helm up.

After dinner we went out on the piazza, for it was warm autumn weather, and the young folks went off in pairs along the beach road, and the tide had turned and was beginning to come in. The morning had been clear and fine, but by four o'clock it began to look like a fog, and the damp came up out of the sea and settled on everything. Jack said he'd go down to his cottage and have a last look, for the wedding was to be at five o'clock, or soon after, and he wanted to light the lights, so as to have things look cheerful.

"I will just take a last look," he said again, as we reached the house. We went in and he offered me another cigar, and I lit it and sat down in the parlour. I could hear him moving about, first in the kitchen and then upstairs, and then I heard him in the kitchen again, and then before I knew anything I heard somebody moving upstairs again. I knew he couldn't have got up those stairs as quick as that. He came into the parlour and he took a cigar himself and, while he was lighting it, I heard those steps again overhead. His hand shook and he dropped the match.

"Have you got in somebody to help?" I asked.

"No," Jack answered sharply, and struck another match.

"There's somebody upstairs, Jack," I said. "Don't you hear footsteps?"

"It's the wind, Captain," Jack answered, but I could see he was trembling.

"That isn't any wind, Jack," I said; "it's still and foggy. I'm sure there's somebody upstairs."

"If you are so sure of it, you'd better go and see for yourself, Captain," Jack answered, almost angrily.

He was angry because he was frightened. I left him before the fireplace and went upstairs. There was no power on earth that could make me believe I hadn't heard a man's footsteps overhead. I knew there was somebody there. But there wasn't. I went into the bedroom and it was all quiet, and the evening light was streaming in, reddish through the foggy air, and I went out on the landing and looked in the little back room that was meant for a servant-girl or a child. And as I came back again I saw that the door of the other room was wide open, though I knew Jack had locked it. He had said the lock was no good. I looked in. It was a room as big as the bedroom, but almost dark, for it had shutters and they were closed.

There was a musty smell, as of old gear, and I could make out that the floor was littered with sea-chests and that there were oil-skins and such stuff piled on the bed. But I still believed that there was somebody upstairs, and I went in and struck a match and looked round. I could see the four walls and the shabby old paper, an iron bed and a cracked looking glass, and the stuff on the floor. But there was nobody there. So I put out the match and came out and shut the door and turned the key. Now, what I am telling you is the truth. When I had turned the key, I heard footsteps walking away from the door inside the room. Then I felt queer for a minute and when I went downstairs I looked behind me, as the men at the wheel used to look behind them on board the *Helen B.*

Jack was already outside on the steps, smoking. I have an idea that he didn't like to stay inside alone.

"Well?" he asked, trying to seem careless.

"I didn't find anybody," I answered, "but I heard somebody moving about."

"I told you it was the wind," said Jack contemptuously. "I ought to know, for I live here and I hear it often."

There was nothing to be said to that, so we began to walk down towards the beach. Jack said there wasn't any hurry, as it would take Miss Mamie some time to dress for the wedding. So we strolled along and the sun was setting through the fog, and the tide was coming in. I knew the moon was full, and that when she rose the fog would roll away from the land, as it does sometimes. I felt that Jack didn't like my having heard that noise, so I talked of other things and asked him about his prospects, and before long we were chatting as pleasantly as possible.

I haven't been at many weddings in my life and I don't suppose you have, but that one seemed to me to be all right until it was pretty near over, and then, I don't know whether it was part of the cere-mony or not, but Jack put out his hand and took Mamie's and held it a minute and looked at her, while the parson was still speaking.

Mamie turned as white as a sheet and screamed. It wasn't a loud scream, but just a sort of stifled little shriek, as if she were half frightened to death, and the parson stopped and asked her what was the matter, and the family gathered round.

"Your hand's like ice," said Mamie to Jack, "and it's all wet!" She kept looking at it, as she got hold of herself again.

"It don't feel cold to me," said Jack, and he held the back of his hand against his cheek. "Try it again."

Mamie held out hers and touched the back of his hand, timidly at first, and then took hold of it.

"Why, that's funny," she said.

"She's been as nervous as a witch all day," said Mrs. Brewster severely.

"It is natural," said the parson, "that young Mrs. Benton should experience a little agitation at such a moment."

Most of the bride's relations lived at a distance and were busy people, so it had been arranged that the dinner we'd had in the middle of the day was to take the place of a dinner afterwards, and that we should just have a bite after the wedding was over, and then that everybody should go home, and the young couple would walk down to the cottage by themselves. When I looked out I could see the light burning brightly in Jack's cottage, a quarter of a mile away. I said I didn't think I could get any train to take me back before half past nine, but Mrs. Brewster begged me to stay until it was time, as she said her daughter would want to take off her wedding dress before she went home, for she had put on something white with a wreath, that was very pretty, and she couldn't walk home like that, could she?

So when we had all had a little supper the party began to break up, and when they were all gone Mrs. Brewster and Mamie went upstairs, and Jack and I went on the piazza to have a smoke, as the old lady didn't like tobacco in the house.

The full moon had risen now and it was behind me as I looked down towards Jack's cottage, so that everything was clear and white, and there was only the light burning in the window. The fog had rolled down to the water's edge and a little beyond, for the tide was high, or nearly, and was lapping up over the last reach of sand within fifty feet of the beach road.

Jack didn't say much as we sat smoking, but he thanked me for coming to his wedding, and I told him I hoped he would be happy, and so I did. I dare say both of us were thinking of those footsteps upstairs just then, and that the house wouldn't seem so lonely with a woman in it. By and by we heard Mamie's voice talking to her mother on the stairs, and in a minute she was ready to go. She had put on again the dress she had worn in the morning.

Well, they were ready to go now. It was all very quiet after the day's excitement, and I knew they would like to walk down that path alone now that they were man and wife at last. I bade them good night, although Jack made a show of pressing me to go with them by the path as far as the cottage, instead of going to the station by the beach road. It was all very quiet, and it seemed to me a sensible way of getting married, and when Mamie kissed her mother good night I just looked the other way, and knocked my ashes over the rail of the piazza. So they started down the straight path to Jack's cottage, and I waited a minute with Mrs. Brewster, looking after them, before taking my hat to go. They walked side by side, a little shyly at first, and then I saw Jack put his arm round her waist. As I looked he was on her left and I saw the outline of the two figures very distinctly against the moonlight on the path, and the shadow on Mamie's right was broad and black as ink, and it moved along, lengthening and shortening with the unevenness of the ground beside the path.

I thanked Mrs. Brewster and bade her goodnight, and though she was a hard New England woman her voice trembled a little as she answered, but being a sensible person she went in and shut the door behind her as I stepped out on the path. I looked after the couple in the distance a last time, meaning to go down to the road, so as not to overtake them; but when I had made a few steps I stopped and looked again, for I knew I had seen something queer, though I had only realized it afterwards. I looked again, and it was plain enough now, and I stood stock-still, staring at what I saw. Mamie was walking between two men. The second man was just the same height as Jack, both being about a half a head taller than she; Jack on her left in his black tailcoat and round hat, and the other man on her right—well, he was a sailor-man in wet oilskins. I could see the moonlight shining on the water that ran down him, and on the little puddle that had settled where the flap of his sou'wester was turned up behind—and one of his wet shiny arms was round Mamie's waist, just above Jack's. I was fast to the spot where I stood, and for a minute I thought I was crazy. We'd had nothing but some cider for dinner and tea in the evening, otherwise I'd have thought something had got into my head, though I was never drunk in my life. It was more like a bad dream after that.

I was glad Mrs. Brewster had gone in. As for me, I couldn't help following the three, in a sort of wonder to see what would happen, to see whether the sailor-man in his wet togs would just melt away into the moonshine. But he didn't.

I moved slowly, and I remembered afterwards that I walked on the grass, instead of on the path, as if I were afraid they might hear me coming. I suppose it all happened in less than five minutes after that, but it seemed as if it must have taken an hour. Neither Jack nor Mamie seemed to notice the sailor. She didn't seem to know that his wet arm was round her, and little by little they got near the cottage, and I wasn't a hundred yards from them when they reached the door. Something made me stand still then. Perhaps it was fright, for I saw everything that happened just as I see you now.

Mamie set her foot on the step to go up, and as she went forward I saw the sailor slowly lock his arm in Jack's, and Jack didn't move to go up. Then Mamie turned round on the step, and they all three stood that way for a second or two. She cried out then—I heard a man cry like that once, when his arm was taken off by a steam crane—and she fell back in a heap on the little piazza.

I tried to jump forward, but I couldn't move, and I felt my hair rising under my hat. The sailor turned slowly where he stood, and swung Jack round by the arm steadily and easily, and began to walk him down the pathway from the house. He walked him straight down that path, as steadily as Fate, and all the time I saw the moonlight shining on his wet oilskins. He walked him through the gate and across the beach road and out upon the wet sand, where the tide was high. Then I got my breath with a gulp and ran for them across the grass and vaulted over the fence and stumbled across the road. But when I felt the sand under my feet, the two were at the water's edge; and when I reached the water they were far out and up to their waists; and I saw that Jack Benton's head had fallen forward on his breast, and his free arm hung limp beside him, while his dead brother steadily marched him to his death. The moonlight was on the dark water, but the fog-bank was white beyond, and I saw them against it, and they went slowly and steadily down. The water was up to their armpits and then up to their shoulders, and then I saw it rise up to the black rim of Jack's hat. But they never wavered; and the two heads went straight on, straight on, till they were under, and there was just a ripple in the moonlight where Jack had been.

It has been on my mind to tell you that story, whenever I got a chance. You have known me, man and boy, a good many years, and I thought I would like to hear your opinion. Yes, that's what I always thought. It wasn't Jim that went overboard, it was Jack, and Jim just let him go when he might have saved him; and then Jim passed himself off for Jack with us, and with the girl. If that's what happened, he got what he deserved. People said the next day that Mamie found it out as they reached the house, and that her husband just walked out into the sea and drowned himself—and they would have blamed me for not stopping him if they'd known that I was there. But I never told what I had seen, for they wouldn't have believed me. I just let them think I had come too late.

When I reached the cottage and lifted Mamie up, she was raving mad. She got better afterwards, but she was never right in her head again.

Oh, you want to know if they found Jack's body? I don't know whether it was his, but I read in a paper at a southern port where I was with my new ship that two dead bodies had come ashore in a gale down east, in pretty bad shape. They were locked together, and one was a skeleton in oilskins.

THE BRUTE

ODGING IN FROM THE rain-swept street, I exchanged a smile and a glance with Miss Blank in the bar of the Three Crows. This exchange was effected with extreme propriety. It is a shock to think that, if still alive, Miss Blank must be something over sixty now. How time passes!

Noticing my gaze directed enquiringly at the partition of glass and varnished wood, Miss Blank was good enough to say, encouragingly,

"Only Mr. Jermyn and Mr. Stonor in the parlour, with another gentleman I've never seen before."

I moved towards the parlour door. A voice discoursing on the other side (it was but a matchboard partition) rose so loudly that the concluding words became quite plain in all their atrocity:

"That fellow Wilmot fairly dashed her brains out, and a good job too!"

This inhuman sentiment, since there was nothing profane or improper in it, failed to do as much as to check the slight yawn Miss

Blank was achieving behind her hand. And she remained gazing fixedly at the windowpanes, which streamed with rain.

As I opened the parlour door the same voice went on in the same cruel strain:

"I was glad when I heard she got the knock from somebody at last. Sorry enough for poor Wilmot, though. That man and I used to be chums at one time. Of course that was the end of him. A clear case if there ever was one. No way out of it. None at all."

The voice belonged to the gentleman Miss Blank had never seen before. He straddled his long legs on the hearthrug. Jermyn, leaning forward, held his pocket handkerchief spread out before the grate. He looked back dismally over his shoulder, and as I slipped behind one of the little wooden tables, I nodded to him. On the other side of the fire, imposingly calm and large, sat Mr. Stonor, jammed tight into a capacious Windsor armchair. There was nothing small about him but his short, white side-whiskers. Yards and yards of extra superfine blue cloth (made up into an overcoat) reposed on a chair by his side. And he must just have brought some liner from sea, because another chair was smothered under his black waterproof, ample as a pall, and made of three-fold oiled silk, double-stitched throughout. A man's handbag of the usual size looked like a child's toy on the floor near his feet.

I did not nod to him. He was too big to be nodded to in that parlour. He was a senior Trinity pilot and condescended to take his turn in the cutter only during the summer months. He had been many times in charge of royal yachts in and out of Port Victoria. Besides, it's no use nodding to a monument. And he was like one. He didn't speak, he didn't budge. He just sat there, holding his handsome old head up, immovable, and almost bigger than life. It was extremely fine. Mr. Stonor's presence reduced old Jermyn to a mere shabby wisp of a man, and made the talkative stranger in tweeds on the hearthrug look absurdly boyish. The latter must have been a few years over thirty, and was certainly not the sort of individual that gets abashed at the sound of his own voice, because gathering me in, as it were, by a friendly glance, he kept it going without a check.

"I was glad of it," he repeated emphatically. "You may be surprised at it, but then you haven't gone through the experience I've had of her. I can tell you, it was something to remember. Of course, I got off scot-free myself—as you can see. She did her best to break

62

up my pluck for me tho'. She jolly near drove as fine a fellow as ever lived into a madhouse. What do you say to that—eh?"

Not an eyelid twitched in Mr. Stonor's enormous face. Monumental! The speaker looked straight into my eyes.

"It used to make me sick to think of her going about the world murdering people."

Jermyn approached the handkerchief a little nearer to the grate and groaned. It was simply a habit he had.

"I've seen her once," he declared, with mournful indifference. "She had a house. . . ."

The stranger in tweeds turned to stare down at him, surprised.

"She had three houses," he corrected authoritatively. But Jermyn was not to be contradicted.

"She had a house, I say," he repeated, with dismal obstinacy. "A great big, ugly, white thing. You could see it from miles away—sticking up."

"So you could," assented the other readily. "It was old Colchester's notion, though he was always threatening to give her up. He couldn't stand her racket any more, he declared; it was too much of a good thing for him; he would wash his hands of her, if he never got hold of another—and so on. I daresay he would have chucked her, only—it may surprise you—his missus wouldn't hear of it. Funny, eh? But with women, you never know how they will take a thing, and Mrs. Colchester, with her moustaches and big eyebrows, set up for being as strong-minded as they make them. She used to walk about in a brown silk dress, with a great gold cable flopping about her bosom. You should have heard her snapping out: 'Rubbish!' or 'Stuff and nonsense!' I daresay she knew when she was well off. They had no children, and had never set up a home anywhere. When in England she just made shift to hang out anyhow in some cheap hotel or boardinghouse. I daresay she liked to get back to the comforts she was used to. She knew very well she couldn't gain by any change. And, moreover, Colchester, though a first-rate man, was not what you may call in his first youth, and, perhaps, she may have thought that he wouldn't be able to get hold of another (as he used to say) so easily. Anyhow, for one reason or another, it was 'Rubbish' and 'Stuff and nonsense' for the good lady. I overheard once young Mr. Apse himself say to her confidentially 'I assure you, Mrs. Colchester, I am beginning to feel quite unhappy about the name she's getting for herself.' 'Oh,' says she, with her deep little hoarse laugh, 'if one took notice of all the silly talk,' and she showed Apse all her ugly false teeth at once. 'It would take more than that to make me lose my confidence in her, I assure you,' says she."

At this point, without any change of facial expression, Mr. Stonor emitted a short sardonic laugh. It was very impressive, but I didn't see the fun. I looked from one to another. The stranger on the hearthrug had an ugly smile.

"And Mr. Apse shook both Mrs. Colchester's hands, he was so pleased to hear a good word said for their favourite. All these Apses, young and old you know, were perfectly infatuated with that abominable, dangerous—"

"I beg your pardon," I interrupted, for he seemed to be addressing himself exclusively to me, "but who on earth are you talking about?"

"I am talking of the Apse family," he answered, courteously.

I nearly let out a damn at this. But just then the respected Miss Blank put her head in, and said that the cab was at the door, if Mr. Stonor wanted to catch the eleven-three up.

At once the senior pilot arose in his mighty bulk and began to struggle into his coat, with awe-inspiring upheavals. The stranger and I hurried impulsively to his assistance, and directly we laid our hands on him he became perfectly quiescent. We had to raise our arms very high, and to make efforts. It was like caparisoning a docile elephant. With a "Thanks, gentlemen," he dived under and squeezed himself through the door in a great hurry.

We smiled at each other in a friendly way.

"I wonder how he manages to hoist himself up a ship's side-ladder," said the man in tweeds; and poor Jermyn, who was a mere North Sea pilot, without official status or recognition of any sort, pilot only by courtesy, groaned.

"He makes eight hundred a year."

"Are you a sailor?" I asked the stranger, who had gone back to his position on the rug.

"I used to be till a couple of years ago when I got married," answered this communicative individual. "I even went to sea first in that very ship we were speaking of when you came in."

"What ship?" I asked, puzzled. "I never heard you mention a ship."

"I've just told you her name, my dear sir," he replied. *"The Apse Family.* Surely you've heard of the great firm of Apse & Sons, ship-owners. They had a pretty big fleet. There was the *Lucy Apse,* and the *Harold Apse,* and *Anne, John, Malcolm, Clara, Juliet,* and so on—no end of *Apses.* Every brother, sister, aunt, cousin, wife—and grandmother too, for all I know—of the firm had a ship named after them. Good, solid, old-fashioned craft they were too, built to carry and to last. None of your new-fangled, labour-saving appliances in them, but plenty of men and plenty of good salt beef and hardtack put aboard—and off you go to fight your way out and home again."

The miserable Jermyn made a sound of approval, which sounded like a groan of pain. Those were the ships for him. He pointed out in doleful tones that you couldn't say to labour-saving appliances, "Jump lively now, my hearties." No labour-saving appliance would go aloft on a dirty night with the sands under your lee.

"No," assented the stranger, with a wink at me. "The Apses didn't believe in them either, apparently. They treated their people well—as people don't get treated nowadays, and they were awfully proud of their ships. Nothing ever happened to them. This last one, the *Apse Family,* was to be like the others, only she was to be still stronger, still safer, still more roomy and comfortable. I believe they meant her to last for ever. They had her built composite—iron, teak-wood, and greenheart, and her scantling was something fabulous. If ever an order was given for a ship in a spirit of pride this one was. Everything of the best. The commodore captain of the employ was to command her, and they planned the accommodation for him like a house on shore under a big, tall poop that went nearly to the mainmast. No wonder Mrs. Colchester wouldn't let the old man give her up. Why, it was the best home she ever had in all her married days. She had a nerve, that woman.

"The fuss that was made while that ship was building! Let's have this a little stronger, and that a little heavier; and hadn't that other thing better be changed for something a little thicker. The builders entered into the spirit of the game, and there she was, growing into the clumsiest, heaviest ship of her size right before all their eyes, without anybody becoming aware of it somehow. She was to be 2,000 tons register, or a little over; no less on any account. But see what happens. When they came to measure her she turned out 1,999 tons and a fraction. General consternation! And they say old Mr. Apse was so annoyed, when they told him, that he took to his bed and died. The old gentleman had retired from the firm twenty-five years before, and was ninety-six years old if a day, so his death wasn't, perhaps, so surprising. Still Mr. Lucian Apse was convinced that his father would have lived to a hundred. So we may put him at the head of the list. Next comes the poor devil of a shipwright that brute caught and squashed as she went off the ways. They called it the launch of a ship, but I've heard people say that, from the wailing and yelling and scrambling out of the way, it was more like letting a devil loose upon the river. She snapped all her checks like pack-threads, and went for the tugs in attendance like a fury. Before anybody could see what she was up to she sent one of them to the bottom, and laid up another for three months' repairs. One of her cables parted, and then, suddenly—you couldn't tell why—she let herself be brought up with the other as quiet as a lamb.

"That's how she was. You could never be sure what she would be up to next. There are ships difficult to handle, but generally you can depend on them behaving rationally. With *that* ship, whatever you did with her, you never knew how it would end. She was a wicked beast. Or, perhaps, she was only just insane."

He uttered this supposition in so earnest a tone that I could not refrain from smiling. He left off biting his lower lip to apostrophize me.

"Eh! Why not? Why couldn't there be something in her build, in her lines corresponding to. . . . What's madness? Only something just a tiny bit wrong in the make of your brain. Why shouldn't there be a mad ship—I mean mad in a ship-like way, so that under no circumstances could you be sure she would do what any other sensible ship would naturally do for you. There are ships that steer wildly, and ships that can't be quite trusted always to stay; others want careful watching when running in a gale; and, again, there may be a ship that will make heavy weather of it in every little blow. But then you expect her to be always so. You take it as part of her character, as a ship, just as you take account of a man's peculiarities of temper when you deal with him. But with her you couldn't. She was unaccountable. If she wasn't mad, then she was the most evil-minded, underhand, savage brute that ever went afloat. I've seen her run in a heavy gale beautifully for two days, and on the third broach to twice in the same afternoon. The first time she flung the helmsman clean over the wheel, but as she didn't quite manage to kill him she had another try about three hours afterwards. She swamped herself fore and aft, burst all the canvas we had set, scared all hands into a panic, and even frightened Mrs. Colchester down there in these beautiful stern cabins that she was so proud of. When we mustered the crew there was one man missing. Swept overboard, of course, without being either seen or heard, poor devil! and I only wonder more of us didn't go.

"Always something like that. Always. I heard an old mate tell Captain Colchester once that it had come to this with him, that he was afraid to open his mouth to give any sort of order. She was as much of a terror in harbour as at sea. You could never be certain what would hold her. On the slightest provocation she would start snapping ropes, cables, wire hawsers, like carrots. She was heavy, clumsy, unhandy—but that does not quite explain that power for mischief she had. You know, somehow, when I think of her I can't help remembering what we hear of incurable lunatics breaking loose now and then."

He looked at me inquisitively. But, of course, I couldn't admit that a ship could be mad.

"In the ports where she was known," he went on, "they dreaded the sight of her. She thought nothing of knocking away twenty feet or so of solid stone facing off a quay or wiping off the end of a wooden wharf. She must have lost miles of chain and hundreds of tons of anchors in her time. When she fell aboard some poor offending ship it was the very devil of a job to haul her off again. And she never got hurt herself—just a few scratches or so, perhaps. They had wanted to have her strong. And so she was. Strong enough to ram Polar ice with. And as she began so she went on. From the day she was launched she never let a year pass without murdering somebody. I think the owners got very worried about it. But they were a stiff-necked generation, all these Apses; they wouldn't admit there could be anything wrong with the *Apse Family*. They wouldn't even change her name. 'Stuff and nonsense,' as Mrs. Colchester used to say. They ought at least to have shut her up for life in some dry dock or other, away up the river, and never let her smell salt water again. I assure you, my dear sir, that she invariably did kill some one every voyage she made. It was perfectly well known. She got a name for it, far and wide."

I expressed my surprise that a ship with such a deadly reputation could ever get a crew.

"Then, you don't know what sailors are, my dear sir. Let me just show you by an instance. One day in dock at home, while loafing on the forecastle head, I noticed two respectable salts come along, one a middle-aged, competent, steady man, evidently, the other a smart, youngish chap. They read the name on the bows and stopped to look at her. Says the elder man: '*Apse Family*. That's the sanguinary female dog' (I'm putting it in that way) 'of a ship, Jack, that kills a man every voyage. I wouldn't sign in her—not for Joe, I wouldn't.' And the other says: 'If she were mine, I'd have her towed on the mud and set on fire, blamme if I wouldn't.' Then the first man chimes in: 'Much do they care! Men are cheap, God knows.' The younger one spat in the water alongside. 'They won't have me—not for double wages.'

"They hung about for some time and then walked up the dock. Half an hour later I saw them both on our deck looking about for the mate, and apparently very anxious to be taken on. And they were."

"How do you account for this?" I asked.

"What would you say?" he retorted. "Recklessness! The vanity of boasting in the evening to all their chums: 'We've just shipped in that there *Apse Family*. Blow her. She ain't going to scare us.' Sheer sailor-like perversity! A sort of curiosity. Well—a little of all that, no doubt. I put the question to them in the course of the voyage. The answer of the elderly chap was:

"'A man can die but once.' The younger assured me in a mocking tone that he wanted to see 'how she would do it this time.' But I tell you what; there was a sort of fascination about the brute."

Jermyn, who seemed to have seen every ship in the world, broke in sulkily:

"I saw her once out of this very window towing up the river; a great black ugly thing, going along like a big hearse."

"Something sinister about her looks, wasn't there?" said the man in tweeds, looking down at old Jermyn with a friendly eye. "I always had a sort of horror of her. She gave me a beastly shock when I was no more than fourteen, the very first day—nay, hour—I joined her. Father came up to see me off, and was to go down to Gravesend with us. I was his second boy to go to sea. My big brother was already an officer then. We got on board about eleven in the morning, and found the ship ready to drop out of the basin, stern first. She had not moved three times her own length when, at a little pluck the tug gave her to enter the dock gates, she made one of her rampaging starts, and put such a weight on the check rope—a new six-inch hawser—that forward there they had no chance to ease it round in time, and it parted. I saw the broken end fly up high in the air, and the next moment that brute brought her quarter against the pierhead with a jar that staggered everybody about her decks. She didn't hurt herself. Not she! But one of the boys the mate had sent aloft on the mizzen to do something, came down on the poop-deck—thump—right in front of me. He was not much older than myself. We had been grinning at each other only a few minutes before. He must have been handling himself carelessly, not expecting to get such a jerk. I heard his startled cry—Oh!—in a high treble as he felt himself going, and looked up in time to see him go limp all over as he fell. Ough! Poor father was remarkably white about the gills when we shook hands in Gravesend. 'Are you all right?' he says, looking hard at me. 'Yes, father.' 'Quite sure?' 'Yes, father.' 'Well, then, good-bye, my boy.' He told me afterwards that for half a word he would have carried me off home with him there and then. I am the baby of the family—you know," added the man in tweeds, stroking his moustache with an ingenuous smile.

I acknowledged this interesting communication by a sympathetic murmur. He waved his hand carelessly.

"This might have utterly spoiled a chap's nerve for going aloft, you know—utterly. He fell within two feet of me, cracking his head on a mooring-bit. Never moved. Stone dead. Nice-looking little fellow, he was. I had just been thinking we would be great chums. However, that wasn't yet the worst that brute of a ship could do. I served in her three years of my time, and then I got transferred to the *Lucy Apse*, for a year. The sailmaker we had in the *Apse Family* turned up there, too, and I remember him saying to me one evening, after we had been a week at sea: 'Isn't she a meek little ship?' No wonder we thought the *Lucy Apse* a dear, meek little ship after getting clear of that big rampaging savage brute. It was like heaven. Her officers seemed to me the restfullest lot of men on earth. To me who had known no ship but the *Apse Family*, the *Lucy* was like a sort of magic craft that did what you wanted her to do of her own accord. One evening we got caught aback pretty sharply from right ahead. In about ten minutes we had her full again, sheets aft, tacks down, decks cleared, and the officer of the watch leaning against the weather rail peacefully. It seemed simply marvellous to me. The other would have stuck for half an hour in irons, rolling her decks full of water, knocking the men about—spars cracking, braces snapping, yards taking charge, and a confounded scare going on after because of her beastly rudder, which she had a way of flapping about fit to raise your hair on end. I couldn't get over my wonder for days.

"Well, I finished my last year of apprenticeship in that jolly little ship—she wasn't so little either, but after that other heavy devil she seemed but a plaything to handle. I finished my time and passed; and then just as I was thinking of having three weeks of real good time on shore I got at breakfast a letter asking me the earliest day I could be ready to join the *Apse Family* as third mate. I gave my plate a shove that shot it into the middle of the table; dad looked up over his paper; mother raised her hands in astonishment, and I went out bare-headed into our bit of garden, where I walked round and round for an hour.

"When I came in again mother was out of the diningroom, and dad had shifted berth into his big armchair. The letter was lying on the mantelpiece.

" 'It's very creditable to you to get the offer, and very kind of them to make it,' he said. 'And I see also that Charles has been appointed chief mate of that ship for one voyage.'

"There was overleaf a PS. to that effect in Mr. Apse's own handwriting, which I had overlooked. Charley was my big brother.

" 'I don't like very much to have two of my boys together in one ship,' father goes on, in his deliberate solemn way. 'And I may tell you that I would not mind writing Mr. Apse a letter to that effect.'

"Dear old dad! He was a wonderful father. What would you have done? The mere notion of going back (and as an officer, too), to be worried and bothered, and kept on the jump night and day by that brute, made me feel sick. But she wasn't a ship you could afford to fight shy of. Besides, the most genuine excuse could not be given without mortally offending Apse & Sons. The firm, and I believe the whole family down to the old unmarried aunts in Lancashire, had grown desperately touchy about that accursed ship's character. This was the case for answering 'Ready now' from your very deathbed if you wished to die in their good grace. And that's precisely what I did answer—by wire, to have it over and done with at once.

"The prospect of being shipmates with my big brother cheered me up considerably, though it made me a bit anxious, too. Ever since I remember myself as a little chap he had been very good to me, and I looked upon him as the finest fellow in the world. And so he was. No better officer ever walked the deck of a merchant ship. And that's a fact. He was a fine, strong, upstanding, suntanned young fellow, with his brown hair curling a little, and an eye like a hawk. He was just splendid. We hadn't seen each other for many years, and even this time, though he had been in England three weeks already, he hadn't showed up at home yet, but had spent his spare time in Surrey somewhere making up to Maggie Colchester, old Captain Colchester's niece. Her father, a great friend of dad's, was in the sugar-broking business, and Charley made a sort of second home of their house. I wondered what my big brother would think of me. There was a sort of sternness about Charley's face which never left it, not even when he was larking in his rather wild fashion.

"He received me with a great shout of laughter. He seemed to think my joining as an officer the greatest joke in the world. There was a difference of ten years between us, and I suppose he remembered me best in pinafores. I was a kid of four when he first went to sea. It surprised me to find how boisterous he could be.

" 'Now we shall see what you are made of,' he cried. And he held me off by the shoulders, and punched my ribs, and hustled me into his berth. 'Sit down, Ned. I am glad of the chance of having you with me. I'll put the finishing touch to you, my young officer, providing you're worth the trouble. And, first of all, get it well into your head that we are not going to let this brute kill anybody this voyage. We'll stop her racket.'

"I perceived he was in dead earnest about it. He talked grimly of the ship, and how we must be careful and never allow this ugly beast to catch us napping with any of her damned tricks.

"He gave me a regular lecture on special seamanship for the use of the *Apse Family*; then changing his tone, he began to talk at large, rattling off the wildest, funniest nonsense, till my sides ached with laughing. I could see very well he was a bit above himself with high spirits. It couldn't be because of my coming. Not to that extent. But, of course, I wouldn't have dreamt of asking what was the matter. I had a proper respect for my big brother, I can tell you. But it was all made plain enough a day or two afterwards, when I heard that Miss Maggie Colchester was coming for the voyage. Uncle was giving her a sea trip for the benefit of her health.

"I don't know what could have been wrong with her health. She had a beautiful colour, and a deuce of a lot of fair hair. She didn't care a rap for wind, or rain, or spray, or sun, or green seas, or anything. She was a blue-eyed, jolly girl of the very best sort, but the way she cheeked my big brother used to frighten me. I always expected it to end in an awful row. However, nothing decisive happened till after we had been in Sydney for a week. One day, in the men's dinner hour, Charley sticks his head into my cabin. I was stretched out on my back on the settee, smoking in peace.

" 'Come ashore with me, Ned,' he says, in his curt way.

"I jumped up, of course, and away after him down the gangway and up George Street. He strode along like a giant, and I at his elbow, panting. It was confoundedly hot. 'Where on earth are you rushing me to, Charley?' I made bold to ask.

" 'Here,' he says.

" 'Here' was a jeweller's shop. I couldn't imagine what he could want there. It seemed a sort of mad freak. He thrusts under my nose three rings, which looked very tiny on his big, brown palm, growling out 'For Maggie! Which!'

"I got a kind of scare at this. I couldn't make a sound, but I pointed at the one that sparkled white and blue. He put it in his waistcoat pocket, paid for it with a lot of sovereigns, and bolted out. When we got on board I was quite out of breath. 'Shake hands, old chap,' I gasped out. He gave me a thump on the back. 'Give what orders you like to the boatswain when the hands turn-to,' says he; 'I am off duty this afternoon.'

"Then he vanished from the deck for a while, but presently he came out of the cabin with Maggie, and these two went over the gangway publicly, before all hands, going for a walk together on that awful, blazing, hot day, with clouds of dust flying about. They came back after a few hours looking very staid, but didn't seem to have the slightest idea where they had been. Anyway that's the answer they both made to Mrs. Colchester's question at tea-time.

"And didn't she turn on Charley, with her voice like an old night cabman's. 'Rubbish. Don't know where you've been! Stuff and nonsense. You've walked the girl off her legs. Don't do it again.'

"It's surprising how meek Charley could be with that old woman. Only on one occasion he whispered to me, 'I'm jolly glad she isn't Maggie's aunt, except by marriage. That's no sort of relationship.' But I think he let Maggie have too much of her own way. She was hopping all over that ship in her yachting skirt and a red tam-o'-shanter like a bright bird on a dead black tree. The old salts used to grin to themselves when they saw her coming along, and offered to teach her knots or splices. I believe she liked the men, for Charley's sake, I suppose.

"As you may imagine, the diabolic propensities of that cursed ship were never spoken of on board. Not in the cabin, at any rate. Only once on the homeward passage Charley said, incautiously, something about bringing all her crew home this time. Captain Colchester began to look uncomfortable at once, and that silly, hard-bitten old woman flew out at Charley as though he had said something indecent. I was quite confounded myself; as to Maggie, she sat completely mystified, opening her blue eyes very wide. Of course, before she was a day older she wormed it all out of me. She was a very difficult person to lie to.

" 'How awful,' she said, quite solemn. 'So many poor fellows. I am glad the voyage is nearly over. I won't have a moment's peace about Charley now.'

"I assured her Charley was all right. It took more than that ship knew to get over a seaman like Charley. And she agreed with me.

"Next day we got the tug off Dungeness; and when the tow-rope was fast Charley rubbed his hands and said to me in an undertone, 'We've baffled her, Ned.'

" 'Look's like it,' I said, with a grin at him. It was beautiful weather, and the sea as smooth as a millpond. We went up the river without a shadow of trouble except once, when off Hole Haven the brute took a sudden sheer and nearly had a barge anchored just clear of the fairway. But I was aft, looking after the steering, and she did not catch me napping that time. Charley came up on the poop, looking very concerned. 'Close shave,' says he.

" 'Never mind, Charley,' I answered, cheerily. 'You've tamed her.'

"We were to tow right up to the dock. The river pilot boarded us below Gravesend, and the first words I heard him say were: 'You may just as well take your port anchor inboard at once, Mr. Mate.'

"This had been done when I went forward. I saw Maggie on the forecastle head enjoying the bustle, and I begged her to go aft, but she took no notice of me, of course. Then Charley, who was very busy with the head gear, caught sight of her and shouted in his biggest voice: 'Get off the forecastle head, Maggie. You're in the way here.' For all answer she made a funny face at him, and I saw poor Charley turn away, hiding a smile. She was flushed with the excitement of getting home again, and her blue eyes seemed to snap electric sparks as she looked at the river. A collier brig had gone round just ahead of us, and our tug had to stop her engines in a hurry to avoid running into her.

"In a moment, as is usually the case, all the shipping in the reach seemed to get into a hopeless tangle. A schooner and a ketch got up a small collision all to themselves right in the middle of the river. It was exciting to watch, and, meantime, our tug remained stopped. Any other ship than that brute could have been coaxed to keep straight for a couple of minutes—but not she! Her head fell off at once, and she began to drift down, taking her tug along with her. I noticed a cluster of coasters at anchor within a quarter of a mile of us, and I thought I had better speak to the pilot. 'If you let her get amongst that lot,' I said quietly, 'she will grind some of them to bits before we get her out again.'

" 'Don't I know her!' cries he, stamping his foot in a perfect fury. And he out with his whistle to make that bothered tug get the ship's head up again as quick as possible. He blew like mad, waving his arm to port, and presently we could see that the tug's engines had been set going ahead. Her paddles churned the water, but it was as if she had been trying to tow a rock—she couldn't get an inch out of that ship. Again the pilot blew his whistle, and waved his arms to port. We could see the tug's paddles turning faster and faster away, broad on our bow.

"For a moment tug and ship hung motionless in a crowd of moving shipping, and then the terrific strain that evil, stony-hearted brute would always put on everything tore the towing-chock clean out. The tow-rope surged over, snapping the iron stanchions of the headrail one after another as if they had been sticks of sealing-wax.

It was only then I noticed that in order to have a better view over our heads, Maggie had stepped upon the port anchor as it lay flat on the forecastle deck.

"It had been lowered properly into its hardwood beds, but there had been no time to take a turn with it. Anyway, it was quite secure as it was, for going into dock; but I could see directly that the tow-rope would sweep under the fluke in another second. My heart flew up right into my throat, but not before I had time to yell out, 'Jump clear of that anchor!'

"But I hadn't time to shriek out her name. I don't suppose she heard me at all. The first touch of the hawser against the fluke threw her down; she was up on her feet again as quick as lightning, but she was up on the wrong side. I heard a horrid, scraping sound, and then that anchor, tipping over, rose up like something alive; its great, rough iron arm caught Maggie round the waist, seemed to clasp her close with a dreadful hug, and flung itself with her over and down in a terrific clang of iron, followed by heavy ringing blows that shook the ship from stern to stem—because the ring stopper held!"

"How horrible!" I exclaimed.

"I used to dream for years afterwards of anchors catching hold of girls," said the man in tweeds, a little wildly. He shuddered. "With a most pitiful howl Charley was over after her almost on the instant. But, Lord! he didn't see as much as a gleam of her red tam-o'-shanter in the water. Nothing! nothing whatever! In a moment there were half-a-dozen boats around us, and he got pulled into one. I, with the boatswain and the carpenter, let go the other anchor in a hurry and brought the ship up somehow. The pilot had gone silly. He walked up and down the forecastle head wringing his hands and muttering to himself, 'Killing women, now! Killing women now!' Not another word could you get out of him.

"Dusk fell, then a night black as pitch; and peering upon the river I heard a low, mournful hail, 'Ship ahoy!' Two Gravesend watermen came alongside. They had a lantern in their wherry, and looked up the ship's side, holding on to the ladder without a word. I saw in the patch of light a lot of loose, fair hair down there."

He shuddered again.

"After the tide turned poor Maggie's body had floated clear of one of them big mooring buoys," he explained. "I crept aft, feeling half-dead, and managed to send a rocket up—to let the other searchers know, on the river. And then I slunk away forward like a cur, and spent the night sitting on the heel of the bowsprit so as to be as far as possible out of Charley's way."

"Poor fellow!" I murmured.

"Yes. Poor fellow," he repeated musingly. "That brute wouldn't let him—not even him—cheat her of her prey. But he made her fast in dock next morning. He did. We hadn't exchanged a word—not a single look for that matter. I didn't want to look at him. When the last rope was fast he put his hands to his head and stood gazing down at his feet as if trying to remember something. The men waited on the main deck for the words that end the voyage. Perhaps that is what he was trying to remember. I spoke for him. 'That'll do, men.'

"I never saw a crew leave a ship so quietly. They sneaked over the rail one after another, taking care not to bang their sea chests too heavily. They looked our way, but not one had the stomach to come up and offer to shake hands with the mate as is usual.

"I followed him all over the empty ship to and fro, here and there, with no living soul about but the two of us, because the old shipkeeper had locked himself up in the galley—both doors. Suddenly poor Charley mutters, in a crazy voice, 'I'm done here,' and strides down the gangway with me at his heels, up the dock, out at the gate, on towards Tower Hill. He used to take rooms with a decent old landlady in America Square, to be near his work.

"All at once he stops short, turns round, and comes back straight at me. 'Ned,' says he, 'I am going home.' I had the good luck to sight a four-wheeler and got him in just in time. His legs were beginning to give way. In our hall he fell down on a chair, and I'll never forget father's and mother's amazed, perfectly still faces as they stood over him. They couldn't understand what had happened to him till I blubbered out, 'Maggie got drowned, yesterday, in the river.'

"Mother let out a little cry. Father looks from him to me, and from me to him, as if comparing our faces—for, upon my soul, Charley did not resemble himself at all. Nobody moved; and the poor fellow raises his big brown hands slowly to his throat, and with one single tug rips everything open—collar, shirt, waistcoat—a perfect wreck and ruin of a man. Father and I got him upstairs somehow, and mother pretty nearly killed herself nursing him through a brain fever."

The man in tweeds nodded at me significantly.

"Ah! there was nothing that could be done with that brute. She had a devil in her."

"Where's your brother?" I asked, expecting to hear he was dead. But he was commanding a smart steamer on the China coast, and never came home now.

Jermyn fetched a heavy sigh, and the handkerchief being now sufficiently dry, put it up tenderly to his red and lamentable nose.

"She was a ravening beast," the man in tweeds started again. "Old Colchester put his foot down and resigned. And would you believe it? Apse & Sons wrote to ask whether he wouldn't reconsider his decision! Anything to save the good name of the *Apse Family!* Old Colchester went to the office then and said that he would take charge again but only to sail her out into the North Sea and scuttle her there. He was nearly off his chump. He used to be darkish iron-grey, but his hair went snow-white in a fortnight. And Mr. Lucian Apse (they had known each other as young men) pretended not to notice it. Eh? Here's infatuation if you like! Here's pride for you!

"They jumped at the first man they could get to take her, for fear of the scandal of the *Apse Family* not being able to find a skipper. He was a festive soul, I believe, but he stuck to her grim and hard. Wilmot was his second mate. A harum-scarum fellow, and pretending to a great scorn for all the girls. The fact is he was really timid. But let only one of them do as much as lift her little finger in encouragement, and there was nothing that could hold the beggar. As apprentice, once, he deserted abroad after a petticoat, and would have gone to the dogs then if his skipper hadn't taken the trouble to find him and lug him by the ears out of some house of perdition or other.

"It was said that one of the firm had been heard once to express a hope that this brute of a ship would get lost soon. I can hardly credit the tale, unless it might have been Mr. Alfred Apse, whom the family didn't think much of. They had him in the office, but he was considered a bad egg altogether, always flying off to race meetings and coming home drunk. You would have thought that a ship so full of deadly tricks would run herself ashore some day out of sheer cussedness. But not she! She was going to last for ever. She had a nose to keep off the bottom."

Jermyn made a grunt of approval.

"A ship after a pilot's own heart, eh?" jeered the man in tweeds. "Well, Wilmot managed it. He was the man for it, but even he, perhaps, couldn't have done the trick without that green-eyed governess, or nurse, or whatever she was to the children of Mr. and Mrs. Pamphilius.

"Those people were passengers in her from Port Adelaide to the Cape. Well, the ship went out and anchored outside for the day. The skipper—hospitable soul—had a lot of guests from town to a fare-well lunch—as usual with him. It was five in the evening before the last shore boat left the side, and the weather looked ugly and dark in the gulf. There was no reason for him to get under way. However, as he had told everybody he was going that day, he imagined it was proper to do so anyhow. But as he had no mind after all these festivities to tackle the straits in the dark, with a scant wind, he gave orders to keep the ship under lower topsails and foresail as close as she would lie, dodging along the land till the morning. Then he sought his virtuous couch. The mate was on deck, having his face washed very clean with hard rain squalls. Wilmot relieved him at midnight.

"The *Apse Family* had, as you observed, a house on her poop. . . . "

"A big, ugly white thing, sticking up," Jermyn murmured sadly, at the fire.

"That's it: a companion for the cabin stairs and a sort of chart-room combined. The rain drove in gusts on the sleepy Wilmot. The ship was then surging slowly to the southward, close hauled, with the coast within three miles or so to windward. There was nothing to look out for in that part of the gulf, and Wilmot went round to dodge the squalls under the lee of that chartroom, whose door on that side was open. The night was black, like a barrel of coal-tar. And then he heard a woman's voice whispering to him.

"That confounded green-eyed girl of the Pamphilius people had put the kids to bed a long time ago, of course, but it seems couldn't get to sleep herself. She heard eight bells struck, and the chief mate come below to turn in. She waited a bit, then got into her dressing gown and stole across the empty saloon and up the stairs into the chartroom. She sat down on the settee near the open door to cool herself, I daresay.

"I suppose when she whispered to Wilmot it was as if some-body had struck a match in the fellow's brain. I don't know how it was they had got so very thick. I fancy he had met her ashore a few times before. I couldn't make it out, because, when telling the story, Wilmot would break off to swear something awful at every second word. We had met on the quay in Sydney, and he had an apron of sacking up to his chin, a big whip in his hand. A wagon-driver. Glad to do anything not to starve. That's what he had come down to.

"However, there he was, with his head inside the door, on the girl's shoulder as likely as not—officer of the watch! The helmsman, on giving his evidence afterwards, said that he shouted several times that the binnacle lamp had gone out. It didn't matter to him, because his orders were to 'sail her close.' 'I thought it funny,' he said, 'that the ship should keep on falling off in squalls, but I luffed her up every time as close as I was able. It was so dark I couldn't see my hand before my face, and the rain came in bucketfuls on my head.'

"The truth was that at every squall the wind hauled aft a little, till gradually the ship came to be heading straight for the coast, without a single soul in her being aware of it. Wilmot himself confessed that he had not been near the standard compass for an hour. He might well have confessed! The first thing he knew was the man on the lookout shouting blue murder forward there.

"He tore his neck free, he says, and yelled back at him: 'What do you say?'

" 'I think I hear breakers ahead, sir,' howled the man and came rushing aft with the rest of the watch, in the 'awfullest blinding deluge that ever fell from the sky,' Wilmot says. For a second or so he was so scared and bewildered that he could not remember on which side of the gulf the ship was. He wasn't a good officer, but he was a seaman all the same. He pulled himself together in a second, and the right orders sprang to his lips without thinking. They were to hard up with the helm and shiver the main and mizzen-topsails.

"It seems that the sails actually fluttered. He couldn't see them, but he heard them rattling and banging above his head. 'No use! She was too slow in going off,' he went on, his dirty face twitching, and the damn'd carter's whip shaking in his hand. 'She seemed to stick fast.' And then the flutter of the canvas above his head ceased. At this critical moment the wind hauled aft again with a gust, filling the sails, and sending the ship with a great way upon the rocks on her lee bow. She had overreached herself in her last little game. Her time had come—the hour, the man, the black night, the treacherous gust of wind—the right woman to put an end to her. The brute deserved nothing better. Strange are the instruments of Providence. There's a sort of poetical justice. . . . "

The man in tweeds looked hard at me.

"The first ledge she went over stripped the false keel off her. Rip! The skipper, rushing out of his berth, found a crazy woman, in a red flannel dressing-gown, flying round and round the cuddy, screeching like a cockatoo.

"The next bump knocked her clean under the cabin table. It also started the sternpost and carried away the rudder, and then that brute ran up a shelving, rocky shore, tearing her bottom out, till she stopped short, and the foremast dropped over the bows like a gangway."

"Anybody lost?" I asked.

"No one, unless that fellow Wilmot," answered the gentleman, unknown to Miss Blank, looking round for his cap. "And his case was worse than drowning for a man. Everybody got ashore all right. Gale didn't come on till next day, dead from the West, and broke up that brute in a surprisingly short time. It was as though she had been rotten at heart. . . . " He changed his tone. "Rain left off. I must get my bike and rush home to dinner. I live in Herne Bay—came out for a spin this morning."

He nodded at me in a friendly way, and went out with a swagger.

"Do you know who he is, Jermyn?" I asked.

The North Sea pilot shook his head, dismally. "Fancy losing a ship in that silly fashion! Oh dear! oh dear!" he groaned in lugubrious tones, spreading his damp handkerchief again like a curtain before the glowing grate.

On going out I exchanged a glance and a smile (strictly proper) with the respectable Miss Blank, barmaid of the Three Crows.

JOHN WILLIAM DEFOREST

A STRANGE ARRIVAL

RIG *BETSY JANE,* OF New Haven, Connecticut, bound for Jamaica, is doing her best to get there.

It is not by any means her "level best," for a fresh tornado has burst from his lair in the Gulf of Mexico, and is blowing all his great guns and marline-spikes down the course of the Gulf Stream, as if he were totally out of patience with that venerable current, and meant to hurricane it off the face of the planet.

The waves rush, rear, tumble, howl, and froth at the mouth, like a mad herd of immeasurable buffaloes. Up goes one to a quivering peak; for a moment it stands, shaking its maniacal head of spray at the heavens; then, with a dying roar, it is trampled upon by its comrades. Onward they climb, roll, reel, topple, and wallow; their panting sides marbled with long streaks and great splashes of foam; their bluish masses continually throwing out new outlines of jagged, translucent edges; their sullen bellows and sharp gasps defying the beak and scream of the tornado. It is a combat which makes little account of man if he comes within range of its fury.

At a distance, the brig appears a stumpy black speck, buffeted, jerked, submerged, and then tossed upward. Now it plunges clean out of sight, as if the depths had gaped beneath it to their trembling base; now it crawls slowly into view again, as if a miracle had saved it for just another moment. You can see, misty miles away, that the craft has lost her topmasts, and that she is in dire trouble.

At hand things appear even worse than afar. The forty horses and mules, which were being transported for hard labor to the sugar-mills of the West Indies, have been drowned at their fastenings, thrown overboard by the sailors, dragged overboard by the billows. Short, frayed tatters of canvas, and loose, unstranding ends of rope, flutter and snap from the remaining yards. The caboose is gone; the bulwarks have taken to swimming; the water sweeps clean from stem to stern. Under a storm-jib, the only sail that can hold, the only sail that the reeling craft can bear, she is running before the gale. Worst of all, one of the dragging topmasts made a parting, traitorous rush at the stern, and stove a fracture through which the Atlantic spurts and foams.

We will wait a night and day, while the tornado dies into a half-gale, and the sea changes from toppling mountains to the sliding hills. Around the wheel, the only upright object on deck, sits a little group of drenched forms and haggard faces, staring with reddened eyes at the restless deserts of ocean. We will spend few words on the black cook, the mulatto cabin boy, the six gaunt and brown New England sailors, the broad-shouldered, hard-featured mate. Our story more nearly concerns Captain Phineas Glover, and his daughter, Mary Anne Glover.

If the little oyster-planting suburb of Fair Haven ever produced a purer specimen of the old-fashioned, commonplace stock Yankee than "Capm Phin Glover," let Fair Haven stand forth and brag of her handiwork in that line, secure from competition. It passed understanding how he could be so yellow, so sandy, so flaxen, after thirty years of exposure to sun, wind, and sea. How was it that pulling at tackles in his youth had left his shoulders so scant, his chest so hollow, and his limbs so lean? We must conclude that Captain Glover was Yankee all through, and that his soul was too stubborn for the forces of nature, beating them in their struggle to refashion his physique.

But tough as was his individuality, a due proportion of it had melted into paternity. As he looked at Mary Anne's round, blond face and ringlets of draggled flaxen, he was evidently thinking mainly of her peril. "O Lord! what made me fetch her?" was the all-absorbing thought of Phineas Glover. The girl, eighteen years old perhaps, was still childlike enough to have implicit trust in a father, and she returned his gaze with a confiding steadiness which enhanced his trouble.

"Pumps are played out, Capm," said the mate, in the hoarse tone of an over-fatigued and desperate man. "The brig will go down in two hours. We must take to the boat."

"It's lucky we had one stowed away," replied Glover, and paused to meditate, his eyes on the waves.

"Shall we get her up and launch her?" asked the mate, sharply, impatient at this hesitation.

"I wish we had n't cut the masts away," sighed the captain, after another pause. "If we had n't, I'd make a sail."

"Make sail to Davy Jones's locker? I tell you we see the Dutchman last night. More 'n one of us see him."

"I seen him," said the cook, with a deprecatory grin. "An' so did Jimmy."

"Ordinarily I don't mind such stories," continued the mate. "But now you see how things is for yourself; you see that something out o' the common has been afoul of us; and my opinion is that it hain't done with the brig yet. Anyway, Dutchman or no Dutchman, this brig is settling."

"I don't believe it, Mr. Brown. Them staves an' bar'ls is a floatin' cargo. She'll go to the water's edge, mebbe, but she won't go a mite farther."

"Now look a here, Capm. I, for one, don't want to resk it."

"Nor I," struck in the sailors, and, in a more humble tone, the black cook.

"Wal," decided the captain, "I sha' n't put my daughter in a boat, in this sea, a thousan' miles from land. She an' I'll stay aboard the brig. If you want to try the boat, try it. I don't say nothin' agin it."

A brief silence, a short, earnest discussion, and the thing was thus settled. The boat was dragged out of the hold and launched; two or three barrels of provisions and water were embarked; the crew, one by one, slid down into the little craft; presently it dropped away to leeward. Phineas and Mary Anne Glover called to the adventurers, "Look us up, if you find help," and waved them a sad farewell. The seamen rose from their seats and returned three encouraging cheers. A little sail was set in the bow of the boat, and it stole, rising and falling, toward the setting sun. Night came down on the rolling, waterlogged, but still floating brig.

"I tell ye them boys had better a great sight hung by us," said Captain Glover to Mary Anne, as they sat on the upper steps of the gangway and looked down upon the water swashing about the cabin. "She hain't settled a hair in the last two hours. The' ain't a speck o' danger o' founderin'. I knew the' wa'n't. Noah's flood could n't founder them staves an' bar'ls."

"Oh dear! I wish I was in Fair Haven," blubbered Mary Anne. "If I could only git back there, I'd stay there."

"Come now, cheer up," returned the father, doing his best to smile. "Why, I've been a sight wus off than this, an' come out on't with the stars an' stripes a flyin'. Las' time I was wrecked, I had to swim ashore on a mule—swum a hundred miles in three days, with nothin' to eat but the mule's ears—an' as for sleepin', sho! Tell ye that mule *was* a kicker. A drove o' sharks was right after us, an' he kicked out the brains o' th' whole boodle of 'em. Stands to reason I could n't sleep much."

"O pa! You *do* tell such stories! I sh'd think you'd be afraid to tell 'em now."

"Wal, you don't b'lieve it. But live an' learn. Tell you, b'fore you git home, you'll b'lieve things you never b'lieved b'fore. Why, I got a new wrinkle no later 'n day b'fore yesterday. Many strange things 's I've seen, I never b'lieved till now in the Flyin' Dutchman. You heard what the men said. Wal, I saw him 's plain 's they did. I'm obleeged to b'lieve in him. I sighted him comin' right up on our larboard bow, 's straight in the wind's eye 's he could steer. He run up till he was a cable's length from us, an' I was jest about to hail him, when he disappeared. Kind o' went up or down, I could n't say which. Anyhow, next minute, he was n't there."

This time Captain Glover spoke with such earnestness that his daughter put faith at least in his sincerity.

"O pa! I wish you would n't scare me so," she whimpered. "It's awful."

"Lord bless you! never mind it, Mary Anne," chirruped the father. "The critter's done all the harm he 's allowed to do. "Tain't in his peajacket to do wus 'n he has. That's jest the reason why he up helm and put out o' sight. Come now, we'll have supper; lots to eat aboard. I reckon we've provisions enough to last three years, an' have a big tuck-out every Thanksgiving. Come, chirk up, Mary Anne. I wish them poor boys was half 's well off's we be. Why, we can be as happy 's Robinson Crusoe."

All night Mary Anne, as she afterwards related, dreamed about the Flying Dutchman. She saw him steer straight over the meadows to the Fair Haven steeple, and knock it prostrate with one glance through his telescope. He carried her away to caverns under the sea which were encrusted with pearls and stored with treasure. He sailed with her so fast around the world that the sun was always setting and yet never got out of sight. His canvas was made of moon-beams, and his hull of the end of a rainbow. When she awoke at daylight, the first words that she heard from her father were, "Wal, if that ain't the Dutchiest Dutchman that ever I did see!"

Leaping up, and steadying herself against the paternal shoulder, she looked across the now gently heaving waters. Was there witch-craft in the world? Had they slept a hundred years in a night, and slept backward at that? Not for two centuries, not since the days of Hendrik Hudson and De Ruyter, had earthly eyes beheld such a sight as now bewildered these two human oysters from Fair Haven. The wildest fancies, the most improbable invention of Capm Phin Glover were left a long ways astern by the spectacle before him.

"I never see the like," he said, quite forgetting his need of rescue in his wonder. "Dunno whether it's a Dutchman or a China-man. The' was a Chinee junk brought to New York that was a mite like it."

Here he suddenly remembered that he was a shipwrecked unfortunate, and burst into a series of shrill yellings, emphasized by wavings of his tarpaulin.

A hundred fathoms distant, right against the broad, dazzling halo of the rising sun, slowly bowing and curvetting on the long, low swell, lay a craft of six or eight hundred tons burden, with a perfectly round bow capped by a lofty forecastle, and a stern which ran up into something like a tower. Two huge but stumpy masts supported the yards of four enormous square sails, while a third mast, singularly short and slender, rose from near the tiller. Two short jibs ran down to a bowsprit which pointed upward at an angle of forty-five degrees; two monstrous tops, fenced around with bulwarks, looked like turrets on stilts. The whole pompous, grotesque edifice was painted bright red, with a wide streak of staring yellow.

It seemed to swarm with men, and they were all in strange, old-fashioned costumes, as if they were revellers in a masked ball, or wax figures escaped out of museums. The queerest hats and high-colored jackets and knickerbocker breeches and long stockings went up and down the shrouds, and glided about the curving decks, and stole out on the pug-nosed bowsprit. On the castle-like poop stood three men in richer vesture than the others, whose hats showed plumes of feathers. Presently these three uncovered their heads, and set their faces steadfastly toward heaven, as if engaging in some act of devotion. This ended, the tallest turned toward the sufferers of the *Betsy Jane*, made them a solemn bow and waved his hand encouragingly.

"Wal, if this don't beat all!" said Phin Glover to his daughter. "Now tell me nothin' happens at sea but what happens in Fair Haven. Now tell me I never swum ashore on a mule."

"What is it, pa?" demanded Mary Anne. "Is it a ship, or a house?"

"I declare I dunno whether it's a meetin'-house afloat or Noah's Ark," responded the hopelessly bewildered skipper. "I never hailed the like before, not even in picters."

By this time a round-shouldered, full-breasted boat, high out of water fore and aft, had been let down the bulging sides of the stranger. Half a dozen of the grotesque sailors swung themselves into it; then came the tall personage who had made the cheering signals to our shipwrecked couple; in another minute the goose-fashioned craft was bobbing under the quarter of the *Betsy Jane*. Phin Glover looked at his rescuers in such amazement that he forgot to speak to them. Even when the tall man stepped from his seat upon the deck of the waterlogged brig, the Yankee skipper could only continue to stare with his mouth open.

The visitor was in every way a remarkable object. A sugar-loaf hat with a feather, a close-fitting doublet of purple velvet, loose breeches of claret-colored silk tying below the knee, silk stockings of a topaz or sherry yellow, broad, square-toed shoes decked with a bow, and a long, straight sword hanging from a shoulder-belt, constituted a costume which even the wonder-hunting Phin Glover had never before beheld, nor so much as constructed out of the rich wardrobe of his imagination. Moreover, this man had a noble form, a stately bearing, and a countenance which was at once stern and sweet. His gray eyes set forth a melancholy yet hopeful light, which seemed to tell a history beyond the natural experience of humanity.

His conduct was as singular as his appearance. After one glance at the Glovers, he knelt down upon the damp deck of the brig, removed his hat, and uttered a prayer in some unknown language. Rising, with a face moistened by tears, he approached Mary Anne, took her trembling hand in his, bowed over it in profound humility and kissed it. Then, before he could be prevented, he in the same manner kissed the horny fist of Captain Glover.

"Seems to me this is puttin' on a leetle too many airs, ain't it?" was the remark of our astonished countryman.

"You are English," returned the other, with a pronunciation which was foreign, and even stranger than foreign. It seemed as if the mould of ages clogged it, as if the dead who have been buried for centuries might have uttered those tones, as if they were meant for ears which have long since been stopped by the fingers of decay.

"No, *sir!*" responded Phin Glover, emphatic with national pride. "Americans! United States of America! Dunno's you ever sailed there," he added, startled and somewhat humbled by a suspicion that there might be countries or ages in which his beloved Union was not, or had not been, famous. He was a good deal confused by what was happening, and could not think in perfectly clear grammar or sense.

"You speak English," continued the stranger. "I also have learned it. During five years I abode in London. Inform me of the state of the gracious Queen Elizabeth."

"Queen Elizabeth!" echoed Captain Phin Glover. "Why, good gracious! you don't mean the old Queen Elizabeth! Come now, you don't mean to say you mean *her!* Why, bless your body! that's all gone by; improved off the face of the earth; holystoned out of creation. Queen Elizabeth! She's dead. Been dead ever s'long. Did n't you know it? Shipmate, tell a fellah; ain't you a jokin'? Where upon earth do you hail from?"

"From Amsterdam. I have voyaged to the Indies and am return-ing to Amsterdam."

"Amsterdam! Queen Elizabeth—The Flyin' Dutchman, as I'm a sinner!" exclaimed Phineas. "Shipmate, *be* you the Flyin' Dutchman?"

"I know not what you mean," answered the stranger. "I am, however, a Hollander, and I am flying from the wrath to come. I am a great criminal who hopes forgiveness."

"That's right—that's orthodox," chimed in Glover, who always went to church in Fair Haven, though indifferent to divine service in foreign parts. "But bless my body! Queen Elizabeth! The Flyin' Dutchman! If this don't beat all! Now tell me I did n't swim ashore on a mule. Tell me I never rigged a jury-mast on an iceberg, an' steered it into the straits of Newfoundland. Shipmate, I'm glad to see ye. What's the news from Amsterdam?"

"Alas! it is long since I was there. I know not how long. When I left, Antwerp had lately been overcome by the Spaniards."

"By the Spaniards? Never heerd of it. Wal, cheer up, shipmate. Since you quit, the Dutch have taken Holland, every speck an' scrap of it."

The stranger's eyes beamed with a joy which was at once patri-otic and religious.

"What might your name be?" was the next remark of our countryman.

"Arendt Albertsen Van Libergen."

Captain Glover was silent; such a long title awed him, as being clearly patrician; moreover, he did not feel capable of pronouncing it, and that was embarrassing.

"You must now come upon my vessel," continued the Hollan-der. "Yours cannot be got to land."

"How 'bout the cargo?" queried Glover. "Bar'ls 'n staves—wal, no use, I s'pose—can't be got up. Some provisions, though. Might take 'em along, 'n allow somethin' for 'em."

"Our provisions never fail," returned Captain Van Libergen. "Come."

They stepped into the boat; the old-time sailors fell back on their old-time oars; in two minutes they were mounting the sides of the *Flying Dutchman*. If Phineas and Mary Anne Glover had been led into the Tower of London or the Museum of Dresden, they could hardly have discovered a more curious medley of antiques than saluted their gaze on this singular craft.

"The bul'arks was five feet high," our countryman subsequently related. "The' was at least three inches through—made for fightin', I should jedge. The' was four big iron guns, 'bout the size o' twenty-four pounders, but the curiousest of shape y' ever see, an' mounted, Lord bless you! Sech carriages 'd make a marine laugh nowadays. Then the' wa' n't less 'n a dozen small brass pieces, dreadful thin at the breech, an' with mouths like a bell. I see some blunderbusses, too, with thunderin' big butts, an' muzzles whittled out like the snouts of dragons. Fact is, the' had all sorts of arms, spears, an' straight broadswords, an' battle-axes on long poles, an' crossbows—y' never see such crossbows in Fair Haven.

"The decks was a sight," our narrator proceeded. "They run scoopin' up for'ard an' scoopin' up aft. The fo'kesle an' the quarter-deck looked at each other like two opposition meetin'-houses. The fore an' main masts was as stumpy's cabbage-stalks. As for her riggin', she was a ship, an' yet she wa' n't a ship. However, on the whole, might 's well call her a ship, considerin' the little mizzen by the tiller. But the' ain't a boy in Fair Haven don't draw better ships on his slate in school-time, when he oughter be mindin' his addition 'n subtraction. As for the crew, y' never see such sailors nowadays, not even in picter-books. The' looked more like briguns in a play than like real seamen. A Weathersfield onion-sloop would n't ship such big-trousered, long stockinged lubbers. Put me in mind o' Greeks, most of anything human. But the' was discipline among 'em. Tell ye the' was mighty ceremonious to the skipper an' his mates. Must allow 'em that credit. The' was discipline."

Phineas Glover's wonder did not abate when he was conducted into the cabin of the Flying Dutchman. All was antique—the carved oaken wainscoting, the ponderous sideboard of Indian wood, the mighty table, set with Delft ware and silver flagons. Amid this venerable, severe elegance stood two gentlemen and a beautiful lady; the former attired much like Van Libergen, the latter in what seemed a court costume of other days.

"These are Adraien Van Vechter and Dircksen Hybertzen, my cousins," said the Flying Dutchman. "And this is Cornelie Van

Vechter, the wife of my cousin. They speak no English, but they desire me to say that they rejoice in your deliverance, and that they are your humble servants."

"When a woman 's as putty as that, an' can smile as sweet as that, she don't need no English to make herself understood," returned Captain Glover, gallantly. "Tell 'em they can't be no humbler servants to us than we be to them."

The lady now advanced to Mary Anne, took her hand with another charming smile, and placed her at table. Van Libergen went through the same gracious formality with Phineas; and the other two Hollanders, after bowing to right and left, seated themselves.

"But before we took a mouthful," relates our minute and veracious countryman, "the Flying Dutchman stood up an' asked a blessing which I thought would last till we got to Amsterdam. Never see a more pious critter. If he could manhandle a blessing that long, he must have had a monstrous gift at prayer."

By the way, Captain Glover was boggled, as we may suppose, by the outlandish names of his new acquaintance, and especially by that of the commandant. The title of a celebrated cheese, which he had partaken of in lager-bier saloons, came to the aid of his memory; and he found it convenient, during his stay on the famous sea-wanderer, to address Arendt Van Libergen as Capm Limburgher.

The meal was served by dark men in white apparel, whom Mary Anne took to be "some kind of Negroes," but whom her father guessed to be ""Lascars." In place of tea and coffee, there were vintages of Spain, taken perhaps from some captured galleon. The glorious old wine! Captain Glover had never tasted the like before, not even at his owner's in New Haven. Under its incitation, he came out strong as a conversationalist, telling the story of his shipwreck and not a little of his previous life, and throwing in some of those apocryphal episodes for which he was celebrated. He was particularly splendid in describing a religious procession which he had seen in Havana.

"Most wonderful sight!" he said. "Two miles of priests, and every one of 'em with a wax candle in his hand, as big—as big as the pillars in front of the State House."

"O pa!" protested the abashed Mary Anne, with an alarmed glance at her august hosts, "you don't mean as big as the pillars in front of the State House."

"Yes, by thunder!" insisted the captain, "*and* fluted from top to bottom."

But, if our countryman slightly surprised his entertainers, they prodigiously and perpetually puzzled him. Their inquiries were all concerning matters so out of date, so far beyond his tether! They asked about the siege of Antwerp, the surrendry of Brussels and Ghent, the reported mutinies of Walloons, the prospect of armed succors from England. After endeavoring to draw some information on these subjects from the abysses of his subjective, and finding that he was floundering into various geographical and chronological errors, he frankly acknowledged that he was not logged up in Dutch politics, having had little chance of late at the newspapers. And when they spoke of the Prince of Parma, William of Orange, Maurice of Nassau, the Earl of Leicester, and Henry of Navarre, he feared that he was not making things very clear to them in asserting that those old cocks were all as dead as General Washington. This statement, however, produced a painful impression upon his auditors.

"Dead!" sighed the beautiful lady. "Then others also have passed away. Are we only to find those we love in the grave?"

"And are we not dead ourselves?" sadly yet firmly replied Captain Van Libergen. "Did not our due term of life long since close? Only the signal mercy of Heaven has preserved us on earth until we could repent of our great sin. Perhaps, when the expiation is complete, we also shall suddenly cease to be."

"Let's hope not," replied Phineas Glover, always cheerful in his views. "But come, about the dates; time of Queen Elizabeth, you say. Why that was settlement of Virginny. That was 1587, wa' n't it, Mary Anne? Wal, if 't was 1587, then as this is the year 1867, 't was two hundred 'n eighty years ago. Why, shipmates, if your log is correct, if you left Amsterdam when you say, you've been on the longest cruise ever I heard of. Two hundred 'n eighty years out o' sight o' land! Jerusalem! I'd ruther live ashore all the while."

When these words were translated to Cornelie Van Vechter, she covered her face with her hands, moaning, "All dead! all dead!"

"I knew it was thus," sighed Arendt Van Libergen, "and yet I weakly hoped that it might be otherwise."

"What! Hain't you kep' no log, shipmate?" demanded Phineas Glover.

"How could we believe it?" replied the Hollander. "How could we believe that we were even as the Everlasting Jew?"

"Everlasting Jew? Wandering Jew, s'pose ye mean. Wal now, Capm Van Limburgher, I'll tell ye what it all means. You're the Flyin' Dutchman; that 's just what you are; now take my word for it, an' be easy; I've heard of ye often, an' dunno but what I've seen ye. You 're monstrous well known to sailors; an' on the whole I 'm glad I 've come acrost ye; though seems to me, 't wa n't quite han'some to sink the *Betsy Jane;* that is, unless you was under some kind o' necessity o' doin' it. Yes, *sir;* you're the Flyin' Dutchman; bet your pile on it, if you're a bettin' man."

"But what in the name of thunder is it all for?" he added, after a moment of curious and puzzled staring at the famous wanderer, "what makes ye go flyin' round, sinkin' ships an' sailin' in the wind's eye, an' raisin ' Nipton generally? Why don't ye go into port? Tell ye the whole United States would turn out to give ye receptions an' hear ye lecter! The Ledger 'd give ye a hundred thousan' dollars for your biography, written by your own fist. Might pile up a million in five years. Must be mighty fond o' cruisin'. Make money by it? Sh'd think y'd want to slosh round on shore, once in a century, at least."

"It is my punishment," replied the rover, with an affecting solemnity and humanity. "I am a great criminal."

"Waterlogged the *Betsy Jane,* certin," muttered Glover, in spite of a jog on the elbow from Mary Anne.

"You shall hear our tale," said Captain Van Libergen, signing to the Hindoo servants to leave the cabin.

"Sh'd be delighted to put it in the papers," observed our country-man. "The Palladium or the Journal would either of 'em snap at it."

"I was mad to be rich," began the Flying Dutchman. "I desired wealth, not for its luxury, but for its power. Sometimes, in the midst of my hardness towards other men as I grasped at gold, it occurred to me that some day a fitting retribution would descend upon my head. A voice within sometimes whispered, 'In that thou art living for thyself alone, thou art denying Him who died for thee; an appointed hour will come when thou wilt be subjected to a last trial; and then, if thou choose the evil, thy punishment will be great.'

"Yet I continued covetous and pitiless, and I made these men who voyage with me like myself. This vessel is freighted with the tears and sweat of the Indies, wrung out by me into gold and precious merchandise. Knowing that the sooner I gained my native land the greater would be my profit, I swore that nothing should detain me on my voyage. Horrible oath! Kept with the faith of a demon! Punished with the wrath of God! On the ninetieth day, when we were within a hundred leagues of Amsterdam, I saw a wreck with two persons upon it. My cousin Cornelie Van Vechter implored me with tears to turn aside and save them. Monstrously cruel, I refused to waste the time, and steered onward. Then, even as we passed, a far-sounding voice, surely not the voice of a mortal, called from the sinking ship, 'Sail forever, without reaching port, until you repent!'

"Cornelie Van Vechter cried: 'It was Christ upon that wreck, and you have forsaken him, and he has doomed you.' Had she been a man, I would have stricken her down, I was so hardened in heart. But she had perceived the truth; she had divined our punishment. Alas! She, the innocent, as so often happens on earth, was fated to share the reward of the guilty. Since that time we have sailed, we have sailed, we have sailed. No land. Nothing but sea. We cannot anywhere find the blessed land. We find nothing but a vast hell of ocean. O, the hell of illimitable ocean! Time, too, was no more. We have kept record of time, without faith in it. For a while we laughed at our calamity, as we had mocked at our sin. We could not believe that our friends were dead; that the world of our time had passed away; that we were strangers to the human race.

"Another horror! We were fated to witness all wrecks that be upon the sea. Wherever a vessel went down, amid howlings of waves and shrieks of sailors, thither we were borne at the speed of lightning, always in the teeth of gales. No struggling and crying of desperate men on the ocean for near three centuries but what these eyes have seen and these ears heard. From tempest to tempest we have flown, always, always beaten by opposing billows, discovering strange seas only to find new horrors. And amidst all this, my heart has remained so hardened that I would not wish to succor one perishing soul.

"At last, wearied with struggling against the Almighty, crazed to see once more the sweet earth for which Christ died, we repented. Yesternight I called my crew together and confessed my sin and besought the mercy of God. A voice answered me from the abysses of the stars, saying, 'Succor those whom I shall send, and find grace!'

"At dawn this morning I beheld you on your wreck, and I turned aside to save you."

During this relation Cornelie Van Vechter wept so piteously that Mary Anne Glover cried aloud in sympathy. Even the commonplace soul of Phineas Glover was moved to suitable thoughts.

"Wal, Capm, it's a most surprisin' providence," he remarked, with solemnity. "An' the' 's one thing, at the end on 't, that p'r'aps you don't see. It's consid'able of a comedown for you to pick up an' make so much of two poor critters like us. We're middlin' sort o' folks, Capen; we ain't lords an' ladies, like what you've asked about; we're no great shakes, an' that 's a fact. I begun my seafarin' life as a cabin boy, an' Mary Anne has shelled her heft in oysters, over an' over. Pickin' *us* up, an' kissin' our hands an' all that, is a kind o' final test of your humility.

"Wal, it's a most edifyin' narrative," he continued, after a thoughtful pause. "It's better 'n many a sermon that I've sot under. I see the moral of it, as plain as a marlinespike in my eye. You want to git to port; you won't help a feller critter in distress; consequently you don't git to port. Why, our great Republic, the United States of America,—dunno 's you ever heerd of it—has had some such dealin's. We run alongside them poor Negroes: we might 'a' helped 'em an' sent 'em to school an' civilized 'em; but all we did was to use em in puttin' money into our puss. Consequently we've had a dreadful long voyage over a sea of troubles, an' hain't got quite into port yit. However, you don't know what I'm jawin' about; an', besides, I'm takin' up the time of the company. Gentlemen, go on!"

No one responding, Captain Glover raised his flagon of Manzanilla to his lips, with the words, "Here's better luck nex' time!"

Thus closed this remarkable breakfast, seldom paralleled, we venture to say, on this planet, however it may be on the others.

Now came an interesting week on the *Flying Dutchman*. What most struck Captain Glover, as he has repeatedly informed us, was the solemnity and religious aspect of all on board.

"They seemed to be awfully convicted, and yet they seemed to entertain a hope," were his words. "They had a kind 'o tender, humble look, mixed with a sort o' trustin' joy. Certinly it was the most interestin' occasion that I ever see or expec' to see. Jest think of the Flyin' Dutchman an' his whole crew gittin' religion together.

Father Taylor would 'a' given his head to be aboard o' that ship in such a season."

Our level-headed skipper took a deep interest also in an examination of the far-famed wanderer's cargo. Arendt Van Libergen led the two Glovers through what portion of the hold was accessible, and showed them such treasures of spice, gums, India silks, gold-dust and ornaments, pearls and precious stones, as no Fair Havener ever gazed upon before.

"Beats the oyster trade, don't it, Mary Anne?" remarked our countryman. "Capen Limburgher, you probably don't realize the value of our American oyster. It's the head sachem of shellfish for cookin' pupposes. Every free native American citizen eats his forty bushels annually. You can estimate by that the importance of the openin' business; an' Fair Haven is the very hub an' centre an' stronghold of it. Nary gal in the village but can knife her sixty quarts daily. Mary Anne here is a splitter at it. It's made heaps of money for the place. But compared with your trade, compared with dealin' in the gold an' silver an' diamond line, sho! Why, Capm Limburgher, you're one of the merchant princes of the earth. Your ship puts me in mind of Zekiel's description of the galleys of Tyre and Sidon. Model about the same, too, I sh'd reckon."

Except by a profound sigh, Arendt Van Libergen made no response to these flatteries. He pushed aside with his foot a bag of gold-dust, as if he considered it dross indeed, and ensnaring dross.

"S'prisin' how well preserved things be," continued Glover. "Now here's this alspice, 's fresh 's if 't was picked this year, 'stead of two hundred an' eighty years ago."

"It is a part of our punishment," returned the Flying Dutchman. "Our wealth was forbidden to decay, and yet we were forbidden to use it. We could gaze upon it in all its freshness, and yet we could not land it at our homes. In the midst of it, we have known that it was not ours. Surrounded by the fruit of our desires, we were under a curse of barrenness."

"And here am I, under a cuss, without a red cent," was the natural reply. "Capm, I declare I'd like to swap cusses with ye."

"Take what pleases you," answered Arendt Van Libergen. "It is now of no value to me."

"Now, really, Capm, don't want to rob ye," protested Phineas

Glover. But, bent downward by his poverty and his avarice, he commenced filling his pockets with gold.

"Catch hold, Mary Anne," he whispered. "Take what's offered ye, 's a good old text."

But in the girl's soul there was a fine emotion which would not permit her to clutch at the wealth which dazzled her eyes. A profound pity for the woes of these fated wanderers had rapidly risen into love as she had watched from day to day the noble bearing and mournful beauty of Arendt Van Libergen. Not for all the treasures that were in his galleon would she have grasped for greed in his presence. She stood upright, her lashes gemmed with tears, gazing at this strangely doomed being.

He caught her glance; he gave her one sad, sweet smile in reward for it; then he selected a string of priceless pearls and placed it around her neck. One of her tears wet his hand, and he murmured, "Thanks for pity."

They now went on deck, Captain Glover's numerous pockets cumbrously stuffed with gold-dust and idols, and Mary Anne bearing naught but the string of pure pearls.

Meantime the *Flying Dutchman* is sailing before a fair wind towards Amsterdam. The curse is lifted; the vessel is not now different from all earthly craft; she no longer flies in the teeth of gales, surrounded forever by billows; she is like other ships in her dependence upon the laws of nature; but she is favored with fortunate breezes and a smooth sea; she seems to know that at last she is bound home.

On a sunlit summer morning—on such a cloudless and dewy morning of grace as forgiven phantom ships are wont to enter port— the *Flying Dutchman* arrived off a low, green coast, within sight of the masts, roofs, and towers of a great city.

"That's Amsterdam," confidently declared Captain Glover, who had never before crossed the ocean. "There the old town is, jest as I left it last, an' jest as you left it, I'll bet a biscuit. There's the State House—I s'pose it is—an' all the meetin'-houses,—the 'Piscopal 'n' the Methodis' 'n' the Congregational. Take the word of an old sailor, you'll find it all right ashore, an' everybody turnin' out to shake hands with ye. See all your friends an' family before night, Miss Van Vechter."

"Will the dead arise to greet us?" sighed Cornelie Van Vechter, when this cheerful prophecy was translated to her.

"Wal, now 'tain't certin they be dead," argued Captain Glover. "There was Joyce Heth, in our country—Barnum did say an' swear she was a hundred an' thirty-two year old—an' she a Negro, with no chance for proper eatin' an' no medicines to speak of. An' there was old Tom Johnson of Fair Haven. *I* never heerd anybody pretend to deny that he was less 'n two hundred. That's a positive, solemn fact," declared the cheerful captain, looking a little embarrassed under the lady's mournful gaze.

"Now in your time," he continued, "folks had powerful constitutions, an' necessarily lived to a good old age. Why, it stands to reason you'll find *some* of 'em all alive an' frisky. An' glad to see ye? Sho!"

"Alas!" murmured the beautiful Hollander, "if they live, they will be broken with years, and they will not know us."

"Let us deceive ourselves with no false hopes," said Ardent Van Libergen. "We are the dead going to the dead."

"Now that ain't my style, Capm Limburgher," protested Glover. "Hope on, hope ever, is my motto. If't had n't been, I never sh'd 'a' come ashore many a time when I've gone to the bottom, or fit with white bears for a squattin' right on an iceberg."

A glance, not of disdain, but of devout pity, fell from the rover's eyes, and silenced the babbling skipper.

A Dutch pilot, who now boarded the vessel, was so dumbfounded at its build and the appearance of its crew, that, while he remained upon it, he did not utter one syllable. He stood blanched with fright at the clumsy tiller, and made signs as to the management of the nondescript rigging. Our garrulous countryman sidled up to him, and sought to engage him in conversation. Whether the pilot understood English or not, he made no reply further than to clatter his teeth with terror.

And now, as they approached the wharves, a strange, awful transformation began to steal upon the crew of the *Flying Dutchman*. The green water of the harbor seemed to commence the dissolution of that charm which had kept them youthful through nearly three centuries. Phineas Glover, glancing at Arendt Van Libergen, noticed that his chestnut hair was streaked with silver, and that his face, lately so smooth and hale, was seamed with wrinkles. Turning to Cornelia Van Vechter, he saw that she too had lost the freshness of her young beauty, and taken on the tints and bearing of middle age.

"I've heerd o' folks gittin' gray in a night," muttered the startled skipper; "but this is the first time I ever see it. Tell me now I never steered an iceberg."

Moment by moment this fearful change of youth into age proceeded. Soon Arendt Van Libergen sat feebly down on the gangway steps, a decrepit, snowy-haired old man, with no beauty but a smile of devout resignation. Cornelie Van Vechter, now an ancient matron, clung to the shoulder of her suddenly venerable husband. Grayheaded sailors, their locks momentarily growing whiter, and their bronzed faces paling to the ashy hue of age, slowly and weakly coiled away ropes which seemed to be falling into dust. The change reached the ship; every fathom toward land opened cracks in the bulwarks; the masts began to drop in dry-rotted slivers; the sails lay on the yards in mouldering rags.

Suddenly terrified, Captain Glover seized Mary Anne, rushed with her to the castle-like quarterdeck, and sought refuge behind the trembling pilot. The girl was crying. "O, he must die!" she whispered; "I shall never see him again."

Looking towards Arendt Van Libergen, Glover beheld him, feeble with extreme age, deadly pale and gasping. Beyond him lay Cornelie Van Vechter, Adraien Van Vechter, Dircksen Hybertzen, and all the sailors, all prostrate, all breathing out their little remaining life, yet all with a sweet smile of resignation on their indescribably ancient features.

At this moment the vessel neared the wharf. With a loud scream the Dutch pilot sprang across decaying timbers, leaped the space between the bulwarks and the shore, and disappeared in the labyrinth of the living city. Over the dust of vanishing planks Phineas Glover and his daughter followed, tumbling upon the flagging of the landing-place. They heard the ship touch behind them, with a soft, rustling noise, as of mere mould and fungus. They turned to gaze at her, but she had disappeared. A great dust filled the air; it hid her, as they thought, from their sight; it descended slowly and noiselessly into the green waters; and when it was gone, nothing was left; the *Flying Dutchman* was no more. But, high above the spot where she had been, sweeping first clearly and then faintly into the heavens, rang a sweet music of many joyous voices, a chant of gratitude and of deliverance.

The Glovers, staring down into the mysteriously whispering wavelets, saw only a cloudy settling of pulverous matter, which each instant grew thinner, and soon was naught. Clear green water, woven through with strands of sunlight, rolled over the last mooring-place of the famous sea-wanderer.

"Wal, that beats square-rigged icebergs," mumbled Captain Glover. "Lord! how full the world is of wonders! yes, and of disappointments! I did expec' to git some kind of commission out of that chap, an' make my fortune. However, I've got some gold-dust an' idols."

He touched his pockets; they were flat against his ribs. He rammed his hands into them; they contained only a corroded solution. He looked for the chain of pearls; it was still around Mary Anne's neck. The wealth which he had hinted his desire for, and which he had so eagerly clutched at, had vanished. Naught remained but the pure offering of gratitude to pity.

Such is the story of the return of the Flying Dutchman from his long cruise, as related to us by the worthy and reliable Captain Phineas Glover of Fair Haven.

SIR ARTHUR CONAN DOYLE

THE CAPTAIN OF
THE *POLE-STAR*

*[Being an extract from the singular journal of
JOHN M'ALISTER RAY, student of medicine.]*

SEPTEMBER 11th.—Lat. 81° 40' N.; long. 2° E. Still lying-to amid enormous ice fields. The one which stretches away to the north of us, and to which our ice-anchor is attached, can not be smaller than an English county. To the right and left unbroken sheets extend to the horizon. This morning the mate reported that there were signs of pack ice to the southward. Should this form of sufficient thickness to bar our return, we shall be in a position of danger, as the food, I hear, is already running somewhat short. It is late in the season, and the nights are beginning to reappear. This morning I saw a star twinkling just over the foreyard, the first since the beginning of May. There is considerable discontent among the crew, many of whom are anxious to get back home to be in time for the herring season, when labor always commands a high price upon the Scotch coast. As yet their displeasure is only signified by sullen

100

countenances and black looks, but I heard from the second mate this afternoon that they contemplated sending a deputation to the captain to explain their grievance. I much doubt how he will receive it, as he is a man of fierce temper, and very sensitive about anything approaching to an infringement of his rights. I shall venture after dinner to say a few words to him upon the subject. I have always found that he will tolerate from me what he would resent from any other member of the crew. Amsterdam Island, at the northwest corner of Spitzbergen, is visible upon our starboard quarter—a rugged line of volcanic rocks, intersected by white seams, which represent glaciers. It is curious to think that at the present moment there is probably no human being nearer to us than the Danish settlements in the south of Greenland—a good nine hundred miles as the crow flies. A captain takes a great responsibility upon himself when he risks his vessel under such circumstances. No whaler has ever remained in these latitudes till so advanced a period of the year.

9 P.M.—I have spoken to Captain Craigie, and though the result has been hardly satisfactory, I am bound to say that he listened to what I had to say very quietly and even deferentially. When I had finished he put on that air of iron determination which I have frequently observed upon his face, and paced rapidly backward and forward across the narrow cabin for some minutes. At first I feared that I had seriously offended him, but he dispelled the idea by sitting down again and putting his hand upon my arm with a gesture which almost amounted to a caress. There was a depth of tenderness too in his wild dark eyes which surprised me considerably.

"Look here, doctor," he said, "I'm sorry I ever took you—I am indeed—and I would give fifty pounds this minute to see you standing safe upon the Dundee quay. It's hit or miss with me this time. There are fish to the north of us. How dare you shake your head, sir, when I tell you I saw them blowing from the masthead?"—this in a sudden burst of fury, though I was not conscious of having shown any signs of doubt. "Two-and-twenty fish in as many minutes, as I am a living man, and not one under ten feet.* Now, doctor, do you think I can leave the country when there is only one infernal strip of

---

* A whale is measured among whalers not by the length of its body, but by the length of its whalebone.

ice between me and my fortune? If it came on to blow from the north tomorrow we could fill the ship and be away before the frost could catch us. If it came on to blow from the south—well, I suppose the men are paid for risking their lives, and as for myself it matters but little to me, for I have more to bind me to the other world than to this one. I confess that I am sorry for *you*, though. I wish I had old Angus Tait who was with me last voyage, for he was a man that would never be missed, and you—you said once that you were engaged, did you not?"

"Yes," I answered, snapping the spring of the locket which hung from my watch-chain, and holding up the little vignette of Flora.

"Curse you!" he yelled, springing out of his seat, with his very beard bristling with passion. "What is your happiness to me? What have I to do with her that you must dangle her photograph before my eyes?"

I almost thought that he was about to strike me in the frenzy of his rage, but with another imprecation he dashed open the door of the cabin and rushed out upon deck, leaving me considerably astonished at his extraordinary violence. It is the first time that he has ever shown me anything but courtesy and kindness. I can hear him pacing excitedly up and down overhead as I write these lines.

I should like to give a sketch of the character of this man, but it seems presumptuous to attempt such a thing upon paper, when the idea in my own mind is at best a vague and uncertain one. Several times I have thought that I grasped the clue which might explain it, but only to be disappointed by his presenting himself in some new light which would upset all my conclusions. It may be that no human eye but my own shall ever rest upon these lines, yet as a psychological study I shall attempt to leave some record of Captain Nicholas Craigie.

A man's outer case generally gives some indication of the soul within. The captain is tall and well formed, with dark, handsome face, and a curious way of twitching his limbs, which may arise from nervousness, or be simply an outcome of his excessive energy. His jaw and whole cast of countenance are manly and resolute, but the eyes are the distinctive feature of his face. They are of the very darkest hazel, bright and eager, with a singular mixture of reckless- ness in their expression, and of something else which I have sometimes thought was more allied with horror than any other emotion. Generally the former predominated, but on occasions, and more particularly when he was thoughtfully inclined, the look of fear would spread and deepen until it imparted a new character to his whole countenance. It is at these times that he is most subject to tempestuous fits of anger, and he seems to be aware of it, for I have known him to lock himself up so that no one might approach him until his dark hour was passed. He sleeps badly, and I have heard him shouting during the night, but his cabin is some little distance from mine, and I could never distinguish the words which he said.

This is one phase of his character, and the most disagreeable one. It is only through my close association with him, thrown together as we are day after day, that I have observed it. Otherwise he is an agreeable companion, well-read and entertaining, and as gallant a seaman as ever trod a deck. I shall not easily forget the way in which he handled the ship when we were caught by a gale among the loose ice at the beginning of April. I have never seen him so cheerful, and even hilarious, as he was that night, as he paced backward and forward upon the bridge amid the flashing of the lightning and the howling of the wind. He has told me several times that the thought of death is a pleasant one to him, which is a sad thing for a young man to say; he cannot be much more than thirty, though his hair and mustache are already slightly grizzled. Some great sorrow must have overtaken him and blighted his whole life. Perhaps I should be the same if I lost my Flora—God knows! I think if it were not for her that I should care very little whether the wind blew from the north or the south tomorrow. There, I hear him come down the companion, and he has locked himself up in his room, which shows that he is still in an unamiable mood. And so to bed, as old Pepys would say, for the candle is burning down (we have to use them now since the nights are closing in), and the steward has turned in, so there are no hopes of another one.

September 12th. —Calm, clear day, and still lying in the same position. What wind there is comes from the southeast, but it is very slight. Captain is in a better humor, and apologized to me at breakfast for his rudeness. He still looks somewhat distrait, however, and retains that wild look in his eyes which in a Highlander would mean that he was "fey"—at least so our chief engineer remarked to me, and he has some reputation among the Celtic portion of our crew as a seer and expounder of omens.

It is strange that superstition should have obtained such mastery over this hard-headed and practical race. I could not have believed to what an extent it is carried had I not observed it for myself. We have had a perfect epidemic of it this voyage, until I have felt inclined to serve out rations of sedatives and nerve tonics with the Saturday allowance of grog. The first symptom of it was that shortly after leaving Shetland the men at the wheel used to complain that they heard plaintive cries and screams in the wake of the ship, as if something were following it and were unable to overtake it. This fiction has been kept up during the whole voyage, and on dark nights at the beginning of the seal-fishing it was only with great difficulty that men could be induced to do their spell. No doubt what they heard was either the creaking of the rudder-chains, or the cry of some passing sea-bird. I have been fetched out of bed several times to listen to it, but I need hardly say that I was never able to distinguish anything unnatural. The men, however, are so absurdly positive upon the subject that it is hopeless to argue with them. I mentioned the matter to the captain once, but to my surprise he took it very gravely, and indeed seemed to be considerably disturbed by what I told him. I should have thought that he at least would have been above such vulgar delusions.

All this disquisition upon superstition leads me up to the fact that Mr. Manson, our second mate, saw a ghost last night—or, at least says that he did, which of course is the same thing. It is quite refreshing to have some new topic of conversation after the eternal routine of bears and whales which has served us for so many months. Manson swears the ship is haunted, and that he would not stay in her a day if he had any other place to go to. Indeed, the fellow is honestly frightened, and I had to give him some chloral and bromide of potassium this morning to steady him down. He seemed quite indignant when I suggested that he had been having an extra glass the night before, and I was obliged to pacify him by keeping as grave a countenance as possible during his story, which he certainly narrated in a very straightforward and matter-of-fact way.

"I was on the bridge," he said, "about four bells in the middle watch, just when the night was at its darkest. There was a bit of a moon, but the clouds were blowing across it so that you couldn't see far from the ship. John M'Leod, the harpooner, came aft from the foc'sle-head and reported a strange noise on the starboard bow. I went forrad and we both heard it, sometimes like a bairn crying and sometimes like a wench in pain. I've been seventeen years to the country and I never heard seal, old or young, make a sound like that. As we were standing there on the foc'sle head the moon came out from behind a cloud, and we both saw a sort of white figure moving across the ice field in the same direction that we had heard the cries. We lost sight of it for a while, but it came back on the port bow, and we could just make it out like a shadow on the ice. I sent a hand aft for the rifles, and M'Leod and I went down on to the pack, thinking that maybe it might be a bear. When we got on the ice I lost sight of M'Leod, but I pushed on in the direction where I could still hear the cries. I followed them for a mile or maybe more, and then running round a hummock I came right on to the top of it standing and waiting for me seemingly. I don't know what it was. It wasn't a bear anyway. It was tall and white and straight, and if it wasn't a man nor a woman, I'll stake my davy it was something worse. I made for the ship as hard as I could run, and precious glad I was to find myself aboard. I signed articles to do my duty by the ship, and on the ship I'll stay, but you don't catch me on the ice again after sundown."

That is his story, given as far as I can in his own words. I fancy what he saw must, in spite of his denial, have been a young bear erect upon its hind legs, an attitude which they often assume when alarmed. In the uncertain light this would bear a resemblance to a human figure, especially to a man whose nerves were already somewhat shaken. Whatever it may have been, the occurrence is unfortunate, for it has produced a most unpleasant effect upon the crew. Their looks are more sullen than before, and their discontent more open. The double grievance of being debarred from the herring fishing and of being detained in what they choose to call a haunted vessel, may lead them to do something rash. Even the harpooners, who are the oldest and steadiest among them, are joining in the general agitation.

Apart from this absurd outbreak of superstition, things are looking rather more cheerful. The pack which was forming to the south of us has partly cleared away, and the water is so warm as to lead me to believe that we are lying in one of those branches of the Gulf Stream which run up between Greenland and Spitzbergen. There are numerous small Medusæ and sea-lemons about the ship, with abundance of shrimps, so that there is every possibility of "fish" being sighted. Indeed, one was seen blowing about dinnertime but in such a position that it was impossible for the boats to follow it.

September 13th.—Had an interesting conversation with the chief mate, Mr. Milne, upon the bridge. It seems that our captain is as great an enigma to the seamen, and even to the owners of the vessel, as he has been to me. Mr. Milne tells me that when the ship is paid off, upon returning from a voyage, Captain Craigie disappears, and is not seen again until the approach of another season, when he walks quietly into the office of the company, and asks whether his services will be required. He has no friend in Dundee, nor does any one pretend to be acquainted with his early history. His position depends entirely upon his skill as a seaman and the name for courage and coolness which he had earned in the capacity of mate, before being trusted with a separate command. The unanimous opinion seems to be that he is not a Scotchman, and that his name is an assumed one. Mr. Milne thinks that he has devoted himself to whaling simply for the reason that it is the most dangerous occupation which he could select, and that he courts death in every possible manner. He mentioned several instances of this, one of which is rather curious, if true. It seems that on one occasion he did not put in an appearance at the office, and a substitute had to be selected in his place. That was at the time of the last Russian and Turkish war. When he turned up again next spring he had a puckered wound in the side of his neck which he used to endeavor to conceal with his cravat. Whether the mate's inference that he had been engaged in the war is true or not I can not say. It was certainly a strange coincidence.

The wind is veering round in an easterly direction, but is still very slight. I think the ice is lying closer than it did yesterday. As far as the eye can reach on every side there is one wide expanse of spotless white, only broken by an occasional rift or the dark shadow of a hummock. To the south there is the narrow lane of blue water which is our sole means of escape, and which is closing up every day. The captain is taking a heavy responsibility upon himself. I hear that the tank of potatoes has been finished, and even the biscuits are running short, but he preserves the same impassable countenance, and spends the greater part of the day at the crow's nest, sweeping

the horizon with his glass. His manner is very variable, and he seems
to avoid my society, but there has been no repetition of the violence
which he showed the other night.

7:30 P. M.—My deliberate opinion is that we are commanded by
a madman. Nothing else can account for the extraordinary vagaries
of Captain Craigie. It is fortunate that I have kept this journal of our
voyage, as it will serve to justify us in case we have to put him under
any sort of restraint, a step which I should only consent to as a last
resource. Curiously enough it was he himself who suggested lunacy
and not mere eccentricity as the secret of his strange conduct. He
was standing upon the bridge about an hour ago, peering as usual
through his glass, while I was walking up and down the quarterdeck.
The majority of the men were below at their tea, for the watches
have not been regularly kept of late. Tired of walking, I leaned
against the bulwarks, and admired the mellow glow cast by the
sinking sun upon the great ice fields which surround us. I was suddenly aroused from the reverie into which I had fallen by a hoarse
voice at my elbow, and starting round I found that the captain had
descended and was standing by my side. He was staring out over the
ice with an expression in which horror, surprise, and something
approaching to joy were contending for the mastery. In spite of the
cold, great drops of perspiration were coursing down his forehead,
and he was evidently fearfully excited. His limbs twitched like those
of a man upon the verge of an epileptic fit, and the lines about his
mouth were drawn and hard.

"Look!" he gasped, seizing me by the wrist, but still keeping
his eyes upon the distant ice, and moving his head slowly in a
horizontal direction, as if following some object which was moving
across the field of vision. "Look! There, man, there! Between the
hummocks! Now coming out from behind the far one! You see her—
you *must* see her! There still! Flying from me, by God, flying from
me—and gone!"

He uttered the last two words in a whisper of concentrated
agony which shall never fade from my remembrance. Clinging to the
ratlines, he endeavored to climb upon the top of the bulwarks as if in
the hope of obtaining a last glance at the departing object. His
strength was not equal to the attempt, however, and he staggered
back against the saloon skylights, where he leaned panting and
exhausted. His face was so livid that I expected him to become

unconscious, so lost no time in leading him down the companion, and stretching him upon one of the sofas in the cabin. I then poured him out some brandy, which I held to his lips, and which had a wonderful effect upon him, bringing the blood back into his white face and steadying his poor shaking limbs. He raised himself up upon his elbow, and looking round to see that we were alone, be beckoned to me to come and sit beside him.

"You saw it, didn't you?" he asked, still in the same subdued awesome tone so foreign to the nature of the man.

"No, I saw nothing."

His head sunk back again upon the cushions. "No, he wouldn't without the glass," he murmured. "He couldn't. It was the glass that showed her to me, and then the eyes of love—the eyes of love. I say, Doc, don't let the steward in! He'll think I'm mad. Just bolt the door, will you?"

I rose and did what he had commanded.

He lay quiet for a while, lost in thought apparently, and then raised himself up upon his elbow again, and asked for some more brandy.

"You don't think I am, do you, Doc?" he asked, as I was putting the bottle back into the after-locker. "Tell me now, as man to man, do you think that I am mad?"

"I think you have something on your mind," I answered, which is exciting you and doing you a good deal of harm."

"Right there, lad!" he cried, his eyes sparkling from the effects of the brandy. "Plenty on my mind—plenty! But I can work out the latitude and the longitude, and I can handle my sextant and manage my logarithms. You couldn't prove me mad in a court of law, could you, now?" It was curious to hear the man lying back and coolly arguing out the question of his own sanity.

"Perhaps not," I said; "but still I think you would be wise to get home as soon as you can, and settle down to a quiet life for a while."

"Get home, eh?" he muttered, with a sneer upon his face. "One word for me and two for yourself, lad. Settle down with Flora— pretty little Flora. Are bad dreams signs of madness?"

"Sometimes," I answered.

"What else? What would be the first symptoms?"

"Pains in the head, noises in the ears, flashes before the eyes, delusions—"

"Ah! what about them?" he interrupted. "What would you call a delusion?"

"Seeing a thing which is not there is a delusion."

"But she *was* there!" he groaned to himself. "She *was* there!" and rising, he unbolted the door and walked with slow and uncertain steps to his own cabin, where I have no doubt that he will remain until tomorrow morning. His system seems to have received a terrible shock, whatever it may have been that he imagined himself to have seen. The man becomes a greater mystery every day, though I fear that the solution which he has himself suggested is the correct one, and that his reason is affected. I do not think that a guilty conscience has anything to do with his behavior. The idea is a popular one among the officers, and, I believe, the crew; but I have seen nothing to support it. He has not the air of a guilty man, but of one who has had terrible usage at the hands of fortune, and who should be regarded as a martyr rather than a criminal.

The wind is veering round to the south tonight. God help us if it blocks that narrow pass which is our only road to safety! Situated as we are on the edge of the main Arctic pack, or the "barrier" as it is called by the whalers, any wind from the north has the effect of shredding out the ice around us and allowing our escape, while a wind from the south blows up all the loose ice behind us and hems us in between two packs. God help us, I say again!

September 14th.—Sunday, and a day of rest. My fears have been confirmed, and the thin strip of blue water has disappeared from the southward. Nothing but the great motionless ice fields around us, with their weird hummocks and fantastic pinnacles. There is a deathly silence over their wide expanse which is horrible. No lapping of the waves now, no cries of seagulls or straining of sails, but one deep universal silence in which the murmurs of the seamen, and the creak of their boots upon the white shining deck, seem discordant and out of place. Our only visitor was an Arctic fox, a rare animal upon the pack, though common enough upon the land. He did not come near the ship, however, but after surveying us from a distance fled rapidly across the ice. This was curious conduct, as they generally know nothing of man, and being of an inquisitive nature, become so familiar that they are easily captured. Incredible as it may seem, even this little incident produced a bad effect upon the crew. "Yon puir beastie kens mair, ay, an sees mair nor you nor me!" was the comment of one of the leading harpooners, and the others nodded their acquiescence. It is vain to attempt to argue against such puerile superstition. They have made up their minds that there is a curse upon the ship, and nothing will ever persuade them to the contrary.

The captain remained in seclusion all day except for about half an hour in the afternoon, when he came out upon the quarter-deck. I observe that he kept his eye fixed upon the spot where the vision of yesterday had appeared, and was quite prepared for another outburst, but none such came. He did not seem to see me although I was standing close beside him. Divine service was read as usual by the chief engineer. It is a curious thing that in whaling vessels the Church of England Prayer book is always employed, although there is never a member of that Church among either officers or crew. Our men are all Roman Catholics or Presbyterians, the former predominating. Since a ritual is used which is foreign to both, neither can complain that the other is preferred to them, and they listen with all attention and devotion, so that the system has something to recommend it.

A glorious sunset which made the great fields of ice look like a lake of blood. I have never seen a finer and at the same time more weird effect. Wind is veering round. If it will blow twenty-four hours from the north all will yet be well.

September 15th.—Today is Flora's birthday. Dear lass! It is well that she can not see her boy, as she used to call me, shut up among the ice fields with a crazy captain and a few weeks' provisions. No doubt she scans the shipping list in the *Scotsman* every morning to see if we are reported from Shetland. I have set an example to the men and look cheery and unconcerned; but God knows, my heart is very heavy at times.

The thermometer is at nineteen Fahrenheit today. There is but little wind, and what there is comes from an unfavorable quarter. Captain is in an excellent humor; I think he imagines he has seen some other omen or vision, poor fellow, during the night, for he came into my room early in the morning, and stooping down over my bunk, whispered, "It wasn't a delusion, Doc; it's all right!" After breakfast he asked me to find out how much food was left, which the second mate and I proceeded to do. It is even less than we had expected. Forward they have half a tank full of biscuits, three barrels of salt meat, and a very limited supply of coffee beans and sugar. In the afterhold and lockers there are a good many luxuries, such as tinned salmon, soups, harricot mutton, etc., but they will go a very short way among a crew of fifty men. There are two barrels of flour in the storeroom, and an unlimited supply of tobacco. Altogether there is about enough to keep the men on half rations for eighteen or twenty days — certainly not more. When we reported the state of things to the captain, he ordered all hands to be piped, and addressed them from the quarterdeck. I never saw him to better advantage. With his tall, well-knit figure, and dark animated face, he seemed a man born to command, and he discussed the situation in a cool, sailor-like way which showed that while appreciating the danger he had an eye for every loophole of escape.

"My lads," he said, " no doubt you think I brought you into this fix, if it is a fix, and maybe some of you feel bitter against me on account of it. But you must remember that for many a season no ship that comes to the country has brought in as much oil-money as the old *Pole-Star*, and every one of you has had his share of it. You can leave your wives behind you in comfort while other poor fellows come back to find their lasses on the parish. If you have to thank me for the one you have to thank me for the other, and we may call it quits. We've tried a bold venture before this and succeeded, so now that we've tried one and failed we've no cause to cry out about it. If the worst comes to the worst, we can make the land across the ice, and lay in a stock of seals which will keep us alive until the spring. It won't come to that, though, for you'll see the Scotch coast again before three weeks are out. At present every man must go on half rations, share and share alike, and no favor to any. Keep up your hearts and you'll pull through this as you've pulled through many a danger before." These few simple words of his had a wonderful effect upon the crew. His former unpopularity was forgotten, and the old harpooner whom I have already mentioned for his superstition, led off three cheers, which were heartily joined in by all hands.

September 16th. — The wind has veered round to the north during the night, and the ice shows some symptoms of opening out. The men are in good humor in spite of the short allowance upon which they have been placed. Steam is kept up in the engine room, that there may be no delay should an opportunity for escape present itself. The captain is in exuberant spirits, though he still retains that wild "fey" expression which I have already remarked upon. This burst of cheerfulness puzzles me more than his former gloom. I cannot understand it. I think I mentioned in an early part of this journal that one of his oddities is that he never permits any person to enter his cabin, but insists upon making his own bed, such as it is, and performing every other office for himself.

To my surprise he handed me the key today and requested me to go down there and take the time by his chronometer while he measured the altitude of the sun at noon. It was a bare little room, containing a washing-stand and a few books, but little else in the way of luxury, except some pictures upon the walls. The majority of these are small cheap oleographs, but there was one watercolor sketch of the head of a young lady which arrested my attention. It was evidently a portrait, and not one of those fancy types of female beauty which sailors particularly effect. No artist could have evolved from his own mind such a mixture of character and weakness. The languid, dreamy eyes, with their drooping lashes, and the broad, low brow, unruffled by thought or care, were in strong contrast with the clean-cut, prominent jaw, and the resolute set of the lower lip. Underneath it in one of the corners was written, "M. B., æt. 19." That any one in the short space of nineteen years of existence could develop such strength of will as was stamped upon her face seemed to me at the time to be well-nigh incredible. She must have been an extraordinary woman. Her features have thrown such a glamour over me that, though I had but a fleeting glance at them, I could, were I a draughtsman, reproduce them line for line upon this page of the journal. I wonder what part she has played in our captain's life. He has hung her picture at the end of his berth, so that his eyes continually rest upon it. Were he a less reserved man I should make some remark upon the subject. Of the other things in his cabin there was nothing worthy of mention—uniform coats, a camp-stool, small looking glass, tobacco box, and numerous pipes, including an Oriental hookah—which, by-the-by, gives some color to Mr. Milne's story about his participation in the war, though the connection may seem rather a distant one.

11:20 P.M.—Captain just gone to bed after a long and interesting conversation on general topics. When he chooses he can be a most fascinating companion, being remarkably well read, and having the power of expressing his opinion forcibly without appearing to be dogmatic. I hate to have my intellectual toes trod upon. He spoke about the nature of the soul, and sketched out the views of Aristotle and Plato upon the subject in a masterly manner. He seems to have a leaning for metempsychosis and the doctrines of Pythagoras. In discussing them we touched upon modern spiritualism, and I made some joking allusion to the impostures of Slade, upon which, to my surprise, he warned me most impressively against confusing the innocent with the guilty, and argued that it would be as logical to brand Christianity as an error because Judas, who professed that religion, was a villain. He shortly afterward bid me goodnight and retired to his room.

The wind is freshening up, and blows steadily from the north. The nights are as dark now as they are in England. I hope tomorrow may set us free from our frozen fetters.

September 17th. —The bogie again. Thank Heaven that I have strong nerves! The superstition of these poor fellows, and the circumstantial accounts which they give, with the utmost earnestness and self-conviction, would horrify any man not accustomed to their ways. There are many versions of the matter, but the sum total of them all is that something uncanny has been flitting round the ship all night, and that Sandie McDonald of Peterhead and "lang" Peter Williamson of Shetland saw it, as also did Mr. Milne on the bridge — so, having three witnesses, they can make a better case of it than the second mate did. I spoke to Milne after breakfast, and told him that he should be above such nonsense, and that as an officer he ought to set the men a better example. He shook his weatherbeaten head ominously, but answered with characteristic caution, "Mebbe aye, mebbe na, doctor," he said; "I didna ca'it a ghaist. I canna' say I preen my faith in sea-bogles an' the like, though there's a mony as claims to ha' seen a' that and waur. I'm no easy feared, but maybe your ain bluid would run a bit cauld, mun, if instead o' speerin' aboot it in daylicht ye were wi' me last night, an' seed an awfu' like shape, white an' grewsome, whiles here, whiles there, an' it greetin' and ca'ing in the darkness like a bit lambie that hae lost its mither. Ye would na' be sae ready to put it a' doon to auld wives' clavers then, I'm thinkin'." I saw it was hopeless to reason with him, so contented myself with begging him as a personal favor to call me up the next time the spectre appeared—a request to which he acceded with many ejaculations expressive of his hopes that such an opportunity might never arise.

As I had hoped, the white desert behind us has become broken by many thin streaks of water which intersect it in all directions. Our latitude today was 80° 52′ N., which shows that there is a strong southerly drift upon the pack. Should the wind continue favorable it will break up as rapidly as it formed. At present we can do nothing but smoke and wait and hope for the best. I am rapidly becoming a fatalist. When dealing with such uncertain factors as wind and ice a man can be nothing else. Perhaps it was the wind and sand of the Arabian deserts which gave the minds of the original followers of Mohammed their tendency to bow to kismet.

These spectral alarms have a very bad effect upon the captain. I feared that it might excite his sensitive mind, and endeavored to conceal the absurd story from him, but unfortunately he overheard one of the men making an allusion to it, and insisted upon being informed about it. As I had expected, it brought out all his latent lunacy in an exaggerated form. I can hardly believe that this is the same man who discoursed philosophy last night with the most critical acumen and coolest judgment. He is pacing backward and forward upon the quarterdeck like a caged tiger, stopping now and again to throw out his hands with a yearning gesture, and stare impatiently out over the ice. He keeps up a continual mutter to himself, and once he called out "But a little time, love—but a little time!" Poor fellow, it is sad to see a gallant seaman and accomplished gentleman reduced to such a pass, and to think that imagination and delusion can cow a mind to which real danger was but the salt of life. Was ever a man in such a position as I, between a demented captain and a ghost-seeing mate? I sometimes think I am the only real sane man aboard the vessel—except, perhaps, the second engineer, who is a kind of ruminant, and would care nothing for all the fiends in the Red Sea so long as they would leave him alone and not disarrange his tools.

The ice is still opening rapidly, and there is every probability of our being able to make a start tomorrow morning. They will think I am inventing when I tell them at home all the strange things that have befallen me.

12 P. M.—I have been a good deal startled, though I feel steadier now, thanks to a stiff glass of brandy. I am hardly myself yet, however, as this handwriting will testify. The fact is that I have gone through a very strange experience, and am beginning to doubt

whether I was justified in branding every one on board as madmen because they professed to have seen things which did not seem reasonable to my understanding. Pshaw! I am a fool to let such a trifle unnerve me; and yet, coming as it does, after all these alarms, it has an additional significance, for I can not doubt either Mr. Manson's story or that of the mate, now that I have experienced that which I used formerly to scoff at.

After all it was nothing very alarming—a mere sound, and that was all. I can not expect that any one reading this, if any one ever should read it, will sympathize with my feelings, or realize the effect which it produced upon me at the time. Supper was over, and I had gone on deck to have a quiet pipe before turning in. The night was very dark—so dark that, standing under the quarter-boat, I was unable to see the officer upon the bridge. I think I have already mentioned the extraordinary silence which prevails in these frozen seas. In other parts of the world, be they ever so barren, there is some slight vibration of the air—some faint hum, be it from the distant haunts of men, or from the leaves of the trees, or the wings of the birds, or even the faint rustle of the grass that covers the ground. One may not actively perceive the sound, and yet if it were withdrawn it would be missed. It is only here in these Arctic seas that stark, unfathomable stillness obtrudes itself upon you in all its gruesome reality. You find your tympanum straining to catch some little murmur, and dwelling eagerly upon every accidental sound within the vessel. In this state I was leaning against the bulwarks when there arose from the ice almost directly underneath me a cry, sharp and shrill, upon the silent air of the night, beginning, as it seemed to me, at a note such as prima donna never reached, and mounting from that ever higher and higher until it culminated in a long wail of agony, which might have been the last cry of a lost soul. The ghastly scream is still ringing in my ears. Grief, unutterable grief, seemed to be expressed in it, and a great longing, and yet through it all there was an occasional wild note of exultation. It shrilled out from close beside me, and yet as I glared into the darkness I could discern nothing. I waited some little time, but without hearing any repetition of the sound, so I came below, more shaken than I have ever been in my life before. As I came down the companion I met Mr. Milne coming up to relieve the watch. "Weel, doctor," he said, "maybe that's auld wives' clavers tae? Did ye no hear it skirling?

Maybe that's a supersteetion? What d'ye think o't noo?" I was obliged to apologize to the honest fellow, and acknowledge that I was as puzzled by it as he was. Perhaps tomorrow things may look different. At present I dare hardly write all that I think. Reading it again in days to come, when I have shaken off all these associations, I should despise myself for having been so weak.

September 18th.—Passed a restless and uneasy night still haunted by that strange sound. The captain does not look as if he had had much repose either, for his face is haggard and his eyes blood-shot. I have not told him of my adventure of last night, nor shall I. He is already restless and excited, standing up, sitting down, and apparently utterly unable to keep still.

A fine lead appeared in the pack this morning, as I had expected, and we were able to cast off our ice-anchor, and steam about twelve miles in a west-sou'-westerly direction. We were then brought to a halt by a great floe as massive as any which we have left behind us. It bars our progress completely, so we can do nothing but anchor again and wait until it breaks up, which it will probably do within twenty-four hours, if the wind holds. Several bladder-nosed seals were seen swimming in the water, and one was shot, an immense creature more than eleven feet long. They are fierce, pugnacious animals, and are said to be more than a match for a bear. Fortunately they are slow and clumsy in their movements, so there is little danger in attacking them upon the ice.

The captain evidently does not think we have seen the last of our troubles, though why he should take a gloomy view of the situation is more than I can fathom since every one else on board considers that we have had a miraculous escape, and are sure now to reach the open sea.

"I suppose you think it's all right now, doctor?" he said, as we sat together after dinner.

"I hope so," I answered.

"We mustn't be too sure—and yet no doubt you are right. We'll all be in the arms of our own true loves before long, lad, won't we? But we musn't be too sure—we mustn't be too sure."

He sat silent a little, swinging his leg thoughtfully backward and forward.

"Look here," he continued; "it's a dangerous place this, even at its best—a treacherous, dangerous place. I have known men cut off very suddenly in a land like this. A slip would do it sometimes—a single slip, and down you go through a crack, and only a bubble on the green water to show where it was that you sank. It's a queer thing," he continued with a nervous laugh, "but all the years I've been in this country I never once thought of making a will—not that I have anything to leave in particular, but still when a man is exposed to danger he should have everything arranged and ready—don't you think so?"

"Certainly," I answered, wondering what on earth he was driving at.

"He feels better for knowing it's all settled," he went on. "Now if anything should ever befall me I hope that you will look after things for me. There is very little in the cabin, but such as it is I should like it to be sold, and the money divided in the same proportion as the oil-money among the crew. The chronometer I wish you to keep yourself as some slight remembrance of our voyage. Of course all this is a mere precaution, but I thought I would take the opportunity of speaking to you about it. I suppose I might rely upon you if there were any necessity?"

"Most assuredly," I answered; "and since you are taking this step, I may as well. . . . "

"You! you!" he interrupted. "*You're* all right. What the devil is the matter with *you?* There, I didn't mean to be peppery, but I don't like to hear a young fellow, that has hardly begun life, speculating about death. Go up on deck and get some fresh air into your lungs instead of talking nonsense in the cabin, and encouraging me to do the same."

The more I think of this conversation of ours the less do I like it. Why should the man be settling his affairs at the very time when we seem to be emerging from all danger? There must be some method in his madness. Can it be that he contemplates suicide? I remember that upon one occasion he spoke in a deeply reverent manner of the heinousness of the crime of self-destruction. I shall keep my eye upon him, however, and though I cannot intrude upon the privacy of his cabin, I shall at least make a point of remaining on deck as long as he stays up.

Mr. Milne pooh-poohs my fears, and says it is only the "skipper's little way." He himself takes a very rosy view of the situation. According to him we shall be out of the ice by the day after tomorrow, pass Jan Meyen two days after that, and sight Shetland in little more than a week. I hope he may not be too sanguine. His opinion may be fairly balanced against the gloomy precautions of the captain, for he is an old and experienced seaman and weighs his words well before uttering them.

The long-impending catastrophe has come at last. I hardly know what to write about it. The captain is gone. He may come back to us again alive, but I fear me—I fear me. It is now seven o'clock in the morning of the 19th of September. I have spent the whole night traversing the great ice-floe in front of us with a party of seamen in the hope of coming upon some trace of him, but in vain. I shall try to give some account of the circumstances which attended upon his disappearance. Should any one ever chance to read the words which I put down, I trust they will remember that I do not write from conjecture or from hearsay, but that I, a sane and educated man, am describing accurately what actually occurred before my very eyes. My inferences are my own, but I shall be answerable for the facts.

The captain remained in excellent spirits after the conversation which I have recorded. He appeared to be nervous and impatient, however, frequently changing his position, and moving his limbs in an aimless way which is characteristic of him at times. In a quarter of an hour he went upon deck seven times, only to descend after a few hurried paces. I followed him each time, for there was something about his face which confirmed my resolution of not letting him out of my sight. He seemed to observe the effect which his movements had produced, for he endeavored by an over-done hilarity, laughing boisterously at the very smallest of jokes, to quiet my apprehensions.

After supper he went on to the poop once more, and I with him. The night was dark and very still, save for the melancholy soughing of the wind among the spars. A thick cloud was coming up from the northwest, and the ragged tentacles which it threw out in front of it were drifting across the face of the moon, which only shone now and again through a rift in the wrack. The captain paced rapidly backward and forward, and then seeing me still dogging him he came across and hinted that he thought I should be better below—which I need hardly say, had the effect of strengthening my resolution to remain on deck.

I think he forgot about my presence after this, for he stood silently leaning over the taffrail, and peering out across the great desert of snow, part of which lay in shadow, while part glittered mistily in the moonlight. Several times I could see by his movements that he was referring to his watch, and once he muttered a short sentence, of which I could only catch the one word, "ready." I confess to having felt an eerie feeling creeping over me as I watched the loom of his tall figure through the darkness, and noted how completely he fulfilled the idea of a man who is keeping a tryst. A tryst with whom? Some vague perception began to dawn upon me as I pieced one fact with another, but I was utterly unprepared for the sequel.

By the sudden intensity of his attitude I felt that he saw something. I crept up behind him. He was staring with an eager, questioning gaze at what seemed to be a wreath of mist, blown swiftly in a line with the ship. It was a dim, nebulous body, devoid of shape, sometimes more, sometimes less apparent, as the light fell on it. The moon was dimmed in its brilliancy at the moment by a canopy of thinnest cloud, like the coating of an anemone.

"Coming, lass, coming," cried the skipper, in a voice of unfathomable tenderness and compassion, like one who soothes a beloved one by some favor long looked for and as pleasant to bestow as to receive.

What followed happened in an instant. I had no power to interfere. He gave one spring to the top of the bulwarks, and another which took him on to the ice, almost to the feet of the pale misty figure. He held out his hands as if to clasp it, and so ran into the darkness with outstretched arms and loving words. I still stood rigid and motionless, straining my eyes after his retreating form, until his voice died away in the distance. I never thought to see him again, but at that moment the moon shone out brilliantly through a chink in the cloudy heaven, and illuminated the great field of ice. Then I saw his dark figure, already a very long way off, running with prodigious speed across the frozen plain. That was the last glimpse which we caught of him—perhaps the last we ever shall. A party was organized to follow him, and I accompanied it, but the men's hearts were not in the work, and nothing was found. Another will be formed within a few hours. I can hardly believe I have not been dreaming, or suffering from some hideous nightmare, as I write these things down.

7:30 P. M.—Just returned dead beat and utterly tired out from a second unsuccessful search for the captain. The floe is of enormous extent, for though we have traversed at least twenty miles of its surface, there has been no sign of its coming to an end. The frost has been so severe of late that the overlying snow is frozen as hard as granite, otherwise we might have had the footsteps to guide us. The crew are anxious that we should cast off and steam round the floe and so to the southward, for the ice has opened up during the night, and the sea is visible upon the horizon. They argue that Captain Craigie is certainly dead, and that we are all risking our lives to no purpose by remaining when we have an opportunity of escape. Mr. Milne and I have had the greatest difficulty in persuading them to wait until tomorrow night, and have been compelled to promise that we will not under any circumstances delay our departure longer than that. We propose therefore to take a few hours' sleep, and then to start upon a final search.

September 20th, evening. —I crossed the ice this morning with a party of men exploring the southern part of the floe, while Mr. Milne went off in a northerly direction. We pushed on for ten or twelve miles without seeing a trace of any living thing except a single bird, which fluttered a great way over our heads, and which by its flight I should judge to have been a falcon. The southern extremity of the ice field tapered away into a long narrow spit which projected out into the sea. When we came to the base of this promontory the men halted, but I begged them to continue to the extreme end of it, that we might have the satisfaction of knowing that no possible chance had been neglected.

We had hardly gone a hundred yards before McDonald of Peterhead cried out that he saw something in front of us, and began to run. We all got a glimpse of it and ran too. At first it was only a vague darkness against the white ice, but as we raced along together it took the shape of a man, and eventually of the man of whom we were in search. He was lying face downward upon a frozen bank. Many little crystals of ice and feathers of snow had drifted on to him as he lay, and sparkled upon his dark seaman's jacket. As we came up some wandering puff of wind caught these tiny flakes in its vortex and they whirled up into the air, partially descended again, and then, caught once more in the current, sped rapidly away in the direction of the sea. To my eyes it seemed but a snowdrift, but many of my companions averred that it started up in the shape of a woman, stooped over the corpse and kissed it, and then hurried away across the floe. I have learned never to ridicule any man's opinion, however strange it may seem. Sure it is that Captain Nicholas Craigie had met with no painful end, for there was a bright smile upon his blue, pinched features, and his hands were still outstretched as though grasping at the strange visitor which had summoned him away into the dim world that lies beyond the grave.

We buried him the same afternoon with the ship's ensign around him, and a thirty-two-pound shot at his feet. I read the burial service, while the rough sailors wept like children, for there were many who owed much to his kind heart, and who showed now the affection which his strange ways had repelled during his lifetime. He went off the grating with a dull, sullen splash, and as I looked into the green water I saw him go down, down, down until he was but a little flickering patch of white hanging upon the outskirts of eternal darkness. Then even that faded away, and he was gone. There he shall lie, with his secret and his sorrows and his mystery all still buried in his breast, until that great day when the sea shall give up its dead, and Nicholas Craigie come out from among the ice with the smile upon his face, and his stiffened arms outstretched in greeting. I pray that his lot may be a happier one in that life than it has been in this.

I shall not continue my journal. Our road to home lies plain and clear before us, and the great ice field will soon be but a remembrance of the past. It will be some time before I get over the shock produced by recent events. When I began this record of our voyage I little thought of how I should be compelled to finish it. I am writing these final words in the lonely cabin, still starting at times and fancying I hear the quick nervous step of the dead man upon the deck above me. I entered his cabin tonight, as was my duty, to make a list of his effects in order that they might be entered in the official log. All was as it had been upon my previous visit, save that the picture which I have described as having hung at the end of his bed had been cut out of its frame, as with a knife, and was gone. With this last link in a strange chain of evidence I close my diary of the voyage of the *Pole-Star*.

[NOTE by Dr. John M'Alister Ray, senior.—I have read over the strange events connected with the death of the captain of the *Pole-Star*, as narrated in the journal of my son. That everything occurred exactly as he describes it I have the fullest confidence, and, indeed, the most positive certainty, for I know him to be a strong-nerved and unimaginative man, with the strictest regard for veracity. Still, the story is, on the face of it, so vague and so improbable, that I was long opposed to its publication. Within the last few days, however, I have had independent testimony upon the subject which throws a new light upon it. I had run down to Edinburgh to attend a meeting of the British Medical Association, when I chanced to come across Dr. P—, an old college chum of mine, now practicing at Saltash, in Devonshire. Upon my telling him of this experience of my son's, he declared to me that he was familiar with the man, and proceeded, to my no small surprise, to give me a description of him, which tallied remarkably well with that given in the journal, except that he depicted him as a younger man. According to his account, he had been engaged to a young lady of singular beauty residing upon the Cornish coast. During his absence at sea his betrothed had died under circumstances of peculiar horror.]

HENRY FIELDING

THE POLICE OFFICER'S TALE

I HAVE SEEN A good many things in my time," said the Police Officer. "Before I came to Burma I was a shoeblack in Auckland, and before that I herded sheep in New South Wales; but the only real adventure that ever happened to me occurred when I was an apprentice on a sailing ship."

"A wreck?" asked the Major.

"No," said the Policeman, "there was no wreck; but we abandoned our ship in mid-ocean and had rather a bad time in open boats till we were picked up. It is not pleasant work navigating the Atlantic in an open boat."

"What made you abandon your ship?" asked the Naval Lieutenant. "Had she sprung a leak, or was it a fire?"

"She was as tight and as firm when we abandoned her as any ship could be," said the Police Officer emphatically. "There was nothing the matter with her alow or aloft, except that which obliged us to leave her."

"I do not understand," said the Lieutenant looking puzzled. "I never heard of a crew abandoning a ship in mid-ocean if she was still tight. Was it mutiny?"

"The captain was a favourite with the crew," said the Police Officer.

The Lieutenant stared. "Was it disease, plague, cholera, yellow fever?"

"No," said the Police Officer, "it was none of those things. In fact it may be said to have been rather an exceptional case. She was a barque belonging to Aberdeen, the *Mary Down*, a wooden ship, one of the last of the old clippers and she had gone to the Mediterranean ports with a cargo of metal and hardware. The last place we touched at was Alexandria and there we filled up with bones for New York."

"Bones?" ejaculated the Cavalry Officer.

"Yes, bones," answered the Police Officer; "they are a very valuable manure, you know. Bones to be ground up into manure, and rags to make paper, these composed a good deal of our cargo. We had a wearisome voyage out of the Mediterranean which is always a tricky place to sail about in. Sometimes we were becalmed, and sometimes we had to take in sail in a desperate hurry when the Levanter came up, so that we were not sorry to pass the Strait and get out into the Atlantic. Two days from Gib we found the Trades and went comfortably bowling along on our course making a good ten knots an hour all day.

"It was the second day out from Gib when I noticed that something was wrong. I was in the second mate's watch, and that night we happened to have the middle watch. The ship was sailing easily upon her course, and there was nothing to do. Presently finding that I had used up my matches I went forward to the forecastle to get a box from my bunk. Coming out I noticed three or four hands clustered together by the shrouds talking earnestly. They stopped, and looked at me rather strangely as I passed. I did not pay much attention and was walking aft lighting my pipe when I felt a touch on the arm: it was Jackson the carpenter, one of the men who had been talking. 'We would like to speak to you a minute, Flisher,' he said.

" 'What's the matter, Jackson?' I asked.

"He did not answer at once and we went back to where the other two men were standing by the shrouds. 'Well?' I asked.

"The three men moved uneasily looking to each other to speak first, but each seeming afraid to do so.

" 'Come,' I said, 'what is it? Have it up.' They looked so serious that I knew it was no little joke that was on.

"Then Jackson, seeing that he was expected to do the talking, took the plug out of his mouth and spitting deliberately over the side, said: 'There's something wrong with this 'ere ship.'

" 'What's wrong?'

" 'She ain't no ship for decent Christian men to sail in,' he said sulkily. 'If I'd ha' known when we was at Alexandry I'm damned if I wouldn't have left there. Skippers has no right to ask men to sail in ships with such a cargo as this.'

"I was considerably surprised at this as the ship was a good one. The forecastle was roomy and dry, and the provisions sound and good. The old man, too, was a capital sailor and, though strict, was not a man to worry his crew; neither were the mates. I had been two voyages already on her and never heard a serious complaint, at least one founded on reason. 'I suppose she's too slow for you, Jackson,' I said. 'You ought to sail on a mail-boat.'

"Jackson shook his head. 'It ain't that she's a bit slow,' he replied. 'She's fast enough for me. Nor 'ave we any complaint against the grog or the old man or the mates. They ain't so bad as times go. No,' and he shook his head still more decidedly; 'it ain't that at all.'

" 'What is it, then?' I asked, a bit angry. 'You aren't afraid to speak of it, are you?'

" 'No,' said Jackson slowly; 'I aren't afraid.' Then he paused and spat again meditatively over the bulwark. 'You aren't seen anythink unusual on this ship, 'ave you, Flisher?'

"I hadn't the faintest idea what the man was driving at. 'Unusual,' I answered, 'no, bar a rat or two, and they can't be unusual, I think.'

" 'Ah,' he said with a tone of conviction; 'well, we 'ave.'

"His tone roused my curiosity. 'What is it, Jackson? What's wrong? Better tell me.'

" 'Ghosts,' said Jackson thickly and glancing apprehensively round, 'ghosts;' and the other men nodded.

"I laughed. The idea of ghosts appeared to me mere childishness. Here were four great hulking men looking as fearful as children.

" 'Oh yes,' growled Jackson, 'you laughs. They don't come aft likely.'

"He spoke so savagely that I stopped. 'What are the ghosts like, Jackson?' I asked. 'Do you mean to say that you've seen them?'

"Jackson nodded. 'Aye, I've seen 'em; we've all seen 'em. Tell him what like they are, Christiansen.'

"The man spoken to was a Dane, a tall, scrambling fair-haired Dane with a weak and wandering blue eye. He was usually the butt of the crew, and it surprised me to hear him appealed to.

" 'Dead men,' answered Christiansen sepulchrally, 'dead men's ghosts. Dere bones are down dere,' and he tapped his feet on the deck, 'but dere spirits, dey are here.' He stopped and looked up into the great mass of white sails that swelled above us. 'De men of all the nations that have fought and died—ah!'

"He gave a nod forward with his head and even in the dusk I saw his eyes distend. We all started and looked across the deck to where Christiansen was looking. It was a clear starlight night and the outline of everything was plain to see; I could even make out from where I stood the break of the poop and the outline of the rail against the sky. I could see nothing unusual and turned again to my companions. They were all bent forward with fearful faces, glaring over the forehatch to the weather-side opposite us. I followed their glances, and again at first I saw nothing, but suddenly I thought that something was moving there. I could not make it out, but there seemed to me two or more figures moving down under the shadow of the bulwarks.

"I ran forward at once to that side but when I came to where they had been they were gone. Near by was the caboose and the carpenter's shop, but the doors of both were closed. I looked up and down but could see nothing.

" 'It's one of the boys fooling,' I said coming back to Jackson, who had not moved.

" 'No it ain't,' said Jackson. 'That ain't no boy; it's a ghost. This place and the fo'ksel is just full of 'em.'

"I confess that it gave me a bit of a turn this sudden disappearance of the figures, but I pretended to laugh. 'They are harmless enough anyhow,' I said. 'Your great lump of flesh isn't afraid of the shadows like that, Jackson? I wouldn't tell the old man, if I were you, that you funked the shadow of the main staysail.'

" 'Look 'ere, Flisher,' said Jackson; 'we've just told you about this because you, being better eddycated than us, we thought you might have some explanation. We did not tell it for you young shaver to laugh at us and say we're afraid. Never you mind if we're afraid or no. These figures, and more figures than them, has been going up and down the decks ever since we left Alexandry. Christiansen seed 'em first, but now we've all seen 'em. We ax you, as one who's been to school and brought up as a gentleman, if you can explain 'em.'

"I was impressed with the earnestness of the men, and perhaps a little flattered at their consulting me. 'No, I can't,' I said. 'I do not believe in ghosts.'

" 'Ah,' said Jackson, 'that's wot they teaches you boys now, is it? Not to believe in ghosts? Well, we sailor-men believe in 'em because we sees 'em. Ay, and we knows the reason too, don't we?'

"Christiansen and the other men grunted an assent. 'It's de bones,' said Christiansen again pointing down the deck.

" 'Bones,' I exclaimed. 'Yes, you said that before. What the devil do you mean?'

" 'Ay, bones,' said Jackson; 'them bones as we took aboard at Alexandry. They was in bags, but *we* knew well enough. Some of the bags bust as they came aboard and we seed the bones. They was men's bones, skulls and things; we seed 'em.'

" 'Ah, we seed 'em,' said Christiansen grimly. 'It was gut to put dem in de bags, but ven de bag broke, den ve see.'

"My blood ran cold at the idea. I had seen the bags loaded, and had in fact helped to tally them, but none broke that I saw. 'Are you sure?' I asked. 'Were they really men's bones?' None of the four sailors condescended to reply and there was a pause. We stood there and looked at each other.

" 'Dere's been a many battle dere in Egypt,' explained Christiansen presently, 'ever since ole Pharaoh's time. Dere's been a many men killed. Dese are de bones. Dere are de skulls and arm and leg bones and all de oder bones down dere. And de spirits, dey are here.'

"He spoke funereally. Overhead the cordage creaked softly as the ship swayed to the breeze, and there came from forward the soft crash of the bows into the seas. 'Look here, I must be off,' I said suddenly, 'or the mate will curse me. Damn your ghosts!' and with that I turned and went aft.

"I crept softly up the gangway to the poop and looked round to see if the mate had missed me. For a moment I did not see him, then as I came past the cabin skylight I suddenly discovered that the skipper was on deck. He and the mate were talking abaft the wheel.

"When the mate saw me he called out to me, 'Flisher.'

" 'Yes, sir,' I answered.

" 'Come here.'

" 'Look here, Flisher,' said the skipper, 'what's all this damned nonsense the hands have got hold of about ghosts? The steward is scared out of his senses.'

" 'I do not know, sir,' I answered. 'The men have just been telling me that there are some ghosts about.'

" 'You haven't seen any, Flisher?' and he looked at me curiously.

"I thought for a moment of the shadows, and then answered, 'No, sir.'

"The skipper nodded and went forward with the mate, and I to leeward again. The steersman was motionless at the wheel and the ship surged steadily forward on her way. There came a rustle and a mutter from aloft as the wind pressed into the sails and the stars danced between the ropes.

"The next day there was no more concealment about it. It was known all over the ship that the forecastle was haunted by ghosts who passed to and fro all the night. It was Hans Christiansen who had first seen them, but by this time there was no one of the crew who had not encountered at least a dozen ghosts. All sorts of tales were current as to their appearance and shape and the stories grew in horror as the day went on. At six bells, as the sun was sinking into a gorgeous sunset far ahead, the crew came aft in a body and complained to the skipper.

" 'Ghosts,' said the old man scornfully when he heard what they had to say, 'ghosts! Who's seen the ghosts?'

"There was a moment's pause among the men and then a sort of grumble. 'We've all seen 'em,' said Jackson who was acting as spokesman for the crew.

" 'Ah,' said the skipper 'you've all seen 'em? And what like are these ghosts that you've all seen? Spirits more like,' he sneered. 'You all drunk enough at Alexandry; a touch of D. T., my men. Now, Jackson, what like was the ghosts *you* seed?'

"Jackson rubbed his head a little confusedly. 'Well, sir,' he said at length, 'I dunno as I seed much. There was something ghost-like I seed pass the deck at night once or twice; but what like it was I don't know. It made me skeered though,' he added reflectively.

" 'They's the spirits of the dead men whose bones are below,' drawled a voice from the crowd, and there followed a hoarse murmur of 'Ay, ay.'

" 'Dead men below?' asked the skipper in surprise.

" 'Them bones, sir, as was loaded at Alexandry,' explained Jackson, 'They say as how they're no bones of beasts but just bones of dead men, skulls and things.'

" 'Say!' roared the skipper. 'Who says that? Who says I've made my ship a damned dead-house? Where's the man? I'd like to see him.'

"The crew looked at each other questioningly. Who was it who had seen them? No one came forward.

" 'Now,' shouted the skipper, 'I'm a waiting. Where's the lubber?'

"Still no one moved.

" 'Where are the mates?' said the skipper, turning furiously to find them both at his elbow. 'You loaded these 'ere bones; did you see anything?'

"The mates shook their heads. 'A bag broke,' said the second mate, 'but there weren't any men's bones in that. I don't believe there are any at all. It's just a lie, sir, a lie to scare the men from their work.'

" 'Ay,' roared the skipper, 'and I'll find the blackguard too! I'll ghost him! I'll teach him to say I've got a damned old graveyard on my ship! Ah—'

"He stopped suddenly as Christiansen half walked, was half jostled forward. 'What have *you* to say, you milk-faced curd-headed son of a Dutchman? Did *you* see the bones?'

" 'Ya,' answered Christiansen, his light blue eyes wandering nervously from the skipper to the mates and from the mates to the topsail. 'I did the skulls see. Ya, dey are dere,' and he pointed forward. 'Mein Gott, yes! I have seed dem.'

"The skipper's rage cooled before this vacillating light-haired Dane with the expressionless face. He stared at him a moment in

129

contempt. 'Oh,' he sneered, 'it was you, was it, who saw the skulls?' Christiansen did not answer. 'Perhaps it was you too who saw the ghosts?'

"Christiansen looked about as if meditating a retreat, but the men behind would not let him pass. 'Speak up, Christiansen,' they said. 'You saw 'em; tell the skipper.'

" 'You were afraid to be alone in the dark, I suppose,' said the skipper scathingly, 'you cur-hearted school-miss. What did you see, you damned long-shore loafer? Are you afraid to speak?'

" 'I saw the ghosts,' explained Christiansen briefly, 'de ghosts of de men that is dead. Dey haf all seen dem,' and he waved his hand to the crew, 'but I seed dem de first. I was alvays gut at seeing the ghosts.'

"A sort of half-concealed pride could be seen in his face, which roused the skipper's rage again to red-heat.

" 'And you believe this Dutchman and his damned lies, you men? You chicken-hearted fools. I'll—' then he suddenly stopped. 'Open the fore-hatch,' he said to the mate.

"The men went forward in a body headed by the mate, and the tarpaulins were removed from the hatch. In a few minutes, the men working very unwillingly, the hatch was open. Down below in the obscurity could be seen the bags in tiers and layers as they had been loaded by the stevedores. Here and there in the dark gleamed a white bone and a strange charnel-house smell came up from below. The men stood round and looked suspiciously and timorously into the hatch.

" 'Fetch up a bag,' said the skipper to the mate. But none of the men would go, and finally with a curse I was ordered to go down. I went and slung six bags into a noose, which were drawn up.

" 'Now,' said the skipper as the bags dropped on deck with a rattle, 'open them bags and let's see Christiansen's skulls.'

"With a draw of his knife the second mate cut the lashing of a bag; he held up the end and the bones fell out. There was a skurry as the men fell back in terror towards the forecastle, their faces blanched and their eyes starting; for out of the bag amid a quantity of bones bleached with age rolled a human skull. Slowly it rolled along the deck turning its eye-sockets this way and that while we all regarded it with horror. Then as the ship lurched it gave a quick movement and stopped just at the feet of Christiansen.

"There was a dead silence. Then Christiansen, who of all present seemed the only one neither frightened nor astonished, stooped and picked up the skull. He raised it carefully in his hands and peered into the empty eyeholes, turning it round and round almost as if with pleasure at seeing a friend. 'Ya,' he said meditating; 'see de large skull of de dead man.' With his finger he traced a mark upon the forehead regretfully. 'Dey cut him dere and he died. Poor fellow!' Then lifting up his eyes he went on in his curious singsong. 'He is de tall soldier dat I seed last night with the great cut upon his face where de blood poured out. He was near the cuddy door; he was cursing dem dat brought his bones out over de sea.'

"To say that the men listened to him in horror would hardly express their state. They were paralysed with fear. I felt afraid myself when I heard the man talking thus to the poor white nameless skull, and even the captain had remained motionless, but as the Dane stopped he suddenly recovered command of himself and stepping forward he struck Christiansen down. The skull rolled out of his hands, and the skipper picked it up and chucked it overboard contemptuously. Then with an oath he turned to his bewildered crew. 'You white-livered lot of curs, you,' he snarled; 'you let a Dane funk you with an old skull. Suppose there is a skull or two aboard, what does it signify? I ain't afraid o' any man alive nor dead either. As to ghosts, that's all his woman's folly,' and he kicked contemptuously the recumbent form of the ghost-seer. 'There ain't no such things. The next man as sees a ghost goes into irons; you know me.' Then he turned on his heel and went aft.

"For a day or two nothing more happened. The crew went about their work all day with sullen faces and during the night watches they clustered together by the forecastle-head and cursed. Christiansen was in his bunk, for the skipper was a strongish chap and he had let Christiansen have it for all he was worth. The skipper was cheerful. 'Ghosts,' he said to the mate with a laugh; 'you try a handspike on the next man who sees a ghost. A bishop with bell and candle don't come up to a marlin-spike in ghost-driving.'

"But the mate was not so happy; he was superstitious as are all seamen. 'Flisher,' he said to me, 'have you seen any of these ghosts?' I told him about the shadows under the forecastle and he shook his head. 'What were they like?' he asked. I could not say; indeed I doubted if I had really seen anything at all. It was that fellow Christiansen; to hear him talk gave one the creeps, and when he said 'Look,' I was ready to believe anything. But I did not really believe in ghosts, I said.

" 'Ah,' said the mate, 'but there is ghosts of course, Flisher. I don't say that I've ever seen them, but lots of my people have. My mother saw a ghost once, a little man in white. Then there's Bible-warrant for it too. You remember that witch of Endor? You don't deny the Bible?'

"I could not do that, I said, but may be there was good religious reason for those ghosts; that time's past now.

" 'And don't you call it reason for these ghosts that we're tak-ing their bones across sea to be manure to tobacco-gardens?' he answered. 'No, no, Flisher, my boy, there's ghosts right enough.'

"I could see that the mate thoroughly believed in the ghosts. As to the men their nerves were stretched to breaking. You could not drop a marlin-spike behind a man without his jumping round with a scared white face on you. And one night, when we were taking in the main-top-gallant sail, the man next me nearly fell off the yard swearing a ghost had touched his face; I had to help him back to the top. When they had nothing to do on deck they collected in little groups and told ghost-stories. All the old ghosts of the sea were resurrected and told of with fear and trembling. The men became possessed, as it were, with ghost-mania.

"On the third or fourth night the breeze suddenly fell. The sky had been overcast all day, and the sun set behind a great purple bank of cloud that hung low upon the horizon. The breeze fell till the sea was one glassy sheet that rolled in league-long undula-tions from horizon to horizon. The night was hot and close like a crowded room. Now and then a great drop of rain fell heavily upon the deck, and far down in the south the lightning played fit-fully, lighting up the broken masses of cloud with sudden vividness. It was a night that unstrung your nerves and made you unhappy and afraid.

"I could hear a man (Williams the cook, I think) telling a ghost story in low and stricken tones to the men. I did not listen much because my nerves were already as tense as I could bear, but in the deadly stillness of the night his words drifted every now and then across to me. He was telling again the old story of the saving of the great ship's company.

" *'Steer Nor'-Nor'-West*. Who had written it upon the slate? The mate rubbed it out but when he came back an hour later to enter upon his log, it was there again: *Steer Nor'-Nor'-West*. The mate rubbed it out a second time and sat down in the dark cuddy to catch the man who wrote it, the man who was playing a joke upon him. As he sat waiting, suddenly a shadowy figure appeared. Whence he came or how the mate could not say, but he was there, writing on the slate; the mate heard the chalk creak. With a bound he was up catching at the man, and finding—nothing! Before him was the empty companion and behind him the empty cuddy, and on the slate were the words again, *Steer Nor'-Nor'-West.'*

"I had heard the story before, and did not care to hear it again. I turned away and looked out at the sea, black as death save where the fitful lightning broke. It was coming nearer and nearer; in the darkness between the flashes the heavens seemed to press right down upon the ship; faint moans, as of dying men came from far away.

"The lad had finished his story and the men sat silently brooding upon it. No one spoke. The creaking of the cordage, as the ship rolled, made the silence even more noticeable. Suddenly I heard a voice low and dreamy come out of the dark close by me. 'Spirits of de dead men,' it moaned, 'spirits of de dead men.' It brought the heart into my mouth, and I turned abruptly. Very dimly I could make out a figure lying on the break of the forecastle peering over into the main deck. It seemed to be gazing at something.

" 'I see dem, the dead men,' it moaned on. 'Dey come up in tens and twenties; dey are dere below. Dey have red coats and blue coats, dose dead soldiers of the wars. Deir faces are bloody with sword-cuts, and dere are holes in dere bodies whence the blood oozes out. Dey look at me mit deir dead eyes.' A cold horror had fallen upon us as Christiansen spoke. My limbs were numbed, and in my ears were strange throbbings. From some inexplicable attraction I crept nearer to the Dane and I found the crew doing the same. No one spoke, or looked except at Christiansen. We became packed as a flock of sheep.

" 'Dere are more and more,' he went on, still in that strange moaning voice. 'De deck is full of dem. Dere are men with black faces and white eyeballs which glare at me. De deck is full of dem; dey throng upon each other.'

"In the pause I heard two bells strike from aft, the sound coming to me as out of a dream. The man next me had caught my arm in a grip that numbed it, but I hardly noticed. The lightning flashed nearer, and in the glare the men's faces, tense and agonised, shone out with a deadly paleness. My temples were bursting.

" 'Dey come up and up; dere are many thousands of dem now. Dey cluster in de rigging. Dere are many dead sailors of de great wars there.'

He now raised himself from his recumbent position and half stood up leaning upon the rail.

" 'Dey come more and more.' He looked away out to sea. 'Dey are passing upon de waters. Dey drive their chariots upon de sea.'

"He rose to his feet, and there was a movement among the men. It was evident their nerves were strung to breaking-point; now and then one gasped as if in agony.

" 'Dey gallop upon the sea. Dey are all dere, de old Pharaoh and his men that died so long ago. Dey look at us with angry eyes as they pass.'

"There was a flicker of phosphorus in a passing wave, glinting as if struck up by horses' hoofs. Here and there across that dark deadly plain there suddenly flashed other phosphorescent gleams. It seemed as if dim forms passed to and fro; I could see them. 'My God!' muttered a man next to me. I would have given worlds to have shouted, to have screamed, but I was held as in a spell.

"Christiansen was standing now leaning over the rail. His arms waved as he spoke, and his voice had become faster and more guttural. 'Dey shake deir heads at me; dey threaten!' he cried. 'Dey say, "why have you taken our bones from deir graves?" Dere is hatred in deir eyes.'

"He was holding now by a foretop-stay; a flash of lightning showed him clearly, glaring down at the sea. 'Do not look so at me,' he cried; 'it was not me! What have I done, den? Mein Gott, to see deir eyes!' He began to gesticulate wildly to the sea. 'Go,' he shrieked, 'go! Dey tear me down!' He planted his feet against the butts in fierce resistance, while the lightning played more and more brightly. His shrieks became wilder and more horrible. 'De dead men take me! Ah, ah, ah!' he screamed, his voice passing far across the sea in unutterable agony. The darkness came down now dense as a veil and we could see no more. We were frozen to stone, while within a hand's grasp of us Christiansen fought with unseen foes. He stamped upon the deck; we heard the groans and panting of the fight. And then the darkness was suddenly lifted again. From the vault above a violet light, ghastly and cold, shone out in unendurable brilliance repeated in throbbing waves of radiance. It showed the ship clear to the trucks, every rope and spar cut in black against the fire; it showed the decks below us, and the sea black and smooth as though cast in black marble, and the stricken faces of the men. And by the rail stood Christiansen, every nerve and muscle strained, his feet braced, his hands gripping fiercely at the stays. He was the central figure, and ere the light had failed, in a moment of time, we saw him drawn from his hold. His feet slipped, his hands were forced from their grip. With one piercing cry of agony he fell before our eyes into the sea.

"Then the night shut down once more, and there burst a roar of thunder as if the universe had broken up. The spell had passed. With inarticulate cries of fear we leapt to our feet and fled. Hither and thither we ran, blinded in a paroxysm of maddening fear. We fell, and picked ourselves up, and fell again. Men met and wrestled and parted; their faces streamed with blood, their breath came hot and quick; till at last in an excess of frenzy they burst suddenly down upon the main-deck and rushed aft for the quarter-boats.

"The first mate, who was on watch, and the skipper hearing the rush of men tried to face them. They were overborne and flung senseless to the deck. With feverish haste the quarter-boats were dropped from the davits and the men fell in. Then without food or water, without compass or chart, they set to work to row away from the ship, bending to their oars like demons.

"All night they rowed. The lightning flashed and the rain poured down, but the men never stopped. They did not look anywhere; their eyes were held to their labouring hands, and thus they did not notice behind them a red glare that rose gradually upon the sky, a glare that was not of the lightning for it was steady. But as the boats increased their distance it fell and fell, until at last the horizon hid it.

"We were picked up two days later, the men exhausted and almost dead. The skipper and the mates were also picked up by another ship. That last flash of lightning had set the *Mary Down* on fire, and the skipper and first mate being disabled the second mate could not put it out single-handed; but they had managed somehow between them to launch the remaining boat in time.

"The *Mary Down* was burnt to the water's edge and then sank. She lies now a thousand fathoms deep beneath the Atlantic and let us hope that the bones have peace at last. They deserve it."

WILHELM HAUFF

THE STORY
OF THE HAUNTED SHIP

M Y FATHER KEPT A small shop at Balsora. He was neither poor nor rich, and was one of those people who are
afraid of venturing anything lest they should lose the
little they possess. He brought me up plainly and virtuously, and
soon I was enabled to assist him in his trade. Scarcely had I reached
my eighteenth year, and hardly had he made his first large specula-
tion, when he died, probably from grief at having confided a thousand pieces of gold to the sea.

I could not help thinking him lucky afterwards on account
of his death, for a few weeks later the news arrived that the ship
to which my father had entrusted his goods had sunk. This mis-
hap, however, did not curb my youthful courage. I converted everything that my father had left into money, and set forth to try my
fortune abroad, accompanied only by my father's old servant, who

from long attachment would not separate himself from me and my fate.

We took ship at Balsora and left the haven with a favourable wind. The ship in which we embarked was bound for India. When we had sailed some fifteen days over the ordinary track, the Captain predicted a storm. He looked very serious, for it appeared that he was not sufficiently acquainted with the course in these parts to await a storm with composure. He had all sail furled, and we drifted along quite gently. The night had fallen. It was cold and clear, and the Captain began to think he had been deceived by false indications of the storm. All at once a ship which we had not observed before drove past at a little distance from our own. Wild shouts and cheers resounded from her deck; at which, in such an anxious hour before a tempest, I wondered not a little. The Captain, who stood by my side, turned as pale as death. "My ship is doomed!" he cried, "Yonder sails death." Before I could question him as to the meaning of this strange exclamation, the sailors came running towards us, howling and crying. "Have you seen it?" they cried. "It is all over with us."

But the Captain caused some consolatory verses to be read out of the Koran, and placed himself at the helm. All in vain! Visibly the storm increased in fury, and before an hour had passed the ship crashed and stuck fast. The boats were lowered, and scarcely had the last sailors saved themselves, when the ship sank before our eyes, and I was launched on the sea, a beggar. Further miseries yet awaited us. The storm raged more furiously; our boat became unmanageable. I had clasped my old servant tightly, and we vowed never to part from one another. At length day broke. But at the first dawn of morning a squall caught the boat in which we were seated and capsized it. I never saw my shipmates again. I was stunned by the shock; when I awoke, I found myself in the arms of my old and faithful servant, who had saved himself on the overturned boat and dragged me after him. The tempest had subsided. Nothing more was seen of our ship. We discovered, however, not far from us another ship, towards which the waves were drifting us. As we drew near I recognized it as the same ship that had dashed past us on the preceding night, and which had terrified our Captain so much. I was inspired with a singular horror at the sight of this vessel. The expression of the Captain which had been so terribly fulfilled, the desolate aspect of the ship, on which, near as we were and loudly as we shouted, no one appeared, frightened me. However, this was our only means of safety, therefore we praised the Prophet who had so wonderfully preserved us.

Over the ship's bow hung a long cable. We paddled with hands and feet towards it in order to grasp it. At length we succeeded. Loudly I raised my voice, but all was silent on board. We then climbed up by the rope, I as the youngest going first. Oh, horror! What a spectacle met my gaze as I stepped upon the deck! The planks were reddened with blood; twenty or thirty corpses in Turkish dresses lay on the deck. Close to the mainmast stood a man, richly attired, a sabre in his hand, but with features pale and distorted; a great nail driven through his forehead pinning him to the mainmast. He also was dead.

Terror shackled my steps. I scarcely ventured to breathe. At last my companion had also come up. He too was struck at the sight of the deck, on which nothing living was to be seen, only so many frightful corpses. After a time we ventured, after having invoked the aid of the Prophet in anguish of heart, to go forward. At each step we glanced around expecting to discover something new and yet more terrible. But all was the same. Far and wide nothing was living but ourselves and the ocean. We dared not even speak aloud, lest the dead Captain spitted to the mast should turn his ghastly eyes upon us, or one of the corpses move its head. At last we reached a hatchway which led to the ship's hold. There we both stopped, involuntarily, and looked at each other, for neither dared to speak his thoughts.

"O Master," said my faithful servant, "something awful has happened here! Yet, though the hold below be full of murderers, I would rather give myself up to their mercy than remain here any longer among these corpses." I thought the same. We grew bold and, full of expectation, descended. But here likewise all was still as death, and only our steps sounded on the ladder. We stood at the door of the cabin. I placed my ear against it and listened. Nothing could be heard. I opened it, and the cabin presented a disorderly appearance. Dresses, weapons, and other things lay in confusion. Everything was out of its place. The crew, or at least the Captain, must have been carousing not long since, for all was still lying about.

We went from place to place and from cabin to cabin, and everywhere found splendid stores of silk, pearls, sugar, and the like. I was beside myself with joy at this sight, for since no one was on board, I thought I had a right to appropriate all to myself; but Ibrahim reminded me that we were doubtless far from land, which we could never reach without the help of man.

We refreshed ourselves with the meats and drinks, of which we found an ample supply, and finally ascended again to the deck. But here we shuddered at the sight of the ghastly corpses. We resolved upon freeing ourselves from them by throwing them overboard. But how awful was the dread which we felt when we found that not one could be moved from his position! So firmly fixed were they to the flooring, that we should have had to take up the planks of the deck in order to remove them, and for this purpose we had no tools. Neither could we loose the Captain from the mainmast, nor wrest his sabre from his rigid grasp.

We passed the day in sad contemplation of our position, and when night began to fall I allowed old Ibrahim to lie down to sleep, while I kept watch on deck spying for some means of deliverance. But when the moon had come out, and I reckoned by the stars that it was about eleven o'clock, such an irresistible sleep took possession of me that I involuntarily fell behind a cask that stood on the deck. However, this was more stupefaction than sleep, for I distinctly heard the sea beating against the side of the ship, and the sails creaking and whistling in the wind. All of a sudden I thought I heard voices and men's footsteps on the deck. I endeavoured to get up to see what it was, but an invisible power held my limbs fettered; I could not even open my eyes. The voices, however, grew more distinct, and it appeared to me as if a merry crew was rushing about on the deck. Now and then I thought I heard the sonorous voice of a commander, and also distinctly the hoisting and lowering of cordage and sails. But by degrees my senses left me, I sank into a deeper sleep, in which I only thought I could hear a clatter of arms, and only awoke when the sun was far above the horizon and scorching my face.

I stared about in astonishment. Storm, ship, the dead, and what I had heard during the night, appeared to me like a dream, but when I glanced around I found everything as on the previous day. Immovable lay the dead; immovable stood the Captain spitted to the mast. I laughed over my dream, and rose up to seek the old man.

He was seated, absorbed in reflection in the cabin. "Oh, Master," he exclaimed, as I entered, "I would rather lie at the bottom of the sea than pass another night in this bewitched ship." I inquired the cause of his trouble, and he thus answered me: "After I had slept some hours, I awoke and heard people running about above my head. I thought at first it was you, but there were at least twenty, rushing to and fro, aloft, and I also heard calling and shouting. At last heavy steps came down the cabin. Upon this I became insensible, and only now and then my consciousness returned for a few moments, and then I saw the same man who is nailed to the mast overhead, sitting there at that table, singing and drinking, while the man in the scarlet dress, who is close to him on the floor, sat beside him and drank with him." Such was my old servant's narrative.

Believe me, my friends, I did not feel at all at ease, for it was no illusion. I had also heard the dead men quite plainly. To sail in such company was gruesome to me. My Ibrahim, however, relapsed into profound meditation. "I have just hit it!" he exclaimed at last. He recalled a little formula, which his grandfather, a man of experience and a great traveller, had taught him, which was a charm against ghosts and sorcery. He likewise affirmed that we might ward off the unnatural sleep during the coming night, by diligently saying verses from the Koran.

The proposal of the old man pleased me. In anxious expectation we saw the night approach. Adjoining the cabin was a narrow berth, into which we resolved to retire. We bored several holes through the door, large enough to overlook the whole cabin; we then locked the door as well as we could inside, and Ibrahim wrote the name of the Prophet in all four corners. Thus we awaited the terrors of the night. It might be about eleven o'clock when I began to feel very drowsy. My companion therefore advised me to say some verses from the Koran, which indeed helped me. All at once everything grew animated above, the cordage creaked, feet paced the deck, and several voices became clearly heard. We had thus sat for some time in intense expectation, when we heard something descending the steps of the cabin stairs. The old man on hearing this commenced to recite the formula which his grandfather had taught him against ghosts and sorcery:

> "If you are spirits from the air,
> Or come from depths of sea,
> Have in dark sepulchres your lair,
> Or if from fire you be.
> Allah is your God and Lord,
> All spirits must obey His word."

I must confess I did not quite believe in this charm, and my hair stood on end as the door opened. In stepped that tall majestic man whom I had seen nailed to the mainmast. The nail still passed through his skull, but his sword was sheathed. Behind him followed another person less richly dressed; him also I had seen stretched on deck. The Captain, for there was no doubt it was he, had a pale face, a large black beard and fiery eyes, with which he looked around the whole cabin. I could see him quite distinctly as he passed our door; but he did not seem to notice the door at all, which hid us. Both seated themselves at the table which stood in the middle of the cabin, speaking loudly and almost shouting to one another in an unknown tongue. They grew more and more hot and excited, until at last the Captain brought his fist down upon the table, so that the cabin shook. The other jumped up with a wild laugh and beckoned the Captain to follow him. The latter rose, tore his sabre out of its sheath, and both left the cabin.

After they had gone we breathed more freely, but our alarm was not to terminate yet. Louder and louder grew the noise on deck. We heard rushing backwards and forwards, shouting, laughing and howling. At last a most fiendish noise was heard, so we thought the deck together with all its sails was coming down on us, clashing of arms and shrieks—and suddenly a dead silence followed. When, after many hours, we ventured to ascend, we found everything as before; not one had shifted his place; all lay as stiff as wood.

Thus we passed many days on board this ship, and constantly steered on an eastern course, where according to my calculation land should be found; but although we seemed to cover many miles by day, yet at night it seemed to go back, for we were always in the same place at the rising of the sun. We could not understand this, except

that the dead crew each night navigated the ship in a directly opposite course with full sails. In order to prevent this, we furled all the
sails before night fell, and employed the same means as we had used
on the cabin door. We wrote the name of the prophet, and the formula prescribed by Ibrahim's grandfather, upon a scroll of parch-
ment, and wound it round the furled sails. Anxiously we awaited the
result in our berths. The noise now seemed to increase more violently than ever; but behold, on the following morning, the sails
were still furled, as we had left them. By day we only hoisted as
many sails as were needed to carry the ship gently along, and thus in
five days we covered a considerable tract.

At last on the sixth morning we discovered land at a short
distance, and thanked Allah and his Prophet for our miraculous
deliverance. This day and on the following night we sailed along a
coast, and on the seventh morning we thought at a short distance we
saw a town. With much difficulty we dropped our anchor, which at
once struck ground, lowered a little boat, which was on deck, and
rowed with all our strength towards the town. After the lapse of half
an hour we entered a river which ran into the sea, and landed. On
entering the gate of the town we asked the name of it, and learnt that
it was an Indian town, not far from where I had intended to land at
first. We went towards a caravanserai and refreshed ourselves after
our adventurous journey. I also inquired there after some wise and
intelligent man, intimating to the landlord that I wished to consult
one on matters relating to sorcery. He led me to some remote street
to a mean-looking house and knocked. I was allowed to enter, and
simply told to ask for Muley.

In the house I met a little old man, with a grey beard and a long
nose, who asked me what I wanted. I told him I desired to see the
wise Muley, and he answered me that he was Muley. I now asked his
advice what I should do with the corpses, and how I was to set about
to remove them from the ship. He answered me that very likely the
ship's crew were spellbound on the ocean on account of some crime;
and he believed the charm might be broken by bringing them on
land, which, however, could only be done by taking up the planks on
which they lay. The ship, together with all its goods, by divine and
human law belonged to me, because I had as it were found it. I was,
however, to keep all very secret, and make him a little present of my
abundance, in return for which he and his slaves would assist me in

removing the dead. I promised to reward him richly, and we set forth followed by five slaves provided with saws and hatchets. On the road the magician Muley could not sufficiently laud the happy thought of tacking the Koran verses upon the sails. He said that this had been the only means of our deliverance.

It was yet early morning when we reached the vessel. We all set to work immediately, and in an hour four lay already in the boat. Some of the slaves had to row them to land to bury them there. They related on their return that the corpses had saved them the trouble of burial, for hardly had they been put on the ground when they crumbled into dust. We continued sawing off the corpses, and before evening all had been removed to land except one, namely he who was nailed to the mast. In vain we endeavoured to draw the nail out of the wood. Every effort could not displace it a hair's-breadth. I did not know what to do, for it was impossible to cut down the mast to bring him to land. Muley, however, devised an expedient. He ordered a slave quickly to row to land, in order to bring him a pot filled with earth. When it was brought, the magician pronounced some mystic words over it, and emptied the earth upon the head of the corpse. Immediately he opened his eyes, heaved a deep sigh, and the wound of the nail in his forehead began to bleed. We now extracted the nail easily, and the wounded man fell into the arms of one of the slaves.

"Who has brought me hither?" he said, after having slightly recovered. Muley pointed to me, and I approached him. "Thanks be to thee, unknown stranger, for thou hast rescued me from a long martyrdom. For fifty years has my corpse been floating upon these waves, and my spirit was condemned to reanimate it each night; but now earth having touched my head, I can return to my fathers reconciled." I begged him to tell us how he had fallen into this awful condition, and he answered, "Fifty years ago I was a man of power and rank, and lived in Algiers. The longing after gain induced me to fit out a vessel in order to engage in piracy. I had already carried on this business for some time, when one day I took on board at Zante a Dervish, who asked for a free passage. My companions and myself were wild fellows, and paid no respect to the sanctity of the man, but rather mocked him. But one day, when he had reproached me in his holy zeal with my sinful mode of living, I became furious at night, after having drunk a great deal with my steersman in my cabin. Enraged at what a Dervish had told me, and what I would not even allow a Sultan to tell me, I rushed upon deck, and plunged my dagger in his breast. As he died, he cursed me and my crew, that we might neither live nor die till our heads should touch the earth. The Dervish died, and we threw him into the sea, laughing at his menaces; but in the very same night his words were fulfilled.

"Some of my crew mutinied against me. We fought with insane fury until my adherents were defeated, and I was nailed to the mainmast. But the mutineers also expired of their wounds, and my ship soon became but an immense tomb. My eyes also grew dim, my breathing ceased, I thought I was dying. But it was only a kind of numbness that seized me. The very next night, and at the precise hour that we had thrown the Dervish into the sea, I and all my companions awoke, we were alive, but we could only do and say what we had said and done on that night. Thus we have been sailing these fifty years unable to live or die: for how could we reach land? It was with a savage joy that we sailed many times with full sail in the storm, hoping that at length we might strike some rock, and rest our wearied heads at the bottom of the sea. We did not succeed. But now I shall die. Thanks once more, my unknown deliverer, and if treasures can reward thee, accept my ship as a mark of my gratitude."

After having said this, the Captain's head fell upon his breast, and he expired. Immediately his body also, like the crew's, crumbled to dust. We collected it in a little urn and buried him on shore. I engaged, however, workmen from the town, who repaired my ship thoroughly. After having bartered the goods which I had on board for others at a great profit, I collected a crew, rewarded my friend Muley handsomely, and set sail towards my native place. I made, however, a detour, and landed on many islands and countries where I sold my goods. The Prophet blessed my enterprise. After a lapse of nine months, twice as wealthy as the dying Captain had made me, I reached Balsora. My fellow citizens were astonished at my riches and my fortune, and did not believe anything else but that I must have found the diamond valley of the celebrated traveller Sinbad. I left their belief undisturbed, but henceforth the young people of Balsora, when they were scarcely eighteen years old, were obliged to go out into the world in order like myself to seek their fortune. But I lived quietly and peacefully, and every five years undertook a journey to Mecca, in order to thank the Lord for His blessing at this sacred shrine, and pray for the Captain and his crew that He might receive them into His Paradise.

WILLIAM HOPE HODGSON

~~~~~~~

THE DERELICT

IT'S *THE MATERIAL,*" said the old ship's doctor. . . . "The *Material*, plus the conditions; and, maybe," he added slowly, "a third factor—yes, a third factor; but there, there. . . ." He broke off his half-meditative sentence, and began to charge his pipe.

"Go on, Doctor," we said encouragingly, and with more than a little expectancy. We were in the smokeroom of the *Sand-a-lea*, running across the North Atlantic; and the doctor was a character. He concluded the charging of his pipe, and lit it; then settled himself, and began to express himself more fully.

"So potent is the share of the *Material* in the production of that thing which we name Life, and so eager the Life-Force to express itself, that I am convinced it would, if given the right conditions, make itself manifest even through so hopeless-seeming a medium as a simple block of sawn wood; but nevertheless this does not bring us one iota nearer to its *explanation*.

"Anyway," he continued, "as I suppose you've guessed, I've a yarn to tell you in support of my impression that life is no more a

147

mystery than fire or electricity and that it can take for its purpose and need, the most incredible and unlikely matter.

"It was when I was a young man," he began again, in his queer level way, between puffs at his pipe, "and that is a good many years ago, gentlemen. I had passed my examination; but was so run down with overwork, that it was decided that I had better take a trip to sea. I was by no means well off, and felt very glad, in the end, to secure a nominal post as a doctor in a sailing passenger-clipper, running out to China.

"The name of the ship was the *Bheotpte*, and soon after I had got all my gear aboard, she cast off, and we dropped down the Thames, and next day were well away out in the Channel.

"The captain's name was Gannington, a very decent man; though quite illiterate. The first mate, Mr. Berlies, was a quiet, sternish, reserved man, very well read. The second mate, Mr. Selvern, was, perhaps, by birth and upbringing, the most socially cultured of the three; but he lacked the stamina and indomitable pluck of the other two. He was more of a sensitive; and emotionally and even mentally, the most alert man of the three.

"On our way out, we called at Madagascar, where we landed some of our passengers; then we ran eastward, meaning to call at North-West Cape; but about a hundred degrees east, we encountered a very dreadful weather, which carried away all our sails and sprung the jibboom and fore t'gallant mast.

"The storm carried us northward for several hundred miles, and when it dropped us finally, we found ourselves in a very bad state. The ship had been strained, and had taken some three feet of water through her seams; the main topmast had been sprung, in addition to the jibboom and fore t'gallant mast; two of our boats had gone, as also one of the pigsties (with three fine pigs), this latter having been washed overboard but some half hour before the wind began to ease, which it did quickly; though a very ugly sea ran for some hours after.

"The wind left us just before dark, and when morning came, it brought splendid weather; a calm, mildly undulating sea, and a brilliant sun, with no wind. It showed us also that we were not alone; for about two miles away to the westward was another vessel, which Mr. Selvern, the second mate, pointed out to me.

" 'That's a pretty rum-looking packet, Doctor,' he said, and handed me his glass. I looked through it, at the other vessel, and saw what he meant; at least, I thought I did.

" 'Yes, Mr. Selvern,' I said, 'she's got a pretty old-fashioned look about her.'

He laughed at me, in his pleasant way.

" 'It's easy to see you're not a sailor, Doctor,' he remarked. 'There's a dozen rum things about her. She's a derelict, and has been floating round, by the look of her, for many a score of years. Look at the shape of her counter, and the bows and cut-water. She's as old as the hills, as you might say, and ought to have gone down to Davy Jones a long time ago.

" 'Look at the growths on her, and the thickness of her standing rigging; that's all salt encrustations, I fancy, if you notice the white color. She's been a small barque; but don't you see she's not a yard left aloft? They've all dropped out of the slings; everything rotted away; wonder the standing rigging hasn't gone too. I wish the Old Man would let us take the boat, and have a look at her; she's well worth it.'

"There seemed very little chance of this, however; for all hands were turned-to and kept hard at it all day long, repairing the damage to the masts and gear, and this took a long while, as you may think. Part of the time I gave a hand, heaving on one of the deck-capstans; for the exercise was good for my liver. Old Captain Gannington approved, and I persuaded him to come along and try some of the medicine, which he did; and we grew very chummy over the job.

"We got talking about the derelict, and he remarked how lucky we were not to have run full tilt on to her, in the darkness; for she lay right away to leeward of us, according to the way that we had been drifting in the storm. He also was of the opinion that she had a strange look about her, and that she was pretty old but on this latter point he plainly had far less knowledge than the second mate; for he was, as I have said, an illiterate man, and he knew nothing of seacraft beyond what experience had taught him. He lacked the book knowledge, which the second mate had, of vessels previous to his day, which it appeared the derelict was.

" 'She's an old 'un, Doctor,' was the extent of his observations in this direction.

"Yet, when I mentioned to him that it would be interesting to go aboard, and give her a bit of an overhaul, he nodded his head, as if the idea had already been in his mind.

" 'When the work's over, Doctor,' he said. 'Can't spare the men now, ye know. Got to get all shipshape an' ready as smart as we can. But we'll take my gig, an' go off in the Second Dog Watch. The glass is steady, an' it'll be a bit of jam for us.'

"That evening, after tea, the captain gave orders to clear the gig and get overboard. The second mate was to come with us, and the skipper gave him word to see that two or three lamps were put into the boat, as it would soon fall dark. A little later, we were pulling across the calmness of the sea with a crew of six at the oars, and making very good speed of it.

"Now, gentlemen, I have detailed to you, with great exactness, all the facts, both big and little, so that you can follow step by step each incident in this extraordinary affair; and I want you now to pay the closest attention.

"I was sitting in the stern-sheets, with the second mate and the captain, who was steering; and as we drew nearer and nearer to the stranger, I studied her with an ever-growing attention, as, indeed, did the captain and the second mate. She was, as you know, the west-ward of us, and the sunset was making a great flame or red light to the back of her, so that she showed a little blurred and indistinct by reason of the halation of the light, which almost defeated the eye in any attempt to see her rotting spars and standing rigging, submerged as they were in the fiery glory of the sunset.

"It was because of the effect of the sunset that we had come quite close, comparatively, to the derelict before we saw that she was surrounded by a sort of curious scum, the color of which was difficult to decide upon, by reason of the red light that was in the atmosphere; but which afterwards we discovered to be brown. This scum spread all about the old vessel for many hundreds of yards, in a huge, irregular patch, a great stretch of which reached out to the eastward, upon our starboard side, some score, or so, fathoms away.

" 'Queer stuff,' said Captain Gannington, leaning to the side, and looking over. 'Something in the cargo as 'as gone rotten an' worked out through 'er seams.'

" 'Look at her bows and stern,' said the second mate; 'just look at the growth of her.'

"There were, as he said, great clumpings of strange-looking sea-fungi under the bows and the short counter astern. From the stump of her jibboom and her cutwater, great beards of rime and marine growths hung downward into the scum that held her in. Her blank starboard side was presented to us, all a dead, dirtyish white, streaked and mottled vaguely with dull masses of heavier color.

" 'There's a steam of haze rising off her,' said the second mate, speaking again; 'you can see it against the light. It keeps coming and going. Look!'

"I saw then what he meant—a faint haze or steam, either suspended above the old vessel, or rising from her; and Captain Gannington saw it also.

" 'Spontaneous combustion!' he exclaimed. 'We'll 'ave to watch w'en we lift the 'atches; 'nless it's some poor devil that's got aboard her; but that ain't likely.'

"We were now within a couple of hundred yards of the old derelict, and had entered into the brown scum. As it poured off the lifted oars, I heard one of the men mutter to himself: 'Damn treacle!' and indeed, it was something like it.

"As the boat continued to forge nearer and nearer to the old ship, the scum grew thicker and thicker; so that, at last, it perceptibly slowed us.

" 'Give way, lads! Put some beef to it!' sung out the captain; and thereafter there was no sound, except the panting of the men, and the faint, reiterated *suck, suck,* of the sullen brown scum upon the oars, as the boat was forced ahead. As we went, I was conscious of a peculiar smell in the evening air, and whilst I had no doubt that the puddling of the scum, by the oars, made it rise, I felt that in some way, it was vaguely familiar; yet I could give it no name.

"We were now very close to the old vessel, and presently she was high above us, against the dying light. The captain called out then to 'in with the bow oars, and stand by with the boathook,' which was done.

" 'Aboard there! Ahoy! Aboard there! Ahoy!' shouted Captain Gannington, but there came no answer, only the flat sound of his voice going lost into the open sea, each time he sang out.

" 'Ahoy! Aboard there! Ahoy!' he shouted, time after time; but there was only the weary silence of the old hulk that answered us; and, somehow as he shouted, the while that I stared up half expectantly at her, a queer little sense of oppression, that amounted almost to nervousness came upon me. It passed, but I remember how I was suddenly aware that it was growing dark. Darkness comes fairly rapidly in the tropics, though not so quickly as many fiction-writers seem to think; but it was not that the coming dusk had preceptibly deepened in that brief time, of only a few moments, but rather that my nerves had made me suddenly a little hypersensitive. I mention my state particularly; for I am not a nervy man, normally, and my abrupt touch of nerves is significant, in the light of what happened.

" 'There's no one aboard there!' said Captain Gannington. 'Give way, men!' For the boat's crew had instinctively rested on their oars, as the captain hailed the old craft. The men gave way again; and then the second mate called out excitedly: 'Why, look there, there's our pigsty! See, it's got *Bheotpte* painted on the end. It's drifted down here, and the scum's caught it. What a blessed wonder!'

"It was as he had said, our pigsty that had been washed over-board in the storm, and it was most extraordinary to come across it there.

" 'We'll tow it off with us, when we go,' remarked the captain, and shouted to the crew to get down to their oars; for they were hardly moving the boat, because the scum was so thick, close in around the old ship, that it literally clogged the boat from going ahead. I remember that it struck me in a half-conscious sort of way, as curious that the pigsty, containing our three dead pigs, had managed to drift so far, unaided, whilst we could scarcely manage to *force* the boat in now that we had come right into the scum. But the thought passed from my mind; for so many things happened within the next few minutes.

"The men managed to bring the boat alongside, within a couple of feet of the derelict, and the man with the boathook hooked on.

" ' 'Ave you got 'old there, forrard?' asked the captain. 'Yessir!' said the bow man; and as he spoke there came a queer noise of tearing.

152

" 'What's that?' asked the captain.

" 'It's tore, sir. Tore clean away!' said the man; and his tone showed that he had received something of a shock.

" 'Get a hold again, then!' said Captain Gannington, irritably. 'You don't s'pose this packet was built yesterday! Shove the hook into the main chains.' The man did so gingerly, as you might say; for it seemed to me, in the growing dusk, that he put no strain on the hook, though, of course, there was no need; you see, the boat could not go very far, of herself, in the stuff in which she was embedded. I remember thinking this, also, as I looked up at the bulging side of the old vessel. Then I heard Captain Gannington's voice:

" 'Lord, but she's old! An' what a color, Doctor! She don't half want paint, do she! . . . Now then, somebody—one of them oars.'

"An oar was passed to him, and he leaned it up against the ancient, bulging side, then he paused, and called to the second mate to light a couple of lamps, and stand by to pass them up; for the darkness had settled down now upon the sea.

"The second mate lit two of the lamps, and told one of the men to light a third, and keep it handy in the boat; then he stepped across, with a lamp in each hand, to where Captain Gannington stood by the oar against the side of the ship.

" 'Now, my lad,' said the captain, to the man who had pulled stroke, 'up with you, an' we'll pass ye the lamps.'

"The man jumped to obey; caught the oar, and put his weight upon it, and as he did so, something seemed to give a little.

" 'Look!' cried the second mate, and pointed, lamp in hand, 'It's sunk in!'

"This was true. The oar had made quite an indentation into the bulging, somewhat slimy side of the old vessel.

" 'Mould, I reckon,' said Captain Gannington, bending towards the derelict, to look. Then to the man:

" 'Up you go, my lad, and be smart. . . . Don't stand there waitin'!'

"At that, the man, who had paused a moment as he felt the oar give beneath his weight, began to shin up, and in a few seconds he was aboard, and leaned over the rail for the lamps. These were passed up to him, and the captain called to him to steady the oar. Then Captain Gannington went, calling me to follow, and after me the second mate.

"As the captain put his face over the rail, he gave a cry of astonishment:

" 'Mould, by gum! Mould . . . Tons of it! . . . Good Lord!'

"As I heard him shout that, I scrambled the more eagerly after him, and in a moment or two, I was able to see what he meant— everywhere that the light from the two lamps struck, there was nothing but smooth, great masses and surfaces of a dirty-white mould.

"I climbed over the rail, with the second mate close behind, and stood upon the mould-covered decks. There might have been no planking beneath the mould, for all that our feet could feel. It gave under our tread, with a spongy, puddingy feel. It covered the deck-furniture of the old ship, so that the shape of each article and fitment was often no more than suggested through it.

"Captain Gannington snatched a lamp from the other man, and the second mate reached for the other. They held the lamps high, and we all stared. It was most extraordinary, and, somehow, most abominable. I can think of no other word, gentlemen, that so much describes the predominant feeling that effected me at the moment.

" 'Good Lord!' said Captain Gannington, several times. 'Good Lord!' But neither the second mate nor the man said anything, and for my part I just stared, and at the same time began to smell a little at the air, for there was again a vague odor of something half familiar, that somehow brought to me a sense of half-known fright.

"I turned this way and that, staring, as I have said. Here and there, the mould was so heavy as to entirely disguise what lay beneath, converting the deck-fittings into indistinguishable mounds of mould, all dirty-white, and blotched and veined with irregular, dull purplish markings.

"There was a strange thing about the mould, which Captain Gannington drew attention to—it was that our feet did not crush into it and break the surface, as might have been expected, but merely indented it.

" 'Never seen nothin' like it before! . . . Never!' said the captain, after having stooped with his lamp to examine the mould under our feet. He stamped with his heel, and the stuff gave out a dull, puddingy sound. He stooped again, with a quick movement, and stared, holding the lamp close to the deck. 'Blest if it ain't a reg'lar skin to it!' he said.

"The second mate and the man and I all stooped, and looked at it. The second mate prodded it with his forefinger, and I remember I rapped it several times with my knuckles, listening to the dead sound it gave out, and noticing the close, firm texture of the mould.

" 'Dough!' said the second mate. 'It's just like blessed dough! . . . Pouf!' He stood up with a quick movement. 'I could fancy it stinks a bit,' he said.

"As he said this, I knew suddenly what the familiar thing was in the vague odor that hung about us—it was that the smell had something animal-like in it; something of the same smell only *heavier*, that you smell in any place that is infested with mice. I began to look about with a sudden, very real uneasiness. . . . There might be vast numbers of hungry rats aboard. . . . They might prove exceedingly dangerous, if in a starving condition, yet, as you will understand, somehow I hesitated to put forward my idea as a reason for caution. It was too fanciful.

"Captain Gannington had begun to go aft, along the mould-covered main deck, with the second mate; each of them holding his lamp high up, so as to cast a good light about the vessel. I turned quickly and followed them, the man with me keeping close to my heels, and plainly uneasy. As we went, I became aware that there was a feeling of moisture in the air, and I remembered the slight mist, or smoke, above the hulk, which had made Captain Gannington suggest spontaneous combustion in explanation.

"And always, as we went, there was that vague animal smell; and suddenly I found myself wishing we were well away from the old vessel.

"Abruptly, after a few paces, the captain stopped and pointed at a row of mould-hidden shapes on either side of the main deck. . . . 'Guns,' he said. 'Been a privateer in the old days, I guess; maybe worse! We'll 'ave a look below, doctor; there may be something worth touchin'. She's older than I thought. Mr. Selvern thinks she's about three hundred years old; but I scarce think it.'

"We continued our way aft, and I remember that I found myself walking as lightly and gingerly as possible; as if I were subconsciously afraid of treading through the rotten, mould-hid decks. I think the others had a touch of the same feeling, from the way that they walked. Occasionally the soft mould would grip our heels, releasing them with a little, sullen suck.

"The captain forged somewhat ahead of the second mate, and I know that the suggestion he had made himself, that perhaps there might be something below, worth the carrying away, had stimulated his imagination. The second mate was, however, beginning to feel somewhat the same way that I did; at least, I have that impression. I think if it had not been for what I might truly describe as Captain Gannington's sturdy courage, we should all of us have just gone back over the side very soon; for there was most certainly an unwholesome feeling aboard that made one feel queerly lacking in pluck, and you will soon perceive that this feeling was justified.

"Just as the captain reached the few, mould-covered steps, leading up on to the short half-poop, I was suddenly aware that the feeling of moisture in the air had grown very much more definite. It was perceptible now, intermittently, as a sort of thin, moist, fog-like vapor, that came and went oddly, and seemed to make the decks a little indistinct to the view, this time and that. Once, an odd puff of it beat up suddenly from somewhere, and caught me in the face, carrying a queer, sickly, heavy odor with it, that somehow frightened me strangely, with a suggestion of a waiting and half-comprehended danger.

"We had followed Captain Gannington up the three mould-covered steps, and now went slowly aft along the raised afterdeck.

"By the mizen-mast, Captain Gannington paused, and held his lantern near it. . . .

" 'My word, mister,' he said to the second mate, 'it's fair thickened up with the mould; why, I'll g'antee it's close on four foot thick.' He shone the light down to where it met the deck. 'Good Lord!' he said. 'Look at the sea-lice on it!' I stepped up; and it was as he had said; the sea-lice were thick upon it, some of them huge, not less than the size of large beetles, and all a clear, colorless shade, like water except where there were little spots of gray in them—evidently their internal organisms.

" 'I've never seen the like of them, 'cept on a live cod!' said Captain Gannington, in an extremely puzzled voice. 'My word, but they're whoppers!' Then he passed on, but a few paces farther aft, he stopped again, and held his lamp near to the mould-hidden deck.

156

" 'Lord bless me, Doctor!' he called out, in a low voice. 'Did you ever see the like of that? Why, it's a foot long, if it's a hinch!'

"I stooped over his shoulder, and saw what he meant; it was a clear, colorless creature, about a foot long, and about eight inches high, with a curved back that was extraordinary narrow. As we stared, all in a group, it gave a queer little flick, and was gone.

" 'Jumped!' said the captain. 'Well, if that ain't a giant of all the sea-lice that I've ever seen! I guess it jumped twenty foot clear.' He straightened his back, and scratched his head a moment, swinging the lantern this way and that with the other hand, and staring about us. 'Wot are *they* doin' aboard 'ere!' he said. 'You'll see 'em (little things) on fat cod, an' such like. . . . I'm blowed, Doctor, if I understand.'

"He held his lamp towards a big mound of the mould, that occupied part of the after portion of the low poop-deck, a little foreside of where there came a two-foot high 'break' to a kind of second and loftier poop, that ran away aft to the taffrail. The mound was pretty big, several feet across, and more than a yard high. Captain Gannington walked up to it.

" 'I reckon this's the scuttle,' he remarked, and gave it a heavy kick. The only result was a deep indentation into the huge, whitish hump of mould, as if he had driven his foot into a mass of some doughy substance. Yet, I am not altogether correct in saying that this was the only result; for a certain other thing happened—from a place made by the captain's foot, there came a little gush of purplish fluid, accompanied by a peculiar smell, that was, and was not, half familiar. Some of the mouldlike substance had stuck to the toe of the captain's boot, and from this, likewise, there issued a sweat, as it were, of the same color.

" 'Well!' said Captain Gannington, in surprise, and drew back his foot to make another kick at the hump of mould; but he paused, at an exclamation from the second mate:

" 'Don't sir!' said the second mate.

"I glanced at him, and the light from Captain Gannington's lamp showed me that his face had a bewildered, half-frightened look, as if it were suddenly and unexpectedly half afraid of something, and as if his tongue had given way to his sudden fright, without any intention on his part to speak.

"The captain also turned and stared at him.

" 'Why, mister?' he asked, in a somewhat puzzled voice, through which there sounded just the vaguest hint of annoyance. "We've got to shift this muck, if we're to get below.'

"I looked at the second mate, and it seemed to me that, curiously enough, he was listening less to the captain, than to some other sound.

"Suddenly, he said in a queer voice: 'Listen, everybody!'

"Yet we heard nothing, beyond the faint murmur of the men talking together in the boat alongside.

" 'I don't hear nothin',' said Captain Gannington, after a short pause. 'Do you, Doctor?'

" 'No,' I said.

" 'What was it you thought you heard?' asked the captain, turning again to the second mate. But the second mate shook his head, in a curious, almost irritable way; as if the captain's question interrupted his listening. Captain Gannington stared a moment at him, then held his lantern up, and glanced about him, almost uneasily. I know I felt a queer sense of strain. But the light showed nothing, beyond the grayish, dirty white of the mould in all directions.

" 'Mister Selvern,' said the captain at last, looking at him, 'don't get fancying things. Get hold of your bloomin' self. Ye know ye heard nothin'?'

" 'I'm quite sure I heard something, sir!' said the second mate. 'I seemed to hear. . . .' He broke off sharply, and appeared to listen, with an almost painful intensity.

" 'What did it sound like?' I asked.

" 'It's all right, Doctor,' said Captain Gannington, laughing gently. 'Ye can give him a tonic when we get back. I'm goin' to shift this stuff.'

"He drew back, and kicked for the second time at the ugly mass, which he took to hide the companionway. The result of his kick was startling; for the whole thing wobbled sloppily, like a mound of unhealthy-looking jelly.

"He drew his foot out of it quickly, and took a step backwards, staring, and holding his lamp towards it.

" 'By gum!' he said, and it was plain that he was genuinely startled. 'The blessed thing's gone soft!'

*

"The man had run back several steps from the suddenly flaccid mound, and looked horribly frightened. Though, of what, I am sure he had not the least idea. The second mate stood where he was, and stared. For my part, I know I had a most hideous uneasiness upon me. The captain continued to hold his light towards the wobbling mound, and stare.

" 'It's gone squashy all through!' he said. 'There's no scuttle there. There's no bally woodwork inside that lot! Phoo! What a rum smell!'

"He walked round to the after side of the strange mound, to see whether there might be some signs of an opening into the hull at the back of the great heap of mould-stuff. And then:

" '*Listen!*' said the second mate, again, and in the strangest sort of voice.

"Captain Gannington straightened himself upright, and there succeeded a pause of the most intense quietness, in which there was not even the hum of talk from the men alongside in the boat. We all heard it—a kind of dull, soft, *Thud! Thud! Thud! Thud!* somewhere in the hull under us, yet so vague that I might have been half doubtful I heard it, only that the others did so, too.

"Captain Gannington turned suddenly to where the man stood:

" 'Tell them. . . .' he began. But the fellow cried out something, and pointed. There had come a strange intensity into his somewhat unemotional face; so that the captain's glance followed his action instantly. I stared, also, as you may think. It was the great mound, at which the man was pointing. I saw what he meant.

"From the two gaps made in the mould-like stuff by Captain Gannington's boot, the purple fluid was jetting out in a queerly regular fashion, almost as if it were being forced out by a pump. My word, but I stared! And even as I stared, a larger jet squirted out, and splashed as far as the man, spattering his boots and trouser-legs.

"The fellow had been pretty nervous before, in a stolid, ignorant way, and his funk had been growing steadily; but, at this, he simply let out a yell, and turned about to run. He paused an instant, as if a sudden fear of the darkness that held the decks between him and the boat had taken him. He snatched at the second mate's lantern, tore it out of his hand, and plunged heavily away over the vile stretch of mould.

"Mr. Selvern, the second mate, said not a word; he was just standing, staring at the strange-smelling twin streams of dull purple that were jetting out from the wobbling mound. Captain Gannington, however, roared an order to the man to come back; but the man plunged on and on across the mould, his feet seeming to be clogged by the stuff, as if it had grown suddenly soft. He zigzagged as he ran, the lantern swaying in wild circles as he wrenched his feet free, with a constant *plop, plop;* and I could hear his frightened gasps, even from where I stood.

" 'Come back with that lamp!' roared the captain again; but still the man took no notice, and Captain Gannington was silent an instant, his lips working in a queer, inarticulate fashion; as if he were stunned momentarily by the very violence of his anger at the man's insubordination. And, in the silence, I heard the sound again: *Thud! Thud! Thud! Thud!* Quite distinctly now, beating, it seemed suddenly to me, right down under my feet, but deep.

"I stared down at the mould on which I was standing, with a quick, disgusting sense of the terrible all about me; then I looked at the captain, and tried to say something, without appearing frightened. I saw that he had turned again to the mound, and all the anger had gone out of his face. He had his lamp out toward the mound, and was listening. There was a further moment of absolute silence; at least, I know that I was not conscious of any sound at all, in all the world, except that extraordinary *Thud! Thud! Thud! Thud!* down somewhere in the huge bulk under us.

"The captain shifted his feet, with a sudden, nervous movement; and as he lifted them, the mould went *plop, plop.* He looked quickly at me, trying to smile, as if he were not thinking anything very much about it. 'What do you make of it, Doctor?' he said.

" 'I think. . . .' I began. But the second mate interrupted with a single word; his voice pitched a little high, in a tone that made us both stare instantly at him.

" 'Look!' he said, and pointed at the mound. The thing was all of a slow quiver. A strange ripple ran outward from it, along the deck, as you will see a ripple run inshore out of a calm sea. It reached a mound a little fore-side of us, which I supposed to be the cabin skylight; and in a moment the second mound sank nearly level with the surrounding decks, quivering floppily in a most extraordinary fashion. A sudden quick tremor took the mould right under the second mate, and he gave out a hoarse cry, and held his arms out on each side of him, to keep his balance. The tremor in the mould spread, and Captain Gannington swayed, and spread his feet with a sudden curse of fright. The second mate jumped across to him, and caught him by the wrist.

" 'The boat, sir!' he said, saying the very thing that I had lacked the pluck to say. 'For God's sake. . . .'

"But he never finished; for a tremendous hoarse scream cut off his words. They hove themselves round, and looked. I could see without turning. The man who had run from us, was standing in the waist of the ship, about a fathom from the starboard bulwarks.

"He was swaying from side to side and screaming in a dreadful fashion. He appeared to be trying to lift his feet, and the light from his swaying lantern showed an almost incredible sight. All about him the mould was in active movement. His feet had sunk out of sight. The stuff appeared to be *lapping* at his legs; and abruptly his bare flesh showed.

"The hideous stuff had rent his trouser-legs away, as if they were paper. He gave out a simply sickening scream, and, with a vast effort, wrenched one leg free. It was partly destroyed. The next instant he pitched face downward, and the stuff heaped itself upon him, as if it were actually alive, with a dreadful savage life. It was simply infernal. The man had gone from sight. Where he had fallen was now a writhing mound, in constant and horrible increase, as the mould appeared to move toward it in strange ripples from all sides.

"Captain Gannington and the second mate were stone silent, in amazed and incredulous horror; but I had begun to reach towards a grotesque and terrific conclusion, both helped and hindered by my professional training.

"From the men in the boat alongside, there was a loud shouting, and I saw two of their faces appear suddenly above the rail. They showed clearly, a moment, in the light from the lamp which the man had snatched from Mr. Selvern; for strangely enough, this lamp was standing upright and unharmed on the deck, a little way fore-side of that dreadful, elongated, growing mound, that still swayed and writhed with an incredible horror.

The lamp rose and fell on the passing ripples of the mould just—for all the world—as you will see a boat rise and fall on little swells. It is of some interest to me now, psychologically, to remember how that rising and falling lantern brought home to me, more than anything, the incomprehensible, dreadful strangeness of it all.

"The men's faces disappeared, with sudden yells, as if they had slipped or been suddenly hurt; and there was a fresh uproar of shouting from the boat. The men were calling to us to come away; to come away. In the same instant, I felt my left boot drawn suddenly and forcibly downward, with a horrible painful grip. I wrenched it free, with a yell of angry fear. Forrard of us, I saw that the vile surface was all a-move, and abruptly I found myself shouting in a queer frightened voice:

" 'The boat, Captain! The boat, Captain!'

"Captain Gannington stared round at me, over his right shoulder, in a peculiar, dull way, that told me he was utterly dazed with bewilderment and the incomprehensibleness of it all. I took a quick, clogged, nervous step towards him, and gripped his arm and shook it fiercely.

" 'The boat!' I shouted at him. 'The boat! For God's sake, tell the men to bring the boat aft!'

"Then the mould must have drawn his feet down; for, abruptly, he bellowed fiercely with terror, his momentary apathy giving place to furious energy. His thick-set, vastly muscular body doubled and whirled with his enormous effort, and he struck out madly, dropping the lantern. He tore his feet free, something ripped as he did so. The *reality* and necessity of the situation had come upon him, brutishly real, and he was roaring to the men in the boat:

" 'Bring the boat aft! Bring 'er aft! Bring 'er aft!'

"The second mate and I were shouting the same thing, madly.

" 'For God's sake be smart, lads!' roared the captain, and he stooped quickly for his lamp, which still burned. His feet were gripped again, and he hove them out, blaspheming breathlessly, and leaping a yard high with his effort. Then he made a run for the side, wrenching his feet free at each step. In the same instant, the second mate cried out something, and grabbed at the captain.

" 'It's got hold of my feet! It's got hold of my feet!' the second mate screamed. His feet had disappeared up to his boot-tops, and Captain Gannington caught him round the waist with his powerful left arm, gave a mighty heave, and the next instant had him free; but both his boot-soles had almost gone.

"For my part, I jumped madly from foot to foot, to avoid the plucking of the mould; and suddenly I made a run for the ship's side. But before I got there, a queer gap came in the mould, between us and the side, at least a couple of feet wide, and how deep I don't know. It closed up in an instant, and all the mould, where the gap had been, went into a sort of flurry of horrible ripplings, so that I ran back from it; for I did not dare to put my foot upon it. Then the captain was shouting at me:

" 'Aft, Doctor! Aft, Doctor! This way, Doctor! Run!' I saw then that he had passed me, and was up on the after raised portion of the poop. He had the second mate thrown like a sack, all loose and quiet, over his left shoulder; for Mr. Selvern had fainted, and his long legs flopped, limp and helpless, against the captain's massive knees as the captain ran. I saw, with a queer unconscious noting of minor details, how the torn soles of the second mate's boots flapped and jigged, as the captain staggered aft.

" 'Boat ahoy! Boat ahoy! Boat ahoy!' shouted the captain; and then I was beside him, shouting also. The men were answering with loud yells of encouragement, and it was plain they were working desperately to force the boat aft, through the thick scum about the ship.

"We reached the ancient, mould-hid taffrail, and slewed about, breathlessly, in the half darkness, to see what was happening. Captain Gannington had left his lantern by the big mound, when he picked up the second mate; and as we stood gasping, we discovered suddenly that all the mould between us and the light was full of movement. Yes, the part on which we stood, for about six or eight feet forrard of us was still firm.

"Every couple of seconds, we shouted to the men to hasten, and they kept calling to us that they would be with us in an instant. And all the time, we watched the deck of that dreadful hulk, I felt, for my part, literally sick with mad suspense, and ready to jump overboard into that filthy scum all about us.

"Down somewhere in the huge bulk of the ship, there was all the time the extraordinary, dull, ponderous *Thud! Thud! Thud! Thud!* growing ever louder. I seemed to feel the whole hull of the derelict beginning to quiver and thrill with each dull beat. And to me, with the grotesque and monstrous suspicion of what made that noise, it was, at once, the most dreadful and incredible sound I have ever heard.

"As we waited desperately for the boat, I scanned incessantly so much of the gray-white bulk as the lamp showed. The whole of the decks seemed to be in strange movement. Forrard of the lamp I could see, indistinctly, the moundings of the mould swaying and nodding hideously, beyond the circle of the brightest rays. Nearer, and full in the glow of the lamp, the mound which should have indicated the skylight, was swelling steadily . There were ugly purple veinings on it, and as it swelled, it seemed to me that the veinings and mottling on it were becoming plainer—rising, as though embossed upon it, as you will see the veins stand out on the body of a powerful full-blooded horse. It was most extraordinary. The mound that we had supposed to cover the companionway had sunk flat with the surrounding mould, and I could not see that it jetted out any more of the purplish fluid.

"A quaking movement of the mould began, away forward of the lamp, and came flurrying away aft towards us; and at the sight of that, I climbed up on to the spongy-feeling taffrail, and yelled afresh for the boat. The men answered with a shout, which told me they were nearer, but the beastly scum was so thick that it was evidently a fight to move the boat at all. Beside me, Captain Gannington was shaking the second mate furiously, and the man stirred and began to moan. The captain shook him awake.

" 'Wake up! Wake up, Mister!' he shouted.

"The second mate staggered out of the captain's arms, and collapsed suddenly, shrieking: 'My feet! Oh, God! My feet!' The captain and I lugged him off the mould, and got him into a sitting position upon the taffrail, where he kept up a continual moaning.

" 'Hold 'em, Doctor,' said the Captain, and whilst I did so, he ran forrard a few yards, and peered down over the starboard quarter rail. 'For God's sake, be smart, lads! Be smart!' he shouted down to the men; and they answered him, breathless, from close at hand; yet still too far away for the boat to be any use to us on the instant.

"I was holding the moaning, half-unconscious officer, and staring forrard along the poop decks. The flurrying of the mould was coming aft, slowly and noiselessly. And then, suddenly, I saw something closer:

164

" 'Look out, Captain!' I shouted; and even as I shouted, the mould near to him gave a sudden peculiar slobber. I had seen a ripple stealing towards him through the horrible stuff. He gave an enormous, clumsy leap, and landed near to us on the sound part of the mould, but the movement followed him. He turned and faced it, swearing fiercely. All about his feet there came abruptly little gapings, which made horrid sucking noises.

" 'Come *back*, Captain!' I yelled. 'Come back, *quick!*' and he stamped insanely at it, and leaped back, his boot torn half off his foot. He swore madly with pain and anger, and jumped swiftly for the taffrail.

" 'Come on, Doctor! Over we go!' he called. Then he remembered the filthy scum, and hesitated, roaring out desperately to the men to hurry. I started down, also.

" 'The second mate?' I said.

" 'I'll take charge, Doctor,' said Captain Gannington, and caught hold of Mr. Selvern. As he spoke, I thought I saw something beneath us, outlined against the scum. I leaned out over the stern, and peered. There was something under the port quarter.

" 'There's something down there, Captain!' I called, and pointed in the darkness.

"He stooped far over, and stared.

" 'A boat, by gum! A *boat!*' he yelled, and began to wriggle swiftly along the taffrail, dragging the second mate after him. I followed.

" 'A boat it is, sure!' he exclaimed, a few moments later, and, picking up the second mate clear of the rail, he hove him down into the boat, where he fell with a crash into the bottom.

" 'Over ye go, Doctor!' he yelled at me, and pulled me bodily off the rail, and dropped me after the officer. As he did so, I felt the whole of the ancient, spongy rail give a peculiar sickening quiver, and begin to wobble. I fell onto the second mate, and the captain came after, almost in the same instant; but fortunately he landed clear of us, on to the fore thwart, which broke under his weight, with a loud crack and splintering of wood.

" 'Thank God!' I heard him mutter. 'Thank God! . . . I guess that was a mighty near thing to goin' to hell.'

"He struck a match, just as I got to my feet, and between us we got the second mate straightened out on one of the after thwarts. We shouted to the men in the boat, telling them where we were, and saw the light of their lantern shining round to tell us they were doing their best, and then, while we waited, Captain Gannington struck another match, and began to overhaul the boat we had dropped into. She was a modern, two-oared boat, and on the stern there was painted *Cyclone Glasgow*. She was in pretty fair condition, and had evidently drifted into the scum and been held by it.

"Captain Gannington struck several matches, and went forrard toward the derelict. Suddenly he called to me, and I jumped over the thwarts to him.

" 'Look, Doctor,' he said; and I saw what he meant—a mass of bones, up in the bow of the boat. I stooped over them and looked. They were the bones of at least three people, all mixed together, in an extraordinary fashion, and quite clean and dry. I had a sudden thought concerning the bones; but I said nothing; for my thought was vague, in some ways, and concerned the grotesque and incredible suggestion that had come to me, as to the cause of that ponderous, dull *Thud! Thud! Thud!* that beat on so infernally within the hull, and was plain to hear even now that we had a sick, horrible, mental picture of that frightful wriggling mound aboard the hulk.

"As Captain Gannington struck a final match I saw something that sickened me, and the captain saw it in the same instant. The match went out, and he fumbled clumsily for another, and struck it. We saw the thing again. We had not been mistaken. . . . A great lip of gray-white was protruding in over the edge of the boat—a great lappet of the mould was coming steadily towards us; a live mess of *the very hull itself*. And suddenly Captain Gannington yelled out, in so many words, the grotesque and incredible thing I was thinking:

" *'She's alive!'*

"I never heard such a sound of *comprehension* and terror in a man's voice. The very horrified assurance of it, made actual to me the thing that, before, had lurked in my subconscious mind. I knew he was right; I knew that the explanation, my reason and my training, both repelled and reached towards, was the true one. . . . I wonder whether anyone can possibly understand our feelings in that moment. . . . The unmitigable horror of it, and the *incredibleness*.

"As the light of the match burned up fully, I saw that the mass of living matter, coming towards us, was streaked and veined with purple, the veins standing out, enormously distended. The whole thing quivered continuously to each ponderous *Thud! Thud! Thud!* of that gargantuan organ that pulsed within the huge gray-white hulk. The flame of the match reached the captain's fingers, and there came to me a little sickly whiff of burned flesh; but he seemed unconscious of any pain. Then the flame went out, in a brief sizzle, yet at the last moment, I had seen an extraordinary raw look, become visible upon the end of that monstrous, protruding lappet. It had become dewed with a hideous, purplish sweat. And with the darkness, there came a sudden charnel-like stench.

"I heard the match-box split in Captain Gannington's hands, as he wrenched it open. Then he swore, in a queer frightened voice; for he had come to the end of his matches. He turned clumsily in the darkness, and tumbled over the nearest thwart, in his eagerness to get to the stern of the boat, and I after him; for he knew that thing was coming towards us through the darkness, reaching over that piteous mingled heap of human bones, all jumbled together in the bows. We shouted madly to the men, and for answer saw the bows of the boat emerge dimly into view, round the starboard counter of the derelict.

" 'Thank God!' I gasped out; but Captain Gannington yelled to them to show a light. Yet this they could not do, for the lamp had just been stepped on, in their desperate efforts to force the boat around to us.

" 'Quick! Quick!' I shouted.

" 'For God's sake be smart, men!' roared the captain; and both of us faced the darkness under the port counter, out of which we knew (but could not see) the thing was coming toward us.

" 'An oar! Smart now; pass me an oar!' shouted the captain; and reached out his hand through the gloom toward the oncoming boat. I saw a figure stand up in the bows, and hold something out to us, across the intervening yards of scum. Captain Gannington swept his hands through the darkness, and encountered it.

" 'I've got it. Let go there!' he said, in a quick, tense voice.

"In the same instant, the boat we were in was pressed over suddenly to starboard by some tremendous weight. Then I heard the captain shout: 'Duck y'r head, Doctor,' and directly afterwards he swung the heavy, fourteen-foot ash oar round his head, and struck into the darkness. There came a sudden squelch, and he struck again, with a savage grunt of fierce energy. At the second blow, the boat righted, with a slow movement, and directly afterwards the other boat bumped gently into ours.

"Captain Gannington dropped the oar, and springing across to the second mate, hove him up off the thwart, and pitched him with knee and arms clear in over the bows among the men; then he shouted to me to follow, which I did, and he came after me, bringing the oar with him. We carried the second mate aft, and the captain shouted to the men to back the boat a little; then they got her bows clear of the boat we had just left, and so headed out through the scum for the open sea.

" 'Where's Tom 'Arrison?' gasped one of the men, in the midst of his exertions. He happened to be Tom Harrison's particular chum; and Captain Gannington answered him briefly enough:

" 'Dead! Pull! Don't talk!'

"Now, difficult as it had been to force the boat through the scum to our rescue, the difficulty to get clear seemed tenfold. After some five minutes pulling, the boat seemed hardly to have moved a fathom, if so much; and a quite dreadful fear took me afresh; which one of the panting men put suddenly into words:

" 'It's got us!' he gasped out; 'same as poor Tom!' It was the man who had inquired where Harrison was.

" 'Shut y'r mouth and *pull!*' roared the captain. And so another few minutes passed. Abruptly, it seemed to me that the dull, ponderous *Thud! Thud! Thud!* came more plainly through the dark, and I stared intently over the stern. I sickened a little; for I could almost swear that the dark mass of the monster was actually *nearer* . . . that it was coming nearer to us through the darkness. Captain Gannington must have had the same thought; for after a brief look into the darkness, he made one jump to the stroke-oar, and began to double bank it.

" 'Get forrid under the thwarts, Doctor!' he said to me, rather breathlessly. 'Get in the bows, an' see if you can't free the stuff a bit round the bows.'

"I did as he told me, and a minute later I was in the bows of the boat, puddling the scum from side to side with the boathook, and trying to break up the viscid, clinging muck. A heavy, almost animal-like odor rose off it, and all the air seemed full of the deadening smell. I shall never find words to tell any one the whole horror of it—the threat that seemed to hang in the very air around us; and, but a little astern, that incredible thing, coming, as I firmly believe, nearer, and the scum holding us like half-melted glue.

"The minutes passed in a deadly, eternal fashion, and I kept staring back.

"Abruptly, Captain Gannington sang out:

" 'We're gaining, lads. Pull!' And I felt the boat forge ahead perceptibly, as they gave way, with renewed hope and energy. There was soon no doubt of it; for presently that hideous *Thud! Thud! Thud! Thud!* had grown quite dim and vague somewhat astern, and I could no longer see the derelict, for the night had come down tremendously dark, and all the sky was thick overset with heavy clouds. As we drew nearer and nearer to the edge of the scum, the boat moved more and more freely, until suddenly we emerged with a clean, sweet, fresh sound, into the open sea.

" 'Thank God!' I said aloud, and drew in the boathook, and made my way aft again to where Captain Gannington now sat once more at the tiller. I saw him looking anxiously up at the sky, and across to where the lights of our vessel burned, and again he would seem to listen intently; so that I found myself listening also.

" 'What's that, Captain?' I said sharply; for it seemed to me that I heard a sound far astern, something between a queer whine and a low whistling. 'What's that?'

" 'It's the wind, Doctor,' he said, in a low voice. 'I wish to God we were aboard.'

"Then, to the men: 'Pull! Put y'r backs into it, or ye'll never put y'r teeth through good bread again!'

"The men obeyed nobly, and we reached the vessel safely, and had the boat safely stowed, before the storm came, which it did in a furious white smother out of the west. I could see it for some minutes beforehand, tearing the sea, in the gloom, into a wall of phosphorescent foam; and as it came nearer, that peculiar whining, piping sound grew louder and louder, until it was like a vast steam-whistle, rushing towards us across the sea.

"And when it did come, we got it very heavy indeed; so that the morning showed us nothing but a welter of white seas; and that grim derelict was many a score of miles away in the smother, lost as utterly as our hearts could wish to lose her.

"When I came to examine the second mate's feet, I found them in a very extraordinary condition. The soles of them had the appearance of having been partly digested. I know of no other word that so exactly describes their condition; and the agony the man suffered must have been dreadful.

"Now," concluded the doctor, "that is what I call a case in point. If we could know exactly what that old vessel had originally been loaded with, and the juxtaposition of the various articles of her cargo, plus the heat and time she had endured, plus one or two other only guessable quantities, we should have solved the chemistry of the Life-Force, gentlemen. Not necessarily the *origin*, mind you; but, at least, we should have taken a big step on the way.

"I've often regretted that gale, you know—in a way, that is, in a way! It was a most amazing discovery; but, at the time, I had nothing but thankfulness to be rid of it. . . . A most amazing chance. I often think of the way the monster woke out of its torpor. And that scum. . . . The dead pigs caught in it. . . . I fancy that was a grim kind of net, gentlemen. . . . It caught many things. . . . It. . . ."

The old doctor sighed and nodded.

"If I could have had her bill of lading," he said, his eyes full of regret. "If—it might have told me something to help. But, anyway. . . ." He began to fill his pipe again. "I suppose," he ended, looking round at us gravely, "I s'pose we humans are an ungrateful lot of beggars, at the best!

"But what a chance! What a chance—eh?"

JONAS LIE

THE CORMORANTS
OF ANDVÆR

OUTSIDE ANDVÆR LIES AN island, the haunt of wild-birds, which no man can land upon, for the sea is never so quiet; the sea-swell girds it round about with sucking whirlpools and dashing breakers.

On fine summer days something sparkles there through the sea-foam like a large gold ring; and, time out of mind, folks have fancied there was a treasure there left by some pirates of old.

At sunset, sometimes, there looms forth from thence a vessel with a castle astern, and a glimpse is caught now and then of an old-fashioned galley. There it lies as if in a tempest, and carves its way along through heavy white rollers.

Along the rocks sit the cormorants in a long black row, lying in wait for dogfish.

But there was a time when one knew the exact number of these birds. There was never more nor less of them than twelve, while

171

upon a stone, out in the sea-mist, sat the thirteenth, but it was only visible when it rose and flew right over the island.

The only persons who lived near the Vær* at winter time, long after the fishing season was over, was a woman and a slip of a girl. Their business was to guard the scaffolding poles for drying fish against the birds of prey, who had such a villainous trick of hacking at the drying-ropes.

The young girl had thick coal-black hair, and a pair of eyes that peeped at folk so oddly. One might almost have said that she was like the cormorants outside there, and she had never seen much else all her life. Nobody knew who her father was.

Thus they lived till the girl had grown up.

It was found that, in the summertime, when the fishermen went out to the Vær to fetch away the dried fish, the young fellows began underbidding each other, so as to be selected for that special errand.

Some gave up their share of profits, and others their wages; and there was a general complaint in all the villages round about that on such occasions no end of betrothals were broken off.

But the cause of it all was the girl out yonder with the odd eyes.

For all her rough and ready ways, she had something about her, said those she chatted with, that there was no resisting. She turned the heads of all the young fellows; it seemed as if they couldn't live without her.

The first winter a lad wooed her who had both house and warehouse of his own.

"If you come again in the summertime, and give me the right gold ring I will be wedded by, something may come of it," said she.

And, sure enough, in the summer time the lad was there again.

He had a lot of fish to fetch away, and she might have had a gold ring as heavy and as bonnie as heart could wish for.

"The ring I must have lies beneath the wreckage, in the iron chest, over at the island yonder," said she, "that is, if you love me enough to dare fetch it."

But then the lad grew pale.

---

* A fishing-station, where fishermen assemble periodically.

He saw the sea-bore rise and fall out there l
foam on the bright warm summer day, and on
cormorants sleeping in the sunshine.

"Dearly do I love thee," said he, "but suc
would mean my burial, not my bridal."

The same instant the thirteenth cormorant rose from his stone
in the misty foam, and flew right over the island.

Next winter the steersman of a yacht came a wooing. For two
years he had gone about and hugged his misery for her sake, and he
got the same answer.

"If you come again in the summertime, and give me the right
gold ring I will be wedded with, something may come of it."

Out to the Vær he came again on Midsummer Day.

But when he heard where the gold ring lay, he sat and wept the
whole day till evening, when the sun began to dance northwestward
into the sea.

Then the thirteenth cormorant arose, and flew right over the
island.

There was nasty weather during the third winter.

There were manifold wrecks, and on the keel of a boat,
which came driving ashore, hung an exhausted young lad by his
knife-belt.

But they couldn't get the life back into him, roll and rub him
about in the boathouse as they might.

Then the girl came in.

" 'Tis my bridegroom!" said she.

And she laid him in her bosom, and sat with him the whole
night through, and put warmth into his heart.

And when the morning came, his heart beat.

"Methought I lay betwixt the wings of a cormorant, and leaned
my head against its downy breast," said he.

The lad was ruddy and handsome, with curly hair, and he
couldn't take his eyes away from the girl.

He took work upon the Vær.

But off he must needs be gadding and chatting with her, be it
never so early and never so late.

So it fared with him as it had fared with the others.

It seemed to him that he could not live without her, and on the
day when he was bound to depart, he wooed her.

"*Thee* I will not fool," said she. "Thou hast lain on my breast, and I would give my life to save thee from sorrow. Thou shalt have me if thou wilt place the betrothal ring upon my finger; but longer than the day lasts thou canst not keep me. And now I will wait, and long after thee with a horrible longing, till the summer comes."

On Midsummer Day the youth came thither in his boat all alone.

Then she told him of the ring that he must fetch for her from among the skerries.

"If thou hast taken me off the keel of a boat, thou mayest cast me forth yonder again," said the lad. "Live without thee I cannot."

But as he laid hold of the oars in order to row out, she stepped into the boat with him and sat in the stern. Wondrous fair was she!

It was beautiful summer weather, and there was a swell upon the sea: wave followed upon wave in long bright rollers.

The lad sat there, lost in the sight of her, and he rowed and rowed till the insucking breakers roared and thundered among the skerries; the groundswell was strong, and the frothing foam spurted up as high as towers.

"If thy life is dear to thee, turn back now," said she.

"Thou art dearer to me than life itself," he made answer.

But just as it seemed to the lad as if the prow were going under, and the jaws of death were gaping wide before him, it grew all at once as still as a calm, and the boat could run ashore as if there was never a billow there.

On the island lay a rusty old ship's anchor half out of the sea.

"In the iron chest which lies beneath the anchor is my dowry," said she; "carry it up into thy boat, and put the ring that thou seest on my finger. With this thou dost make me thy bride. So now I am thine till the sun dances northwestward into the sea."

It was a gold ring with a red stone in it, and he put it on her finger and kissed her.

In a cleft on the skerry was a patch of green grass. There they sat them down, and they were ministered to in wondrous wise, how he knew not nor cared to know, so great was his joy.

"Midsummer Day is beauteous," said she, "and I am young and thou art my bridegroom. And now we'll to our bridal bed."

So bonnie was she that he could not contain himself for love.

But when night drew nigh, and the sun began to dance out into the sea, she kissed him and shed tears.

"Beauteous is the summer day," said she, "and still more beauteous is the summer evening; but now the dusk cometh."

And all at once it seemed to him as if she were becoming older and older and fading right away.

When the sun went below the sea-margin there lay before him on the skerry some mouldering linen rags and nought else.

Calm was the sea, and in the clear Midsummer night there flew *twelve* cormorants out over the sea.

MORGAN ROBERTSON

FROM THE DARKNESS
AND THE DEPTHS

I HAD KNOWN HIM for a painter of renown—a master of his art, whose pictures, which sold for high prices, adorned museums, the parlors of the rich, and, when on exhibition, were hung low and conspicuous. Also, I knew him for an expert photographer— an "art photographer," as they say, one who dealt with this branch of industry as a fad, an amusement, and who produced pictures that in composition, lights, and shades rivaled his productions with the brush.

His cameras were the best that the market could supply, yet he was able, from his knowledge of optics and chemistry, to improve them for his own uses far beyond the ability of the makers. His studio was filled with examples of his work, and his mind was stocked with information and opinions on all subjects ranging from international policies to the servant-girl problem.

176

He was a man of the world, gentlemanly and successful, about sixty years old, kindly and gracious of manner, and out of this kindliness and graciousness had granted me the compliment of his friendship, and access to his studio whenever I felt like calling upon him.

Yet it never occurred to me that the wonderful and technically correct marines hanging on his walls were due to anything but the artist's conscientious study of his subject, and only his casual mispronunciation of the word "leeward," which landsmen pronounce as spelled, but which rolls off the tongue of a sailor, be he former dock rat or naval officer, as "looward," and his giving the long sounds to the vowels of the words "patent" and "tackle," that induced me to ask if he had ever been to sea.

"Why, yes," he answered. "Until I was thirty I had no higher ambition than to become a skipper of some craft; but I never achieved it. The best I did was to sign first mate for one voyage—and that one was my last. It was on that voyage that I learned something of the mysterious properties of light, and it made me a photographer, then an artist. You are wrong when you say that a searchlight cannot penetrate fog."

"But it has been tried," I remonstrated.

"With ordinary light. Yes, of course, subject to refraction, reflection, and absorption by the millions of minute globules of water it encounters."

We had been discussing the wreck of the *Titanic*, the most terrible marine disaster of history, the blunders of construction and management, and the later proposed improvements as to the lowering of boats and the location of ice in a fog.

Among these considerations was also the plan of carrying a powerful searchlight whose beam would illumine the path of a twenty-knot liner and render objects visible in time to avoid them. In regard to this I had contended that a searchlight could not penetrate fog, and if it could, would do as much harm as good by blinding and confusing the watch officers and lookouts on other craft.

"But what other kind of light can be used?" I asked, in answer to his mention of ordinary light.

"Invisible light," he answered. "I do not mean the Röntgen ray, nor the emanation from radium, both of which are invisible, but neither of which is light, in that neither can be reflected nor

177

refracted. Both will penetrate many different kinds of matter, but it needs reflection or refraction to make visible an object on which it impinges. Understand?"

"Hardly," I answered dubiously. "What kind of visible light is there, if not radium or the Röntgen ray? You can photograph with either, can't you?"

"Yes, but to see what you have photographed you must develop the film. And there is no time for that aboard a fast steamer running through the ice and the fog. No, it is mere theory, but I have an idea that the ultraviolet light—the actinic rays beyond the violet end of the spectrum, you know—will penetrate fog to a great distance, and in spite of its higher refractive power, which would distort and magnify an object, it is better than nothing."

"But what makes you think that it will penetrate fog?" I queried. "And if it is invisible itself, how will it illumine an object?"

"As to your first question," he answered, with a smile, "it is well known to surgeons that ultraviolet light will penetrate the human body to the depth of an inch, while the visible rays are reflected at the surface. And it has been known to photographers for fifty years that this light—easily isolated by dispersion through prisms—will act on a sensitized plate in an utterly dark room."

"Granted," I said. "But how about the second question? How can you see by this light?"

""There you have me," he answered. "It will need a quicker development than any now known to photography—a traveling film, for instance, that will show the picture of an iceberg or a ship before it is too late to avoid it—a traveling film sensitized by a quicker acting chemical than any now used."

"Why not puzzle it out?" I asked. "It would be a wonderful invention."

"I am too old," he answered dreamily. "My life work is about done. But other and younger men will take it up. We have made great strides in optics. The moving picture is a fact. Colored photographs are possible. The ultraviolet microscope shows us objects hitherto invisible because smaller than the wave length of visible light. We shall ultimately use this light to see through opaque objects. We shall see colors never imagined by the human mind, but which have existed since the beginning of light.

"We shall see new hues in the sunset, in the rainbow, in the flowers and foliage of forest and field. We may possibly see creatures in the air above never seen before.

"We shall certainly see creatures from the depths of the sea, where visible light cannot reach—creatures whose substance is of such a nature that it will not respond to the light it has never been exposed to—a substance which is absolutely transparent because it will not absorb, and appear black; will not reflect, and show a color of some kind; and will not refract, and distort objects seen through it."

"What!" I exclaimed. "Do you think there are invisible creatures?"

He looked gravely at me for a moment, then said: "You know that there are sounds that are inaudible to the human ear because of their too rapid vibration, others that are audible to some, but not to all. There are men who cannot hear the chirp of a cricket, the tweet of a bird, or the creaking of a wagon wheel.

"You know that there are electric currents much stronger in voltage than is necessary to kill us, but of wave frequency so rapid that the human tissue will not respond, and we can receive such currents without a shock. And I *know*"—he spoke with vehemence—"that there are creatures in the deep sea of color invisible to the human eye, for I have not only felt such a creature, but seen its photograph taken by the ultraviolet light."

"Tell me," I asked breathlessly. "Creatures solid, but invisible?"

"Creatures solid, and invisible because absolutely transparent. It is long since I have told the yarn. People would not believe me, and it was so horrible an experience that I have tried to forget it. However, if you care for it, and are willing to lose your sleep tonight, I'll give it to you."

He reached for a pipe, filled it, and began to smoke; and as he smoked and talked, some of the glamor and polish of the successful artist and club-man left him. He was an old sailor, spinning a yarn.

"It was about thirty years ago," he began, "or, to be explicit, twenty-nine years this coming August, at the time of the great Java earthquake. You've heard of it—how it killed seventy thousand people, thirty thousand of whom were drowned by the tidal wave.

"It was a curious phenomenon; Krakatoa Island, a huge conical mountain rising from the bottom of Sunda Strait, went out of existence, while in Java a mountain chain was leveled, and up from the bowels of the earth came an iceberg—as you might call it—that floated a hundred miles on a stream of molten lava before melting.

"I was not there; I was two hundred miles to the sou'west, first mate of one of those old-fashioned, soft-pine, centerboard barkentines—three sticks the same length, you know—with the mainmast stepped on the port side of the keel to make room for the centerboard—a craft that would neither stay, nor wear, nor scud, nor heave to, like a decent vessel.

"But she had several advantages; she was new, and well painted, deck, topsides, and bottom. Hence her light timbers and planking were not water-soaked. She was fastened with 'trunnels,' not spikes and bolts, and hemp–rigged.

"Perhaps there was not a hundredweight of iron aboard of her, while her hemp rigging, though heavier than water, was lighter than wire rope, and so, when we were hit by the backwash of that tidal wave, we did not sink, even though butts were started from one end to the other of the flimsy hull, and all hatches were ripped off.

"I have called it the backwash, yet we may have had a tidal wave of our own; for, though we had no knowledge of the frightful catastrophe at Java, still there had been for days several submarine earthquakes all about us, sending fountains of water, steam bubbles, and mud from the sea bed into the air.

"As the soundings were over two thousand fathoms in that neighborhood, you can imagine the seismic forces at work beneath us. There had been no wind for days, and no sea, except the agitation caused by the upheavals. The sky was a dull mud color, and the sun looked like nothing but a dark, red ball, rising day by day in the east, to move overhead and set in the west. The air was hot, sultry, and stifling, and I had difficulty in keeping the men—a big crew—at work.

"The conditions would try anybody's temper, and I had my own troubles. There was a passenger on board, a big, fat, highly educated German—a scientist and explorer—whom we had taken aboard at some little town on the West Australian coast, and who was to leave us at Batavia, where he could catch a steamer for Germany.

"He had a whole laboratory with him, with scientific instruments that I didn't know the names of, with maps he had made, stuffed beasts and birds he had killed, and a few live ones which he kept in cages and attended to himself in the empty hold; for we were flying light, you know, without even ballast aboard, and bound to Batavia for a cargo.

"It was after a few eruptions from the bottom of the sea that he got to be a nuisance; he was keenly interested in the strange dead fish and nondescript creatures that had been thrown up. He declared them new, unknown to science, and wore out my patience with entreaties to haul them aboard for examination and classification.

"I obliged him for a time, until the decks stank with dead fish, and the men got mutinous. Then I refused to advance the interests of science any farther, and, in spite of his excitement and pleadings, refused to litter the decks any more. But he got all he wanted of the unclassified and unknown before long.

"Tidal wave, you know, is a name we give to any big wave, and it has no necessary connection with the tides. It may be the big third wave of a series—just a little bigger than usual; it may be the ninth, tenth, and eleventh waves merged into one huge comber by uneven wind pressure; it may be the back-wash from an earthquake that depresses the nearest coast, and it may be—as I think it was in our case—a wave sent out by an upheaval from the sea bed. At any rate, we got it, and we got it just after a tremendous spouting of water and mud, and a thick cloud of steam on the northern horizon.

"We saw a seeming rise to the horizon, as though caused by refraction, but which soon eliminated refraction as a cause by its becoming visible in its details—its streaks of water and mud, its irregular upper edge, the occasional combers that appeared on this edge, and the terrific speed of its approach. It was a wave, nothing else, and coming at forty knots at least.

"There was little that we could do; there was no wind, and we headed about west, showing our broadside; yet I got the men at the downhauls, clew-lines, and stripping lines of the lighter kites; but before a man could leave the deck to furl, that moving mountain hit us, and buried us on our beam-ends just as I had time to sing out: 'Lash yourselves, every man.'

"Then I needed to think of my own safety and passed a turn of the mizzen gaff-topsail downhaul about me, belaying to a pin as the cataclysm hit us. For the next two minutes—although it seemed an hour, I did not speak, nor breathe, nor think, unless my instinctive grip on the turns of the downhaul on the pin may have been an index of thought. I was under water; there was roaring in my ears, pain in my lungs, and terror in my heart.

"Then there came a lessening of the turmoil, a momentary quiet, and I roused up, to find the craft floating on her side, about a third out of water, but apt to turn bottom up at any moment from the weight of the water-soaked gear and canvas, which will sink, you know, when wet.

"I was hanging in my bight of rope from a belaying pin, my feet clear of the perpendicular deck, and my ears tortured by the sound of men overboard crying for help—men who had not lashed themselves. Among them I knew was the skipper, a mild-mannered little fellow, and the second mate, an incompetent tough from Portsmouth, who had caused me lots of trouble by his abuse of the men and his depending upon me to stand by him.

"Nothing could be done for them; they were adrift on the back wall of a moving mountain that towered thirty degrees above the horizon to port; and another moving mountain, as big as the first, was coming on from starboard—caused by the tumble into the sea of the uplifted water.

"Did you ever fall overboard in a full suit of clothes? If you did, you know the mighty exercise of strength required to climb out. I was a strong, healthy man at the time, but never in my life was I so tested. I finally got a grip on the belaying pin and rested; then, with an effort that caused me physical pain, I got my right foot up to the pinrail and rested again; then, perhaps more by mental strength than physical—for I loved life and wanted to live—I hooked my right foot over the rail, reached higher on the rope, rested again, and finally hove myself up to the mizzen rigging, where I sat for a few moments to get my breath, and think, and look around.

"Forward, I saw men who had lashed themselves to the starboard rail, and they were struggling, as I had struggled, to get up to the horizontal side of the vessel. They succeeded, but at the time I had no use for them. Sailors will obey orders, if they understand the orders, but this was an exigency outside the realm of mere seamanship.

"Men were drowning off to port; men, like myself, were climbing up to temporary safety afforded by the topsides of a craft on her beam ends; and aft, in the alleyway, was the German professor, unlashed, but safe and secure in his narrow confines, one leg through a cabin window, and both hands gripping the rail, while he bellowed like a bull, not for himself, however—but for his menagerie in the empty hold.

"There was small chance for the brutes—smaller than for ourselves, left on the upper rail of an overturned craft, and still smaller than the chance of the poor devils off to port, some of whom had gripped the half-submerged top-hamper, and were calling for help.

"We could not help them; she was a Yankee craft, and there was not a life buoy or belt on board; and who, with another big wave coming, would swim down to looward with a line?

"Landsmen, especially women and boys, have often asked me why a wooden ship, filled with water, sinks, even though not weighted with cargo. Some sailors have pondered over it, too, knowing that a small boat, built of wood, and fastened with nails, will float if waterlogged.

"But the answer is simple. Most big craft are built of oak or hard pine, and fastened together with iron spikes and bolts— sixty tons at least to a three-hundred-ton schooner. After a year or two this hard, heavy wood becomes water-soaked, and, with the iron bolts and spikes, is heavier than water, and will sink when the hold is flooded.

"This craft of ours was like a small boat—built of soft light wood, with trunnels instead of bolts, and no iron on board except the anchors and one capstan. As a result, though ripped, twisted, broken, and disintegrated, she still floated even on her beam-ends.

"But the soaked hemp rigging and canvas might be enough to drag the craft down, and with this fear in my mind I acted quickly. Singing out to the men to hang on, I made my way aft to where we had an ax, lodged in its beckets on the after house. With this I attacked the mizzen lanyards, cutting everything clear, then climbed forward to the main.

"Hard as I worked I had barely cut the last lanyard when that second wave loomed up and crashed down on us. I just had time to slip into the bight of a rope, and save myself; but I had to give up the ax; it slipped from my hands and slid down to the port scuppers.

"That second wave, in its effect, was about the same as the first, except that it righted the craft. We were buried, choked, and half drowned; but when the wave had passed on, the main and mizzenmasts, unsupported by the rigging that I had cut away, snapped cleanly about three feet above the deck, and the broad, flat-bottomed craft straightened up, lifting the weight of the foremast and its gear, and lay on an even keel, with foresail, staysail, and jib set, the fore gaff-topsail, flying jib, and jib-topsail clewed down and the wreck of the masts bumping against the port side.

"We floated, but with the hold full of water, and four feet of it on deck amidships that surged from one rail to the other as the craft rolled, pouring over and coming back. All hatches were ripped off, and our three boats were carried away from their chocks on the house.

"Six men were clearing themselves from their lashings at the fore rigging, and three more, who had gone overboard with the first sea, and had caught the upper gear to be lifted as the craft righted, were coming down, while the professor still declaimed from the alley.

" 'Hang on all,' I yelled; 'there's another sea coming.'

"It came, but passed over us without doing any more damage, and though a fourth, fifth, and sixth followed, each was of lesser force than the last, and finally it was safe to leave the rail and wade about, though we still rolled rails under in what was left of the turmoil.

"Luckily, there was no wind, though I never understood why, for earthquakes are usually accompanied by squalls. However, even with wind, our canvas would have been no use to us; for, water-logged as we were, we couldn't have made a knot an hour, nor could we have steered, even with all sail set. All we could hope for was the appearance of some craft that would tow the ripped and shivered hull to port, or at least take us off.

"So, while I searched for the ax, and the professor searched into the depths under the main hatch for signs of his menagerie—all drowned, surely—the remnant of the crew lowered the foresail and jibs, stowing them as best they could.

"I found the ax, and found it just in time; for I was attacked by what could have been nothing but a small-sized sea serpent, that had been hove up to the surface and washed aboard us. It was only about six feet long, but it had a mouth like a bulldog, and a row of spikes along its back that could have sawed a man's leg off.

"I managed to kill it before it harmed me, and chucked it overboard against the protests of the professor, who averred that I took no interest in science.

" 'No, I don't,' I said to him. 'I've other things to think of. And you, too. You'd better go below and clean up your instruments, or you'll find them ruined by salt water.'

"He looked sorrowfully and reproachfully at me, and started to wade aft; but he halted at the forward companion, and turned, for a scream of agony rang out from the forecastle deck, where the men were coming in from the jibs, and I saw one of them writhing on his back, apparently in a fit, while the others stood wonderingly around.

"The forecastle deck was just out of water, and there was no wash; but in spite of this, the wriggling, screaming man slid head-first along the break and plunged into the water on the main deck.

"I scrambled forward, still carrying the ax, and the men tumbled down into the water after the man; but we could not get near him. We could see him under water, feebly moving, but not swimming; and yet he shot this way and that faster than a man ever swam; and once, as he passed near me, I noticed a gaping wound in his neck, from which the blood was flowing in a stream—a stream like a current, which did not mix with the water and discolor it.

"Soon his movements ceased, and I waded toward him; but he shot swiftly away from me, and I did not follow, for something cold, slimy, and firm touched my hand—something in the water, but which I could not see.

"I floundered back, still holding the ax, and sang out to the men to keep away from the dead man; for he was surely dead by now. He lay close to the break of the topgallant forecastle, on the starboard side; and as the men mustered around me I gave one my ax, told the rest to secure others, and to chop away the useless wreck pounding our port side—useless because it was past all seamanship to patch up that basketlike hull, pump it out, and raise jury rigging.

"While they were doing it, I secured a long pike pole from its beckets, and, joined by the professor, cautiously approached the body prodding ahead of me.

"As I neared the dead man, the pike pole was suddenly torn from my grasp, one end sank to the deck, while the other raised above the water; then it slid upward, fell, and floated close to me. I seized it again and turned to the professor.

" 'What do you make of this, Herr Smidt?' I asked. 'There is something down there that we cannot see—something that killed that man. See the blood?'

"He peered closely at the dead man, who looked curiously distorted and shrunken, four feet under water. But the blood no longer was a thin stream issuing from his neck; it was gathered into a misshapen mass about two feet away from his neck.

" 'Nonsense,' he answered. 'Something alive which we cannot see is contrary to all laws of physics. Der man must have fallen und hurt himself, which accounts for der bleeding. Den he drowned in der water. Do you see?—mine Gott! What iss?'

"He suddenly went under water himself, and dropping the pike pole, I grabbed him by the collar and braced myself. Something was pulling him away from me, but I managed to get his head out, and he spluttered:

" 'Help! Holdt on to me. Something haf my right foot.'

" 'Lend a hand here,' I yelled to the men, and a few joined me, grabbing him by his clothing. Together we pulled against the invisible force, and finally all of us went backward, professor and all, nearly to drown ourselves before regaining our feet. Then, as the agitated water smoothed, I distinctly saw the mass of red move slowly forward and disappear in the darkness under the forecastle deck.

" 'You were right, mine friend,' said the professor, who, in spite of his experience, held his nerve. 'Dere is something invisible in der water—something dangerous, something which violates all laws of physics und optics. Oh, mine foot, how it hurts!'

" 'Get aft,' I answered, 'and find out what ails it. And you fellows,' I added to the men, 'keep away from the forecastle deck. Whatever it is, it has gone under it.'

"Then I grabbed the pike pole again, cautiously hooked the barb into the dead man's clothing, and, assisted by the men, pulled him aft to the poop, where the professor had preceded, and was examining his ankle. There was a big, red wale around it, in the middle of which was a huge blood blister. He pricked it with his knife, then rearranged his stocking and joined us as we lifted the body.

" 'Great God, sir!' exclaimed big Bill, the bosun. 'Is that Frank? I wouldn't know him.'

"Frank, the dead man, had been strong, robust, and full-blooded. But he bore no resemblance to his living self. He lay there, shrunken, shortened, and changed, a look of agony on his emaciated face, and his hands clenched—not extended like those of one drowned.

" 'I thought drowned men swelled up,' ventured one of the men.

" 'He was not drowned,' said Herr Smidt. 'He was sucked dry, like a lemon. Perhaps in his whole body there is not an ounce of blood, nor lymph, nor fluid of any kind.'

"I secured an iron belaying pin, tucked it inside his shirt, and we hove him overboard at once; for, in the presence of this horror, we were not in the mood for a burial service. There we were, eleven men on a waterlogged hulk, adrift on a heaving, greasy sea, with a dark-red sun showing through a muddy sky above, and an invisible *thing* forward that might seize any of us at any moment it chose, in the water or out; for Frank had been caught and dragged down.

"Still, I ordered the men, cook, steward, and all, to remain on the poop and—the galley being forward—to expect no hot meals, as we could subsist for a time on the cold, canned food in the storeroom and lazaret.

"Because of an early friction between the men and the second mate, the mild-mannered and peace-loving skipper had forbidden the crew to wear sheath knives; but in this exigency I overruled the edict. While the professor went down into his flooded room to doctor his ankle and attend to his instruments, I raided the slop chest, and armed every man of us with a sheath knife and belt; for while we could not see the creature, we could feel it—and a knife is better than a gun in a hand-to-hand fight.

"Then we sat around, waiting, while the sky grew muddier, the sun darker, and the northern horizon lighter with a reddish glow that was better than the sun. It was the Java earthquake, but we did not know it for a long time.

"Soon the professor appeared and announced that his instruments were in good condition, and stowed high on shelves above the water.

" 'I must resensitize my plates, however,' he said. 'Der salt water has spoiled them; but mine camera merely needs to dry out; und mine telescope, und mine static machine und Leyden jars— why, der water did not touch them.'

" 'Well, ' I answered. 'That's all right. But what good are they in the face of this emergency? Are you thinking of photographing anything now?'

" 'Perhaps. I haf been thinking some.'

" 'Have you thought out what that creature is—forward, there?'

" 'Partly. It is some creature thrown up from der bottom of der sea, und washed on board by der wave. Light, like wave motion, ends at a certain depth, you know; und we have over twelve thousand feet beneath us. At that depth dere is absolute darkness, but we know that creatures live down dere, und fight, und eat, und die.'

" 'But what of it? Why can't we see that thing?'

" 'Because, in der ages that haf passed in its evolution from der original moneron, it has never been exposed to light—I mean visible light, der light that contains der seven colors of der spectrum. Hence it may not respond to der three properties of visible light—reflection, which would give it a color of some kind; absorption, which would make it appear black; or refraction, which, in der absence of der other two, would distort things seen through it. For it would be transparent, you know.'

" 'But what can be done?' I asked helplessly, for I could not understand at the time what he meant.

" 'Nothing, except that der next man attacked must use his knife. If he cannot see der creature, he can feel it. Und perhaps —I do not know yet—perhaps, in a way, we may see it—its photograph.'

"I looked blankly at him, thinking he might have gone crazy, but he continued.

" 'You know,' he said, 'that objects too small to be seen by the miscroscope, because smaller than der amplitude of der shortest wave of visible light, can be seen when exposed to der ultraviolet light—der dark light beyond der spectrum? Und you know that this light is what acts der most in photography? That it exposes on a sensitized plate new stars in der heavens invisible to der eye through the strongest telescope?'

" 'Don't know anything about it,' I answered. 'But if you can find a way out of this scrape we're in, go ahead.'

" 'I must think,' he said dreamily. 'I haf a rock-crystal lens which is permeable to this light, und which I can place in mine camera. I must have a concave mirror, not of glass, which is opaque to this light, but of metal.'

" 'What for?' I asked.

" 'To throw der ultraviolet light on der beast. I can generate it with mine static machine.'

" 'How will one of our lantern reflectors do? They are of polished tin, I think.'

" 'Good! I can repolish one.'

"We had one deck lantern larger than usual, with a metallic reflector that concentrated the light into a beam, much as do the present day searchlights. This I procured from the lazaret, and he pronounced it available. Then he disappeared, to tinker up his apparatus.

"Night came down, and I lighted three masthead lights, to hoist at the fore to inform any passing craft that we were not under command; but, as I would not send a man forward on that job, I went myself, carefully feeling my way with the pike pole. Luckily, I escaped contact with the creature, and returned to the poop, where we had a cold supper of canned cabin stores.

"The top of the house was dry, but it was cold, especially so as we were all drenched to the skin. The steward brought up all the blankets there were in the cabin—for even a wet blanket is better than none at all—but there were not enough to go around, and one man volunteered, against my advice, to go forward and bring aft bedding from the forecastle.

"He did not come back; we heard his yell, that finished with a gurgle; but in that pitch black darkness, relieved only by the red glow from the north, not one of us dared to venture to his rescue. We knew that he would be dead, anyhow, before we could get to him; so we stood watch, sharing the blankets we had when our time came to sleep.

"It was a wretched night that we spent on the top of that after house. It began to rain before midnight, the heavy drops coming down almost in solid waves; then came wind, out of the south, cold and biting, with real waves, that rolled even over the house, forcing us to lash ourselves. The red glow to the north was hidden by the rain and spume, and, to add to our discomfort, we were showered with ashes, which, even though the surface wind was from the south, must have been brought from the north by an upper air current.

"We did not find the dead man when the faint daylight came; and so could not tell whether or not he had used his knife. His body must have washed over the rail with a sea, and we hoped the invisible killer had gone, too. But we hoped too much. With courage born of this hope a man went forward to lower the masthead lights, prodding his way with the pike pole.

"We watched him closely, the pole in one hand, his knife in the other. But he went under at the fore rigging without even a yell, and the pole went with him, while we could see, even at the distance and through the disturbed water, that his arms were close to his sides, and that he made no movement, except for the quick darting to and fro. After a few moments, however, the pike pole floated to the surface, but the man's body, drained, no doubt, of its buoyant fluids, remained on the deck.

"It was an hour later, with the pike pole for a feeler, before we dared approach the body, hook on to it, and tow it aft. It resembled that of the first victim, a skeleton clothed with skin, with the same look of horror on the face. We buried it like the other, and held to the poop, still drenched by the downpour of rain, hammered by the seas, and choked by ashes from the sky.

"As the shower of ashes increased it became dark as twilight, and though the three lights aloft burned out at about midday, I forbade a man to go forward to lower them, contenting myself with a turpentine flare lamp that I brought up from the lazaret, and filled, ready to show if the lights of a craft came in view. Before the afternoon was half gone it was dark as night, and down below, up to his waist in water, the German professor was working away.

"He came up at supper-time, humming cheerfully to himself, and announced that he had replaced his camera lens with the rock crystal, that the lantern, with its reflector and a blue spark in the focus, made an admirable instrument for throwing the invisible rays on the beast, and that he was all ready, except that his plates, which he had resensitized—with some phosphorescent substance that I forget the name of, now—must have time to dry. And then, he needed some light to work by when the time came, he explained.

" 'Also another victim,' I suggested bitterly; for he had not been on deck when the last two men had died.

" 'I hope not,' he said. 'When we can see, it may be possible to stir him up by throwing things forward; then when he moves der water we can take shots.'

" 'Better devise some means of killing him,' I answered. 'Shooting won't do, for water stops a bullet before it goes a foot into it.'

" 'Der only way I can think of,' he responded, 'is for der next man—you hear me all, you men—to stick your knife at the end of the blood—where it collects in a lump. Dere is der creature's stomach, and a vital spot.'

" 'Remember this, boys,' I laughed, thinking of the last poor devil, with his arms pinioned to his side. 'When you've lost enough blood to see it in a lump, stab for it.'

"But my laugh was answered by a shriek. A man lashed with a turn of rope around his waist to the stump of the mizzenmast, was writhing and heaving on his back, while he struck with his knife, apparently at his own body. With my own knife in my hand I sprang toward him, and felt for what had seized him. It was something cold, and hard, and leathery, close to his waist.

"Carefully gauging my stroke, I lunged with the knife, but I hardly think it entered the invisible fin, or tail, or paw of the monster; but it moved away from the screaming man, and the next moment I received a blow in the face that sent me aft six feet, flat on my back. Then came unconsciousness.

"When I recovered my senses the remnant of the crew were around me, but the man was gone—dragged out of the bight of the rope that had held him against the force of breaking seas, and down to the flooded main deck, to die like the others. It was too dark to see, or do anything; so, when I could speak I ordered all hands but one into the flooded cabin where, in the upper berths and on the top of the table, were a few dry spots.

"I filled and lighted a lantern, and gave it to the man on watch with instructions to hang it to the stump of the mizzen and to call his relief at the end of four hours. Then, with doors and windows closed, we went to sleep, or tried to go to sleep. I succeeded first, I think, for up to the last of consciousness I could hear the mutterings of the men; when I awakened, they were all asleep, and the cabin clock, high above the water, told me that, though it was still dark, it was six in the morning.

"I went on deck; the lantern still burned at the stump of mizzenmast but the lookout was gone. He had not lived long enough to be relieved, as I learned by going below and finding that no one had been called.

"We were but six, now—one sailor and the bos'n, the cook and steward, the professor and myself."

The old artist paused, while he refilled and lighted his pipe. I noticed that the hand that held the match shook perceptibly, as though the memories of that awful experience had affected his nerves. I know that the recital had affected mine; for I joined him in a smoke, my hands shaking also.

"Why," I asked, after a moment of silence, "if it was a deep-sea creature, did it not die from the lesser pressure at the surface?"

"Why do not men die on the mountaintops?" he answered. "Or up in balloons? The record is seven miles high, I think; but they lived. They suffered from cold, and from lack of oxygen—that is, no matter how fast, or deeply they breathed, they could not get enough. But the lack of pressure did not trouble them; the human body can adjust itself.

"Conversely, however, an increase of pressure may be fatal. A man dragged down more than one hundred and fifty feet may be crushed; and a surface fish sent to the bottom of the sea may die from the pressure. It is simple; it is like the difference between a weight lifted from us and a weight added."

"Did this thing kill any more men?" I asked.

"All but the professor and myself, and it almost killed me. Look here."

He removed his cravat and collar, pulled down his shirt, and exposed two livid scars about an inch in diameter, and two apart.

"I lost all the blood I could spare through those two holes," he said, as he readjusted his apparel, "but I saved enough to keep me alive."

"Go on with the yarn," I asked. "I promise you I will not sleep tonight."

"Perhaps I will not sleep myself," he answered, with a mournful smile. "Some things should be forgotten, but as I have told you this much I may as well finish, and be done with it.

"It was partly due to a sailor's love for tobacco, partly to our cold, drenched condition. A sailor will starve quietly, but go crazy if deprived of his smoke. This is so well known at sea that a skipper, who will not hesitate to sail from port with rotten or insufficient food for his men, will not dare take a chance without a full supply of tobacco in the slop chest.

"But our slop chest was under water, and the tobacco utterly useless. I did not use it at the time, but I fished some out for the others. It did not do; it would not dry out to smoke, and the salt in it made it unfit to chew. But the bos'n had an upper bunk in the forward house, in which was a couple of pounds of navy plug, and he and the sailor talked this over until their craving for a smoke overcame their fear of death.

"Of course, by this time, all discipline was ended, and all my commands and entreaties went for nothing. They sharpened their knives, and, agreeing to go forward, one on the starboard rail, the other on the port, and each to come to the other's aid if called, they went up into the darkness of ashes and rain. I opened my room window, which overlooked the main deck, but could see nothing.

"Yet I could hear; I heard two screams for help, one after the other—one from the starboard side, the other from the port, and knew that they were caught. I closed the window, for nothing could be done. What manner of thing it was that could grab two men so far apart nearly at the same time was beyond all imagining.

"I talked to the steward and cook, but found small comfort. The first was Japanese, the other Chinese, and they were the old-fashioned kind—what they could not see with their eyes, they could not believe. Both thought that all those men who had met death had either drowned or died by falling. Neither understood—and, in fact, I did not myself—the theories of Herr Smidt. He had stopped his cheerful humming to himself now, and was very busy with his instruments.

" 'This thing,' I said to him, 'must be able to see in the dark. It certainly could not have heard those two men, over the noise of the wind, sea, and rain.'

" 'Why not?' he answered, as he puttered with his wires. 'Cats and owls can see in the dark, und the accepted explanation is that by their power of enlarging der pupils they admit more light to the retina. But that explanation never satisfied me. You haf noticed, haf you not, that a cat's eyes shine in der dark, but only when der cat is looking at you?—that is, when it looks elsewhere you do not see der shiny eyes.'

" 'Yes,' I answered, 'I have noticed that.'

" 'A cat's eyes are searchlights and they send forth a visible light as do fireflies and certain fish in der upper tributaries of der

193

Amazon which haf four eyes, der two upper of which are searchlights, der two lower of which are organs of percipience or vision. But visible light is not der only light. It is possible that the creature out on deck generates an invisible light, and can see by it.'

" 'But what does it all amount to?' I asked impatiently.

" 'I haf told you,' he answered calmly. 'Der creature may live in an atmosphere of ultraviolet light, which I can generate mineself. When mine plates dry, und it clears off so I can see what I am doing, I may get a picture of it. When we know what it is, we may find means of killing it.'

" 'God grant that you succeed,' I answered fervently. 'It has killed enough of us.'

"But, as I said, the thing killed all but the professor and myself. And it came about through the other reason I mentioned—our cold, drenched condition. The cold, canned food was palling upon us all. We had a little light through the downpour of ashes and rain about midday, and the steward and cook began talking about hot coffee.

"We had the turpentine torch for heating water, and some coffee high and dry on a shelf in the steward's storeroom, but not a pot, pan, or cooking utensil of any kind in the cabin. So these two poor lads, against my expostulations—somewhat faint, I admit, for the thought of a hot drink took away some of my common sense—went out on the deck and waded forward, waist-deep in the water, muddy now, from the downfall of ashes.

"I could see them as they entered the galley to get the coffee-pot, but, though I stared from my window until the blackness closed down, I did not see them come out. Nor did I hear even a squeal. The thing must have been in the galley.

"Night came on, and, with its coming, the wind and rain ceased, though there was still a slight shower of ashes. But this ended toward midnight, and I could see stars overhead and a clear horizon. Sleep, in my nervous, overwrought condition, was impossible; but the professor, after the bright idea of using the turpentine torch to dry out his plates, had gone to his fairly dry berth, after announcing his readiness to take snapshots about the deck in the morning.

"But I roused him long before morning. I roused him when I saw through my window the masthead and two side lights of a steamer approaching from the starboard, still about a mile away. I had not dared to go up and rig that lantern at the mizzen stump; but now I nerved myself to go up with the torch, the professor following with his instruments.

" 'You cold-blooded crank,' I said to him, as I waved the torch. 'I admire your devotion to science, but are you waiting for that thing to get me?'

"He did not answer, but rigged his apparatus on the top of the cabin. He had a Wimshurst machine—to generate a blue spark, you know—and this he had attached to the big deck light, from which he had removed the opaque glass. Then he had his camera, with its rock-crystal lens.

"He trained both forward, and waited, while I waved the torch, standing near the stump with a turn of rope around me for safety's sake in case the thing seized me; and to this idea I added the foolish hope, aroused by the professor's theories, that the blinding light of the torch would frighten the thing away from me as it does wild animals.

"But in this last I was mistaken. No sooner was there an answering blast of a steam whistle, indicating that the steamer had seen the torch, than something cold, wet, leathery, and slimy slipped around my neck. I dropped the torch, and drew my knife, while I heard the whir of the static machine as the professor turned it.

" 'Use your knife, mine friend,' he called. 'Use your knife, und reach for any blood what you see.'

"I knew better than to call for help, and I had little chance to use the knife. Still, I managed to keep my right hand, in which I held it, free, while that cold, leathery thing slipped farther around my neck and waist. I struck as I could, but could make no impression; and soon I felt another stricture around my legs, which brought me on my back.

"Still another belt encircled me, and, though I had come up warmly clad in woolen shirts and monkey jacket, I felt these garments being torn away from me. Then I was dragged forward, but the turn of rope had slipped down toward my waist, and I was merely bent double.

"And all the time that German was whirling his machine, and shouting to strike for any blood I saw. But I saw none. I felt it going, however. Two spots on my chest began to smart, then burn as though hot irons were piercing me. Frantically I struck, right and left, sometimes at the coils encircling me, again in the air. Then all became dark.

"I awakened in a stateroom berth, too weak to lift my hands, with the taste of brandy in my mouth and the professor standing over me with a bottle in his hand.

" 'Ach, it is well,' he said. 'You will recover. You haf merely lost blood, but you did the right thing. You struck with your knife at the blood, and you killed the creature. I was right. Heart, brain, und all vital parts were in der stomach.'

" 'Where are we now?' I asked, for I did not recognize the room.

" 'On board der steamer. When you got on your feet und staggered aft, I knew you had killed him, and gave you my assistance. But you fainted away. Then we were taken off. Und I haf two or three beautiful negatives, which I am printing. They will be a glorious contribution to der scientific world.'

"I was glad that I was alive, yet not alive enough to ask any more questions. But next day he showed me the photographs he had printed."

"In Heaven's name, what was it?" I asked excitedly, as the old artist paused to empty and refill his pipe.

"Nothing but a giant squid, or octopus. Except that it was bigger than any ever seen before, and invisible to the eye, of course. Did you ever read Hugo's terrible story of Gilliat's fight with a squid?"

I had, and nodded.

"Hugo's imagination could not give him a creature—no matter how formidable—larger than one of four feet stretch. This one had three tentacles around me, two others gripped the port and starboard pinrails, and three were gripping the stump of the mainmast. It had a reach of forty feet, I should think, comparing it with the beam of the craft.

"But there was one part of each picture, ill defined and missing. My knife and right hand were not shown. They were buried in a dark lump, which could be nothing but the blood from my veins. Unconscious, but still struggling, I had struck into the soft body of the monster, and struck true."

ELIZABETH STUART PHELPS WARD

KENTUCKY'S GHOST

TRUE? EVERY SYLLABLE.

That was a very fair yarn of yours, Tom Brown, very fair for a landsman, but I'll bet you a doughnut I can beat it.

It was somewhere about twenty years ago that we were laying in for that particular trip to Madagascar.

We cleared from Long Wharf in the ship *Madonna*, which they tell me means My Lady, and a pretty name it was; it was apt to give me that gentle kind of feeling when I spoke it, which is surprising when you consider what a dull old hull she was, never logging over ten knots, and uncertain at that. It may have been because of Moll's coming down once in a while in the days that we lay at dock, bringing the boy with her, and sitting up on deck in a little white apron, knitting. She was a very good-looking woman, was my wife, in those days, and I felt proud of her—natural, with the lads looking on.

I used to speak my thought about the name sometimes, when the lads weren't particularly noisy, but they laughed at me mostly. I was rough enough and bad enough in those days; as rough as the

197

rest, and as bad as the rest, I suppose, but yet I seemed to have my notions a little different from the others. "Jake's poetry," they called 'em.

We were loading for the East Shore trade. There isn't much of the genuine, old-fashioned trade left in these days, except the whisky branch. We had a little whisky in the hold, I remember, that trip, with a good stock of knives, red flannel, handsaws, nails, and cotton. We were hoping to be at home again within the year. We were well provisioned, and Dodd the cook made about as fair coffee as you're likely to find in the galley of a trader. As for our officers, when I say the less said of them the better, it ain't so much that I mean to be disrespectful as that I mean to put it tenderly. Officers in the merchant service, especially if it happens to be the African service, are quite often brutal men, and about as fit for their positions as if they'd been imported for the purpose a little indirect from Davy Jones's locker.

Well, we weighed, along the last of the month, in pretty good spirits. The *Madonna* was as seaworthy as any eight-hundred-tonner in the harbour, even if she was clumsy; we turned in, some sixteen of us or thereabouts, into the fo'castle—a jolly set, mostly old messmates, and well content with one another; and the breeze was stiff from the west, with a fair sky.

The night before we were off, Molly and I took a walk upon the wharves after supper. I carried the baby. A boy, sitting on some boxes, pulled my sleeve as we went by, and asked me, pointing to the *Madonna*, if I would tell him the name of the ship.

"Find out for yourself," said I, not overpleased to be interrupted.

"Don't be cross with him," says Molly. The baby threw a kiss at the boy, and Molly smiled at him through the dark. I don't suppose I should ever have remembered the lubber from that day to this, except that I liked the looks of Molly smiling at him through the dark.

My wife and I said good-bye the next morning in a little sheltered place among the lumber on the wharf; she was one of your women who never like to do their crying before folks.

She climbed on the pile of lumber and sat down, a little flushed and quivery, to watch us off. I remember seeing her there with the baby till we were well down the channel. I remember noticing the bay as it grew cleaner, and thinking that I would break off swearing; and I remember cursing Bob Smart like a pirate within an hour.

The breeze held steadier than we'd looked for, and we'd made a good offing and discharged the pilot by nightfall. Mr. Whitmarsh, the mate, was aft with the captain. The boys were singing a little; the smell of the coffee was coming up, hot and homelike, from the galley. I was up in the maintop when all at once there came a cry and a shout; and, when I touched deck, I saw a crowd around the fore-hatch.

"What's all this noise for?" says Mr. Whitmarsh, coming up and scowling.

"A stowaway, sir! A boy stowed away!" said Bob, catching the officer's tone quick enough. He jerked the poor fellow out of the hold, and pushed him along to the mate's feet.

I say "poor fellow", and you'd never wonder why if you'd seen as much of stowing away as I have.

I'd as lief see a son of mine in a Carolina slave-gang as to see him lead the life of a stowaway. What with the officers feeling that they've been taken in, and the men, who catch their cue from their superiors, and the spite of the lawful boy who was hired in the proper way, he don't have what you may call a tender time.

This chap was a little fellow, slight for his years, which might have been fifteen. He was palish, with a jerk of thin hair on his forehead. He was hungry, and homesick, and frightened. He looked about on all our faces, and then he cowered a little, and lay still just as Bob had thrown him.

"We—ell," says Whitmarsh, very slow, "if you don't repent your bargain before you go ashore, my fine fellow,——— me, if I'm mate of the *Madonna!* and take that for your pains!"

Upon that he kicks the poor little lubber from quarterdeck to bowsprit and goes down to his supper. The men laugh a little, then they whistle a little, then they finish their song quite gay and well acquainted, with the coffee steaming away in the galley. Nobody has a word for the boy—bless you, no!

I'll venture he wouldn't have had a mouthful that night if it had not been for me; and I can't say as I should have bothered myself about him, if it had not come across me sudden, while he sat there rubbing his eyes quite violent, that I had seen the lad before; then I remembered walking on the wharves, and him on the box, and Molly saying softly that I was cross to him.

Seeing that my wife had smiled at him, and my baby thrown a kiss at him, it went against me not to look after the little rascal a bit that night.

"But you've got no business here, you know," said I. "Nobody wants you."

"I wish I was ashore!' said he, 'I wish I was ashore!"

With that he begins to rub his eyes so very violent that I stopped. There was good stuff in him too; for he choked and winked at me, and made out that the sun was on the water and he had a cold in the head.

I don't know whether it was on account of being taken a little notice of that night, but the lad always hung about me afterwards; chased me round with his eyes in a way he had, and did odd jobs for me without the asking.

One night before the first week was out, he hauled alongside of me on the windlass. I was trying a new pipe so I didn't give him much notice for a while.

"You did this job up shrewd, Kent," said I, by and by, "How did you steer in?" For it did not often happen that the *Madonna* got out of port with a stowaway in her hold.

"Watch was drunk; I crawled down ahind the whisky. It was hot and dark. I lay and thought how hungry I was," says he.

"Friends at home?" says I.

Upon that he gives me a nod, very short, and gets up and walks off whistling.

The first Sunday out that chap didn't know any more what to do with himself than a lobster just put on to boil. Sunday's cleaning day at sea, you know. The lads washed up, and sat round, little knots of them, mending their trousers. Bob got out his cards. Me and a few mates took it comfortable under the to'gallant fo'castle (I being on watch below), reeling off the stiffest yarns we had in tow. Kent looked on a while, then listened to us a while, then walked off.

By and by says Bob, "Look over there!" and there was Kent, sitting curled away in a heap under the stern of the long-boat. He had a book. Bob crawls behind and snatches it up, unbeknown, out of his hands; then he falls to laughing as if he would strangle, and gives the book a toss to me. It was a bit of Testament, black and old. There was writing on the yellow leaf which ran:

"Kentucky Hodge,
"from his Affecshunate mother
"who prays, For you evry day, Amen."

The boy turned red, then white, and straightened up quite
sudden, but he never said a word, only sat down again, and let us
laugh it out. I've lost my reckoning if he ever heard the last of it. He
told me one day how he came by the name, but I forget exactly.
Something about an old uncle died in Kentucky, and the name was
moniment-like, you see. He used to seem cut up a bit about it at first,
for the lads took to it famously; but he got used to it in a week or
two, and seeing as they meant him no unkindness, took it quite
cheery.

One other thing I noticed was that he never had the book about
after that. He fell into our ways next Sunday more easy.

They don't take the Bible as a general thing, sailors don't;
though I will say that I never saw the man at sea who didn't give it
the credit of being an uncommon good yarn.

But I tell you, Tom Brown, I felt sorry for that boy. It's punishment enough for a little scamp like him leaving the honest shore,
and folks at home that were a bit tender of him maybe, to rough it on
a trader, learning how to slush down a back-stay, or tie knots with
frozen fingers in a snow-squall.

But that's not the worst of it, by no means. If ever there was a
cold-blooded, cruel man, with a wicked eye and a fist like a mallet,
it was Job Whitmarsh. And I believe, of all the trips I've taken, him
being mate of the *Madonna*, Kentucky found him at his worst. Bra-
dley the second mate was none too gentle in his ways, but he never
held a candle to Mr. Whitmarsh. He took a spite to the boy from the
first, and he kept it up to the last.

I've seen him beat that boy till the blood run down in little
pools on deck; then send him up, all wet and red, to clear the to'sail
halliards; and when, what with the pain and faintness, he dizzied a
little, and clung to the ratlines, half blind, he would have him down
and flog him till the cap'n interfered—which would happen occasionally on a fair day when he had taken just enough to be good-
natured. He used to rack his brains for the words he slung at the boy
working quiet enough beside him. If curses had been a marketable
article, Whitmarsh would have made his fortune. Then he used to

kick the lad down the fo'castle ladder; he used to work him, sick or well, as he wouldn't have worked a dray-horse; he used to chase him all about the deck at the rope's end; he used to mast-head him for hours on the stretch; he used to starve him out in the hold. It didn't come in my line to be over-tender, but I turned sick at heart, Tom, more than once, looking on helpless, and me a great stout fellow.

I remember a thing McCallum said one night; McCallum was a Scot, an old fellow with grey hair; told the best yarns on the fo'castle.

"Mark my words, shipmates," says he. "When Job Whitmarsh's time comes to go as straight to hell as Judas, that boy will bring his summons." Dead or alive, that boy will bring his summons."

One day I recollect that the lad was sick with fever, and took to his hammock. Whitmarsh drove him on deck, and ordered him aloft. I was standing near by, trimming the spanker. Kentucky staggered for'ard a little and sat down. There was a rope's-end there, knotted three times. The mate struck him.

"I'm very weak, sir," says he.

He struck him again. He struck him twice more. The boy fell over a little, and lay where he fell.

I don't know what ailed me, but all of a sudden I seemed to be lying off Long Wharf, with Molly in a white apron with her shining needles, and the baby a-play in his red stockings about the deck.

"Think if it was him!" says she, or she seems to say, "Think if it was *him!*"

And the next I knew I'd let slip my tongue in a jiffy, and given it to the mate in a way I'll bet Whitmarsh never got before. And the next I knew after that they had the irons on me.

"Sorry about that, eh?" said he, the day before they took 'em off.

"*No*, sir," says I. And I never was. Kentucky never forgot that. I had helped him occasional in the beginning—learned him how to veer and haul a brace, let go or belay a sheet—but let him alone generally speaking, and went about my own business. That week in irons I really believe the lad never forgot.

One Saturday night, when the mate had been uncommon furious that week—Kentucky turned on him, very pale and slow (I was up in the mizzen-top, and heard him quite distinct).

"Mr. Whitmarsh," says he, "Mr. Whitmarsh,"—he draws his breath in—"Mr. Whitmarsh"—three times—"you've got the power and you know it, and so do the gentlemen who put you here; and I'm only a stowaway boy, and things are all in a tangle, but *you'll be sorry yet for every time you've laid your hands on me!*"

He hadn't a pleasant look about the eyes either, when he said it.

Fact was, that first month on the *Madonna* had done the lad no good. He had a surly, sullen way with him, some'at like what I've seen about a chained dog. At the first, his talk had been clean as my baby's, and he would blush like any girl at Bob Smart's stories; but he got used to Bob, and pretty good, in time, at small swearing.

I don't think I should have noticed it so much if it had not been for seeming to see Molly and the knitting-needles, and the child upon the deck, and hearing her say, "Think if it was *him!*"

Well, things went along just about so with us till we neared the Cape. It's not a pretty place, the Cape, on a winter's voyage. I can't say as I ever was what you may call scared after the first time rounding it, but it's not a pretty place.

I don't seem to remember much about Kent till there come a Friday at the first of December. It was a still day, with a little haze, like white sand sifted across a sunbeam on a kitchen table. The lad was quiet-like all day, chasing me about with his eyes.

"Sick?" says I.

"No," says he.

"Whitmarsh drunk?" says I.

"No," says he.

A little after dark I was lying on a coil of ropes, napping it. The boys were having the Bay of Biscay quite lively, and I waked up on the jump in the choruses. Kent came up. He was not singing. He sat down beside me, and first I thought I wouldn't trouble myself about him, and then I thought I would.

So I opens one eye at him encouraging. He crawls up a little closer to me. It was rather dark where we sat, with a great greenish shadow dropping from the mainsail. The wind was up a little, and the light at helm looked flickery and red.

"Jake," says he all at once, "where's your mother?"

"In heaven!" says I, all taken aback.

"Oh!" says he. "Got any women-folks at home that miss you?" asks he, by and by.

Said I, "Shouldn't wonder."

After that he sits still a little with his elbows on his knees; then he peers at me sidewise a while; then said he, "I s'pose *I've* got a mother to home. I ran away from her."

That was the first time he had ever spoke about his folks since he came aboard.

"She was asleep down in the south chamber," says he. "I got out the window. There was one white shirt she'd made for meetin' and such. I've never worn it out here. I hadn't the heart. It has a collar and some cuffs, you know. She had a headache making of it. She's been follering me round all day, sewing that shirt. When I come in she would look up bright-like and smiling. Father's dead. There ain't anybody but me. All day long she's been follering of me round."

So then he gets up, and joins the lads, and tries to sing a little; but he comes back very still and sits down. We could see the flickery light upon the boys' faces, and on the rigging, and on the cap'n, who was damning the bosun a little aft.

"Jake," says he, quite low, "look here. I've been thinking. Do you reckon there's a chap here—just one, perhaps—who's said his prayers since he came aboard?"

"*No!*" said I, quite short: for I'd have bet my head on it.

I can remember, as if it was this morning, just how the question sounded, and the answer. I can't seem to put it into words how it came all over me. The wind was turning brisk, and we'd just eased her with a few reefs; Bob Smart, out furling the flying jib, got soaked; me and the boy sitting silent, were spattered. I remember watching the curve of the great swells, mahogany colour, with the tip of white, and thinking how like it was to a big creature hissing and foaming at the mouth, and thinking all at once something about Him holding of the sea in a balance, and not a word bespoke to beg His favour respectful since we weighed our anchor, and the cap'n yonder calling on Him just that minute to send the *Madonna* to the bottom, if the bosun hadn't disobeyed his orders about the squaring of the after-yards.

"From his Affecshunate mother who prays, For you evry day, Amen," whispers Kentucky, presently, very soft, "The book's tore up. Mr. Whitmarsh wadded his old gun with it. But I remember."

Then said he, "It's almost bedtime at home. She's setting in a little rocking-chair, green one. There's a fire, and the dog. She sets all by herself."

Then he begins again: "She has to bring in her own wood now. There's a grey ribbon on her cap. When she goes to meetin' she wears a grey bonnet. She's drawed the curtains and the door is locked. But she thinks I'll be coming home sorry some day—I'm sure she thinks I'll be coming home sorry."

Just then there comes the order, "Port watch ahoy! Tumble up there lively!" so I turns out, and the lad turns in, and the night settles down a little black, and my hands and head are full. Next day it blows a clean, all but a bank of grey, very thin and still which lay just abeam of us.

The sea looked like a great purple pincushion, with a mast or two stuck in on the horizon for the pins. "Jake's poetry," the boys said that was.

By noon that little grey bank had grown up thick, like a wall. By sundown the cap'n let his liquor alone, and kept the deck. By night we were in chop-seas, with a very ugly wind.

"Steer small, there!" cries Whitmarsh, growing hot about the face—for we made a terribly crooked wake, with a broad sheer, and the old hull strained heavily, "Steer small there, I tell you! Mind your eye now, McCallum, with your fore-sail! Furl the royals! Send down the royals! Cheerily, men! Where's that lubber Kent? Up with you, lively now!"

Kentucky sprang for'ard at the order, then stopped short. Anybody as knows a royal from an anchor wouldn't have blamed the lad. It's no play for an old tar, stout and full in size, sending down the royals in a gale like that; let alone a boy of fifteen years on his first voyage.

But the mate takes to swearing and Kent shoots away up—the great mast swinging like a pendulum to and fro, and the reef-points snapping, and the blocks creaking, and the sails flapping to that extent as you wouldn't consider possible unless you'd been before the mast yourself. It reminded me of evil birds I've read of, that stun a man with their wings.

Kent stuck bravely as far as the crosstrees. There he slipped and struggled and clung in the dark and noise a while, then comes sliding down the backstay.

"I'm not afraid, sir," says he; "but I cannot do it."

For answer Whitmarsh takes to the rope's-end. So Kentucky is up again, and slips and struggles and clings again, and then lays down again.

At this the men begin to grumble a little.

"Will you kill the lad?" said I. I get a blow for my pains, that sends me off my feet none too easy; and when I rub the stars out of my eyes the boy is up again, and the mate behind him with the rope. Whitmarsh stopped when he'd gone far enough. The lad climbed on. Once he looked back. He never opened his lips; he just looked back. If I've seen him once since, in my thinking, I've seen him twenty times-up in the shadow of the great grey wings, looking back.

After that there was only a cry, and a splash, and the *Madonna* racing along with the gale at twelve knots. If it had been the whole crew overboard, she could never have stopped for them that night.

"Well," said the cap'n, "you've done it now."

Whitmarsh turned his back.

By and by, when the wind fell, and the hurry was over, and I had the time to think a steady thought, being in the morning watch, I seemed to see the old lady in the grey bonnet setting by the fire. And the dog. And the green rocking-chair. And the front door, with the boy walking in on a sunny afternoon to take her by surprise.

Then I remember leaning over to look down, and wondering if the lad were thinking of it too, and what had happened to him now, these two hours back, and just about where he was, and how he liked his new quarters, and many other strange and curious things.

And while I sat there thinking, the Sunday-morning stars cut through the clouds, and the solemn Sunday-morning light began to break upon the sea.

We had a quiet run of it, after that, into port, where we lay about a couple of months or so, trading off for a fair stock of palm oil, ivory, and hides. The days were hot and purple and still. We hadn't what you might call a blow till we rounded the Cape again, heading for home.

It was just about the spot that we lost the boy that we fell upon the worst gale of the trip. It struck us quite sudden. Whitmarsh was a little high. He wasn't apt to be drunk in a gale, if it gave him warning sufficient.

Well, somebody had to furl the main-royal again, and he pitched on to McCallum. McCallum hadn't his beat for fighting out the royal in a blow.

206

So he piled away lively, up to the to'-sail yard. There, all of a sudden, he stopped. Next we knew he was down like lightning.

His face had gone very white.

"What's up with *you?*" roared Whitmarsh.

Said McCallum, *"There's somebody up there, sir."*

Screamed Whitmarsh, "You're an idiot!"

Said McCallum, very quiet and distinct: "There's somebody up there, sir. I saw him quite plain. He saw me. I called up. He called down. Says he, *'Don't you come up!'* and hang me if I'll stir a step for you or any other man tonight."

I never saw the face of any man alive go the turn that mate's face went. If he wouldn't have relished knocking the Scotchman dead before his eyes, I've lost my guess. Can't say what he would have done to the old fellow, if there'd been any time to lose.

He'd the sense left to see there wasn't overmuch, so he orders out Bob Smart direct.

Bob goes up steady, with a quid in his cheek and a cool eye. Half-way amid to'-sail and to'gallant he stops, and down he comes, spinning.

"Be drowned if there ain't!" said he. "He's sitting square upon the yard. I never see the boy Kentucky, if he isn't sitting on that yard. *'Don't you come up!'* he cries out, *'don't you come up!'* he cries out, 'don't you come up!' "

"Bob's drunk, and McCallum's a fool!" said Jim Welch, standing by. So Welch volunteers up, and takes Jaloffe with him. They were a couple of the coolest hands aboard—Welch and Jaloffe. So up they goes, and down they comes like the rest, by the run.

"He beckoned of me back!" says Welch. "He hollered not to come up! not to come up!"

After that there wasn't a man of us would stir aloft, not for love nor money.

Well, Whitmarsh he stamped, and he swore, and he knocked us about furious; but we sat and looked at one another's eyes, and never stirred. Something cold, like a frostbite, seemed to crawl along from man to man, looking into one another's eyes.

"I'll shame ye all, then, for a set of cowardly lubbers!" cries the mate; and what with the anger and the drink he was as good as his word, and up the ratlines in a twinkle.

207

In a flash we were after him—he was our officer, you see, and we felt ashamed—me at the head, and the lads following after.

I got to the futtock shrouds, and there I stopped, for I saw him myself—a palish boy, with a jerk of thin hair on his forehead; I'd have known him anywhere in this world or t'other. I saw him just as distinct as I see you, Tom Brown, sitting on that yard quite steady with the royal flapping like to flap him off.

I reckon I've had as much experience fore and aft, in the course of fifteen years at sea, as any man that ever tied a reef-point in a nor'easter; but I never saw a sight like that, not before nor since.

I won't say that I didn't wish myself on deck; but I stuck to the shrouds, and looked on steady.

Whitmarsh, swearing that the royal should be furled, went on and went up.

It was after that I hear the voice. It came from the figure of the boy upon the upper yard.

But this time it says, *"Come up! Come up!"* And then, a little louder, *"Come up! Come up! Come up!"* So he goes up and next I knew there was a cry—and next a splash—and then I saw the royal flapping from the empty yard, and the mate was gone, and the boy.

Job Whitmarsh was never seen again.

HENRY VAN DYKE

MESSENGERS
AT THE WINDOW

THE LIGHTHOUSE ON THE Isle of the Wise Virgin—formerly called the Isle of Birds—still looks out over the blue waters of the Gulf of Saint Lawrence; its white tower motionless through the day, like a seagull sleeping on the rock; its great yellow eye wide-open and winking, winking steadily once a minute, all through the night. And the birds visit the island,—not in great flocks as formerly, but still plenty of them; long-winged waterbirds in the summer, and in the spring and fall short-winged landbirds passing in their migrations—the children and grandchildren, no doubt, of the same flying families that used to pass there fifty years ago, in the days when Nataline Fortin was "The Keeper of the Light." And she herself,—that brave girl who said that the light was her "law of God," and who kept it, though it nearly broke her heart—Nataline is still guardian of the island and its flashing beacon of safety.

Not in her own person, you understand, for her dark curly hair long since turned white, and her brown eyes were closed, and she was laid at rest beside her father in the little graveyard behind the chapel at Dead Men's Point. But her spirit still inhabits the island and keeps the light. The son whom she bore to Marcel Thibault was called Baptiste, after her father, and he is now the lighthousekeeper; and her granddaughter, Nataline, is her living image; a brown darling of a girl, merry and fearless, who plays the fife bravely all along the march of life.

It is good to have some duties in the world which do not change, and some spirits who meet them with a proud cheerfulness, and some families who pass on the duty and the cheer from generation to generation—aristocrats, first families, the best blood.

Nataline the second was bustling about the kitchen of the lighthouse, humming a little song, as I sat there with my friend Baptiste, snugly sheltered from the night fury of the first September storm. The sticks of sprucewood snapped and crackled in the range; the kettle purred a soft accompaniment to the girl's low voice; the wind and the rain beat against the seaward window. I was glad that I had given up the trout fishing, and left my camp on the *Sainte-Marguérite-en-bas*, and come to pass a couple of days with the Thibaults at the lighthouse.

Suddenly there was a quick blow on the window behind me, as if someone had thrown a ball of wet seaweed or sand against it. I leaped to my feet and turned quickly, but saw nothing in the darkness.

"It is a bird, m'sieu'," said Baptiste, "only a little bird. The light draws them, and then it blinds them. Most times they fly against the big lantern above. But now and then one comes to this window. In the morning sometimes after a big storm we find a hundred dead ones around the tower."

"But, oh," cried Nataline, "the pity of it! I can't get over the pity of it. The poor little one—how it must be deceived—to seek light and to find death! Let me go out and look for it. Perhaps it is not dead."

She came back in a minute, the raindrops shining on her cheeks and in her hair. In the hollow of her firm hands she held a feathery brown little body, limp and warm. We examined it carefully. It was stunned, but not killed, and apparently neither leg nor wing was broken.

"It is a white-throat sparrow," I said to Nataline, "you know the tiny bird that sings all day in the bushes, *sweet-sweet-Canada, Canada, Canada?*"

"But yes!" she cried, "he is the dearest of them all. He seems to speak to you—to say, 'be happy.' We call him the *rossignol*. Perhaps if we take care of him, he will get well, and be able to fly tomorrow— and to sing again."

So we made a nest in a box for the little creature, which breathed lightly, and covered him over with a cloth so that he should not fly about and hurt himself. Then Nataline went singing up to bed, for she must rise at two in the morning to take her watch with the light. Baptiste and I drew our chairs up to the range, and lit our pipes for a good talk.

"Those small birds, m'sieu'," he began, puffing slowly at his pipe, "you think, without doubt, that it is all an affair of chance, the way they come—that it means nothing, that it serves no purpose for them to die?"

Certain words in an old book, about a sparrow falling to the ground, came into my mind, and I answered him carefully, hoping, perhaps, that he might be led on into one of those mystical legends which still linger among the exiled children of Britanny in the new world.

"From our side, my friend, it looks like chance—and from the birds' side, certainly, like a very bad chance. But we do not know all. Perhaps there is some meaning or purpose beyond us. Who can tell?"

"I will tell you," he replied gravely, laying down his pipe, and leaning forward with his knotted hands on his knees. "I will tell you that those little birds are sometimes the messengers of God. They can bring a word or a warning from Him. That is what we Bretons have believed for many centuries at home in France. Why should it not be true here? Is He not here also? Those birds are God's *coureurs des bois*. They do His errands. Would you like to hear a thing that happened in this house?"

This is what he told me.

My father, Marcel Thibault, was an honest man, strong in the heart, strong in the arms, but, in the conscience—well, he had his little weaknesses, like the rest of us. You see his father, the old

Thibault, lived in the days when there was no lighthouse here, and wrecking was the chief trade of this coast.

It is a cruel trade, m'sieu'—to live by the misfortune of others. No one can be really happy who lives by such a trade as that. But my father—he was born under that influence; and all the time he was a boy he heard always people talking of what the sea might bring to them, clothes and furniture, and all kinds of precious things—and never a thought of what the sea might take away from the other people who were shipwrecked and drowned. So what wonder is it that my father grew up with weak places and holes in his conscience?

But my mother, Nataline Fortin—ah, m'sieu', she was a straight soul, for sure—clean white, like a wild swan! I suppose she was not a saint. She was too fond of singing and dancing for that. But she was a good woman, and nothing could make her happy that came from the misery of another person. Her idea of goodness was like this light in the lantern above us—something faithful and steady that warns people away from shipwreck and danger.

Well, it happened one day, about this time forty-eight years ago, just before I was ready to be born, my father had to go up to the village of *La Trinité* on a matter of business. He was coming back in his boat at evening, with his sail up, and perfectly easy in his mind—though it was after sunset—because he knew that my mother was entirely capable of kindling the light and taking care of it in his absence. The wind was moderate, and the sea gentle. He had passed the *Point du Caribou* about two miles, when suddenly he felt his boat strike against something in the shadow.

He knew it could not be a rock. There was no hardness, no grating sound. He supposed it might be a tree floating in the water. But when he looked over the side of the boat, he saw it was the body of a dead man.

The face was bloated and blue, as if the man had been drowned for some days. The clothing was fine, showing that he must have been a person of quality; but it was disarranged and torn, as if he had passed through a struggle to his death. The hands, puffed and shapeless, floated on the water, as if to balance the body. They seemed almost to move in an effort to keep the body afloat. And on the little finger of the left hand there was a great ring of gold with a red stone set in it, like a live coal of fire.

When my father saw this ring a passion of covetousness leaped upon him.

"It is a thing of price," he said, "and the sea has brought it to me for the heritage of my unborn child. What good is a ring to a dead man? But for my baby it will be a fortune."

So he luffed the boat, and reached out with his oar, and pulled the body near to him, and took the cold, stiff hand into his own. He tugged at the ring, but it would not come off. The finger was swollen and hard, and no effort that he could make served to dislodge the ring.

Then my father grew angry, because the dead man seemed to withhold from him the bounty of the sea. He laid the hand across the gunwale of the boat, and, taking up the axe that lay beside him, with a single blow he chopped the little finger from the hand.

The body of the dead man swung away from the boat, turned on its side, lifting its crippled left hand into the air, and sank beneath the water. My father laid the finger with the ring upon it under the thwart, and sailed on, wishing that the boat would go faster. But the wind was light, and before he came to the island it was already dark, and a white creeping fog, very thin and full of moonlight, was spread over the sea like a shroud.

As he went up the path to the house he was trying to pull off the ring. At last it came loose in his hand; and the red stone was as bright as a big star on the edge of the sky, and the gold was heavy in his palm. So he hid the ring in his vest.

But the finger he dropped in a cluster of blueberry bushes not far from the path. And he came into the house with a load of joy and trouble on his soul; for he knew that it is wicked to maim the dead but he thought also of the value of the ring.

My mother Nataline was able to tell when people's souls had changed, without needing to wait for them to speak. So she knew that something great had happened to my father, and the first word she said when she brought him his supper was this:

"How did it happen?"

"What has happened?" said he, a little surprised, and putting down his head over his cup of tea to hide his face.

"Well," she said in her joking way, "that is just what you haven't told me, so how can I tell you? But it was something very bad or very good, I know. Now which was it?"

"It was good," said he, reaching out his hand to cut a piece from the loaf, "it was as good . . . as good as bread."

"Was it by land," said she, "or was it by sea?"

He was sitting at the table just opposite that window, so that he looked straight into it as he lifted his head to answer her.

"It was by sea," he said smiling, "a true treasure of the deep."

Just then there came a sharp stroke and a splash on the window, and something struggled and scrabbled there against the darkness. He saw a hand with the little finger cut off spread out against the pane.

"My God," he cried, "what is that?"

But my mother, when she turned, saw only a splotch of wet on the outside of the glass.

"It is only a bird," she said, "one of God's messengers. What are you afraid of? I will go out and get it."

She came back with a cedar-bird in her hand—one of those brown birds that we call *recollets* because they look like a monk with a hood. Her face was very grave.

"Look," she cried, "it is a *recollet*. He is only stunned a little. Look, he flutters his wings, we will let him go—like that! But he was sent to this house because there is something here to be confessed. What is it?"

By this time my father was disturbed, and the trouble was getting on top of the joy in his soul. So he pulled the ring out of his vest and laid it on the table under the lamp. The gold glittered, and the stone sparkled, and he saw that her eyes grew large as she looked at it.

"See," he said, "this is the good fortune that the waves brought me on the way home from *La Trinité*. It is a heritage for our baby that is coming."

"The waves!" she cried, shrinking back a little. "How could the waves bring a heavy thing like that? It would sink."

"It was floating," he answered, casting about in his mind for a good lie, "it was floating—about two miles this side of the *Pointe du Caribou*—it was floating on a piece of . . . "

At that moment there was another blow on the window, and something pounded and scratched against the glass. Both of them were looking this time, and again my father saw the hand without the little finger—but my mother could see only a blur and a movement.

He was terrified, and fell on his knees praying. She trembled a little, but stood over him brave and stern.

"What is it that you have seen," said she, "tell me, what has made you afraid?"

"A hand!" he answered, very low, "a hand on the window."

"A hand!" she cried, "then there must be someone waiting outside. You must go and let him in."

"Not I," whispered he, "I dare not."

Then she looked at him hard, and waited a minute. She opened the door, peered out, trembled again, crossed the threshold, and returned with the body of a blackbird.

"Look," she cried, "another messenger of God—his heart is beating a little. I will put him here where it is warm—perhaps he will get well again. But there is a curse coming upon this house. Confess. What is this about hands?"

So he was moved and terrified to open his secret halfway.

"On the rocks this side of the point," he stammered, "as I was sailing very slowly . . . there was something white . . . the arm and hand of a man . . . this ring on one of the fingers. Where was the man? Drowned and lost. What did he want of the ring? It was easy to pull it. . . ."

As he said this, there was a crash at the window. The broken pane tinkled upon the floor. In the opening they both saw, for a moment, a hand with the little finger cut off and the blood dripping from it.

When it faded, my mother Nataline went to the window, and there on the floor, in a little red pool, she found the body of a dead cross-bill, all torn and wounded by the glass through which it had crashed.

She took it up and fondled it. Then she gave a great sigh, and went to my father Marcel and kneeled beside him.

(You understand, m'sieu', it was he who narrated all this to me. He said he never should forget a word or a look of it until he died—and perhaps not even then.)

So she kneeled beside him and put one hand over his shoulder, the dead cross-bill in the other.

"Marcel," she said, "thou and I love each other so much that we must always go together—whether to heaven or to hell—and very soon our little baby is to be born. Wilt thou keep a secret from me now? Look, this is the last messenger at the window—the blessed bird whose bill is twisted because he tried to pull out the nail from the Saviour's hand on the cross, and whose feathers are always red because the blood of Jesus fell upon them. It is a message of pardon that he brings us, if we repent. Come, tell the whole of the sin."

At this the heart of my father Marcel was melted within him, as a block of ice is melted when it floats into the warmer sea, and he told her all of the shameful thing that he had done.

She stood up and took the ring from the table with the ends of her fingers, as if she did not like to touch it.

"Where hast thou put it," she asked, "the finger of the hand from which this thing was stolen?"

""It is among the bushes," he answered, "beside the path to the landing."

"Thou canst find it," said she, "as we go to the boat, for the moon is shining and the night is still. Then thou shalt put the ring where it belongs, and we will row to the place where the hand is—dost thou remember it?"

So they did as she commanded. The sea was very quiet and the moon was full. They rowed together until they came about two miles from the *Point du Caribou*, at a place which Marcel remembered because there was a broken cliff on the shore.

When he dropped the finger, with the great ring glittering upon it, over the edge of the boat, he groaned. But the water received the jewel in silence, with smooth ripples, and a circle of light spread away from it under the moon, and my mother Nataline smiled like one who is well content.

"Now," she said, "we have done what the messengers at the window told us. We have given back what the poor man wanted. God is not angry with us now. But I am very tired—row me home, for I think my time is near at hand."

The next day, just before sunset, was the day of my birth. My mother Nataline told me, when I was a little boy, that I was born to good fortune. And, you see, m'sieu', it was true, for I am the keeper of her light.

MARY S. WATTS

THE VOODOO-WOMAN

EN OR TWELVE YEARS ago I spent a summer on an island of the Maine coast which I shall here call Northport. It was an isolated place; I must reach it from the mainland by catboat, with my trunk nicely adjusted in the midst—a fashion of travel that seemed to me then in the last degree adventurous. One can hardly overstate the wonder and delight with which a landward-dwelling person makes the acquaintance of the sea. I passed whole days exploring my island, in a continual foolish beatific surprise at this altered face of Nature—the vast, dominant water, the tides coming and going with an ordered mystery. There was a sharp fragrance in the Northern woods; I liked the clean, weedless forest floor and the austere pines marching on either hand. It was not a luxuriant soil—Northport is as near solid rock, I think, as any land can be—yet it was covered with a lean and sober vegetation. Blueberries grew in the uplands, and I sometimes made a show of picking them, carrying a tin pail with a book in the bottom of it; but the bushes can have suffered little by me, for I believe a more deliberate and conscienceless idler never existed.

217

These pursuits must have made me pretty unsociable, for I do not remember exchanging a word with anyone, except my hosts at the farmhouse where I lodged, until the day, a fortnight or so after my arrival, when I fell in with Cap'n Jonathan Starr. I found him comfortably disposed upon a natural bench of stone commanding a wide view from the summit of one of Northport's many headlands; this and its twin slanted to the sea by long and noble reaches, to inclose a bay fit for the galleys of Aeneas; and the grave trees collected on its shore might very well figure the sacred grove, dark with an awful shadow. There was a sky of steadfast blue; white clouds, white sails, went to and fro along the horizon; the picture did not lack a classic outline—always excepting, that is, the singularly ill-assorted detail of Cap'n Jonathan Starr callously chewing tobacco in the foreground. The old man had been convoyed thither in my sight by a little brisk, acid granddaughter; I had heard her shrilling orders at him as I drew near.

"Now, Gran'pa, here's your tobacco. Here's your cane. Here's your cushion. Now, I'm going to pick berries; and don't you stir till I come back, hear?"

After which she whisked out a pan from somewhere, fell on her knees beside the nearest bush, and in a twinkle the berries were bounding against the tin.

"Is this Christmas Cove?" I asked of this queer travesty of Little Nell.

She tilted her chin, appraised me in one brief glance, and returned to her task, flinging a "yes" at me over her shoulder. Her grandfather was more lenient.

"Fine day, ain't it?" he said amiably, and made room for me beside him on the bench. He was a small, stoop-shouldered mariner, with mild blue eyes and that arrangement of beard behind, not on, the chin that makes one think of a halo in the wrong place. He was not garrulous, but showed a pleasant willingness to talk as soon as the berry-picker, of whom he plainly stood in some awe, had, going from bush to bush, picked herself out of sight.

"Literary, ain't ye?" he asked, after we had exchanged names, glancing at the book in my lap. "I read a good deal myself, off and on. It's about all I'm good for, now." His eyes wandered to the sea with a wistfulness I found rather touching.

"You've always been a sailor, Cap'n Starr?"

"Man and boy, sixty-odd years." He shifted his quid and spat thoughtfully. "But I'm done now. I've made my last v'y'ge—till I clear for up yonder, that is—maybe I ought to say *down* yonder. Person kind of sails under sealed orders, that trip."

"You must have started out young."

"Rising thirteen, I was. Seems like yesterday sometimes, and then again like ever such a long time. I'm fond of sitting here and watching the boats go out, and thinking of old days. Lord! what a man sees going up and down the almighty waters for sixty years!" He shook his head. " 'He bringeth 'em to their desired haven,' " he quoted, with a perfect unabashed reverence. Doubtless he had fared hard on many a rigorous cruise, and fronted death a thousand times; doubtless, too, he had spent his pay in devious ways, and lived the life of Jack ashore—but I think I have seldom seen old age wear a face at once so brave and so simple.

"How did you happen to go to sea, Cap'n Starr?"

"Why, I ran away, like more than one boy before and since," he answered. "And a strange trip it was, too. You'd have thought I'd not care to go again. But I did. That's the way with the sea; it takes hold of you, and it won't let go. I tried schoolteaching once—but I couldn't stick to it. Not but what I was a pretty good teacher; you wouldn't think it to hear me now, but I was."

I told him I had noticed he spoke like an educated man; an awkward speech, but I believe it gratified him.

"Travel's a good schoolmaster," said he. "I've been lots of places."

"Yes? Tell me about your first voyage, Cap'n Starr; you said it was a queer one."

"There ain't much to tell," he said, with a careful pretense of disinclination to talk, although I could see the question pleased him mightily. "I stowed away on the bark *Laughing Sallie*, out o' here for the Wind'ard Isles, Cap'n Jed Slocum. They found me along the second day, when I couldn't hold out any longer. I'll bet I was the sickest boy this side the Horn—and Slocum the maddest man. He gen'ally knew pretty well what he wanted, and if there was one thing on earth he *didn't* want, it was me. However, there I was, and there I had to stay. He hadn't any notion of putting in somewhere and landing me—couldn't take all that trouble for a boy, you know. He said he guessed my folks would make it lively for me when I got home, but, in case they didn't, he'd take care of *his* end of the job, anyhow. And he did. He was a hard man.

"Slocum owned the *Laughing Sallie*, and worked her himself, trading to the islands. Lots of men did that in those days. He'd take down a cargo of rosin, pitch, salt fish, turpentine, hides, tallow—anything and everything that they didn't grow down there—and come back loaded up with sugar and coffee and spices, and sometimes mahogany logs, but not often, because the bark wasn't built to carry lumber. The *Laughing Sallie* was named after Slocum's wife, they said. If he was the same kind of man ashore that he was afloat, I guess she didn't have much to laugh at. A hard man he was, Jed Slocum, and he came to a hard end.

"He always had trouble shipping a crew, partly, of course, because his vessel had the name of being a regular floating hell—excuse me, ma'am—for hard work, hard words, and poor feed; but largely because, though he was accounted a good seaman, he was so tarnation reckless. He'd crowd on in the face of a gale fit to blow the teeth down your throat; he was always in a blind, stampeding fury to get where he was going. He wouldn't be beat by wind nor weather; say 'shorten sail' to him and get a black eye. The *Laughing Sallie* never was known to come home with all hands; and right at the beginning of this very cruise, off Hatteras in a storm, one of the starboard watch went overboard. I remember his name was Charlie Mason, and he'd lost two fingers of his left hand, cut off by pirates in the China Seas, he said. But he was spry aloft as any ten-fingered man you ever saw. As if that wasn't enough, within a day's sail of the Bahamas we were made to lay to, with a shot across our bows, by the British line-frigate *Scorpion*, forty-eight guns. She sent a lieutenant and some marines aboard us and took off three men. Stood us down they were British deserters—and I do believe one of 'em was; but, of the others, one was a Glo'ster man that had been with Slocum two cruises, and the other Ned Morris, that we all knew and had grown up with right here around Northport and Boothbay. The English used to do that way in the old days before the war, you know. Losing four men left us so short-handed we were all nearly worked to death—Slocum, too. I'll give him his due, he pitched in with the rest. It didn't improve his temper any. Fortunately, the weather held on good, or I don't know where we'd have been. About three days later we spoke the brig *Dolly Madison*, four weeks out from New Bedford for Valparaiso, with a cargo of rum. Slocum knew her skipper, and had a boat lowered to make him a call and see if he couldn't borrow a hand. But it turned out the *Dolly Madison* wasn't any better off than ourselves, for the *Scorpion* had held her up, too; I think they had lost two men. The *Madison's* captain advised Slocum to put into Port Barrancos, because it was plain the bark couldn't be handled in comfort, the fix we were in. 'And,' says he, 'there's always scores and scores of seamen hanging round Barrancos looking for berths. You can't do better.' 'I can't do worse,' says Slocum, grumbling, but he gave in after a while, when the *Madison's* skipper (his name, I think, was McDermott, or maybe McDonough) said that was what *he* meant to do. They were in the same box together, and misery loves company.

"You see, Port Barrancos was what they call nowadays 'wide open.' There was nothing much to the island except the grand, big harbor; it was the largest of a little group, some of 'em just points of rock sticking up out of the water, with a bunch of palm-trees on top, that sailors used to call the Hen-and-Chickens—on the charts they put it down Barrancos Cays. It was a place of call for ships from all over the world—not the little outlying islands, where only a few fishermen and such lived, although I've touched there to get fresh fruit and turtle-eggs, but Port Barrancos itself. It belonged to Spain then, and there was a big town, all low houses, white and many-colored, and a fortress—built, I guess, in Diego Columbus' time—at the entrance to the harbor; and what with the sugar trade, and slaves, and ships calling in from every quarter of the globe, I tell you, Port Barrancos was a stirring place in those days. I'll bet it had more liquor shops and dancehalls and pawnbrokers and gambling-dives to the square yard than any other town of equal size on the face of the earth—every one of 'em jammed to the doors with sailormen, mostly drunk and raising hell—excuse me, ma'am. There was all the tongues of the Tower o' Babel to be heard there, and you might take your choice of complexions, ranging from coal-black to pink-and-white with blue eyes. The natives are kind of coffee-colored, with straight hair. As for law and order, why, the fellow with the most money got it, and the rest had to shift for themselves, every man for his own hand, and Somebody take the hindmost!

"Take it altogether, you can see why a sober, steady man like Slocum wasn't very keen to turn what men he had loose in Port

Barrancos; but, in the pinch, he couldn't help himself. We made the island next day, and came to anchor just inside the lower tip of the crescent (that's the shape of the bay), under the guns of the Morro. The *Dolly Madison* was berthed a little farther along, as I remember, near a dock where there was a big sugar warehouse. Of course, I was about crazy to go ashore, and they let me without any fuss, although all but the two men that rowed Slocum's gig were expressly forbid to stir off the vessel. Nobody was caring much about me, you know; boys are cheap and plentiful, and I hadn't been wanted, in the first place.

"I've been in Port Barrancos since many times, but it never looked so wonderful and interesting to me again after that first day. I dawdled along the streets, staring and listening like an idiot, I guess, until I came to the market-house. It was built over a whole square, with two streets through, crossing in the middle. The people had dozens of little hole-in-the-wall stalls where they sold their stuff, dickering and screeching—you never heard the beat of it! By and by I came to the fruit-stands, and then my mouth surely did begin to water. There were pineapples and oranges, and hunks of sugarcane, and round, potato-looking things they call sapodillas, which I afterwards found out ain't all they're cracked up to be—but it all looked good to me then. I hadn't any money, so I just must take it out in looking. After a while I noticed a young colored woman in one of the booths eying me pretty hard, and then making believe to be busy with her fruit, and then sizing me up again. She saw I had caught her at it, and sung out: 'Leetle boy-ee! Come-a here, leetle boy-ee!'

"I went up, and she reached around behind her and brought out a basket of figs and held it toward me.

" 'You lak' feeg, eh?' says she, talking like that.

"Boylike, I wasn't going to acknowledge I hadn't any money, so I said, 'Thank ye, ma'am, I never eat 'em,' aching for a taste all the while.

"She began to laugh. 'You got no money, eh? You tak' heem, so,' and she shoved the basket into my hands.

"I wondered how on earth she knew I hadn't, and what she meant by making me a present of the fruit. But in a minute she said, 'You nice-a leetle boy-ee—pretty leetle boy-ee. I lak' you. You stop here?' and handed out a stool.

"Now, I wasn't particular about being called a 'nice-a leetle boy-ee'— that kind of talk 'most always makes a boy uncomfortable—but I thought she meant well in her outlandish fashion, so I answered, 'Much obliged, ma'am,' and sat down, and she showed me how to peel the figs, which, of course, I didn't know anything about. I took a good look at her. She was very tall and slim, quick as a fish in her movements, and had on a neat blue cotton dress, and a turban of pale-yellow muslin wound about her head, and long gold earrings. She was a real pretty, light, tawny shade, and was always nodding and smiling with her big black eyes, and showing her white, shiny, pointed teeth like a cat's. But what gave me a sort of turn was when all at once she pulled out her left arm from under the folds of her skirt, where she had kept it all this time, doing everything skillfully with her right, and I saw she hadn't any hand on it! She must have been born that way, for there was no mark of its being cut off; her arm was round and smooth over the end like a broom-handle, with just one or two little folds or pleats in the skin.

"You wouldn't think it, but, ma'am, the thing had a kind of creepiness about it; I hated to look at it, but couldn't help myself, somehow. She saw me and didn't seem to mind; she got out a piece of thin paper and some tobacco, and rolled a cigarette and began to smoke, looking sideways at me and laughing. Then she leaned over and blew a cloud of the warm smoke around my head, and says she: 'You come-a with me, leetle boy-ee, eh?'

"I tried to answer and tell her I must go back to the ship, but I only mumbled something; I felt dazed and wanted to lie down somewhere and go to sleep. But when presently she got up and said in her cool, soft voice, 'You follow, leetle boy-ee,' I got up, too, and trailed after her, as you do in dreams.

"I didn't know how far we walked or which way, but, in a little, we got down to the waterside and found a boat, and got in, nobody paying any attention to us. She made me sit in the bow, and rowed herself, handily as a man, with her stump-wrist stuck through a thong of leather on one of the oars—she went fast, too. After a while she began to sing in time to her stroke, and then either I fell asleep or lost consciousness some other way, for the next thing I knew, the keel of the boat was bumping on shingle, and she was getting out with the painter in her hand and pulling us up on a beach. I sat up and rubbed my eyes. We were in a kind of harbor, where a little river came down, widening to the sea; in places the palms and green tropic stuff grew almost into the water; the tide was coming in; there was a great long arm of land stretching out that made what you might call a natural breakwater, and I could hear the surf humming outside of it, and, where it narrowed and flattened, see the clouds of spray roll up, and hang, and fall. There were two big palms, as like as twins, standing at the very point, shaking about in the wind.

"That was the noisiest place to be so lonesome I ever saw. The breakers thumped outside the bar; the huge wind whistled among the trees; all kinds of birds squawked and chittered overhead in the jungle, and underfoot it seemed to be alive with creeping and rustling things.

" 'Where is this?' says I, staring around and beginning to be uneasy. 'I want to go back to the ship.'

" 'Dis nice-a place,' said the woman, in her gibberish. 'You come-a see my house. Look, Barrancos, look!' She pointed, and, sure enough, a long way off, I could just make out a little dim spot on the skyline that might have been Port Barrancos or Port Anything-you-please, for all I could tell.

" 'I want to go back,' says I, cruelly scared, but fighting it down the best I could. There was something in that clamorous, empty shore, the sea shouting and flinging on the bar, not another human being in sight (not even a sail) except the tall yellow woman—there was something in it, I say, that chilled the heart. 'Won't you please take me back, ma'am?' says I.

" 'You go back, one leetle time,' says she; 'follow now.' She started off into the woods, and I behind her like a dog.

"If it was noisy on the beach, it was ten times worse inland. There was some kind of bird that shrieked and laughed like a mad-man in the trees. I saw I couldn't tell you how many big, fat snakes curled up on logs, and one hanging down from a tree like a curtain-tassel, with a flat head shaped like a spade. They never offered to move—just watched us with their dull, fixed eyes. The ground was a bog of tepid black slime; there were long vines that caught you around the neck and ankles; and it was dark and stunk foully, like a sick man's breath.

"All at once we came to a clearing where there was a shack such as the natives put up, thatched with banana-leaves, without any windows, and a blanket hanging in front of a hole in one side for a door. Outside there was a kettle swung on three sticks over a dead fire. The woman turned around and says, 'You mak' fire now,' and went inside the hut and pulled the blanket to. So I got to work with a pile of leaves and sticks, and pretty soon had a good blaze going. Once I peeped into the pot; it was about half full of stuff like grayish jelly; it quivered when I joggled it. All this while—only a few minutes—I could hear the woman gabbling fast in a low voice; once or twice I thought I heard some one else speak, but that may have been fancy. Anyway, she came out at last and took me by the hand and pulled me inside. There wasn't anything there; only the four bare walls and dirt floor, and in one corner a live black chicken that sat without moving. 'You look here,' said the woman, and picked up a dirty rag off the floor. There was a hole about two feet square and I don't know how deep, full to the brim of gold and silver coins; I never saw so much money together before nor since—and the queer thing is, I was too much of a boy and too frightened to care anything about it!

" 'My, that's real pretty, ma'am,' I said at last, seeing she expected me to say something.

" 'You no want some, leetle boy-ee? You tak' some, eh?'

" 'Thank ye kindly, ma'am, I don't care for any,' says I—and I meant it. I'd always been brought up to think it was kind of low to take money you hadn't earned from any one.

" 'Oh, yes; you tak' some,' she said eagerly. And with that she thrust her stump in among the coins up to the elbow and churned them all about, then grabbed out a big handful. 'You tak' heem,' she said, and stuffed them into my pockets in spite of me. 'Now, not say no more; hush now.' She laid her finger on her lip, took the black cock under her arm, and went outside, where the fire was burning strong and the kettle bubbling. She pulled me over to it, and suddenly, before my eyes, plumped the chicken, live as it was, into the boiling mess. It came once to the top, with a horrid croak; and, before I could gather myself together, she had me by the wrist, holding it over the pot and sawing at it with a knife. The blood spurted and ran down. I cried out—I struggled like a rat—and saw a big black man standing grinning with little red eyes the other side of the fire!

"And that's the last I knew, ma'am. The whole thing wheeled around me into blackness, in a muck of fire and blood, and my own screams ringing in my ears!

*

"When I came to, I was lying across a couple of barrels in the broiling sun on the waterfront at Port Barrancos. I sat up. I felt a little weak and giddy, but otherwise as good as ever. At first I was in a kind of daze, not remembering where I was nor what had happened; and when, little by little, it all came back to me, I thought I'd been having a bad dream. Then, as I stretched and gaped, I felt a hot twinge of pain in my wrist, and, looking, saw it was bound up in a bit of rag. That brought me up all standing. I took the rag off, and there was the cut, but not a real bad one. I studied a good while over it, gave it up at last, started along the quay, and, by good luck, fell in with a man peddling oranges out of a boat, and persuaded him to set me across to the *Laughing Sallie*. As we came near, one of the men was leaning over the side, so I hailed him. He stared at me for a minute without answering; then, 'Why, Johnny,' says he, 'where you been all day and all night? We made sure you were drowned or knocked on the head.'

" 'I ain't been away all day and night,' says I. 'I don't know what you're talking about.' Then the orange-man struck in and said he wanted something for putting me over; so the seaman (his name was Matthew Friend), knowing I never had any money, good-naturedly went down into his pocket and gave him some small silver. 'I wouldn't wonder if you'd had a touch o' sun, my lad,' says he, eying me; 'you look kind of peaked. Where'd you go yesterday?'

" 'Nowhere, I tell you,' says I, puzzled. 'How could I? I went ashore this morning.'

"There was an old sailor aboard, named Cobb, that came up and looked me over. 'This is Wednesday, Johnny,' said he; 'what day was it you left the ship?'

"It was Tuesday morning! Where had I been all that time? I, for one, never knew.

" 'Take him below, Matt,' says old Cobb, seeing how frightened and bewildered I was; 'no need for skipper to see him yet awhile.' So Friend heaved me up in his arms, and, lo and behold, a handful of gold and silver dropped out of my jacket pocket and rolled all about the decks!

"The men were hardly more thunderstruck than I. I had forgotten all that part of my adventure. The mate and another seaman came running at the sound, and everybody stood staring. No one moved to touch it for a minute, they were all so surprised. Then

Matthew Friend set me down roughly, and says he, 'Why, ye limb, did you have all that and let me pay your boat-hire? I'll. . . . '

" 'Hold on, hold on, Matt,' says the mate, who was a hatchet-faced, keen sort of fellow. 'Maybe it ain't good.'

"Old Cobb stooped down and picked up a piece, bit it pretty hard, and rang it on the deck. 'That's gold, for sure, Mr. Cannon,' said he. 'I guess it's Spanish money; I never saw any like it before.'

" 'It's what they call a piece-of-eight,' said Mr. Cannon, squinting his eyes to examine it. 'It's dated 1612—they don't coin 'em any more.' Then he wheeled round on me. 'Where'd you get this? Did you steal it? Where've you been?'

" 'Speak up and tell the truth, Johnny,' said another man.

" 'Or I'll take a rope to you,' added Friend, by way of encouragement.

"So I told them the whole story then and there, not being at all unwilling, but certain that no one would believe me.

"At first no one did. They asked all manner of questions, at which the mate, especially, was very artful, to trap me; but when I stuck to the same tale, without altering it or contradicting myself, first one and then another began to trust me—the more as it wasn't to be believed that I would cut my own wrist, or that I could invent such a yarn, anyhow. And one thing fell out very strangely to confirm me, as it were. When I described the place where the woman had taken me, one of the seamen cried out that he knew the spot, and that it was on an island called Dos Hermanos (on account of the twin palms), ten or twelve miles southeast by south from Barrancos, and that he had landed there to take turtles. 'I could find my way to it blindfold,' said he. 'They do say the buccaneers used that harbor in old days to dock and repair their ships.'

" 'To be sure,' said Mr. Cannon; 'that would account for Johnny's treasure—likely they buried it there. They were great hands to bury money.'

"Old Cobb shook his head. 'How d'ye account for the black wench?' said he. 'I'll tell you what *I* b'lieve. Whether that treasure was stowed away by pirates or not, she come at it by foul means, and you may lay to it, she's a voodoo.'

" 'What's that?' said I, who didn't know a voodoo from a lobster-pot.

" 'Why, a witch, sonny. They're always looking out for children, and when they catch 'em, nobody ever hears of 'em again. They want 'em to kill and eat, or else to use in their spells somehow—maybe to raise the devil. I guess that's what she wanted of you, only her magic didn't work for once.'

" 'Don't see why,' said Friend, surveying me. 'Johnny ain't no angel.'

" 'Yes; but he didn't want to take her money, d'ye see? Maybe that kept her charms from working.'

" 'But, look here, didn't the boy say he saw a black man? Maybe that *was* the devil, shipmates.'

" 'More like her lover come home to dinner,' said Mr. Cannon, and they all laughed. Nevertheless I could see my story had made a kind of stir in the men's minds. I was about the most important person in the ship that day; every man, at one time or another, took me aside and made me tell him about it all over again, and asked to see the money, and offered to take care of it for me. Next to me in popularity was Abel Harper, the man that knew where the island was. And as soon as Slocum returned, which he did at noon, in a biting bad temper, not having been able to sign on anybody, they had me aft into the cabin.

"My, my, money's a queer thing! Here it had gone and turned a lot of as honest sailormen as ever were seen into no better than a shipload of pirates. However the mulatto woman had come by her holeful of treasure in the beginning, it was hers now—but nobody gave that a second thought. From that minute no man trusted his fellow or spoke his thought outright—and the secret seemed to level away all distinctions between captain and crew. Yes, ma'am, there wasn't much discipline left on board the *Laughing Sallie* when the treasure-hunting fever took 'em all. I called it a secret, because when the skipper of the *Dolly Madison* came aboard for a sociable time that evening, word was passed for'ard that nothing was to be said about me or my adventure. But a seaman don't naturally hold in a secret any more than a sieve does water, and I am certain some of ours must have let something leak out, by what happened afterwards. Of course, I knew that something was in the wind, but not just what it was until we stood out of Barrancos harbor the next morning at the turn of the tide. There wasn't any grumbling about being short-handed, either, you may be sure—the shorter the better, everybody thought, and worked with a will. We fetched the island about midday, and one of the men gave me a hand up into the rigging to take a look at it.

" 'Is that the place, Johnny?' he asked.

"At first I didn't recognize it, but by and by, when we opened the bay and saw the two palms standing where the spray blew over them, I knew it, and dropped down on the deck, shaking. You see, I thought maybe they'd want me to go ashore and guide 'em to the shack. And, let alone the fact that I had been too scared and stupefied to take any marks of the road to it, the mere notion of going back there put me in a cold sweat. But, as it turned out, nothing was further from their minds. They wanted no boys along. Abel Harper said the island was small, and that you could go all over it in an hour, although he himself had never been away from the shore. Slocum anchored inside the bar, feeling his way with the line, at a place Harper pointed out, about three hundred yards from the river's mouth. Then, while the men were clearing away our long-boat, what does he do but call me to help him lug out a lot of muskets, cutlasses, and ammunition from the lazaret—pretty nearly all vessels carried arms of some kind in those days.

"Now, ain't money a queer thing? As if any amount of powder and shot could do any damage to devils and witches! However, the skipper called all hands aft, dealt out the weapons, and then made a short speech, winding up with: 'My lads, for my part, I don't take any stock in devils, or voodoos either, and would be willing to meet the whole bilin' of 'em just as I am. But in case we find other company here, which I think very likely, I propose to make it as pleasant for them as they will for us. What I want to say, in particular, is this: one man must stay here to watch the ship, and you may decide that by lot amongst yourselves, the man that stays getting an equal share with the rest. I can't say fairer than that.'

"Well, there was a good deal of growling over this among the four seamen, for the skipper and mate were out of the drawing, and nobody disputed for a moment that *they* were to go. But at last they all wrote their names on bits of paper and made me draw one out of a hat with my eyes shut. The lot fell to Matthew Friend; he took it good-natured enough, only, as they shoved off, he called out, 'It's share and share alike, ain't it, Cap'n, without any difference 'twixt officers and men?' Slocum grunted out that we'd see about that, which was all the satisfaction Friend got out of him. We watched 'em land and haul the boat up above high tide; then, after some looking around and arguing, they struck a path into the jungle, and in a little were out of sight. They went in single file, Harper leading, then the skipper, then Cobb, then a young seaman whose name I don't remember on account of our always calling him 'Harelip' (he had one), and Mr. Cannon bringing up the rear with a cutlass in his hand. After they had disappeared, Friend says to me coolly, 'Well, Johnny, I guess I'll be leaving you directly.'

" 'Why,' says I, 'what are you going to do? You ain't going, too?'

" 'Ain't I, though?' says Matthew Friend. 'Wait and see. I ain't any notion of staying here and twiddling my thumbs. The ship's as safe as Noah's Ark, and, even if she wasn't, what could one man do? I'm going to swim ashore, and you can come, too, if you like.'

" 'It's mutiny,' says I.

" 'Mutiny be—somethinged!' said he. 'If you come to that, what are we doing here, anyhow? Whose money is that, hey? 'Tain't ours. And what d'ye call taking money that ain't yours? All I'm sure of is, I'm going to have my share.'

"This was the only time I ever heard one of them doubtful about the rights of the case. Friend took off his coat and shirt and made a bundle of them with a pistol wrapped up in the middle, and tied it on top of his head to keep it dry; then he took his knife between his teeth, and dropped over the side. He swam, I should judge, two thirds of the way, and then, all at once, while I was hanging over the rail, sniffling, for I was frightened and lonesome— on a sudden, I say, he gave a short cry, threw his hands up, struggled a minute, and went under!

"I was nigh about crazy. I remember I ran up and down screaming and beating my hands together. Then I thought maybe he was fooling, and shouted to him to drop it. Then I sat down and watched the spot until my eyes all but dropped out of my head. He never came up, so I knew he was gone for good—poor Matt Friend, that was always so jolly and kind and didn't knock me around as much as the rest. I began to cry and act wild again out of sheer terror and helplessness. I never knew whether he had cramps or whether a shark took him—he would have acted the same in either case. At last I got kind of exhausted, and crawled into the shade of the deckhouse and went to sleep.

"I waked up, not knowing what time of day it was, and cried some more. I watched the beach for a long while, but nothing was to be seen except some big turtles; then I felt hungry and went down and got a biscuit. There was nobody to forbid me, so I wandered all over the ship. In the captain's cabin I found the log, and read it up, just out of boy's curiosity, you know. Slocum was a methodical man; the last entry was that very morning. "April 1st: Latitude so-and-so . . . Longitude so-and-so. When . . . " There it ended in a great blot of black stain. It was blood, and I remembered he had gashed his thumb cutting a pen, and was binding it up in a rag when he came on deck to look at the island. All Fools' Day—queer, when you come to think it over.

"As I was looking at the book, I thought I heard a step on deck, and flew out of there in a panic, though I'd have almost been willing to take a flogging to see them come back. But it wasn't anybody. I found a telescope in the mate's berth, and played with that awhile, watching the shore; then I got hungry again, and ate some more biscuit and some cheese and fruit I found in the galley. It was while I was doing this I heard two pistol- or gun-shots, far away but perfectly distinct, and ran to look. There was nothing in sight, but, after a great while, I heard three more, and none after that, though I watched and listened until it was too dark and coming on to blow too hard for me to see or hear anything. I was afraid to go below, because I'd got a horrid kind of feeling that some one was peeking at me through the skylights. It was cooking hot in the fo'c'sle, anyhow. I got a blanket out of my bunk and curled up behind the forehatch; I went to sleep and slept sound, all but a dream I had that Matt Friend was coming over the side with his drowned eyes staring and his wet hands clutching. It waked me up, and I threw out my hand and, sure enough, touched something deadly cold! I gave a screech fit to raise the dead in good earnest; and then I saw 'twasn't anything but a coil of chain-cable!

"In the morning the wind had gone down some, but the decks were blown full of leaves and rubbish, and by the foot of the mainmast I found a dead bird. I swept everything up clean, and started a fire in the galley and put the kettle on. 'The men'll want something hot, they'll be so tired,' says I to myself, watching the beach. But they never came, and I had to eat breakfast alone, after all. That was the longest day I ever put through. I kept the spyglass by me and watched the sea as well as land, for it came into my head maybe that the voodoo-woman might come along, in case she wasn't at home already. I went and got a musket and some powder and shot, and laid them ready to my hand—though what I expected to do it would be hard to say. She never came, though, nor anybody else. There I stayed alone, with the flat glare of water all around, and the everlasting noisy solitude of the land—and the morning and the evening was the second day, as the Book says. As hot and shadeless as it was, I remember how afraid I was of the coming night, and how it came at last all at once, black and sudden, the way it does in the tropics, while I was still straining my eyes landward and hoping against hope. You see, by that time I felt pretty sure the devils had got Slocum and his men, in spite of their guns. What else could have happened? If there'd been other men on the island, and the skipper's party had had a fight, it stood to reason they couldn't all have killed one another. Somebody ought to have turned up before now. And what was going to become of *me*? I slept on deck again, but not very sound, and when the first peep of light came, I was up and searching the shore with my glass; there wasn't a sign of life. Then I took a squint seaward— being still on the lookout for the voodoo—and there was a sail!

"It was a good-sized ship, slipping through the water at a lively gait. What was more, by the way she tacked and veered, I could see she was making for the island. I could have cried for joy. I didn't know who she was or what she was, and I didn't care; I would have welcomed the *Flying Dutchman*, if she would have taken me away from that awful island. But when she got near enough I recognized her lines and rigging. It was the *Dolly Madison*. She must have seen us lying inside the bar, but whether her skipper suspected something was up, from the strange, still, unpeopled look of us, or was getting ready for trouble on his own hook, I can't say; anyway, he hove to about a quarter of a mile off shore, and directly I saw them lowering a boat. The men plainly had their instructions, for they came on very slow, half a dozen pulling, as many more armed to the teeth, the same way Slocum's party had been. They made the harbor entrance without any trouble, and, coming to a standstill, one stood up in the stern and hailed us: 'Ho, the bark ahoy!'

"I flourished my arm by way of answer, and the man, whom I took for one of the mates, bawled again: 'Ho, the *Laughin' Sallie!* Anything the matter?'

"I screamed out to him to come on board, please, sir, and after a pause, during which the men all turned around to point and stare, talking together, he gave an order, and they rowed up under our stern, still very wary, however. I went aft and waited for 'em, hanging over the rail; the men gaped up at the ship and me for a minute in silence. At last, 'Where's Cap'n Slocum, sonny?' asked the mate.

" 'He's gone ashore.'

" 'Well, then, where's your crew?'

" 'They're gone, too, all except Matt Friend, and he's drowned,' says I, wiping my eyes on my sleeve.

" 'D'ye mean to say you're all alone?'

" 'Yes, sir.'

" 'When did the cap'n and crew leave you?'

"I told him. The mate, after some further hesitation, came over the side, with the armed men after him.

" 'Now, look here, sonny,' said he, taking me by the shoulder. 'Tell us all about it from the beginning. What did Cap'n Slocum go ashore for? And what's happened since?'

"I told him that, too, faithfully. When I came to the treasure part, the men exchanged glances. After I had finished, the mate of the *Madison* stood silent, scowling to himself. Then he beckoned to one of the sailors.

" 'What d'ye make of it, Isr'l?'

"Isr'l scratched his head, looked around aloft, walked to the side and spat deliberately, then says he: 'Boy's lyin'.'

" 'I ain't,' says I, as mad as hops. The mate believed me, anyhow. After some more thinking, he made me tumble into his boat along with the rest, and, leaving the *Laughing Sallie* to mind herself for a while, ordered the men to pull for the beach. We made a landing as near the other boat as we could, and found it lying on the sand, just as it had been left, with the oars in the bottom. The mate told off a couple of men to stand by with guns and watch the beach, while the rest searched the island; I was to go with them, much against my will. The weapons they carried gave me no confidence; Slocum had been armed, too.

"We started into the jungle at the same place Slocum and his party had entered. They had made quite a distinct path. It wound about a good deal, and we judged they must have got confused somehow, for the path crossed on itself several times. The sailors kept asking me, 'Do you remember this place, Johnny?' 'Did you see that when you were here before?' but I was as much at a loss as any one.

"At last we came to an open space, where a great tribe of carrion-crows got up with a *whuzz-z-z* and settled in the trees all around. There was a man lying on his back in the middle; he hadn't any face or hands left, but, by his clothes, I knew him for that young fellow we called Harelip. The men turned him over; there were no marks of violence on him. It was awful, the hot, still, murky forest, the mutilated corpse, and the crows sitting around eying us, impatient to begin again. It looked bad—bad. 'We'll come back and bury him,' says the mate at length, in a low voice. 'Come on, men.' They fixed up a scarecrow with a shirt on two sticks to keep the birds away from the poor fellow's body, and left him.

"A few hundred yards more brought us, unexpectedly, to the beach, and we found that we had got clear across the island. There was a strip of smooth sand, all over foot marks going every which way, but not a vestige of human life otherwise. We shouted, and even fired off a gun or two, but nobody answered. I think the men were pretty near as uneasy as I by this time; they kept close together, and we all talked in whispers.

"We turned back into the jungle and followed the track a ways without anything happening, until we were brought up sudden by hearing a voice off to the right. It was mumbling something in a rapid and hurried undertone, every now and then going up in a screech. The mate called out, and it stopped for a minute, then began again. When we got to the spot, we found that sailor I told you about, Abel Harper, kneeling on the ground, scratching it with a stick, like he wanted to dig a hole and bury something, and talking to himself all the time. 'Cover it up, cover it up, cover it up!' he kept saying. He was stark mad and just not quite dead, as we could see, from hunger and thirst. We tried every way we knew to get something sensible out of him, but he wouldn't say a word except that: 'Cover it up, cover it up, cover it up!' Abel Harper never did get back his mind, nor could tell anything of what had happened. He had to be put in an asylum, and lived to be an old man. I used to go and see him when I came off a cruise.

"It wasn't far from there that we at last found the rest. The place looked to me like the clearing where the voodoo-woman's shack had stood, but there was nothing but a pile of charred sticks and ashes there; and the ground around all mummicked up with footprints, some of boots, some of bare feet, and some like cattle-hoofs. The bodies of old Cobb and Mr. Cannon were lying to one side across each other; they hadn't any wounds on 'em, as far as we could make out, but they must have been dead the whole two days, and were pretty far gone.

"We found Slocum sitting bolt upright, dead, with his back against a tree, and his gun rested on a forked twig, pointing to the front; it had been fired. The men said by signs about the body he must have outlasted the others; they thought he hadn't been dead but a few hours. His face was horribly distorted, as if he had died in great pain, but somehow he didn't look frightened—not he! Game to the last, he was. His whole body was as rigid as a handspike; he had such a grip of the gun they couldn't unbend his dead fingers; so they dug a prodigious deep hole, and buried him just as he was. There, on that cursed island, sits Jed Slocum, with his gun across his knee, waiting for the judgmentday."

Cap'n Starr was silent; and, glancing around, I saw Little Nell returning with a burden of berries that might have been the entire annual output of Northport Island. My companion made certain small movements suggestive of the private in the front rank who suddenly encounters the eye of his drill-sergeant fixed upon him.

"There comes Nellie!" said he.

Nellie! Here was an absurd coincidence. The youngster came toward us, rigidly leaning her little body aslant from the weight of the pail, her mouth primly compressed. I was conscious of a great desire to stand well with Nellie.

"You've got ever so many berries—it's wonderful, for such a little girl," I said, in abject propitiation.

She looked at me. "That's what I went for," she said—and the conversation was left without a leg to stand on! I thought I detected a glint of friendly and appreciative amusement in Cap'n Starr's gentle blue eyes.

"You boarding with Cap'n Pearce?" the child asked, with unexpected interest. I meekly acknowledged that I was.

"They have supper at five o'clock," remarked Little Nell abstractedly. "I guess it's 'most five now. Cap'n Pearce's awful particular about folks being on time to their meals." Her grandfather and I rose to our feet with a machine-like unanimity.

"I'd like to come again and sit with you awhile, Cap'n Starr," I said, "and hear the rest of your story—for I'm sure there's more of it. I'd like to know what became of the *Laughing Sallie;* and did no one ever go back there and try again for the treasure?"

"The *Laughing Sallie?*" said he. "Well, to be sure, that would be a long story all by itself. A lot of cruising that old hooker did, and many a port she touched at before she ripped the bottom-boards out of her at last on a reef down toward Salt Cay Bank. I'll tell you about her some day. But the treasure—no, I never heard of anybody offering to meddle with *that* again. For all I know, it's down there still on Barrancos Cay."

RICHARD MIDDLETON

THE GHOST SHIP

FAIRFIELD IS A LITTLE village lying near the Portsmouth Road about halfway between London and the sea. Strangers who find it by accident now and then call it a pretty, old-fashioned place; we who live in it and call it home don't find anything very pretty about it, but we should be sorry to live anywhere else. Our minds have taken the shape of the inn and the church and the green, I suppose. At all events, we never feel comfortable out of Fairfield.

Of course the Cockneys, with their vasty houses and noise-ridden streets, can call us rustics if they choose, but for all that Fairfield is a better place to live in than London. Doctor says that when he goes to London his mind is bruised with the weight of the houses, and he was a Cockney born. He had to live there himself when he was a little chap, but he knows better now. You gentlemen may laugh—perhaps some of you come from London way—but it seems to me that a witness like that is worth a gallon of arguments.

Dull? Well, you might find it dull, but I assure you that I've listened to all the London yarns you have spun tonight, and they're absolutely nothing to the things that happen at Fairfield. It's because of our way of thinking and minding our own business. If one of your Londoners were set down on the green of a Saturday night when the ghosts of the lads who died in the war keep tryst with the lasses who lie in the churchyard, he couldn't help being curious and interfering, and then the ghosts would go somewhere where it was quieter. But we just let them come and go and don't make any fuss, and in consequence Fairfield is the ghostliest place in all England. Why, I've seen a headless man sitting on the edge of the well in broad daylight, and the children playing about his feet as if he were their father. Take my word for it, spirits know when they are well off as much as human beings.

Still, I must admit that the thing I'm going to tell you about was queer even for our part of the world, where three packs of ghost-hounds hunt regularly during the season, and blacksmith's great-grandfather is busy all night shoeing the dead gentlemen's horses. Now that's a thing that wouldn't happen in London, because of their interfering ways, but blacksmith he lies up aloft and sleeps as quiet as a lamb. Once when he had a bad head he shouted down to them not to make so much noise, and in the morning he found an old guinea left on the anvil as an apology. He wears it on his watch chain now. But I must get on with my story; if I start telling you about the queer happenings at Fairfield I'll never stop.

It all came of the great storm in the spring of '97, the year that we had two great storms. This was the first one, and I remember it very well, because I found in the morning that it had lifted the thatch of my pigsty into the widow's garden as clean as a boy's kite. When I looked over the hedge, widow—Tom Lamport's widow that was— was prodding for her nasturtiums with a daisy-grubber. After I had watched her for a little I went down to the "Fox and Grapes" to tell landlord what she had said to me. Landlord he laughed, being a married man and at ease with the sex. "Come to that," he said, "the tempest has blowed something into my field. A kind of a ship I think it would be."

I was surprised at that until he explained that it was only a ghost ship and would do no hurt to the turnips. We argued that it had been blown up from the sea at Portsmouth, and then we talked of something else. There were two slates down at the parsonage and a big tree in Lumley's meadow. It was a rare storm.

I reckon the wind had blown our ghosts all over England. They were coming back for days afterwards with foundered horses and as footsore as possible, and they were so glad to get back to Fairfield that some of them walked up the street crying like little children. Squire said that his great-grandfather's great-grandfather hadn't looked so dead beat since the Battle of Naseby, and he's an educated man.

What with one thing and another, I should think it was a week before we got straight again, and then one afternoon I met the landlord on the green and he had a worried face. "I wish you'd come and have a look at that ship in my field," he said to me, "it seems to me it's leaning real hard on the turnips. I can't bear thinking what the missus will say when she sees it."

I walked down the lane with him, and sure enough there was a ship in the middle of his field, but such a ship as no man had seen on the water for three hundred years, let alone in the middle of a turnip field. It was all painted black and covered with carvings, and there was a great bay window in the stern for all the world like the Squire's drawing-room. There was a crowd of little black cannon on deck and looking out of her portholes, and she was anchored at each end to the hard ground. I have seen the wonders of the world on picture-postcards, but I have never seen anything to equal that.

"She seems very solid for a ghost ship," I said, seeing the landlord was bothered.

"I should say it's a betwixt and between," he answered, puzzling it over, "but it's going to spoil a matter of fifty turnips, and missus she'll want it moved." We went up to her and touched the side, and it was as hard as a real ship. "Now there's folks in England would call that very curious," he said.

Now I don't know much about ships, but I should think that that ghost ship weighed a solid two hundred tons, and it seemed to me that she had come to stay, so that I felt sorry for the landlord, who was a married man. "All the horses in Fairfield won't move her out of my turnips," he said, frowning at her.

Just then we heard a noise on her deck, and we looked up and saw that a man had come out of her front cabin and was looking down at us very peaceably. He was dressed in a black uniform set out with rusty gold lace, and he had a great cutlass by his side in a brass sheath. "I'm Captain Bartholomew Roberts," he said, in a gentleman's voice, "put in for recruits. I seem to have brought her rather far up the harbor."

"Harbor!" cried landlord; "why, you're fifty miles from the sea."

Captain Roberts didn't turn a hair. "So much as that, is it?" he said coolly. "Well, it's of no consequence."

Landlord was a bit upset at this. "I don't want to be unneighbourly," he said, "but I wish you hadn't brought your ship into my field. You see, my wife sets great store on these turnips."

The captain took a pinch of snuff out of a fine gold box that he pulled out of his pocket, and dusted his fingers with a silk handkerchief in a very genteel fashion. "I'm only here for a few months," he said, "but if a testimony of my esteem would pacify your good lady I should be content." And with the words he loosed a great gold brooch from the neck of his coat and tossed it down to landlord.

Landlord blushed as red as a strawberry. "I'm not denying she's fond of jewellery," he said, "but it's too much for half a sackful of turnips." And indeed it was a handsome brooch.

The captain laughed. "Tut, man," he said, "it's a forced sale, and you deserve a good price. Say no more about it." And nodding good-day to us, he turned on his heel and went into the cabin. Landlord walked back up the lane like a man with a weight off his mind. "That tempest has blowed me a bit of luck," he said, "the missus will be main pleased with that brooch. It's better than blacksmith's guinea, any day."

Ninety-seven was Jubilee year, the year of the second Jubilee, you remember, and we had great doings at Fairfield, so that we hadn't much time to bother about the ghost ship, though anyhow it isn't our way to meddle in things that don't concern us. Landlord, he saw his tenant once or twice when he was hoeing his turnips and passed the time of day, and landlord's wife wore her new brooch to church every Sunday. But we didn't mix much with the ghosts at any time, all except an idiot lad there was in the village, and he didn't know the difference between a man and a ghost, poor innocent! On Jubilee Day, however, somebody told Captain Roberts why the church bells were ringing, and he hoisted a flag and fired off his guns like a loyal Englishman. 'Tis true the guns were shotted, and one of the round shot knocked a hole in Farmer Johnstone's barn, but nobody thought much of that in such a season of rejoicing.

It wasn't till our celebrations were over that we noticed that anything was wrong in Fairfield. 'Twas shoemaker who told me first about it one morning at the "Fox and Grapes." "You know my great-great-uncle?" he said to me.

"You mean Joshua, the quiet lad," I answered, knowing him well.

"Quiet!" said shoemaker indignantly. "Quiet you call him, coming home at three o'clock every morning as drunk as a magistrate and waking up the whole house with his noise."

"Why, it can't be Joshua!" I said, for I knew him for one of the most respectable young ghosts in the village.

"Joshua it is," said shoemaker, "and one of these nights he'll find himself out in the street if he isn't careful."

This kind of talk shocked me, I can tell you, for I don't like to hear a man abusing his own family, and I could hardly believe that a steady youngster like Joshua had taken to drink. But just then in came butcher Aylwin in such a temper that he could hardly drink his beer. "The young puppy! the young puppy!" he kept on saying; and it was some time before shoemaker and I found out that he was talking about his ancestor that fell at Senlac.

"Drink?" said shoemaker hopefully, for we all like company in our misfortunes, and butcher nodded grimly.

"The young noodle," he said, emptying his tankard.

Well, after that I kept my ears open, and it was the same story all over the village. There was hardly a young man among all the ghosts of Fairfield who didn't roll home in the small hours of the morning the worse for liquor. I used to wake up in the night and hear them stumble past my house, singing outrageous songs. The worst of it was that we couldn't keep the scandal to ourselves, and the folk at Greenhill began to talk of "sodden Fairfield," and taught their children to sing a song about us:

"Sodden Fairfield, sodden Fairfield, has no use for bread-and-butter;
Rum for breakfast, rum for dinner, rum for tea, and rum for supper!"

We are easy-going in our village, but we didn't like that.

Of course we soon found out where the young fellows went to get the drink, and landlord was terribly cut up that his tenant should have turned out so badly, but his wife wouldn't hear of parting with the brooch, so that he couldn't give the Captain notice to quit. But as time went on, things grew from bad to worse, and at all hours of the day you would see those young reprobates sleeping it off on the village green. Nearly every afternoon a ghost wagon used to jolt down to the ship with a lading of rum, and though the older ghosts seemed inclined to give the Captain's hospitality the go-by, the youngsters were neither to hold nor to bind.

So one afternoon when I was taking my nap I heard a knock at the door, and there was parson looking very serious, like a man with a job before him that he didn't altogether relish. "I'm going down to talk to the Captain about all this drunkenness in the village, and I want you to come with me," he said straight out.

I can't say that I fancied the visit much myself, and I tried to hint to parson that as, after all, they were only a lot of ghosts, it didn't very much matter.

"Dead or alive, I'm responsible for their good conduct," he said, "and I'm going to do my duty and put a stop to this continued disorder. And you are coming with me, John Simmons." So I went, parson being a persuasive kind of man.

We went down to the ship, and as we approached her I could see the Captain tasting the air on deck. When he saw parson he took off his hat very politely, and I can tell you that I was relieved to find that he had a proper respect for the cloth. Parson acknowledged his salute and spoke out stoutly enough. "Sir, I should be glad to have a word with you."

"Come on board, sir; come on board," said the Captain, and I could tell by his voice that he knew why we were there. Parson and I climbed up an uneasy kind of ladder, and the Captain took us into the great cabin at the back of the ship, where the bay window was. It was the most wonderful place you ever saw in your life, all full of gold and silver plate, swords with jewelled scabbards, carved oak chairs, and great chests that looked as though they were bursting with guineas. Even parson was surprised, and he did not shake his head very hard when the Captain took down some silver cups and poured us out a drink of rum. I tasted mine, and I don't mind saying that it changed my view of things entirely. There was nothing betwixt and between about that rum, and I felt that it was ridiculous to blame the lads for drinking too much of stuff like that. It seemed to fill my veins with honey and fire.

Parson put the case squarely to the Captain, but I didn't listen much to what he said; I was busy sipping my drink and looking through the window at the fishes swimming to and fro over land-lord's turnips. Just then it seemed the most natural thing in the world that they should be there, though afterwards, of course, I could see that that proved it was a ghost ship.

But even then I thought it was queer when I saw a drowned sailor float by in the thin air with his hair and beard all full of bubbles. It was the first time I had seen anything quite like that at Fairfield.

All the time I was regarding the wonders of the deep, parson was telling Captain Roberts how there was no peace or rest in the village owing to the curse of drunkenness, and what a bad example the youngsters were setting to the older ghosts. The Captain listened very attentively, and only put in a word now and then about boys being boys and young men sowing their wild oats. But when parson had finished his speech he filled up our silver cups and said to parson, with a flourish, "I should be sorry to cause trouble anywhere where I have been made welcome, and you will be glad to hear that I put to sea tomorrow night. And now you must drink me a prosper-ous voyage." So we all stood up and drank the toast with honour, and that noble rum was like hot oil in my veins.

After that Captain showed us some of the curiosities he had brought back from foreign parts, and we were greatly amazed, though afterwards I couldn't clearly remember what they were. And then I found myself walking across the turnips with parson, and I was telling him of the glories of the deep that I had seen through the window of the ship. He turned on me severely. "If I were you, John Simmons," he said, "I should go straight home to bed." He has a way of putting things that wouldn't occur to an ordinary man, has parson, and I did as he told me.

Well, next day it came on to blow, and it blew harder and harder, till about eight o'clock at night I heard a noise and looked out into the garden. I dare say you won't believe me, it seems a bit tall even to me, but the wind had lifted the thatch of my pigsty into the widow's garden a second time. I thought I wouldn't wait to hear what widow had to say about it, so I went across the green to the "Fox and Grapes," and the wind was so strong that I danced along on tiptoe like a girl at the fair. When I got to the inn landlord had to help me shut the door; it seemed as though a dozen goats were pushing against it to come in out of the storm.

"It's a powerful tempest," he said, drawing the beer. "I hear there's a chimney down at Dickory End."

"It's a funny thing how these sailors know about the weather," I answered. "When Captain said he was going tonight, I was thinking it would take a capful of wind to carry the ship back to sea, but now here's more than a capful."

"Ah, yes," said landlord, "it's tonight he goes true enough, and, mind you, though he treated me handsome over the rent, I'm not sure it's a loss to the village. I don't hold with gentrice who fetch their drink from London instead of helping local traders to get their living."

"But you haven't got any rum like his," I said, to draw him out.

His neck grew red above his collar, and I was afraid I'd gone too far; but after a while he got his breath with a grunt.

"John Simmons," he said, "if you've come down here this windy night to talk a lot of fool's talk, you've wasted a journey."

Well, of course, then I had to smooth him down with praising his rum, and Heaven forgive me for swearing it was better than Captain's. For the like of that rum no living lips have tasted save mine and parson's. But somehow or other I brought landlord round, and presently we must have a glass of his best to prove its quality.

"Beat that if you can!" he cried, and we both raised our glasses to our mouths, only to stop halfway and look at each other in amazement. For the wind that had been howling outside like an outrageous dog had all of a sudden turned as melodious as the carol-boys of a Christmas Eve.

"Surely that's not my Martha," whispered landlord; Martha being his great-aunt that lived in the loft overhead.

We went to the door, and the wind burst it open so that the handle was driven clean into the plaster of the wall. But we didn't think about that at the time; for over our heads, sailing very comfortably through the windy stars, was the ship that had passed the summer in landlord's field. Her portholes and her bay window were blazing with lights, and there was a noise of singing and fiddling on her decks. "He's gone," shouted landlord above the storm, "and he's taken half the village with him!" I could only nod in answer, not having lungs like bellows of leather.

In the morning we were able to measure the strength of the storm, and over and above my pigsty there was damage enough wrought in the village to keep us busy. True it is that the children had to break down no branches for the firing that autumn, since the wind had strewn the woods with more than they could carry away. Many of our ghosts were scattered abroad, but this time very few came back, all the young men having sailed with Captain; and not only ghosts, for a poor half-witted lad was missing, and we reckoned that he had stowed himself away or perhaps shipped as cabin boy, not knowing any better.

What with the lamentations of the ghost-girls and the grumblings of families who had lost an ancestor, the village was upset for a while, and the funny thing was that it was the folk who had complained most of the carryings-on of the youngsters, who made most noise now that they were gone. I hadn't any sympathy with shoemaker or butcher, who ran about saying how much they missed their lads, but it made me grieve to hear the poor bereaved girls calling their lovers by name on the village green at nightfall. It didn't seem fair to me that they should have lost their men a second time, after giving up life in order to join them, as like as not. Still, not even a spirit can be sorry for ever, and after a few months we made up our mind that the folk who had sailed in the ship were never coming back, and we didn't talk about it any more.

And then one day, I dare say it would be a couple of years later, when the whole business was quite forgotten, who should come trapesing along the road from Portsmouth but the daft lad who had gone away with the ship, without waiting till he was dead to become a ghost. You never saw such a boy as that in all your life. He had a great rusty cutlass hanging to a string at his waist, and he was tattooed all over in fine colours, so that even his face looked like a girl's sampler. He had a handkerchief in his hand full of foreign shells and old-fashioned pieces of small money, very curious, and he walked up to the well outside his mother's house and drew himself a drink as if he had been nowhere in particular.

The worst of it was that he had come back as soft headed as he went, and try as we might we couldn't get anything reasonable out

245

of him. He talked a lot of gibberish about keel-hauling and walking the plank and crimson murders—things which a decent sailor should know nothing about, so that it seemed to me that for all his manners Captain had been more of a pirate than a gentleman mariner. But to draw sense out of that boy was as hard as picking cherries off a crabtree. One silly tale he had that he kept on drifting back to, and to hear him you would have thought that it was the only thing that happened to him in his life. "We was at anchor," he would say, "off an island called the Basket of Flowers, and the sailors had caught a lot of parrots and we were teaching them to swear. Up and down the decks, up and down the decks, and the language they used was dreadful. Then we looked up and saw the masts of the Spanish ship outside the harbour. Outside the harbour they were, so we threw the parrots into the sea and sailed out to fight. And all the parrots were drownded in the sea and the language they used was dreadful." That's the sort of boy he was, nothing but silly talk of parrots when we asked him about the fighting. And we never had a chance of teaching him better, for two days after he ran away again, and hasn't been seen since.

That's my story, and I assure you that things like that are happening at Fairfield all the time. The ship has never come back, but somehow as people grow older they seem to think that one of these windy nights she'll come sailing in over the hedges with all the lost ghosts on board. Well, when she comes, she'll be welcome. There's one ghost-lass that has never grown tired of waiting for her lad to return. Every night you'll see her out on the green, straining her poor eyes with looking for the mast-lights among the stars. A faithful lass you'd call her, and I'm thinking you'd be right.

Landlord's field wasn't a penny the worse for the visit, but they do say that since then the turnips that have been grown in it have tasted of rum.